BLOOD OF THE
DRAGON THRONE

All who feel they've had to be somehow more
in order to fit in.

Shadow Dragon Saga

Curse of the Dragon Shadow

Legend of the Dragon Soul

Rise of the Dragon Sworn

Blood of the Dragon Throne

Reign of the Dragon Born

Secret of the Dragon Crown

First Edition
Published by Fairies and Fantasy Pty Ltd 2024

ISBN: 978-1-922390-95-0 (paperback)

www.selinafenech.com

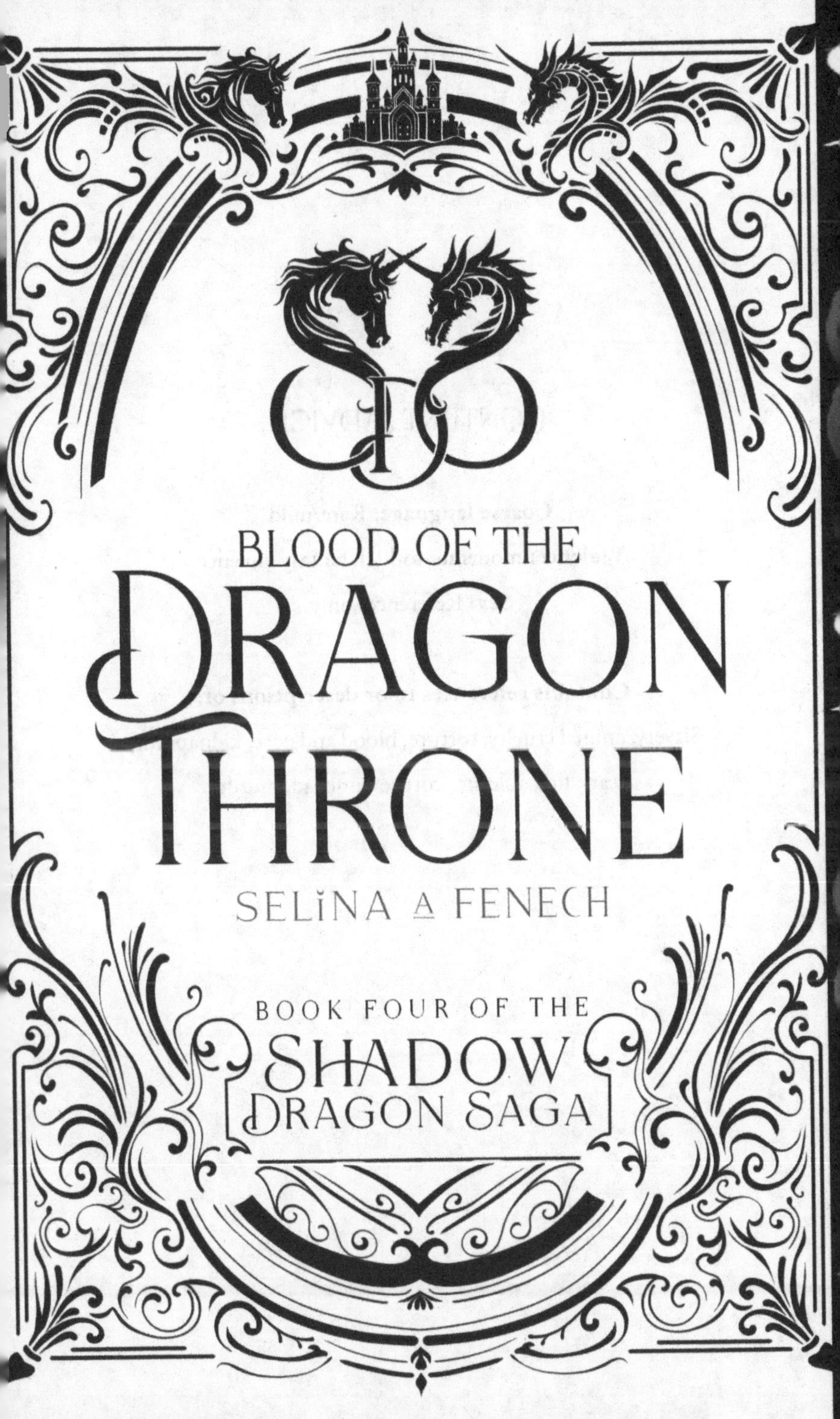

BLOOD OF THE DRAGON THRONE

SELINA A FENECH

BOOK FOUR OF THE SHADOW DRAGON SAGA

Content Advice

Coarse language: Rare/mild

Violence: moderate-to-high fantasy violence

Sex: References only

Contains references to or descriptions of:

Slavery, animal cruelty, torture, blood and gore, kidnapping,
scars, fire, ableism, corpses/undead, murder.

CONTENTS

Dragon Keeps

1. Braigwenkeep (Trade Hub)
2. Nevrynkeep (Mining)
3. Ardahnkeep (Trade Harbor, Old Rolanian Capital)
4. Tjollaskeep (Mining)
5. Salixkeep (Fishing)
6. Ulfrenkeep (Mining)
7. Ylvakeep (Farming)
8. Leskakeep (Farming)
9. Pryshakeep (Farming)
10. Dastmyrkeep (Glass)
11. Tarrickeep (Mining)
12. Gerichkeep (Lumber)
13. Skaellakeep (Farming)
14. Idrakeep (Penal)
15. Hjelzahnkeep (Training)
16. Eslindekeep (Incomplete)

NORTHERN ALDERKIN DEPTHS
(Nerrun Deemfret)
Gris Holen
(15)
Sunborn Range
Stonewing Crest
(4)
CENTRAL ALDERKIN DEPTHS
(Luns Deemfret)
Eishowl Peaks
(6)
Bovin Steppes
(13)
(5)
Unicorn Tears River
The Red Cliffs
SOUTHERN ALDERKIN DEPTHS
(Sons Deemfret)
Erst Holen
Talon Bluffs
Lorg Sesstra
(8)
Nord Myrr
Lorg Eldstrom
Lorg Draeka
Draeskull Crags
Starris River
(3)
Grand Holen
(9)
EYLE NORDCREST
(14)
Seasong Shores
Serpents Ruil
Mestra's Horn
EASTERN ALDERKIN DEPTHS
(Ilst Deemfret)
DRAEKHAN'S REST
(7)
Etherflame Plains
DRAEKHANHELM
SKYBREAK SEA

ALDERKIN DEPTHS
Relic Lower
Wet Descent
Whisperwind Passage
UPSLOPE
DragonMaw Descent
Upper Flats
Stores
1.
The Curtain
Relic Upper
2.
12.
3.
9.
The Grand Arch
11.
Flowstone Steps
Delver's Circuit
Crystalline Reservoir
STONESHIELD GATE
Livestock
Rock Farm

THE UNDERCITY
Mushroom Farms
CURSED DEPTHS
DOWNSLOPE
ohans' Den
UNICORN GATE
FIRSTMAN'S PASS
5.
7.
10.
8.
4.
6.
1. Temple Tower
2. Grand Column
3. Frostwork Column
4. Dragonwing Tower
5. Satinstraw Tower
6. Slowflow Flats
7. Rimstone Flats
8. Shimmervein Tower
9. Grand Arch Markets
10. Downslope Markets
11. Curtain Markets
12. Sinking Stream Lake

ONE

Kess lay on her back on the damp stone floor and shivered as Riony paced the claustrophobic cell.

"Could you have possibly, even if trying, gotten us into a worse mess than this?" Riony thrust both palms against the wooden door holding them inside.

Too solid. It didn't budge, didn't even rattle.

Kess blinked, slow and sluggish, staring at the dark stain marking the back of Riony's shirt. "I'm sorry."

Kess had done her best to investigate every corner of the room she could through hazy, doubled vision and with limbs that refused to move.

More a disused root cellar than dungeon, chilled and musty, it had been chiseled deep into solid stone and closed off with a door neither rodents nor thieves could penetrate.

Shelving lined two sides of the room, empty of anything except the curls of old onion skins and cobwebs. Only the floor was storage now, for strewn bouquets and Kess's limp body.

She needed to focus, find a way out, find anything she could turn to her advantage. But her eyes kept returning to Riony, to the rusty color marring the fabric of her back.

Riony spoke over her shoulder, keeping her back to Kess. "This is all your fault."

"I'm sorry." Kess's head pounded.

Searing points of pain ached throughout her skull, and shame hurt her even deeper.

She won't even look at me. Kess didn't blame her.

How long had they been in there? She'd tried to mark the days at first, in her brief moments of waking and lucidity. Soft scratches in the dust of the disused shelves. The tally lines doubled, tripled in her blurred vision. Days, weeks, months, she couldn't count the crookedly marked lines.

A dull beam of natural light reached in from a narrow ventilation shaft in the ceiling high above, the only thing marking day or night which seemed to turn from one to the other every time she blinked. She spent most of her time lost and paralyzed in nightmares, as the morass mercy carpeting the floor oozed its soapy, peppery scent into her lungs.

Days and nights and days and nights, all filled with nauseating visions of a blade, her blade, slicing deep into Riony's back. Clasped within her fingers as she plunged it in.

That didn't happen. It was just a dream. Riony is here.

"I can't think straight. Can you help me? Move me away from the morass mercy, please, Pony." The old name slipped out over Kess's numb lips.

Riony loomed in the space, monstrously tall between the walls closing in on all sides. "I'm not your Pony and I'll never carry you. Ever again."

Kess's eyes closed, too heavy, for too long. Tears squeezed from the corners.

She was small again, in a fine dress of embroidered silver velvet, upon a bed of soft down and plush cushions.

On her lap, she held a broad-paged book filled with illustrations of all the breeds of dragons, both naturally occurring, and hybrids bred by humans. A childish picture book, simple in its descriptions. She'd read other far more complicated texts on all aspects of dragon riding and breeding.

But she had a soft spot for this tome and its naturalistic depictions of dragons that were so much more fluid and powerful than the stiff technical illustrations in her other books.

"One day I'll have my own dragon." Kess said it as a promise, a truth held deep in her fluttering heart. "An etherdart maybe. I'd like something fast, though."

Sitting cross-legged beside her, Riony dutifully looked over the page Kess presented. "I thought snowflames were faster?"

Kess tsked. "Yes, obviously, but they burn out fast too. I need a dragon who will stay with me, be my companion in combat and honor as long as possible. The Dragon King's steed is his original and been with him over eighty years!"

She turned the pages slowly, a strange churning of nerves in her stomach as she shared her beloved book with Riony, as though she were sharing some deep, dark secret. A ridiculous feeling. She was only sharing her future.

"I'm going to be a great dragonrider. One of the best. They'll write ballads about my adventures!" Kess leaned back against the headboard and turned her face upward as though she could see the sky she would one day soar in.

"Those are some big dreams."

Kess closed the book with a pout. "Not just a dream. It's my future. Don't you have plans for your future?"

Even before she'd finished the sentence, Kess could see the deep, scalding shimmer of sadness and fury in Riony's eyes.

That was the moment Kess had realized, through all her designs for her own destiny, the person she was closest to

had no future beyond what her masters set for her. All her churning worry turned solid and settled hard in her stomach.

"You'll probably still be with me anyway. I'll still need you, even when I have a dragon." Which was the second stupidest thing Kess had said within minutes.

Riony opened her mouth to speak, and blood dripped from the corner of her lips, staining her shirt.

Kess's whole body shook, a chill rattling through her uncontrollably, and her eyes peeled open. She was confused to find herself lying on a floor surrounded by bundles of smelly herbs.

It felt so real. Where am I?

"Try to stay awake, would you? This isn't the time to be dozing off." There was a tenderness beneath Riony's terse words that Kess didn't deserve.

"I'm sorry." Kess's lips barely parted around the words, her voice hoarse. Pain throbbed behind her eyes.

"Is that all you can say to me?"

There was so much more Kess wanted to say. "I'm sorry."

For everything. So many things. Too many things.

Riony dropped onto her haunches beside Kess, glaring critically. "Your apologies don't mean anything. It's too late now."

All tenderness in her tone had fled. Since being stuck there together, she'd had none of her usual smirking,

obscene humor. No carefree bravado. Her words now only held a deathly finality that made Kess shiver.

She held her breath for a long moment as though it could clear her lungs and head of the sedative permeating the room, then pushed her words out in a rush. "A promise then. That I won't call you Pony, ever again. I know you hate it, that you always hated it."

"And you kept on using it anyway. Nice."

Kess's throat clogged, and the words rattled around within her head.

Because it was a good way to ensure you hated me in return. I'm sure you did anyway, how could you not? But it was better to make sure. Then I'd never had reason to hope for anything more.

Riony stood up again, irises of enigmatic hue scowling down. "Promises are also useless. It's too late, Kess."

It's too late.

A pain like a dagger to the heart choked Kess and she sobbed out the words, "Can I ever make it up to you?"

It's too late.

Footsteps echoed down, muffled through the solid door, and they both turned to the sound.

A jangle of keys, the click of a lock, the creaking whine of old hinges, and Kife stood in the threshold.

He held a scarf over his mouth and nose, forehead

wrinkled as he glared down at Kess, and Kess alone.

Riony was gone.

Of course. Because she's dead.

"What a disgusting mess." Kife reached down for Kess's ankle as she wept soundlessly against the filthy ground.

He dragged her out of the room, pushing the door loosely closed behind him to separate them from the pungent herbs. Grasping her under the arms he hefted her roughly upward. He propped her up on the steep stairs, a couple higher than where he stood so they were almost eye to eye.

"Hey, wake up!" Kife slapped her across the cheek, as though the addition of physical pain would do anything to ease the effects of the morass mercy.

It only added spite into the swirl of emotions and nightmares blurring Kess's thoughts.

Kife was pacing the short length of his step, shouting, but Kess couldn't quite make the sounds turn into coherent words.

Something about silvernix. Expenses. Running out. Kill those guards if they ask for a bribe again. Crooks, everywhere.

Kess's eyelids drooped again but didn't close. Out there on the dark stairs, the air was clear, and slowly the edges of reality firmed themselves in Kess's perception.

The sting on her already bruised cheek was real.

The weak ache in her joints and long bones from a body

wrought motionless and underfed for too long was real.

And Riony was really ...

"I can't get an audience! Not even with one of King Draekhan's advisors, or any of the Firsts." Kife's words became clear as a ringing bell.

Good. Kess knew what would happen once he had the ear of the Dragon King, what Kife had planned.

Her memories cleared too, reminding her of how her brother would appear at irregular times to throw her scraps and abuse her for all his failures.

Memories of how she'd been entombed in her prison.

The flare, set off from the discarded saddlebags of an untamed dragon. A rider finding them, offering a favor to a downed fellow rider to bring them to the capital. Kife telling those they met along the way that Kess was unwell. How nobody questioned a dragonrider bringing a restrained and senseless girl into the city with him.

Kife threw his arm out in frustration and Kess flinched away from it.

"It's utter disrespect. How dare they turn away a Heithorn?" He still wore his dragonrider armor, red and blue, the colors of Skaella the First.

A finely crafted sword and collection of daggers, all with the Heithorn crest on the pommel, were on display along his belt, as though his presentation as a lordly dragonrider would grant him access to the king himself.

Kess closed her eyes for a long moment, wishing Riony would appear again, would come back to her, and wondering what Riony would do if she were there, and not gone forever.

Riony wouldn't give up.

"So, you're a reject as usual." She smirked at her brother. "What do you expect me to do about it?"

"As if you could do anything. It's your fault to begin with. You put such a stain upon our family name that I'm not being taken seriously by anybody."

"Then get rid of me if I'm such a thorn in your side." Kess bared her teeth, baiting, willing him to step closer.

Kife continued to pace. His long braid of charcoal hair swung at his back. The smaller side braids leading to the larger central one that ran down the top of his head weren't as neatly done as in the past and the stubble over his jaw was no longer neatly trimmed.

"Oh no, little sis. I'm keeping you around until you can see me in possession of a dragon once more, until you can see me capture the unidragon, so you can watch as I get everything you could never have. And once I have claimed every dream you once had as my own, then, maybe, I'll put you out of your misery."

Kess rolled her eyes at him. "So much melodrama. Only the dishonorable would need to gloat to a captive

audience. But you never understood honor."

Kife stilled, turning on her with knife-thin eyes.

Kess rasped her words through a jeering grin. "Even our parents could see that. I wasn't the only child they were isolating away from the eyes of nobility."

Kife stalked to her in two swift steps and leaned down, his finger jabbing forward and mouth opened.

Kess didn't wait to hear whatever he planned to say. As soon as he was within reach, she threw her arms up as fast as she could.

Blessed sun, they're so slow.

Her joints cracked and muscles ached at being forced into action. They lolled more than struck, one aiming for Kife's throat, the other aiming lower.

If she could have killed him right there, she would have. For herself. And for Riony. But her body barely responded to her demands.

Kife hissed as she clawed weakly against him. There was a brief flurry of limbs as she grasped and scratched, and he kept her fingernails off his neck and eyes. Then he caught her by one wrist and threw her down the few steps to the landing.

Kess smacked onto her stomach, one hand pinned beneath her, fist closed tight. Bitter triumph shot through her aching heart.

Kife stomped down to her. "Don't push me, Kessara, or maybe I'll simply forget that you are down here."

He grabbed her by the ankle and dragged her back into her prison.

As he closed the door and locked it, Kess remained face down, resting her forehead against the floor and breathing hard. The cloying spice of the morass mercy invaded her again.

A slow, dully echoing clap filled the space. Riony crouched beside her. "Great work. Very effective. You know he's going to miss it as soon as he takes his belt off, if not before."

Kess rolled over onto her back, revealing the slim dagger clutched to her chest. "Hopefully that will be too late."

Kess knew she was speaking to a ghost, or some figment of her broken mind, but she didn't care. She didn't blame Riony for haunting her. If anything, it was a comfort she didn't deserve, to not be alone.

With senses already swimming, Kess groaned into a sitting position and shuffled over to the door. The lock—or *locks* in her blurring vision—were just above head height, and it took three tries to get the dagger into the right one.

"What are you even going to do if you get that open?" Riony folded her arms, eyebrows raised skeptically. "Going to go try to get yourself a dragon again?"

Her one dream, all she'd ever wanted. Not anymore.

"No. Dracuni is still out there."

"So you're going to keep hunting her instead?" Riony was suddenly much closer, a wrathful spirit.

Kess's hand slipped, and she almost dropped the dagger. She tried to focus on working the lock. "No. I mean she's out there, without you to protect her."

"So you're going to?"

"If I have to. If I can." If it was too late to do anything else for Riony, for any apologies or promises, the one thing Kess could do was continue to protect the unidragon in her stead.

Although Kess doubted Riony's remaining companions would let her anywhere near them. *They must think I did it, that I killed her.*

Sweat beaded up all over Kess's chilled skin at the sheer exertion of simply keeping her hands up above her head. The lock refused to give.

Somewhere from high above, the howl of a wolf filtered down through the earth to her.

"Did you hear that?" Kess's hand jiggling the blade stilled, and the dagger slipped free of the lock.

"I didn't hear anything." Riony turned her face up toward the narrow ventilation shaft, the faint light setting her red hair aflame.

Was the air clearer up there? Is that why the morass

mercy wasn't affecting Riony?

No. No. She's not really here.

Was Griskin really there, or was that a desperate dream as well? It wasn't the only time she'd heard him call. Had he followed her? Found her? Couldn't reach her?

She hoped he was okay. That she hadn't lost him too.

Kess tried to lift her arm with the dagger back to the lock again, but it rolled droopily against the wall. She gritted her teeth, her eyes hot with defeat.

"I can't do this, not with all the morass mercy in here."

The weedy bouquets had lost some potency since she'd first been thrown in there. Faded enough that she could stay awake, but still messing up her ability to function, physically and mentally. Kess grasped at the nearest bundle of leaves and limply flung it to the other end of the room.

It wasn't far enough. But there were no windows or holes to dispose of the sedative foliage through. She pushed away another posy. Her efforts seemed to only stir up the scent even more.

Kess held Riony in a pleading gaze. "It's too much ... Too hard. I don't know if I can take any more."

Riony smirked in reply. "I don't want to hear the details of your love life, Kess."

Kess coughed out a laugh that quickly devolved into heaving sobs. "What am I going to do without you?"

Riony didn't offer an answer. She lowered down to sit cross-legged in front of Kess, watching dutifully as Kess decided her future.

And Kess knew exactly what she was going to do.

"I'm going to kill him. I'm going to kill Kife."

In revenge for what he did to Riony.

To stop him before he told anyone about Dracuni.

And before he killed her first.

TWO

Zarram Dragonhold was the largest dragon breeding, raising, and housing facility in the capital, with over two dozen breeders stabled and hatchery facilities large enough to raise over thirty hatchlings at a time.

But there was one dragon Dashiel Zarram cared about more than any of the other stock. Their stomach churned at the thought that very soon, the bond they had developed with that dragonling would be severed for good.

Dashiel skipped to keep up with their father's thunderous stride. "If I can show you the progress I've made with training Shiff, you'll see—"

"No. This little ... *experiment* of yours has gone on long enough." The giant of a man, built like a fortress tower, solid and grim, wiped his forehead and continued marching.

The stockyards sweltered in the midday heat as the Zarram siblings followed their father along on his daily inspection. Bovin lowed, jostling against each other in the tight pens.

Across on their father's other side, Vance gave Dashiel a gruff *told you so* expression. Their older brother had a build as equally intimidating as their father's, broad-shouldered in a way that threatened doorways and with a jawline cut from a wood block.

Dashiel refused to be intimidated, despite being the smallest and slimmest of the family. "Shiff isn't just an experiment. I really think there is intelligence within her. And emotions! That feel almost human, and it's like I am connecting with them."

Their father heaved to a stop then and rounded on Dashiel, looming over. "Intelligence? Emotion? Dragons are savage beasts. And your pet must be tamed before she becomes a threat."

"Pabba, please."

Their father raised a stern eyebrow.

"Fadda," Dashiel corrected themselves, switching to the Taen term.

Despite being Rolanian themselves, their father pushed them toward Taenish culture in all ways. As the only

Rolanian dragonlords in the city, they did their best to fit in as their station in society rose.

All three of them wore their hair in intricate Taenish braids that made their natural curls less obvious. Their father and Vance had matching earthy-brown locks, streaked pale from silvernix usage, a signifier of their wealth and station. Dashiel kept their loose caramel curls shorter, a flop of gold standing upon their head, corralled by a few braids along each side.

Vance was in all ways his father, but Dashiel had always been a neat blend of both their parents. Sharp angled yet pretty. Shoulders wider than most women, but more curves than most men.

Dashiel was the youngest too, at twenty-one. There was a good eight years' gap from Dashiel to Vance. They had a few sisters between them who had left for marriages designed to strengthen the Zarram name, but Vance and Dashiel remained at home.

Dashiel looked up into their father's eyes with a pleading determination.

The man scoffed and turned away, heading toward the dual-gate vestibule that led from the stockyards into the hatchery.

Dashiel tilted their head to Vance, mouthing, *Can you talk to him?*

"Because he listens to me when? This is up to you."
Vance huffed a wry laugh and patted Dashiel on the back
in a way that made them stumble forward three steps.

The siblings caught up as their father waited for the
guard to open the interior gate. The solid steel barrier rose
slowly into the recess above as the guard cranked the wheel.
Lord Zarram tsked at the grinding gears. Something had
gone wrong in the mechanism a while ago, meaning the
gate only stayed open with direct intervention, so they had
to have a guard on staff there at all times.

Dashiel knew the expense frustrated their father, but
they hadn't been able to find anyone with the skills to
repair it.

Vance closed the outer door behind them, cutting them
off from the burned orange heat and smelly haze. Only a
thin stream of light shined through a barred grate above.

As the inner gate screeched slowly upward, Lord Zarram
turned to Dashiel. "Your investment into the king's riders
is coming up. Your shimmerdart is a fine creature. The best
of the current generation to raise for your steed. We can't
waste her on these dangerous ideas of yours."

Dashiel had picked the hatchling for that very reason.
She was glorious, large for her kind, bright and curious right
from the egg. She should have been tamed on her day of
hatching, but the newborn had looked into Dashiel's eyes

with such knowing and fear that Dashiel couldn't bring themselves to hammer the spike.

They separated the dragonling from the others, worried it could become dangerous, and then they spent all their free hours together in the weeks since then, only to find the dragonling to be gentler than they could have imagined.

And the idea of taming the creature hurt more than ever.

The gate was fully opened and Lord Zarram turned to leave.

Dashiel grasped his arm. "I can't. Fadda. I can't do it. Please don't make me tame her."

Their father's mouth twitched and he looked away. "You can have until your investment. You will tame her then, alongside the other new recruits taming their chosen hatchlings."

The man strode away, waving one hand dismissively to signal that the discussion was over.

"I think that went as well as could have been hoped," Vance muttered.

Dashiel gave him a flat look. "Yes. Fantastic. I'm thrilled."

Vance leaned to one side, rubbing his thigh with a soft groan. "Come, Dash. You've a bright future. You made it through trials and into the king's own dragonriders! You'll be training with the best after investment."

"Not the best. You won't be there."

Vance let go of his leg and straightened up again. "I had my chance and lost it. I'm stuck here with Pabba now. But you ... You know how the other dragonlords look at us, even when the king himself favors our broods. It's up to you now to destroy their expectations."

The guard waited, straining slightly to keep the gate opened until the siblings stepped through. He cleared his throat softly.

They got moving again. Dashiel hated walking under the drop-gate, always worried the guard might let go and the solid metal would come rushing down and crush them. They took a hurried step to the other side.

A birdlike cry of steel rushing closed followed the siblings as they wandered through the hatchery. Servants sorted and turned eggs on their warming beds. They would be hatching soon, bred specially for the king's newest recruits to select from.

Vance and Dashiel reached the stables for the full-sized dragons. They lined a long hallway, with a fight deck opening into the sky at the end. The siblings stopped in front of a beautiful golden etherflame, dully chewing at a slab of meat in its trough.

"You know ... I didn't want to tame Viska either, at the time." Vance stepped into the stall and placed a hand onto the bright scales of the dragon's cheek.

It didn't respond.

Dashiel raised their eyebrows. "I did *not* know that."

"I didn't take as long as you have to get around to it. Only a couple of days. I fought Fadda over it, questioning why it had to be done, whether we could try another way. I had all these wild ideas. I think it was Eslinde's influence, really."

Dashiel grinned. "I bet."

Vance gave them a quelling glare. "But there's no other way. If you want a dragon that can be flown, that follows orders without question, it must be tamed."

Was it the only way? Dashiel reached a hand to the stake in Viska's forehead. She was such an incredible creature, mostly etherflame, but with just a little snowshimmer in her line a few generations back that made her sleeker and faster than usual for that species. What could she have been if all her autonomy hadn't been taken away by that sharp metal in her brain?

"The Rebel Riders don't tame their dragons," Dashiel said.

"The Rebel Riders are stories." Vance leaned against the stable wall and folded his arms. "Should I have left home to go and become a fictional character to save one dragon from taming?"

"There are rumors that they're real. Eslinde used to believe it." Dashiel mimicked Vance's pose, across on the other side of the stall, trying to look as imposing.

"And that's exactly the kind of influence I was talking about. She always had such rebellious stories and ideas." Vance shook and lowered his head, a soft smile across his lips as he stared at the floor. Then his eyebrows lowered. "But things change."

"You ever find out why she stopped coming around?" Dashiel asked gently.

Vance rumbled a growling grunt.

"It's been, what, five years?"

"Eight." The word jumped from Vance's mouth. "Doesn't matter. I'm sure she's busy. I wouldn't expect her to indulge us with her company like she did when we were young."

Dashiel had always wanted to know what had stopped Eslinde from visiting. It was strange that she didn't even come around to check on or fly her dragon. It was kept a few stalls down, a fine snowshimmer. Eslinde would have had the resources to stable it herself, so it was an honor that she trusted the Zarrams with the keeping of her dragon.

Servants moved around, loading bovin meat from a cart into feeding troughs, and a few people walked in from the entrance.

Dashiel raised their eyebrows. "You wouldn't like to see her again?"

"It's not something I think about."

A grin split Dashiel's lips and they straightened up.

"That's a shame, because she's coming up behind you now."

"How dumb do you think I—"

"Oh, Viska is so big now!" a wispy feminine voice exclaimed.

The woman and her grayglim and handmaiden attendants stopped at the entrance to the dragon's stall.

Vance shot forward from his leaning pose, almost stumbling as he righted himself.

Dashiel subdued a chuckle and moved to greet Eslinde. It had been so long since she'd visited the dragonhold, or been seen at all, that Dashiel was taken aback by how different she looked now.

She must be around thirty years old, but time seemed to have treated her badly. Her skin was sallow and pale, and her austere gray gown, sparkling with highlights of decadent gold, hung on a narrow frame. Hair like a silver beam of moonlight was tied back from her face in a simple braided bun, highlighting sunken cheeks and shadowed eyes.

She was a ghost of her past self.

"What are you, umm, why ... grace us with your presence?" Vance cleared his throat after the stumble of words and shot Dashiel a look of murderous intent.

She gave a wan smile. "I came to congratulate Dashiel on their upcoming investment."

"Me? I thought you might have come to visit—"

Vance slapped a hand over Dashiel's shoulder and squeezed.

"Your dragon," Dashiel coughed the words out.

A slight frown passed over her face and she shook her head. "I'm sure you are looking after her well."

"Always," Vance replied.

Eslinde placed one hand across her chest and gave a slight bow. Earrings of spiraling silver and glass swung as she straightened up again. "Congratulations, Dashiel. I heard you had the highest scores of the current recruits, highest of any since your brother."

Dashiel bowed in return, lowering from the waist far deeper than Eslinde had. Then with a bright smile, they asked, "Will we see you at the ceremony?"

Eslinde lifted one shoulder. "Perhaps. Perhaps I will come along. It has been a while. Maybe it will feel different now."

"You never did like watching the tamings. You don't have to attend." Vance shot Dashiel a look, his tone defensive.

Eslinde waved one hand limply, her fingers skeletal. She looked up at Viska's taming spike, the end of it exposed between golden scales. "I used to watch, make myself watch and wonder how it must feel. A metal stake, right through into the brain. And I did feel it, so deeply."

Dashiel shivered, swallowing hard.

Shaking her head, she toyed with one of her earrings. "Now ... now I look at the spike and pretend it's just jewelry there on their forehead. Nothing terrible. Just a decoration over their scales. And I no longer feel it."

A deep, sinking sadness washed over Dashiel. From the silence all around, they wondered if Vance felt it too. The young woman who had once influenced them both with her fiery, rebellious heart was utterly gone. *What happened to her?*

The awkward silence expanded and then cracked as Eslinde muttered, "I'll see you there, then."

Turning, she strode toward the exit, her gown trailing behind her and attendants in tow, all silent and gray, like a procession of spirits.

Vance exhaled audibly.

"Don't be down, brother. It looks like you'll be seeing her again soon," Dashiel teased.

"Yes. At your investment. Where you'll be taming your dragonling. Good times for all," Vance growled back.

Dashiel's playful tone dropped. "Thanks for the reminder."

"I'm sorry. She's just..." Vance paced a small circle on the ground. "She doesn't look well, does she?"

Dashiel pulled their lips in. "No, she doesn't."

Eslinde looked as unwell as somebody with a wealth of silvernix at their disposal could look. An unwellness of the heart, a wasting away of a soul that the magical healing fluid couldn't repair. The Eslinde they used to know would never turn away from trouble, never pretend a cruelty was something lesser to protect herself.

Just jewelry there on their forehead.

Dashiel's eyes widened as the idea hit. "Oh. Oh!"

"What is it?" Vance turned expectantly toward the entrance of the stables, as though Eslinde was returning.

"I've got to go. There's something I need to try." Dashiel bounced with excitement, bounding away down the hall backward, grinning at their brother on the way.

Vance took a few steps as though to follow, then gave up. "Try what? Is this some new wild experiment?"

"I'll show you soon. If it works." They turned and waved over their shoulder.

Vance called out, "Are we going to regret this?"

Dashiel's exuberant jog slowed then. Would they?

It was just an idea, for now. A concept they could toy with to avoid facing a fate they didn't want. But if it came to following through, if Dashiel pretended to tame a dragon but left it wild and was found out, it could destroy everything the Zarrams had built as a family.

THREE

The door burst open, clattering against the empty shelves. Kess would have flinched, but her body was paralyzed by hunger and the morass mercy. She blinked up at the shadowed wraith filling the doorway.

"Still alive?" Kife snarled. "Could have done me a favor and passed away quietly, but you can't even do that one thing right, little sis."

It had been an eternity since he had last visited, last thrown her the crusts of old bread or left a bucket of water. Kess was as surprised as he was that she still lived. She was sure she'd joined Riony's ghost in an endless limbo of nightmares long ago.

He didn't come inside or try to drag Kess out.

Does he know I have his dagger?

Do I still have his dagger? Kess couldn't feel her own fingers, let alone the weapon she had tucked into the waistband of her pants during a dream long ago.

Does he even care if I did? He hadn't tried to take it back, hadn't called her out. Why would he need to? She was no threat. She was lucky to have enough strength to roll her eyes at him.

Which she did. Maybe if she taunted him enough, he'd try to finish her off once and for all. If Kess could summon the strength to stab him back at the same time, she'd call it a win.

From the way he stalked back and forth in the landing beyond the doorway, whiplike braid swinging, and sword drawn, maybe that time had finally come.

"I'm done with this whole razed affair! It's time to start fresh, without bad luck jinxing my every plan." He leveled the sword her way.

A trickle of fresh air flowed through the open door to Kess, and she tried to suck it in, help her body reawaken from the stupor it had been in.

"Giving up? Can't blame you. If I had your face, I would've given up long ago," Kess slurred.

Sitting behind her in the corner, knees up and legs splayed cavalierly, Riony chuckled.

Kife slashed his sword through the air but remained outside the small chamber. "I'm not giving up. I just feel like killing you might brighten my mood."

"I'm sure it'll help greatly. Good plan. Go ahead, then."

Riony laughed again, a soft rustle of breath. "Subtle, Kess, very subtle."

"Shh!" Kess frowned, then shook her pounding head. "No. Doesn't matter. He can't hear you."

Riony was only there to haunt Kess.

"That's exactly the problem," Kife said, as though she were speaking to him. He spat the words, jabbing his sword as though at imaginary enemies. "What good is this knowledge of the silvernix creature if I can't get the ear of the Dragon King? No way will I share it with anybody else. If I just had a dragon again, I could go after it myself, get proof ..."

"Proof?" Kess turned her head toward him, and it wobbled, skull pressed against the stone. Maybe she wasn't ready to die, not if she could conceive a way out of her cell. A sly smile spread over her lips. "Then you might as well kill me. I'll never tell anyone what I know. You can't use me for leverage to get your way in."

Kife's pacing ceased, and he glowered at Kess. She worried she'd gone too far, too unsubtle again for the outcome she desired.

But Kife was as familiar with subtlety as a blunt axe.

"You'll do whatever I need you to do." He lunged forward and grabbed her around the ankle.

Kess's throbbing head ached and swirled as Kife dragged her across the ground. Dried bundles of morass mercy rustled around her, kicking up their scent.

"Are you really taking me out of here?" There was a desperation in Kess's voice, and she twisted it around into a snarl to hide her hopes. "I won't say anything, even if you do get us in front of the king."

Kife's grin was viciously triumphant. "You keep your mouth shut all you want. I can still use you as *leverage*. I'll tell them you're a criminal, a traitor to the kingdom, who I caught scheming the king's downfall. *That* might get me an audience. Any way I can get in front of the king is worth it."

And anything that gets me away from the morass mercy is worth it.

"Even if you leave me behind?" Riony's eyes glinted like sharp knives from the shadowed corner of the cell.

A juddering shiver shook through Kess's chest. She rolled droopily, arms flopping in a weak attempt to reach for the ghost. "No, I won't!"

Kife laughed at her futile struggling. He got her out of the room and kicked the door closed behind him.

She was out. Kess closed her eyes and tried to think clear thoughts and breathe clear air, but the lingering effect of the sedative was drawing her under again. Her body didn't feel like her own.

The sway of Kife lifting her swung her whole world into dizziness and her head felt fractured and disjointed from her body. "You razing stink, Kess."

She sank away into a dark hollow. Swallowed into nothingness, only brief snatches of reality filtered through to her.

A stairwell, damp and slimy like the throat of a monster. Daylight. *Daylight!* A glare that burned her eyes and forced tears from between her lashes.

Rattling, bumping, thumping. Kess awoke sprawled on the hard bench of a carriage. It beat her back like a wooden bat and the motion stirred sickness in her shriveled stomach.

Stay awake.

Kife was right across from her, turned to the window. There was a jagged press of metal beneath Kess's clothing. The dagger was still there. She fumbled for it, eyes on her brother, on his neck, trying to calculate whether she could draw fast enough, whether her hands still knew how to throw, and exactly which of the three blurred copies of the man to aim at.

A large bump made Kess's whole body lurch and

head flare with pain. She grunted and Kife turned to her. Turning her eyes quickly away, she stilled, and pretended to be squinting out the window instead of focusing on him. The buildings they passed by had wreaths of dried wheat and gold ribbons hung on their doors.

Summers End? It's been months ... I missed my eighteenth birthday.

A dry, rasping sob crumpled within Kess's throat as grief hit her. Not because of the birthday or the duration of her imprisonment, but how for some of that time she'd heard the distant echoes of a wolf howling. He'd been there, trying to find her, reach her.

But she hadn't heard Griskin for a while now. She worried at first that something had happened, whether a city guard had captured him or worse. But she knew the truth. He wasn't going to wait for her forever.

Griskin has abandoned me too.

"It's what you deserve," Riony said, sitting shoulder to shoulder with Kife across the carriage like best buddies.

Riony would never.

Was any of this real? Had Griskin ever come to Draekhanhelm and called to her through the night?

Even so far away from morass mercy, Kess's head still felt steeped in the stuff. It had soaked through every fiber of her and left her stained forever. She tried to stay awake, tried to draw the small dagger and carve it into Kife's flesh, but she slipped away again.

"You're such a dead weight, Kess." Kife dumped her unceremoniously on the floor.

She gasped as pain shocked her into consciousness. Her eyes swiveled, trying to orient herself in the space. A coolly lit chamber, expansive, with a vaulted ceiling and ornate columns, all in a pale marble, shot through with silver.

Lamps flickered with a pale-blue light from sconces. Fine wooden chairs, glassy with polish, lined the wall, as though this were some kind of waiting parlor.

Or audience chambers.

Kess frowned, worried her brother had gotten closer to meeting the king than she'd hoped he would. How long would she last if presented as some kind of assassin plotting Yeonard Draekhan's death?

Kife hadn't bothered putting Kess down onto a chair, although they were all empty. She had been dumped in the middle of the floor on the cold marble. He strode over and pushed a set of double doors open.

Then he swore and kicked at the threshold. "It took the last of my silvernix to bribe my way in, and the King isn't even here?"

Glancing over the unoccupied chairs again, and through the opened doors ahead into a grand chamber with dais and throne all cold and bare, a smile cracked Kess's lips. The whole place was empty. No king, no audiences, no guards. Just an empty space that was otherwise closed except to an idiot who spent silvernix on a guard to get in.

She chuckled. "That's probably the *only* reason you got this far. What a joke. Better luck next time, brother."

Kife dropped into a chair and folded his arms like a displeased infant. "No. This is going to work. We're staying right here until someone, anyone, arrives who will listen."

Kess managed to roll over onto one side and lift her head, a feat so impressive by recent standards that she took courage. Maybe she would take her revenge that day. "I have never heard a dumber plan in my life. Could you be more desperate?"

His sharp eyes locked on her. "I should have kept some of the morass mercy around to shut you up."

"Because you're too useless to shut me up yourself."

"I'm serious, Kess, close that mouth of yours or—"

"What? You're pathetic. You couldn't even defeat a Rolanian slave in a sword fight." Kess let a mocking giggle roll from her mouth and reached one hand to her waist.

"Shut up!"

"I so greatly enjoyed watching from atop *your* dragon as she beat your ass up and down."

"Enough!" he roared and was on his feet, storming

across the floor her way.

Kess wrapped a hand around the hilt of the dagger, warmed from her body.

Kife bent down, grasping her by the straps of the leather vest that was once Riony's. He dragged her up off the floor, face-to-face with him.

Pulling the stolen blade free, Kess swung. It glanced feebly off the scales forming Kife's dragonrider armor. Her fingers were too numb to maintain their grip, and the blade slipped free and clattered on the tiles. Kife kicked it away and it spun across the glossy stone into a corner.

Kife raised an eyebrow and smirked. "If I thought you had any chance at all of hurting me, I would have taken that off you when you stole it. But it was far more fun to see you think you had hope."

He released one hand and then slapped the back of it hard across Kess's face. The crack of knuckle against cheekbone echoed around them.

In reply, a high, outraged voice struck through the air like a bell. "What are you doing to her?"

Whether he'd intended to all along or was startled into it, Kife dropped Kess. She collapsed hard, like a pile of bones.

A gasp of indignation followed, then the same voice again snapped, "Yensen!"

A flurry of motion appeared at Kife's side. A grayglim warden, clad in armor of smoke-colored scales and silk, had Kife locked in a grapple from behind before Kess could even shake off the stun of failing her strike, of being thrown to the ground.

Four others had also entered the room. A woman in a sweeping gown of gray and gold rushed toward Kess, before being pulled back by an older man at her side.

"Careful, this may be some sort of trap," he said in a tone that suggested he was actually excited by the prospect.

"She's hurt, look at her!"

There were a couple of handmaidens behind them as well, but Kess could only stare at the woman with the starlight hair, pulled into a tight, braided bun.

She looks like 'the guest.'

The mysterious visitor to Heithorn estate for the months leading up to the birth of her child. A child that was stolen and took everything good from Kess's life with her.

But she also looked so different, Kess wasn't sure. It may have been that age had narrowed down her cheeks and all the roundness of youth and pregnancy she'd had was replaced with a boney fragility. But there was also something so different in how she carried herself. None of the haughty attitude of the young woman awaiting birth. Only a grim chill of despair and apathy.

"Let me go. I can explain." Kife at least had the dignity to not try to escape the grayglim's hold. He remained still, chin raised.

The woman looked between him and Kess, assessing, as she tapped a finger to the corner of her mouth. "And what explanation could you have for this display of barbarity? I'd expect far more from a Heithorn."

It is her.

Kess glanced at her brother. Had he realized yet who she was? Just some dragonlord lady. That's how he'd described the guest when Kess had fished for any information he might have. And from the confused look on his face, he had never taken much notice of the guest.

"I'm sorry, do I know you?" He huffily jostled one constrained arm.

"Clearly not. But you are the Heithorn son?"

"Finally!" he groaned out the word. "Yes, last remaining of a noble family. It's wonderful to meet someone who recognizes it! You don't know how long I've been trying to speak to someone with some power around here."

The woman inclined her head, very slightly, and made no order to her grayglim to loosen his hold. Instead, she turned back toward Kess, stepping free from the gentle hold of the elderly man beside her. He muttered and grumbled warnings again.

She waved him off. "It's fine."

"Do beware, Milady," Kife said. "That girl is dangerous. A traitor to the kingdom."

"I'm not. Please, he's lying to get his way," Kess countered. Her eyes rolled back, and she shook her head, trying to stay conscious.

"This girl? She's too weak to stand." The guest leaned down, grasping Kess by her hands and tugging. "I can tell a person who has been abused and imprisoned for a long time. And I can tell when someone is trying to feed me lies."

When Kess made no attempt to get her legs under her, even with assistance, the woman frowned. "Jillisa, Olva, come and help me, please."

"If you'll just let me explain." Kife's voice rose louder, snapping in frustration. "I have important secrets that I must share with the king himself. If you can arrange an audience, you'll be rewarded, I promise!"

Kess tightened her grasp around the woman's fingers, still within hers. She couldn't let Kife get to her, get to the king through her.

The handmaidens bent down on either side, lifting Kess from the ground and bringing her over onto a chair. Kess kept her hold on the woman, meeting eyes as pale and silver as her hair.

As the handmaidens stepped back, Kess pulled the

guest closer and whispered, "I know something too. About somebody you once lost."

Those ardent eyes snapped open.

Kess rasped, "But you have to make him leave. I won't tell you unless you make Kife leave."

"Someone I once lost?" The look the guest gave Kess was so intense it rattled her.

Kess nodded.

"What is she saying?" Kife leaned forward in the grayglim's hold. "Don't listen to anything that comes out of that girl's mouth."

The guest addressed her grayglim. "Yensen, could you escort Lord Heithorn out, please?"

There was hesitation then, a faltering of the man's impassive expression. "You aren't to be left unprotected."

"I'm well accompanied here." Eslinde gestured to the three others in the room. "Do as I say."

The man nodded once, a strand of long ebony hair falling loose over his face.

"You can't just ... How dare you!" Kife screeched as Yensen muscled him toward the door. "I'll have you pay for this one day, when I get—"

"You threaten Eslinde the First so freely, boy?" The elderly man stepped forward, his gray robes swishing.

The *oh shit* expression on Kife's face would have brought

Kess great joy in a normal situation. But she was too busy reeling herself.

Eslinde the First was the guest? The youngest of the Dragon King's first generation of heirs was the woman who had been hidden away at their isolated estate to give birth in secrecy?

That meant ... Kess's head drooped and bobbed as a hysterical chuckle burbled from her.

Oh Riony, it wasn't enough to have a live pet with silvernix blood. You had to have a stolen heir as your sister as well?

Over Eslinde's shoulder, the redhead smirked in return. "Guess I'm just lucky? If only that luck kept me alive."

When the grayglim had Kife out of the room, Eslinde the First muttered, "Such a dreadful man. What has been going on between you two that he has treated you like this?"

Kess shrugged and almost slid off her chair. "This is pretty normal, actually."

"And all you deserve," Riony added cheerily.

"I know we never met formally, but ..." Eslinde reached out and helped stabilize Kess, frowning deeply. She looked down at Kess's legs. "I remember you now. And I am interested to hear what you remember of me and those I may have lost."

The child who became Riony's sister. If this woman, the guest, had been any other dragonlord lady, Kess could have told her, could have assumed it wouldn't come to anything. Who had the resources to be chasing a single child across the wastes of the rev blighted world? Kess and Kife had tried and failed already.

But one of the Firsts would have all the resources required to reclaim their child.

Riony sat down in the seat beside her with a prolonged sigh. "And you're going to hand my sister over to this woman? Thanks, Kess. You just keep on hitting new lightless depths, don't you?"

Kess flinched away. She didn't want that. She didn't want to hurt Riony again, alive or dead. "I was mistaken. You aren't who I thought you were. I can't … I don't know anything."

Her words were an unconvincing stumble, but her head drummed with agony and she couldn't think.

Eslinde straightened to her full height away from Kess. She blinked dully. "Really?"

"Your Highness." The older, robed man shuffled closer, although he kept some distance between himself and Kess, wrinkling his nose at the state of her.

Wisps of white hair trailed down each side of his head from a shiny bald top. "What with all this excitement, shall I cancel your meeting? Or will you still be able to meet with Lady Hjelzahn?"

A shiver jolted Kess's back against the chair. There were a lot of Hjelzahns, generations of them, since Hjelzahn the First. But there was one Kess never wanted to see again.

Kess choked on her words. "Lady Hjelzahn? Kverra Hjelzahn?"

"The same." Eslinde shrugged, keeping assessing eyes on Kess as she spoke to the man. "Well, Falden, it all depends on whether this girl has anything to tell me or not."

"Here? You're meeting her here?" Kess asked breathily.

Eslinde replied, "What does that matter to you?"

Because that grayglim noblewoman who seemed immune to pain would no doubt kill Kess as soon as given the opportunity. Because that woman seemed intent upon killing her own children, who both Lyrrin and Dracuni were likely to still be with. Because every part of Kess's drugged and confused mind screamed in fear at the thought of seeing that strange, cold woman again.

"You can't. Don't meet with her. We have to go before she arrives, please."

"Why? What do you have to tell me that gives me a reason to listen to any of this nonsense?"

There was only one thing. The only leverage Kess had to offer, to gain Eslinde's favor and keep herself away from Lady Hjelzahn, away from Kife. And she grieved for what consequences saying it might bring.

Kess reached out and grasped Eslinde's hands again with every scrap of her remaining strength, dragging her down so their faces were only a breath away.

She whispered, "Your daughter is still alive."

FOUR

Kess expected the revelation that her child was still alive might have caused some joy or relief in the princess. Instead, Eslinde's expression was one of naked fear.

Worried the woman had misheard her somehow, Kess raised her voice. "She isn't dead, your—"

"Quiet!" Eslinde pressed her fingers over Kess's mouth and gave her a sharp look, before checking over her shoulders to see how close her entourage were.

The two handmaidens—one with skin aged like the bark of an oak and a stoic, motherly air, and the other young and wide-eyed as though everything around her were new and exciting—were a respectful space back, hovering in readiness to respond to any need that arose.

The older man, Falden, in his noble robes, also maintained a distance, eyeing the utter state of filth Kess displayed with thinly veiled disgust.

Eslinde remained frozen in position with her fingers shushing Kess for a long moment. Her eyes darted as though working through a multitude of thoughts.

The door clicking closed made both her and Kess jump.

Kess leaned sideways to see whether Lady Hjelzahn approached, but found instead the princess's grayglim, Yensen, returning. Whether he had ejected Kife from the palace onto the street himself or handed him over to other guards to expel, he'd returned with an eager speed.

Kess wondered if she should have asked for more, had Kife thrown in a dungeon. But she also didn't want to push Kife into sharing his knowledge of Dracuni in desperation.

There was concern on the grayglim's face as he took in Kess and her proximity to Eslinde. His dark eyes also fell on the dagger which lay in the corner.

"All's well?" he asked.

Eslinde's eyelids fluttered as she side-eyed him but otherwise didn't acknowledge the man.

"We need to go," Kess urged again in a whisper.

"Yes, some privacy is required." Eslinde nodded once and rose up tall, away from Kess. "Olva, Jillisa, help her to my chambers."

They bobbed a curtsy in time together, then each took Kess by an arm.

Their first attempt to assist Kess from the seat left her hanging like a spent scarecrow between them. They moved in closer, propping themselves under a shoulder each.

"Oh goodness, goodness, goodness," the older handmaiden said, turning her nose away.

"Falden?" Eslinde waved the man closer. "Would you wait here and give Lady Hjelzahn my apologies that I won't be able to meet with her today."

"Of course, Your Highness. Unless you need some assistance with this ... situation?" He gestured to Kess, forehead wrinkled.

"Oh, it's nothing. She's an old friend come upon hard times, that's all. Something of a misunderstanding."

"Hmm, quite." Falden settled himself into one of the chairs with a soft groan. Boney knees poked from under his robes.

As she turned to leave, Eslinde paused, then addressed him again. "And could you also check on what records or information we have on the Heithorn family, please?"

His eyes sparkled and thin lips pulled into a smile. "Always happy to assist."

Eslinde nodded, then broke into a long, elegant stride, leading the way out of the audience chambers.

Following behind, Kess tried to keep her head up as she was jostled between the two handmaidens. But her arms ached from the strain of hanging in their grasp and it felt as though her skull had been hollowed out and filled with hot lead.

The grayglim remained close at their heels as their procession wove through the corridors of the palace.

Kess took in what she could of the grand space. Surfaces of glossy marble and obsidian were brightened by flickering lamps and colossal windows of clear glass and steel. Dark wood furniture was made decadent with golden accents and silver upholstery.

Guards in dragon scale armor were posted at regular intervals as Eslinde led them down a long hall, through a tiled courtyard with precisely trimmed hedges, and into a labyrinth of corridors, carved out with large niches, each holding lifelike statues of ancient heroes.

A few other servants rushed about, all Rolanian and all wearing a uniform similar to the women carrying Kess—neat tunics and kirtles in charcoal gray.

Kess tried to keep her bearings, to work out how she could follow this path back to an exit if she had a chance, but a few turns along, her head whirled.

They ascended three flights of stairs, handmaidens huffing and muttering under their breaths, and their

journey came to an end in what seemed to be a poorly managed library.

The chamber was of the same, stark glossy stone as the rest of the palace. The only thing that added color and texture to the room were the bookshelves that lined the walls, filled so completely that the books were wedged in at odd angles in every gap and spilled onto the floor in towering piles.

The vast space only held a few pieces of furniture, their black and silver forms reflecting on slick dark tiles, and all piled in a mess of books.

"Put her on the lounge," Eslinde said and then paced, chewing on a nail as the handmaidens moved aside a few leatherbound tomes and sat Kess down.

Kess's eyelids were drooping and she screwed them shut, then forced them open again to refresh them. The plush cushions beneath her were so soft against her body—that had forgotten any feeling other than hard and cold—that she almost broke down. It was only Riony's steady glare from the armchair opposite that kept Kess composed.

"I'm sorry I told," Kess whispered.

Eslinde spoke over her, tone commanding. "She needs food, clean clothing. Now please, both of you."

She herded her handmaidens back out through the door they'd just come in, then ran up against the grayglim as though hitting a wall.

"Wait outside too, Yensen."

He tilted his head, almost apologetically. "I can't leave you alone with her, Your Highness."

Eslinde drew herself up straight, barely coming to the man's shoulders. "You can and you will. She deserves some privacy and dignity in this moment. Or are you going to give the poor child a sponge bath?"

He frowned awkwardly under thick eyebrows, high cheekbone twitching. "The Heir Killer is still unknown and becoming bolder. This could all be a ruse. This girl could be a threat."

"Her?" There was laughter in the princess's voice. "She's no Heir Killer. And from the looks of things, she's been held captive right through when Skaella was assassinated last week. She's nothing but bruised skin and bones and has no weapons and can't even walk. What do you think she's going to do?"

A breathy, sobbing laugh broke from Kess and she slid down onto her side. She'd been underestimated her whole life but had to admit the princess's estimations felt crushingly accurate in that moment.

A deep, stubborn inner voice that had driven her on her whole life revived from within the shadows of her mind.

I'll show them. I'll show them all.

Eslinde continued her rant, jabbing a finger into the man's breastplate. "And you, you're nothing more than a jailer acting under my parents' orders."

Yensen looked pained. "Your Highness, I'm not—"

"Prove it then! Go on, get out!"

Yensen cast a concerned look toward Kess, then the princess, then Kess again, and then stepped out of the room.

Eslinde closed the door behind him, none too gently, then hurried back to Kess's side.

She knelt before the lounge, and her pale eyes looked deep into Kess's, searching. "You are the Heithorn daughter, aren't you? They kept you away from me as much as they kept me away from you during my stay. What was it ... Kessara?"

Kess wobbled a nod.

"And my child ... a daughter too? How, how do you know she lived?" Despite the closed door, Eslinde still kept her voice barely above a whisper.

Kess blinked, confused for a moment. Did she know for sure? It was just a guess really, based on age and circumstance. However, looking into the princess's face, she could see the same almond shape to her eyes as Lyrrin had, the same pouting, petal lips.

"I know. I've seen her."

"Recently? She's grown?" Eslinde's chest heaved with labored breath.

Across in the armchair, Riony leaned forward, resting her elbows on her knees and locking on Kess with an accusing glare. "Go ahead. Tell her. Let her know aaaaall about my sister and her unnaturally blue eyes and her strange, clawed hands. The Dragon King's daughter is going to love that. I'm sure she's going to make sure Lyrrin stays safe and well."

Kess pulled her lips in and kept them closed tight. She turned her eyes away, staring at the blurring floor beneath her.

Eslinde grasped Kess's wrist, pulling her attention back again. "Is she still at Heithorn estate? Where is she? What happened to her?"

The hammering of questions made Kess flinch, her head about to crack like an egg.

"If you tell her anything, you might as well stab me in the back again," Riony snarled.

"It wasn't me. Riony, I didn't ..."

Eslinde glanced over her shoulder, following Kess's eyeline. She frowned. "What are you talking about? Who's Riony?"

Kess crumpled into a gasping fit of hysteria. "A ghost. She's haunting me, for all I did to her."

Eslinde raised an eyebrow. "A ghost?"

A light rapping echoed from the door and Eslinde

rose back to her feet, brushing her dress down. "Come."

The older handmaiden returned, a neatly folded stack of clothing balanced in her hands. "I've a selection for the child, should be some that fit."

Yensen peered in through the opened door, but Eslinde strode over and closed it on him. "Olva, could you check over her, please? She's behaving oddly. Speaking of ghosts. Could she be unwell, beyond her physical injuries?"

"Ghosts, you say?" Olva placed the clothing down on a low table wrought of black metal and glass beside a stack of books.

She moved close to Kess, pressing her face tight within her gnarled fingers and pulling her eyelids back. "Hmm, yes. I thought I noted a familiar scent ... beneath the *other* smells. Been a long time since I've worked with herbs myself, but there are some fragrances you'll always remember."

Eslinde drifted behind the woman, clasping her hands together. "An herb? Has she been drugged somehow?"

"For certain. It's a nasty sedative that healers only used if they couldn't get their hands on anything else. Terrible side effects. Prolonged headaches, withering, hallucinations."

Eslinde's nervous fidgeting ceased and a dull sadness washed over her face. "Hallucinations?"

The handmaiden released Kess from her tight grip.

"Some silvernix should clear any long-term effects right up, though. Shall I fetch some?"

The corner of Eslinde's mouth twitched and she stared down at Kess for a long moment. "So be it."

As the older handmaiden went out, the younger came in, hefting a silver tray filled with steaming bowls, bread rolls, and fruit.

Once the door was closed to the grayglim again, Eslinde scrubbed her face with her hands and muttered, "It wasn't even real. Just hallucinations."

"Pardon, Your Highness?" The handmaiden placed the tray onto the table beside the clothing with a soft rattle of crockery.

"It's nothing." Eslinde peered at Kess as though she were a piece of trash she was eager to dispose of.

She will. She'll get rid of me if I can't provide enough information for her to believe me.

In a moment of panic, Kess blurted, "The redheaded girl and her family, they took the b—"

"*Bath!*" Eslinde practically shouted. "Jillisa, go and draw one, please."

The handmaiden had frozen with a serving lid held high in one hand. Blinking a couple of times, she curtsied and vanished into a side room. The burbles of running water emerged soon after.

"Careful!" Eslinde hissed near Kess's ear. "Nobody knows, nobody is to know there *ever* was a child! Only my parents and those from the Heithorn estate who didn't know my identity."

Kess nodded vaguely. Of course it was a secret. Why would a first heir travel all the way to the middle of nowhere to give birth? The Heithorn midwife was good, but the Dragon King himself no doubt would have had better.

"Not the biggest secret out there," Riony said. "Once this woman starts searching for Lyrrin, how long do you think it will be before she finds out about Dracuni? You might as well tell her now and get it over with."

"I won't tell," Kess mumbled to the ghost.

Or hallucination. Is that what she was? She seemed so real. Or maybe that's just what Kess wanted, for Riony to still be real.

The world all around her appeared like a view through a twisted mirror and Kess's whole body felt turned inside out.

"Could it be true? My heart feels taut like a bowstring." Eslinde kneeled beside Kess again, elbows on the lounge and palms on her forehead. "The redheaded girl ... there was one there, at the birth. The midwife's daughter and assistant. But no, they were all killed, weren't they?"

Kess opened her mouth to reply, leaned forward, and dry heaved over the side of the seat.

Eslinde jumped away, then when she realized Kess had nothing inside her to expel, tentatively returned. She brushed a hand gently over Kess's cheek where it was still hot and thrumming from being backhanded.

In a gentle voice, she said, "It's alright. We'll have you fixed up soon."

Tears welled up in the corners of Kess's eyes at the small act of kindness.

And then Eslinde continued. "And then you will tell me what you know. This isn't just some sickness. I can sense you are hiding something from me, and I will have the truth from you. All of it."

A chill rushed down Kess's spine as Eslinde strode over to the bathroom doorway. Jillisa met her there, sleeves rolled up as she wiped her hands.

"This girl, Kessara, will be my guest for a while. Prepare the spare room for her and ..."

Eslinde swung back around to Kess. "Do you have any belongings to fetch?"

Nothing that wasn't on Griskin, somewhere far across the land. She hoped he would find a way to rid himself of the saddles and bags he no longer needed weighing him down. She hoped he would be okay without her.

He would be. He'd probably be better.

"No. I have nothing," Kess said, tongue thick and

voice heavy.

Reality slid away from Kess again like an avalanche down a snowy mountain. There were murmurings from the princess about keys and locks as Kess was hauled into a steaming tub and scrubbed brusquely.

The water sloshed and hot wafts of soapy fragrance made Kess sure she was back in her cell again, surrounded by morass mercy.

The next Kess opened her eyes, she was dried and dressed in a soft nightgown and being lowered onto something soft. A cushion strewn daybed in a smaller room that was filled with even more books than the last.

Eslinde brought a blanket up around her and whispered, "I'll be keeping you near, to make sure you and your information remains safe. What you know ... it's very dangerous information to have. People have been killed for that knowledge in the past."

And then, despite the new faces and clean clothing and washed body, Kess was aware enough to realize she'd traded one prison for another.

The older handmaiden arrived, flanked by four guards. She held a palm-sized coffer. When she handed it to Eslinde, the guards bowed and withdrew from the chambers.

Eslinde clicked the latch and pulled from inside a single tiny vial of opalescent fluid.

The royals must still have a plentiful supply if they're willing to spend some on me.

Riony lay on the daybed beside her, hands behind her head and taking up most of the room. "Perhaps you'll waste the last of the kingdom's supply just as you wasted the last of the Heithorn wealth."

Had Riony ever been that cruel? Maybe she wasn't real, but she seemed so tangible, like Kess could reach out and touch her. But maybe she was just a hallucination.

A hallucination born from the ailment she was about to be cured of.

Panic spiked through Kess and she thrashed her arms weakly, trying to pull herself up and away from Eslinde's approach.

"No, no I don't—"

"It's okay, this will make you feel better."

I don't want to. I don't want to lose her again.

But the single drop of silvernix wet her forehead and the room lit with the glow of it streaming throughout her body, casting shadows from the towers of books. All the turmoil within her head seemed to retract like the tide of a stormy sea, all of the aches and confusion washed away as the healing light flowed through her veins.

She rolled to her side, arms reaching out, trying to touch the body that she was sure had been right beside her on the daybed. There was nobody there.

As the shimmer sizzling from her flesh dulled, Kess pulled herself upright, staring beyond the princess and handmaiden in front of her, checking every corner of the room for the familiar face, the smirk, and the tumble of red hair.

Nothing. Riony was gone.

Even the drug-twisted, cruel visage had been the only steady piece of Kess's existence these last months, and the real Riony ... Kess could feel the truth. Riony was the only good thing ever in Kess's life. The one truly good person. And she was gone.

Something cracked apart in Kess's core and she slumped back onto the bed, chest heaving and great clumps of tears rushing from her eyes.

"Did it not work? What's wrong with her?" The handmaiden shuffled in and pressed a crepey hand to Kess's forehead.

There was a long silence, and the princess's words came through muffled by the hum of Kess's cries. "She's grieving."

There was a deep sadness in her tone. A *knowing*.

"Your Highness?"

"Come. Give her space."

The click of a lock followed them from the room, and Kess was alone.

Thin streams of morning light woke Kess. Her eyes peeled open, puffy and sore, and her head ached dreadfully. But for the first time in months, it wasn't from the effects of morass mercy. It came from a night spent crying uncontrollably into a soft pillow.

She hadn't cried like that since Kife abandoned her in the wilds. Since the day Riony had first abandoned her, fleeing Heithorn estate with her family.

She's gone. She's gone. The thoughts that had tormented her all night continued repeating in a way Kess couldn't banish. Whether Riony had been a ghost or hallucination, it didn't matter. Kess couldn't bring herself to believe Riony lived. With the effects of the drug expelled from her system, she remembered everything clearly now.

The knife in Riony's back, right into her heart. The way she had fallen and not moved again. The cries of her friends, *She's not breathing, she's not ...*

Grunting fiercely, Kess squeezed her head between her palms and refocused.

She's gone ... So, what are you going to do about it?

"I'm getting out of here. And I'm going to kill Kife," Kess growled the pledge to herself.

Shifted into a sitting position, Kess took stock of herself and her surroundings.

The silvernix had healed all her ailments, but she'd lost weight and muscle while lying wasted and starved on the cell floor. She brought a leg up and began going through the motions of her exercises, her tendons feeling stiff and tight.

From her disjointed memories of the night before, and the number of books filling the space, Kess assumed this was Eslinde's spare room. There were a couple more bookshelves, although far more books on the floor than in them, a wardrobe, side tables, and the low daybed.

Beyond that, the room was shadowed. There were unlit lamps on each wall, but they contained no oil reservoir. Instead, each was topped with a bulb of glass.

Kess had heard stories of such an invention, illumination powered by the collected lightning breath of snowshimmer dragons. She imagined that destructive energy flowing through those lamps and balked at the idea of touching them.

One wall was split by a section of floor-to-ceiling glass. Morning light came in between crisscrossed, tightly spaced metal bars, and Kess could see a balcony beyond.

She made her way over to the doors, running her hands up to the handle, but it didn't turn. It seemed locked, completely and firmly, but there was no keyhole visible. Kess pressed her face against the glass to get the most she

could from the view.

It was a long way down to the courtyard below. Too far to risk jumping even if she could get onto the balcony.

Beyond the courtyard were rooftops of the rest of the palace and all of the capital dragonkeep below. The sky seemed filled with dragons, transferring people and goods across the city or to other keeps. There was one gap in the aerial traffic, and Kess's breath caught as another wave of grief washed over her.

This time, not hers. It came from the colossal, shadowy mass that descended upon the city below.

The shadow dragon.

All riders and fliers gave it distance, but there was no urgency or worry in their movements. And Kess knew too, that as the shadow dragon roared its mournful cry, it would find no dead within the city's fortified walls to raise.

Still, every part of Kess recoiled from the sight of it, and she turned away, continuing her investigation of the room.

The solitary armoire, glossy with dark enamel, stood beside a matching dresser. Elegant knotwork surrounded the mirror with a single ring of gold around the edge.

On the tabletop was a glass pitcher of water, one stack of unfamiliar clothing, and another of the mixed leathers and garments Kess had arrived in, cleaned and folded. A small object glinted on the top of the stack.

Kess moved closer, lifting herself into the seat in front of the mirror, pointedly avoiding looking at herself. She could feel that her hair had been washed, but not combed or braided. She'd been cleaned of the filth and lingering scent of morass mercy and she didn't really care otherwise how she appeared.

She could only stare at the item lying on the armored vest Riony had given her.

The acorn pendant. She must have had it in her pocket the whole time. She reached for it tentatively, worried that it wasn't real. It was silky soft under her touch, polished by its previous owner's fingers.

Kess's hands trembled as she fastened the pendant around her neck.

Touching the quality hide of the armored vest, Kess considered putting it on too. But if Eslinde the First and her grayglim decided they no longer needed her, Kess doubted the leather armor would save her.

She had no other belongings there worth taking, no weapons, and she couldn't see much within the room she could easily fashion into a blade.

Kess was halfway across the room toward the only other doorway when raised voices pierced through from the room beyond. Something smashed, and a woman screamed.

FIVE

Kess froze, casting a look around the room again for anything she could use as a weapon.

Then a woman shrieked, "Eslinde! You're being unreasonable!"

"*Unreasonable?* You've lied to me for eight years! Tell me the truth!"

"There's nothing to say. Put that down! Don't you—"

Another crash and jingle of breaking glass echoed.

Kess moved to the doorway between her room and the argument and pressed her ear close.

"Stop this nonsense! How dare you treat me like this?"

"What are you going to do? What else do I have that you can take from me?" That was Eslinde's voice, although high and fierce with none of the restraint she'd had the day before.

"Who has been filling your head with these ideas?" The second woman's voice was much like Eslinde's, with only a slightly deeper warble differentiating them.

"Wouldn't you like to know? I'm sure you'll find out through one of your spies soon enough, Mother."

Kess tried to imagine the second woman from her memories of her time at Heithorn estate so long ago. The mother who had trailed the guest around as surely as their bodyguard. Short, pink-skinned and fine-boned, with a sweep of long black hair streaked white down the front, and apparently no older than her adult daughter.

That lack of age gap made some sense now. As the Dragon King's wife, the woman was surely being kept young on regular doses of silvernix just as he was.

The Dragon King's wife. Queen Vellira. Razed earth. Kess worried at her lip, hoping she hadn't made an enemy of one of the most powerful people in Elundrae.

"Enough of this, Eslinde. Whoever it is, they're lying to you."

"You're the liar. You took my baby away. You told me she was dead when she wasn't. You ... you *expected* her to be dead. You didn't just order the deaths of the midwife and her assistant, did you? You ordered hers, too."

There was another rattle of crockery and a gasp.

"I only did what I had to do to keep you safe."

"Just admit it!"

"Fine!" The word rang through the air, leaving a silence behind it. "I lied about the baby being dead. That useless guard was supposed to dispose of it and the witnesses—which was *required* to clean up the mess *you* made—but somehow the fool got himself skewered and the midwife ran off with the child."

"How could you?"

"How could I? Easily. I was protecting you!"

Stomping footsteps punctuated the words. "You were protecting yourself. If you had any love for me, you would have let me keep my daughter."

"Oh no. Don't pretend you're so naïve. You *know* that was never a possibility," the mother's words huffed with a cold, dry humor.

"Something, *something* could have been arranged."

"Exactly. I tried to arrange the best outcome for all of us out of an awful situation. My only mistake was bringing some thuggish dragonrider as our guard. But who would have thought the midwife had it in her to kill the man? I should have brought a grayglim along instead but needed someone ... more disposable."

"Disposable? I can't believe you. Those were people's lives. All those people ..."

"Don't blame me, you spoiled girl. If it weren't for me and what I did, you'd be among those bodies."

A long silence followed, then voices too soft for Kess to hear. She held her breath, listening closer and hearing only a few thumping sounds.

The door at Kess's ear opened too quickly for Kess to back away. She caught herself before falling to the ground and looked up at Eslinde.

"You were listening, then?"

Kess lifted a shoulder. "Obviously."

Eslinde's face was tight and jittery with emotion as she glared down. The room behind her was empty, the mother gone. The princess ran her hands down her silver silk gown as though smoothing wrinkles that weren't there, squared her shoulders, and turned away.

"Come on then. There is food."

She strode away toward the table where a small feast had been laid out, notably missing a couple of glasses that lay shattered across the room.

Halfway there, she stopped and glanced over her shoulder. "Do you ... require assistance?"

"No." Kess scowled as she pulled herself across the polished stone around stacks of books.

The long nightgown caught beneath her as she moved, making the entire process painful. She missed Griskin so much, for so many reasons. A flush of heat rose over her cheeks as the princess watched her climb into the chair opposite her at the table.

Then Kess saw the food and realized how hungry she was and didn't care anymore what the princess thought of her. Light streamed in through the window beside them onto plates piled with crusty bread, surrounded by chutneys and pickles, a side of smoked fish as long as Kess's arm, fresh fruit, and toasted nuts. The selection overwhelmed the small table.

A wheel of soft cheese large enough to feed a family had a dainty knife stuck into the top, and other vessels with lids steamed, filling the air with aromas of honey and spiced meat.

Eslinde didn't touch the feast. She stared at the closed door her mother had recently passed through. "It's true. Blessings from the sun, it is true. My daughter is alive and ..."

Kess spread a slice of creamy cheese over the still warm bread. She took her first bite with her eyes closed, letting it melt in her mouth before rapidly demolishing the rest.

Eslinde's attention turned to her, a soft line between her eyebrows. "Where is she? Which dragonkeep?"

Kess chewed the last bite of bread as she opened the lids on one metal pot after another, peering inside at the stewed meats and creamy oats. "She's not in any dragonkeep."

"Another dragonlord's estate, then? Where did the midwife take her?"

Kess shook her head as she spooned a bowl full of a bit of everything, buying time. She had to be careful not to share too much, only enough to stay in the princess's favor without providing enough to allow her to actually find Lyrrin, and then Dracuni.

"I'm not sure exactly where she is. She's traveling Elundrae."

Eslinde shot from her chair. "On *foot*? Out *there*?"

Mouth filled to bursting, Kess just nodded.

Grasping the sides of her head in her hands, Eslinde paced. "What am I going to do?"

Keeping one eye on the woman's back, Kess rearranged the plates and cutlery before her, moving things around to cover her actions.

The heady scent of spiced milk tea sent Kess's nostalgia spiraling, and she reached for the metal teapot. After washing down another greedy bite, she slowed down, giving the panicking woman a thoughtful look.

"You are Eslinde the First, right? What can't you do?"

Eslinde stilled and gave Kess a withering look. "Travel outside this city, fly my dragon, even leave this room without spies and guards surrounding me."

She flung a hand toward the entrance, and Kess imagined the grayglim on the other side.

A piece of Kess's crumpled heart softened toward the woman. She put down her spoon, despite the food she'd eaten so far only awakening her appetite more.

"But you're Eslinde *the First*," she said again, fidgeting with the long sleeves of the nightgown. "Why would you be treated like that?"

Eslinde returned to her chair. Her silver hair hung loose, not yet braided for the day, and swung around her narrow face.

She rubbed her forehead again with boney fingers, then sighed. "Do you know that I was never meant to be born? There were meant to be no other first-generation heirs after Ylva."

Kess raised her eyebrows. There were a couple of decades between Eslinde and the heir prior to her, but nothing had ever been said publicly about the reasons for that. Most assumed it was because the previous queen had fallen from favor, and it took a while before Yeonard Draekhan took a wife again.

Eslinde held a slice of the crusty bread and picked at it, popping one shred into her mouth for every other few she tossed onto her plate. "My siblings decided fifteen of them was enough, especially once they started having their own children, and those children had children. There were worries about inheritance becoming complicated, *if* Father ever passed away."

"That's so unlikely?" Kess asked.

Eslinde barked a single *ha!*

"So what happened?" Kess hadn't been born yet when the Dragon King remarried and Eslinde was born, but from all she'd heard in the stories that reached Heithorn estate, it seemed as though both those events had been widely celebrated.

"My mother happened. Yeonard Draekhan's first wife, reborn! Or so he believed. He's absolutely besotted with her, so anything she wants, she gets. She wanted an heir, she got one. Only I wasn't the perfect child she'd hoped for." Eslinde's lips twisted into a smile so sly and rebellious it looked entirely out of place.

It vanished again and her voice became somber. "So when I got pregnant young to the wrong person, my mother had all the resources she needed to make it go away."

"That's why you came all the way out to the middle of nowhere to give birth?"

"An isolated estate of a reclusive, minor dragonlord family—"

"Minor?" Kess bristled.

"—where it was unlikely anyone would recognize me. It was perfect. The lord and lady knew, but they were well paid to keep the secret, even from their own children, which it seems they did."

Eslinde chewed on a crumb thoughtfully. "What happened to your parents? Neither you nor your brother were meant to leave your estate."

"Yeah ... Long story." Kess jabbed a spoon into her bowl of mixed foods and filled her mouth again to avoid saying more.

"Regardless, you brought me news that my mother wasn't able to make everything go away, and I'm grateful. Now we must make sure nobody else finds out. You heard my mother. She wasn't wrong. It's only thanks to her privilege that I'm only paying for my mistakes with my freedom, and not my life."

Kess continued eating, as though her curiosity was only casual. "Just from an unwanted pregnancy? Who was the father?"

"It doesn't matter. He's dead." Eslinde's lips drew thin, and she stared at her plate, scattered with a confetti of bread crumbs. "I have shared with you. Now tell me about my daughter. I want to know everything."

Kess looked over at the shards of glass glittering between piles of books across the room. "She's a lot like you in some ways."

"Is she healthy? Safe?"

Kess imaged the Hjelzahn siblings and Niskina and Dracuni, and how they all looked after Lyrrin and each other. And how Riony had cared for the girl, had run across a burning slaver camp filled with revs to leap onto a cage held in the air by a dragon to save her.

Wondering whether there was any chance Riony was still there looking after the princess's daughter only made Kess's eyes water. She blinked the threat of tears away.

"It's been a while since I saw her, but she was as healthy and well protected as could be hoped."

"How long has it been?"

Kess shrugged. She hadn't bothered for years to keep track of the days or dates other than by having a rough sense of seasons passing. All she knew was it was summer before and it was Summer's End now. "Weeks? Months, maybe?"

Eslinde's shoulders sagged, and she stared out the window over the city. "Anything could have happened out there since then."

Kess found it hard to swallow the spoonful of soft oats she'd just taken. "She's a tough kid, just like ... the people who raised her."

"The midwife and her husband?"

Kess thought on that for a moment. When she'd stolen Dracuni from Riony's small rooms in the undercity, there was no sign of the parents. She hadn't really considered much of it then, too focused on her own all-consuming goal.

When did Riony lose them? And how? Kess didn't have to wonder whether it hurt Riony more than Kess's loss of her own parents.

She muttered, "I don't think the parents are around anymore."

"Gone?" Eslinde pressed a hand to her heart. "I'll never get to thank them for saving my daughter."

Kess sniffed and cleared her throat. "They called her Lyrrin."

"Lyrrin," Eslinde repeated in a whisper. Then she leaned forward, hands splayed on the table and an eager brightness in her eyes. "How do you know all of this? Did you spend time with her?"

Kess dug through the food in her bowl, mixing it into a pasty slop in her nervous motions. "I saw her around sometimes."

"Were you friends?"

"Sure."

Leaning back away from Kess, Eslinde gave her an appraising look down her nose. "Don't lie to me, Kessara."

Kess's shoulders tensed, and if she could have marched away from the table, she would have. She wanted to hide from what she'd done, the suffering she'd caused. But she had nobody to make it all go away.

So she faced it and spoke the truth. "I know what I know because I spent most of last year hunting your daughter and her group across Elundrae."

"*Hunting* her? Why?" Eslinde shot to her feet and

snatched a sea-green teacup from the table with a look on her face that precisely matched Lyrrin's expression before the child threw one of her exploding rocks.

"Not *her* exactly."

Eslinde's arm lowered. "Not her? Then who?"

Kess knew she was getting dangerously close to truths she needed to keep hidden. She skirted around them again. "A bounty. I thought ... I was doing the right thing. Something important. I was wrong. I was only hurting ... everybody."

"At least you're being honest now." Eslinde's steely gaze was so intense that Kess had to turn away.

She shrugged. "Yeah, well, I just wanted you to know that if I couldn't catch her, she's not going to be easy to find."

"You might have given up, but I won't."

Kess recoiled, lips twisted in a snarl.

Hands trembling, the princess thumped the teacup back onto the table again, then swept away to the chamber exit.

She paused at the door, running her hand over the decorative stone archway at the side. There was a strange chorus of clunking metal around Kess, from the main door and the barred window beside her and through passages to the other rooms.

Kess caught a glimpse of the grayglim at the door as the princess stepped outside. After the door closed, the percussion of clicks sounded again.

"I have *not* given up," Kess muttered to herself.

Giving the window a skeptical glare, Kess tested it. Again, there was a handle, but no keyhole and no give at all in her attempts to get it open. Spurred on by spite, Kess worked her way around the entire collection of chambers, through the living room, the bathroom, changing room, a small office, Eslinde's bedroom—sheets and blankets strewn in disarray and dotted with books—and back to where she started.

Every exterior exit was locked shut in some way Kess couldn't comprehend or affect.

With a sigh, she settled again at the table. She wasn't giving up. She hadn't. Things had just *changed*.

At least she was awake and lucid again now. She could plan her escape, and revenge, and then ...?

Kess's face wrinkled and her chest ached, still too hurt in a way that silvernix hadn't repaired. She couldn't imagine a future anymore beyond the immediate.

There was nothing left for her out in the world. Griskin had left her, which was for the best. Kess couldn't even bring herself to care about owning a dragon anymore.

Kess's hand wrapped around the acorn hung at her neck. Even if Riony had survived, it didn't matter to Kess's future. Any offer Riony had been making to Kess, Kife had destroyed the chance of Kess taking.

She would hate me more than ever.

But if she was alive ...

Kess refused to entertain the idea, but still it stoked an ember within her, renewing her energy.

Kess removed the cheese knife that she'd tucked away into her nightgown sleeve. She'd hidden it, expecting all the cutlery to be cleared away, to not allow Kess a single option of weapon. But clearly Kess wasn't considered any threat.

With how dull and round the cheese knife was, they were probably right.

The windowsill beside the breakfast spread had some rough-hewn stone, contrasting the polished marble around it. Kess moved her chair closer and began working the metal of the blunt blade against it, slowly working it toward a point.

She still had one goal. To kill Kife. That was enough to keep her going for now.

The hard metal worked much more slowly than the bone Kess was used to sharpening. She gazed out the window as she worked, trying to get a sense of the layout of the palace.

The window looked over the same courtyard as the one in the spare room Kess had awoken in. A parade of at least a dozen grayglim were passing through in two neat rows, flanking three white-haired men within their ranks.

Kess had never seen Yeonard Draekhan, the Dragon

King, in person herself. But she'd seen enough depictions of his unique, dragon tooth-shaped crown, of his hawklike profile stamped onto the backs of sovs, to identify him immediately.

It was hard to believe it was him, despite the evidence. He looked remarkably young for one hundred and twenty-something. Not much older than Kess's parents last time she saw them. Not much older than Eslinde.

Hair as white as snow hung in an intricate tapestry of braids down to his waist, over an ornamental breastplate and shoulder armor in gold. Silver robes spilled from beneath.

The men on either side of him were also obviously heirs as well, based on the milky shade of their hair, but Kess didn't know which. She had always been more interested in studying dragons than the history of the royal line.

The flash of movement drew Kess's eye to another window across the open space.

And a woman's cold eyes stared back. Kess shivered and pulled herself quickly out of sight.

But she knew in her chilled stomach that Lady Hjelzahn had already seen her.

SIX

"It's not going to work," Vance said, inspecting the fake taming stake.

"It will." Dashiel tried to reclaim the device they'd spent so long crafting.

Vance held it out of reach. "And what if it doesn't? What then? If something goes wrong, if it's found out that you faked the taming of a dragon, that you are *keeping* an untamed dragon, that would be the end of your dragonrider career."

Hunt? Catch?

Beside them, the shimmerdart lifted her head from the stone floor of her stall, watching Dashiel's grasping jumps with bright eyes. Almost a month old, she was growing fast, already hound-sized, with a mottled pattern of icy blue and earthy purple scales.

The stall was built for a full-grown flamesong dragon, and despite being large for her type, the dragonling seemed tiny in the space. But Dashiel refused to put her in the battery cages with the tamed dragonlings being raised.

Shiff needed room to move, and the difference in how strong she grew compared to those confined to only moving when told to do so in training was significant.

The modern stalls upstairs for full-grown dragons had no doors—there was no need with tamed beasts—but these older ones in the lower, underground levels had heavy drop-gates of solid steel, from when their family used to breed flamesongs.

The unstable combination of seasong and etherflame were massive, with extraordinarily powerful dragonfire, but had a nasty habit of spontaneously combusting and taking out everything around them. Some breeders still raised them for industry, but Zarram Dragonhold focused on riding dragons these days.

The stalls were mostly empty, only used for long-term storage, and hiding untamed dragonlings.

The eagerness in Shiff's eyes stung Dashiel. They hadn't had as much time to spend with her while preparing for investment, and although they'd left a range of blankets and ropes and balls on the stone floor of the stall to keep the dragonling amused, they could feel how much she missed them.

Dashiel stilled and folded their arms. "I know it's a risk to our family, faking the taming. But I can't do that to Shiff, I won't. She's like family too. I can feel her thoughts, her emotions."

Vance scoffed, relaxing his raised arm.

Dashiel took the bait and leaped for the taming spike, just out of reach again.

Shiff growled and circled around the siblings, fluttering her still-forming wings.

Dashiel grunted at their brother, pointing at the stake vehemently. "It's either this, or I take Shiff and we try our luck out in the world where no one will force me to stab her in the brain and leave her senseless."

Vance gave the small dragonling a gruff look that bordered on sympathetic. "Where would you go? The dragonling is still growing. How would you feed her, or yourself?"

"We could head out into the wilds. Hunt together."

Vance's eyebrow inched up dramatically. "You'd really try that? What do you know about hunting?"

"I'd work it out!"

"Yes, I suppose you probably would. You somehow manage to work most things out." Vance sighed and brought

his arm down, holding the stake out. "I think I would prefer if you stayed and worked out how to keep your dragon out of trouble here, where I can help keep you *both* out of trouble."

Dashiel took back the taming spike, inspecting it to be sure their brother hadn't damaged the fragile construction. "Thanks."

"It looks well made. If it works how you propose, it should go smoothly. But you're going to have to swap it out for the real stake at some point too without anyone noticing."

"I've been practicing. Watch." Dashiel picked up a chewed splinter of old bone from the floor around the same size as a spike.

Dashiel wore their full rider armor in the king's colors—silver and red—prepared for the ceremony. Steel bracers at their forearms were two sizes too large, taken from Vance's collection, with a tight layer of leather beneath to shield their skin. Dashiel tucked the spike into one bracer, then did a quick swap, hiding the bone away in the other bracer and drawing the fake.

Mine! Shiff huffed, standing up on back legs and clawing softly at Dashiel's thighs.

With a short whistle from Dashiel, the dragonling stilled again, sitting as neat and still as a tamed hatchling. Smiling, Dashiel redrew the bone and tossed it across the stall. Shiff trilled as she chased after it.

Vance sighed. "I suppose we're lucky nobody will be standing too close."

"It wasn't that bad." Dashiel pushed the fake spike carefully back into their bracer, wary not to crush the soft metal. "I've thought of everything. There's even a bundle of ash inside, to simulate the smoke from the seared wound."

Clapping Dashiel on the back, Vance said, "Well, let's go and see whether today is the last day for Zarram Dragonhold's respectability. Collect that wild beast of yours."

The dragonling gnawed on her bone with a feral growl.

Nerves hit Dashiel like a wall. "Is it time already?"

"You're about to become one of the Dragon King's riders."

It took a couple of worryingly long minutes to convince Shiff to relinquish her bone, then Dashiel scooped the bundle of silky scales and leather into their arms.

The dragonling's claws wrapped around Dashiel's arm, a companionable touch, but still tight enough that the growing dragon's strength was evident. The tips of her talons pressed between the scales of Dashiel's armor like pincers.

A shiver of nerves washed over Dashiel, then came back mirrored from the dragonling.

Worried? Why?

"It's going to be okay," they said to both her and themselves.

The Zarram siblings walked in silence up the cold stone stairs into the upper levels. When they reached the hatchery, the other new riders being invested that day were already there, eagerly pawing over the newborn hatchlings on offer.

It was one of the great honors bestowed upon those who succeeded in passing rider trials. The opportunity to choose their own dragon.

They didn't truly own the creature. It was bought by the Dragon King and the silvernix required for its taming provided by the Dragon King and it and its rider would serve the Dragon King.

But still the new riders' excitement was clear as they squabbled over which hatchling they considered best. They would be spending the next year with those dragonlings, training the tamed beasts to react to their commands, until they were large enough to fly.

As each rider made their selection, a servant took it away to prepare for the ceremony.

One of the Zarram servants approached Dashiel to take Shiff, wary of how much larger the dragonling was compared to those that had hatched that day.

Dashiel swallowed and whispered close to the dragonling, "Remember what we practiced. Calm and still."

Calm and still. Shiff agreed, but there was a begrudging tone to her thoughts.

Stars, I hope this goes well.

"That's a big beast you've chosen there." Jurge, one of the new recruits, watched as Shiff was taken away.

"Nepotism in action." Zyla approached on Dashiel's other side, her smile teasing but warm on her umber face.

Of the ten other riders being invested that day, Dashiel liked the two of them best. Although just out of her teens, Zyla's braided hair was the salt and pepper of a Taen dragonlord line, while Jurge's hair was all midnight, never touched by a heritage of silvernix usage.

He was a smaller pale-skinned man who had worked his way up from a common Taen family through sheer grit. Zyla, on the other hand, was the fourth rider for the Dragon King among her siblings.

"Like you can talk, Zee," Dashiel teased back.

At the entrance to the hatchery, a woman with arms and thighs like tightly packed bedrolls cleared her throat.

The nervous chatter ceased and the dragonrider recruits stood at attention.

Mestra Lerris looked over them with a glimmer in her eye, that from experience could have been either pride or a joyful readiness to beat obedience into her fresh squad.

"Today you become dragonriders, of the highest order," she barked.

Dashiel was surprised by even that level of rallying support.

Turning on her heel, Mestra Lerris ordered them in line behind her with a sharp snap of, "But you still have a long way to go. Don't embarrass me."

Wide-eyed like a hunted rabbit, Dashiel sought their brother.

Vance leaned on a wall across the hatchery, beyond the discarded broken shells and unwanted dragonlings on the raised platform the new riders had chosen from.

He lifted his chin, wry humor on his lips as he mouthed, "Good luck."

Marching alongside Zyla and Jurge, Dashiel tried to settle their nerves.

Their path to the parade grounds led the group up to the next level and along an exterior corridor with archways open to the view of Draekhanhelm dragonkeep beyond.

The late afternoon sun cast orange light over the city, unusually warm for early autumn. A waft of smoke rose from the Rolanian quarter down the hill to the west. Dashiel could hear the echo of a hundred voices chanting but couldn't make out the words.

Jurge craned to look. "Another riot?"

Zyla kept her eyes forward and tsked. "Can't go a week lately without either the penniless criminals or sun-touched religious nuts making a mess of our streets."

Or both at once, against each other, Dashiel thought.

There were plenty of middle-class Taens who believed the Rolanians and their sinful ways were somehow behind the undead blight growing worse.

Even with the king's favor, the Zarram family had been on the receiving end of threats for not having been "born blessed" like the Taens believed themselves.

Dashiel had learned enough of his peers' religion to fit in, how they believed they were chased from their ancestral home by demons freezing the land to ice. But in their hardship to escape across the sea, they were blessed by the sun and delivered to new homelands where all the abundance that existed was a gift for their use.

A homeland that had before been Rolanian, but as the Taens learned first how to tame dragons, Rolanians became yet another resource the Taens had the privilege of owning.

When revenants began appearing across Elundrae, it wasn't long before those who considered their mythology to be fact saw it as the return of demons, come to punish the unworthy.

A Taen must be honorable to be worthy of the sun's blessings, and any who fail in life thus were never honorable or worthy, and Rolanians didn't even start out with a chance.

"Maybe I should have joined the city guard, they seem to be getting more action these days," Jurge said.

Through the smoke below, the dark silhouettes of

small treedarts dashed from building to building, through the narrow streets and across rooftops toward the unrest, carrying armored soldiers. A crude and simple steed, barely larger than a full-grown wolf, they suited in-city use for policing people rather than revenants.

The new dragonriders' march turned the corner away from the sight, up one more wide set of stairs and out onto the vast flat rooftop of Zarram Dragonhold.

The stone was baked hot underfoot. Marble columns with sleek shafts and capitals carved to form swooping dragons lined the long parade grounds. Crowds of dragonlords, the families of recruits, and older troops of dragonriders filled stands behind those columns, sheltered from the blazing heat by a fluttering silk canopy.

Gold and black pennants with Zarram's crest alternated with silver and red pennants along the top and swirled in the hot wind.

Behind the stands, neatly ordered rows of unmoving dragons sat, saddled with ornate palanquins, the means of transport for all the guests in attendance.

Down the center of the parade grounds, there were ten pedestals, each with a squirming dragonling chained on top and a steel mallet beside them.

Dashiel took a long deep breath and took up position beside Shiff.

She was being good, still and calm. Perhaps too calm compared to the other as-yet-untamed dragonlings, but at least she wasn't drawing attention. Dashiel snuck a training treat from their pocket and gave it to her.

"Good work," they whispered.

A man Dashiel didn't recognize, wearing long ceremonial robes of silver satin, strode down the line, followed by two armored guards. He carried an embossed metal chest and handed taming spikes to each new rider.

Throughout this, the king's proxy delivered a speech. Dashiel had heard it all before, the tale of the first taming, the honor and glory of being a king's rider. Dashiel was too focused on the taming spike being handed to them to listen properly.

A sweat broke out over the back of their neck. Holding that sharp blade of metal, the tip glistening in silvernix, and standing before all those eyes staring down, Dashiel's fingers felt clumsy, their plans miserably ill-conceived.

Are they going to see?

Dashiel cast their gaze over the crowd. They were far closer than Dashiel had thought they would be, and in the front row, sitting straight-backed on velvet cushions, sat Eslinde.

There was no comfort from the familiar face. She was the Dragon King's daughter, after all. What would she think if she saw Dashiel refusing the ceremonial stake provided by the king himself for something they'd snuck in?

The Eslinde they'd once known, wild and rebellious, would cheer, but Dashiel wasn't entirely sure she was still like that.

Eslinde's gaze had a brightness to it that Dashiel hadn't noticed the last time she visited. As though some fire in her had awakened again. Beside her, off the end of the stand in her own separate wooden chair, sat a girl closer to Dashiel's age. A narrow, pretty face was pinched with a shrewd gaze, glaring at a point in the opposite stands.

"Rider Targe!" An announcer's call rang across the grounds, and the first rider raised their mallet.

Rider Targe pressed the tip of the stake to the dragonling's forehead and struck.

The blow was clean, the spike sinking straight down to the cap in one swift motion.

Dashiel had seen tamings gone wrong, where the spike turned crooked or had been hammered in slowly, the hatchling crying all the while. But even this made them sick to the marrow of their bones.

A shimmer through the scales of the silvernix taking effect was followed by a rise of dark smoke. The dragonling slumped, lifeless but not dead, as the announcer called on the next rider.

Dashiel looked away, unable to watch as rider after rider hammered the sharp metal into the hatchling's brains, trying to settle the surge of acid in their stomach. They had to act fast, swap the stakes, or Shiff would suffer the same fate.

Fingers trembling, Dashiel shifted position as though standing at attention with both hands clasped before them. As their hands joined, they shoved the provided stake up into the gap of their bracer.

But they pushed too fast, too hard, nerves overtaking their control. The sharp tip of the spike sliced through the leather between it and their skin, and then through their skin as well.

Dashiel's eyes shot wide. *It's over, I've messed it all up.*

Gulping through panic, Dashiel watched their hands, waiting to see the bright flash of light sparkle from their skin as the silvernix met it, the sign that would give away to everyone in attendance that something strange was occurring, that the rider before them had used the precious silvernix the king had provided on themselves instead of the intended purpose.

But nothing happened.

"Rider Brellson!" the announcer called.

Beside Dashiel, Jurge drove their spike neatly into their dragonling's head. Dark smoke twisted skyward.

Stars, stars, I'm next!

Dashiel rushed to draw their fake spike from their other bracer, their hands rattling like a sand serpent's tail. Hot liquid trickled within the torn leather of their other arm from the stinging wound.

"Rider Zarram!"

Dashiel turned pleading eyes to Shiff and whispered, "Hammer, strike, sleep."

She tilted her head, round eyes reflecting the clear sky above. ***Boring game, again?***

Dashiel placed the fake spike against her forehead and raised the mallet. "Yes, again, like we practiced. Hammer, strike, sleep, until you are back in your stall, and you win."

Please let this work.

Dashiel landed a blow with the mallet, making it look strong. But only a little strength was required.

The stake they'd created folded into itself on impact, telescoping down as the soft metal squashed into itself, leaving only a flat round lump beneath the cap. A few short teeth around the edge of that cap bit down into the dragonling's scales, too shallow to pierce through, but enough, hopefully enough, to hold.

Just a piece of jewelry, decorating the dragonling's forehead.

The puff of ash was less convincing than Dashiel planned, bursting out, then sinking rather than rising skyward, but it was done.

The dragonling slumped, a close approximation of the other hatchlings around them.

Hammer, strike, sleep. Shiff's thought came through as a whisper.

Dashiel exhaled a long sigh. "Good girl."

Nobody cried foul. Nobody rushed to inspect the deception they'd committed, but Dashiel continued to shake anxiously, their arm stinging.

The final two riders repeated the taming process, with only one fumbling their strike. Their dragonling squealed, and Shiff opened one eyelid, their emotions flaring with concern.

Hammer, strike, sleep game?

Dashiel's heart hurt. They whispered, "Yeah. They aren't ... playing as well as you."

She closed her eye and lay still again, as though in competition with the others.

Dashiel wondered whether they could have saved every dragonling there that day, what lengths that would have taken.

There was no way. I'm lucky to still have Shiff.

As the ceremony completed with another speech, servants came along and unchained the newly tamed dragons, taking them away. As one unlocked Shiff, Dashiel reached forward and collected the dragonling themselves.

"I'll take her, thanks."

The final announcement ended with a polite applause, and the audience rose, shifting to either leave or spread down onto the parade grounds to congratulate the new recruits.

Dashiel didn't linger like the rest of their squad, instead rushing with Shiff back to the stairs to the hatchery below.

Vance waited there, leaning in the shade of a column. "I can't believe you pulled that off."

"Shh! Come with me!"

Dashiel led the way, hurrying down the long corridor and to the levels below and Shiff's private stall, Vance close behind.

Dashiel placed Shiff, still acting convincingly limp, onto a blanket. The second she reached the ground, one eyelid cracked open, and then her eyes sprung wide.

She stretched, flexing her claws on the rough woven wool. *Game finished?*

Dashiel nodded.

Hate hammer, strike, sleep.

"It's okay, Shiff. We won't have to practice that one ever again." Dashiel patted her forehead, checking the cap of the fake spike was firmly attached.

"What is it? Did something go wrong?" Vance grumbled as he closed the gate behind them. "We should be up there celebrating with the others. We'll be missed."

"This went wrong," Dashiel said, pulling the real stake

from their bracer with a wince.

"What?" Vance leaned closer, peering at the metal, and then his eyebrows snapped together in a frown. "Is that *blood*?"

Dashiel unbuckled the bracer and held out their arm, showing Vance the torn leather beneath. "It went right through."

"No, it mustn't have. Otherwise ..." Vance reached for the stake. "Give me that."

Holding it close to his face, Dashiel's brother tentatively touched the remaining silvernix at the pointed end.

Nothing happened.

"What in the stars light?"

"Could it be fake?" Dashiel asked. "Or ... I don't know, expired?"

Vance shook his head. "It couldn't be ... not if it's the same silvernix used for the other tamings. They all worked. Without silvernix, there would have been nine dead dragonlings up there."

"Just mine, then? Some kind of sabotage?" Dashiel took the spike back.

There had to be some mistake. They rubbed their hand over the iridescent coating again more thoroughly. Maybe contact with more of the substance would force it to work. But still the silvernix had no effect.

But the rubbing action over the spike caused the steel there to roll and ripple. Looking more closely, Dashiel scratched their thumb over the area, and a thin leafing of metal peeled away to reveal what seemed to be a smoky crystal beneath, glowing dully.

"Umm ..." Dashiel said, holding it to Vance to see, speechless.

Vance's usually passive face was twisted in fierce confusion. "What is that? What's the symbol carved there?"

"And why is it *glowing*?" Dashiel shook it in emphasis.

The mechanism for the gate clicked, and it rolled upward.

"Shiff! Sleep!" Dashiel hissed and hid the strange taming spike in their remaining bracer.

Their dragon huffed, but quickly curled up on a blanket.

White-faced, Dashiel turned to find their father at the door.

The man huffed. "Don't look at me like that."

"Umm ..." Dashiel said again, unable to say anything else. They swallowed, trying to process too many worries at once.

Lord Zarram's eyes had the soft hint of sympathy beneath bushy eyebrows. "I know that was difficult for you, what you did up there. But you did the right thing today, and I'm proud of you."

Dashiel coughed. "Right. Yeah. The right thing. That's what I did."

Vance and Dashiel exchanged side-eyed looks.

Brightening, Lord Zarram said, "Plus, I've heard the king is very happy with this brood and their riders, and the other dragonlords are hearing it too. We'll have our most profitable year ever from this."

Ah, yes, Pabba's main concern as always.

"Come on, enough sulking down here in the dark. Come and celebrate in the sun with the other blessed souls." Lord Zarram put a heavy arm over Dashiel's shoulders and dragged them toward the stairs.

Dashiel tried to pull away from their father's grip. "Actually, I think maybe I might stay down here ..."

"You will come and celebrate, and you will be seen behaving as you should." Lord Zarram squeezed Dashiel's shoulder a little tighter. "As fine as today has been, we must still be careful. The higher we rise, Rolanian blood into a Taen world, the further we can fall. Any scandal could ruin us."

SEVEN

Kess measured out the distance across the parade grounds with her eyes, gauging whether she had a chance of hitting her brother.

He sat in the stand opposite, glaring back at Kess with equal animosity, as though each of them could kill the other through force of will alone.

Even with her best throwing knives, even when she was at her peak, she would have been lucky to bridge that distance and land a killing hit. Since being held prisoner by Kife, her once strong arms had been left weakened.

Over the last few days spent in Eslinde's chambers, Kess had continued to refine the point on her stolen cheese knife and practiced throwing it at the back wall of the opened wardrobe. Whether the unfamiliar blade or wasted muscles were the cause, her aim was currently abysmal, only hitting her target once in every few throws.

The dropping sun hadn't yet delivered any relief from the heat. The rooftop was sweltering, a hot breeze blasting in with the ever-present tang of smoke. Kess fidgeted with the heavy skirt of the gown she'd been given. She'd worn her own leather pants beneath, feeling more secure that way, but regretted it now as her legs swam in sweat.

The braids done by the handmaidens that morning, far more intricate than she'd ever worn, with layers of swooping thin plaits intertwined with thicker weaves and glittering beads, was pulled too tight, leaving her temples aching.

Still, Kess had let them dress her like a doll for the chance to leave the palace. She'd hoped for an opportunity to slip away and escape, but a shot at getting rid of Kife was even better.

He doesn't seem too happy about seeing me again.

Every day Kife was alive and angry increased the risk of him telling somebody about Dracuni.

Kess twisted in her seat, looking over her shoulder at the grayglim watching Eslinde from a few paces away. Yensen, who remained by her side every day, every moment the princess stepped out of her chambers.

He wore the typical smoky-gray armor all of his rank

wore, with a high-collared breastplate of dragon scale, lose silk sleeves between well-fitted shoulder guards and bracers, and leather boots so soft Kess could hardly hear when the man moved.

He seemed the same age as Eslinde, with long narrow eyes and silky black hair, held only in two plain braids on each side of his head.

Maybe I can ask Eslinde to send her shadow to go and kill Kife for me.

She'd need a good reason, though, and one that wasn't, 'Because he needs to die before he tells anyone there's a living creature with silvernix blood.'

She could tell the princess Kife was a threat to Lyrrin, but that was only in a roundabout way, and Eslinde was very good at sniffing out half-truths.

Anyway, Kess still hoped to be the one to spill Kife's blood herself. She'd wait for her chance.

It was unlikely Kife knew Kess would be at the dragonrider investment. Maybe he thought the Dragon King himself would be in attendance, but Yeonard Draekhan had sent a representative for this ceremony, as Eslinde assured Kess he did for most minor affairs such as this.

Eslinde was only attending herself because she knew one of the riders being invested that day. And she insisted Kess should stay with her.

"Ah, there they are!" Eslinde fanned her sweat-shimmered face with a hand.

The new recruits marched down the center of the rooftop parade.

Eslinde pointed to one with golden tanned skin and a mop of caramel curls. "That's Dashiel Zarram. Their family owns this dragonhold. And their brother …"

Eslinde craned her neck, looking around the stands. She muttered, "Their father is over there. No. I can't see Vance."

There was a soft note of disappointment in her voice.

Kess squinted through the hot light at the rider, who waited through the opening speech beside the pedestal with their dragonling. A *big* dragonling.

The rider seemed nervous. Their features, angular jaw, full lips, and eyes lined with thick lashes, kept twisting between an awkward frown and solemn composure. More interestingly, they were clearly Rolanian.

Kess had known of some Rolanians who had risen into roles of dragonriders, back in her life at Heithorn estate. She'd sought out stories about them, telling herself it was for no real reason, just curiosity, and hadn't shared any of that information or the hopes behind it with Riony. Those stories were still too few and far between.

But if the Zarrams owned this dragonhold, they weren't just riders, but dragonlords. Owners of their own dragons.

And plenty of them, from the size of the facilities.

Rolanian dragonlords?

The princess's eyes were still seeking the missing brother, and Kess gave her an appraising look. "How do you know the Zarrams?"

"Through breeding, mostly."

Kess's eyebrows rose.

"*Dragons*, Kessara." The princess sighed. "The Zarrams are some of the best breeders and trainers in Elundrae, and they've always had excellent stock. My family would often visit to trade. Vance, Dash, and I became friends young. Although I haven't seen them much lately."

Kess turned back to the proceedings right as the first rider struck the stake into their hatchling.

Unprepared, she gasped a loud intake of air.

Eslinde turned fully her way. Kess slowly let the air out again as casually as she could until the princess's eyes were off her again.

As the next rider, then the next tamed their hatchlings, a hot sickness rose in Kess's throat.

The rider would raise their mallet, and Kess could feel Dracuni clinging to her in the cave filled with spiders, feel her heart beating against her chest.

The mallet would strike down, and Kess remembered Dracuni trying to comfort her, help her, as her life bled

out of her broken legs.

The newly tamed hatchlings fell still, one after another.

Is Dracuni still safe, out there, without Riony to look after her?

Kess's eyes stung and she willed away the wetness forming there.

Dracuni must be getting big now. Soon enough, she'd be able to protect herself. At least from a single human hunter, a single rival dragon. Not from the full might of the Dragon King if he knew she existed.

There had been no news or rumors in court yet about the existence of a silvernix-blooded creature, from what Kess had heard from Eslinde, so that at least was a good sign.

As the tamings continued, Kess noticed Eslinde's gaze wasn't on the riders and dragonlings before them.

The princess watched the sky. Kess's eyes followed, seeing only the wisps of swirling darkness rising from each taming. It was better than seeing the taming itself, but a heavy weight of grief filled Kess at the sight.

Was that dark smoke really the essence that formed the shadow dragon? Had each hatchling tamed that day strengthened it more?

How many other dragons were tamed that day, for other riders, or industry, in other dragonkeeps, all across Elundrae?

Only one hatchling didn't send a curl of black mist skyward. Dashiel's. There was a puff of a smokelike cloud, but it passed quickly and didn't rise as though there was a destination it sought.

Kess tried to get a better look at Dashiel's dragonling, but the ceremony ended, and the audience were on their feet, descending the stone amphitheater and mingling in the central area.

A number of dragonlords in decadent gold-embroidered finery swarmed upon Eslinde, which in turn drew her grayglim close to her back.

Off to the side in her separate seat, Kess quietly brought her hands to the wheels attached to the wooden chair and rolled herself away.

Eslinde had provided the mobile chair for Kess that morning, announcing that she had the finest engineering minds in the capital develop it.

The best Kess could say of the contraption was that it moved. The wheels turned clunkily when she pushed them, and considerable effort was required to get even a short distance.

Maybe that's just my wasted arms.

Kess would work on rebuilding her strength. And begrudgingly admitted the chair would help. There was none of the touch and response fluidity she had with

Griskin, but at least she was moving and not on the floor.

And she could see her target. Kife lurked beside a column on the other side.

I just have to get close enough to kill him.

She figured at least he wouldn't expect it, here and now, so she'd have that advantage. Kess didn't care about the witnesses or consequences. It didn't matter what happened to her as long as he was gone too.

But getting close wasn't going to be easy.

The crowd parted and reformed around her, switching places as people went from greeting one acquaintance to another, cutting off Kess's slow moving progress.

Servants appeared with trays of chilled drinks, the glasses glistening with condensation. Kess swallowed a dry mouth and pushed on. A man with skin like uncooked pastry exclaimed in loud insult as Kess's rolling chair butted up against him.

"You stepped in front of me," Kess hissed, trying to readjust her angle and go around where the human equivalent of dough remained planted in her path.

Hushed whispers went up all around Kess as she tried to maneuver through the crowd. The looks of disgust thrown her way were far louder.

Almost every head of hair on that rooftop was brightened by the use of silvernix. All people who lived with every benefit

that wealth offered. Straight-backed, strong, and youthful.

In a land where money bought health, and only the dishonorable were poor, Kess's body made her a visual target of shame.

Kess smirked as her eyes landed on Kife, not far away. *I'll give them something to really gossip about.*

Leaning forward, Kess lifted the hem of her skirt, seeking the knife hidden in her boot. Before her fingers could close on it, a long-legged body stopped in front of her.

"It seems Eslinde has a new friend. I don't believe we've met."

Kess straightened, taking in the man in front of her. He had a long diamond-shaped face spotted with coal-dark eyes, pure-white hair braided into a thick rope down his neck, and a grayglim at his back.

Another First?

"No, we haven't met," Kess replied.

"You make it sound as though that's by design." The man gave a self-deprecating laugh.

Kess didn't miss the sly glint in his eyes. She'd spent the last five years in the wilds with lowlifes and snakes and recognized danger in human form when she saw it.

Kess tried to roll past the man. "Excuse me, I—"

"Haven't a moment for Ulfren the First?" He shifted in front of her and offered an almost imperceptible bow.

Kess attempted a polite smile with lips that were pulling into a cringe.

Not just any first heir, but first in line to the throne. Kess opened her mouth to introduce herself in return but wasn't sure it was the best idea. Beyond Ulfren's waist, Kife moved, getting farther away in the crowd. Kess swore under her breath.

"Your Highness. I'm sorry, I'm really nobody important and need to go."

"Nonsense! You seem terribly important to Eslinde. Where in Elundrae did she dig you up from?" The man peered down at Kess, making no effort at all to bridge the gap between their heights.

"Oh, just some smelly hole." Kess stuttered out a laugh, but her hands had gone rigid around the wheels at her sides.

Ulfren's black-hole gaze assessed her again.

Kess tried to do the math at what true age Ulfren was based on her knowledge of the Firsts. Ulfren wasn't the firstborn of the heirs, but the eldest brother had died of natural causes some time ago.

Ulfren looked older than his own father, but not the seventy or so years he probably was. More middle-aged. His loose-fitting gray trousers and coat had a metallic green trim of geometric knotwork sparkling around the hems and collar.

"And now that you've been dug up, what relationship do you have to Eslinde?"

Kess tried to draw herself taller in her chair. She played her tone off light the way he was. "Are you so curious of all her friends?"

"She hardly has any these days, which is why you are a curiosity indeed." Placing a long-fingered hand across his chest, Ulfren tilted his head in a show of sympathy that read as utterly fake.

A shiver ran down Kess's back under his dark gaze.

Ulfren's voice dropped low. "I just want to be sure she's not getting herself into any trouble. Again."

EIGHT

gain? Does Ulfren know about the pregnancy? Kess's mouth went dry. Her world was falling far too quickly into a sea of secrets and scandals she hadn't nearly enough knowledge of.

"What sort of trouble do you mean?" she asked innocently.

"Knowing Eslinde, it could take many forms." Ulfren rubbed his chin, shaking his head softly. "What she really needs, poor thing, is somebody who will keep an eye on her. For her own good."

Kess raised her eyebrows, although still attempting to peer past the man to keep an eye on her brother.

Ulfren continued. "Perhaps, if you're spending so much time with her, you could be that person. If you could get any information back to me on trouble Eslinde might be falling into, I would reward you well for helping me keep my sister safe."

That got Kess's full attention. A reward? She wondered just how big of a reward was on offer—assassinating a problematic brother, for example—and what she'd have to do to receive it. But if it was one First asking her to spy upon another, she assumed the reward involved had to be substantial.

Either that or Ulfren the First would have me quietly disposed of after I'm no longer useful. That's the more likely outcome.

Before Kess could respond, Eslinde swept in beside them. "Ulfren, lovely to see you. I heard you're staying in the capital for a while."

"Not as long as your stay has been." Ulfren rasped an unfriendly chuckle.

Eslinde only smiled courteously in return. "Might I steal this lovely girl from you now? We have people to see."

"Of course. It was an honor to meet Kessara Heithorn." Ulfren gave her a mockingly low bow, eyes locked on her as she flinched at her full name tumbling from his mouth.

He knew all along? What spies does he already have?

Eslinde's hands gripped the back of Kess's chair. "May I?"

"Sure. Yes," Kess said, eager to be away from the man too. The offended glances Kess received as Eslinde pushed

her through the dwindling guests were muted compared to when the princess wasn't at her back and grayglim trailing behind.

"What did my brother want from you?" Eslinde asked once they'd crossed to the other side of the rooftop.

"I didn't really speak to him for long."

Eslinde tsked under her breath, then in a brighter voice said, "There they are!"

"Eslinde, you made it!" Dashiel hurried toward them in a loping jog, the stemmed glass in their hand spilling a sparkling liquid along the way.

"Congratulations again, Dashiel." Eslinde leaned into a polite embrace which was offered enthusiastically but awkwardly, a fumble of long limbs.

Eslinde's grayglim gave Dashiel a reproachful glare, as though he could force Dashiel a respectful distance away with his eyes alone.

A much larger man followed at a slower, uneven pace. The structure of his face was similar to Dashiel's, but with any soft feminine curves removed from the lips and cheeks, and darker hair tumbling in loose braids over his outrageously wide shoulders.

Eslinde's smile widened. "And Vance. Good to—"

"Nice to see—" he said at the same time.

"—again so soon."

"Your Highness." He cleared his throat and leaned back as though wary an awkward embrace was in his future as well.

"This is Kessara." Eslinde stepped back behind the wheeled chair.

"Kess is fine," she said, fussing with her skirts as though they could hide the fact she wasn't standing to greet them.

Dashiel beamed at her. "A new friend? Is it you who has brightened our princess's mood so much?"

"Oh, I don't think that's it, exactly." Kess glanced back at Eslinde, who had seemed somewhat more lively compared to when they'd first met.

Keen to change the subject, Kess said, "I liked your dragonling selection. A shimmerdart? Large one too."

"You could tell all that from the stando?" Dashiel's throat worked as they swallowed hard.

"I ... umm. I like dragons."

Dashiel laughed and rubbed the back of their head. "Yeah. I like dragons too. We have some really special ones at the moment. Oh! How about a tour of our stock?"

Kess looked over at the stairs leading down from the rooftop grounds. Her wheeled chair was clunky enough on a smooth stone surface. She wasn't ready to test it on steps. "I don't think I can."

Dashiel had already begun leading the way and turned

back. "Eslinde will come along too, right?"

Eslinde's gaze fluttered over Vance before replying, "I have time. Let's. It's far too hot up here."

Vance grumbled, eyeing the wheeled chair pointedly, "I don't think that's what Kess means, Dash."

"Oh. I see."

Kess waited for the flicker of revulsion over their expression, but it didn't come.

Dashiel put their glass, still mostly full, down on a passing servant's tray. "We can help you get down the stairs. If that's okay?"

A sneer twitched on Kess's lips, but as all three awaited her reply, she nodded.

It took a few mortifying moments at the top of the stairs discussing the best way to manage their descent. There were offers to carry Kess, but she worked out she could carefully roll the chair down the steps one at a time as long as she had someone assisting to make sure the chair didn't run away on her.

Dashiel volunteered, and they traveled down three long flights of stairs that way before they reached a flight deck lined with rows of stalls. The difference in temperature from the rooftop to there was shocking and the sweat over Kess's skin chilled. Her arms shook from the effort and it had been a slow process.

Kess struggled to meet any of their gazes as she clunked down the final step. "Sorry. I'm not used to this yet."

Vance leaned close and bent as though to adjust his shoes. His voice was low and gruff. "I don't show many people this."

He lifted the hem of his pants, revealing a metal joint where his ankle should be, connected to a carved wooden foot and shin. Their gazes met, and Kess sought answers in the intensity of his look.

He shrugged and straightened back up. "Sometimes things are gone in a way even silvernix can't repair. And that's not our fault. It'd be a better world if everyone understood that."

Kess's mouth popped open, but words refused to be formed, so she closed it.

Eslinde's eyelids fluttered again, as though looking at Vance and trying hard not to look at him at the same time.

Half her mouth lifted in a sad-looking smile. "He's still one of the best dragonriders in Elundrae, regardless."

Vance just grunted and gave Dashiel a shove on the shoulder. "Go on, go show off your dragons."

Smiling radiantly, Dashiel took them across to the first stall where a glistening green and black seasong dragon filled the space.

As beautiful a specimen as the dragon was, Kess found

herself more interested in the furtive glances being passed between Eslinde and Vance. One would stare at the other, then quickly away when the other would look at them.

There was an almost tangible chemistry between them—one neither seemed to want acknowledged. Something far more private, even forbidden.

Could he be Lyrrin's father?

A Rolanian amputee getting a First princess pregnant would be a scandal. Eslinde said Lyrrin's father was dead, but she could have lied about that to protect the identity of the man.

And if it was Vance, did he even know there was a pregnancy?

Eslinde had arrived at Heithorn estate to be sequestered until the birth when she was only just showing. She said only those at the estate and her parents knew. But Kess couldn't trust the princess was telling the whole truth.

She couldn't trust anyone around her, not Eslinde, not the Zarram siblings. No matter how kind these dragonlords seemed, everyone had their own secrets and motivations. Kess's meeting with Ulfren was only a reminder of that.

They moved along to the next stall, where a dragon with scales the color of a golden sunrise curled restfully.

"Viska here has a little snowflame in her background, but we've been breeding back in more and more etherflame, for the size and extended lifespan." Dashiel patted the dragon on its crown of horns.

"She's beautiful. Her fire, is it more a liquid flame or fire blast?" Kess wheeled herself closer, taking in the size of the dragon's talons and thick leather of her golden wings.

"Fire blast, hotter than usual for a purebred ether, but it doesn't seem to weaken her as fast as snowflame's breath does," Dashiel replied.

A soft smile reached Kess's eyes, imagining the powerful creature in action. "And does the presence of snowshimmer in her line make her fast?"

"Does it ever." Vance smirked. "You're as keen on dragons as Dash, aren't you?"

Kess's smile faltered. "I wanted to be a rider ... once."

Wanted it more than anything.

Kess could only find a hollow inside her where that desire once was. She pushed her chair back away from the dragon.

Vance had his eyes on Eslinde again, then returned them to Kess, frowning softly. "How about you take Viska out for a fly? Dash can show you how fast she is."

"That sounds amazing. Although ..." Kess looked to Eslinde for an answer, expecting the princess to protest the offer that would take Kess out of her control.

But Eslinde shared a similar soft frown as Vance.

Raze them both, is that pity? Kess's nose crumpled.

"I suppose Dashiel could bring you back to the palace. We will meet you at the upper flight deck," Eslinde said.

Her grayglim had flown them both there, boxed into a palanquin on a slow, old etherflame. Kess hated flying that way, sitting locked in a container as the air rushed by around them, out of reach. Even if the journey back to the palace was short, Kess was excited at the idea of flying the incredible golden creature before her.

Still tamed, but in so much better condition than Kife's dragon had been. Viska was clearly well cared for, evident in that she'd even been given a name.

Dashiel had a grin splitting ear to ear and was already in the process of saddling up the dragon. They shared knowing looks with Vance, that Vance pointedly ignored.

Was the princess trying to get some time alone with Vance? That wasn't possible anyway with the grayglim always lurking at her shoulder.

It was only once Kess had been given a set of goggles and climbed up into the saddle behind Dashiel that the thought hit her that Vance and Eslinde's looks of concern weren't pity, that this wasn't a scheme to allow the two of them time together, but something more malicious.

Panic rose within Kess, her mind serving images of being thrown from a dragon's back again and again.

"Perhaps I shouldn't," she called down. "What about

the chair?"

Eslinde flapped a hand. "Yensen will carry it back."

Yensen gave her a flat look that suggested he didn't think that was part of his job description but didn't argue.

"Don't worry, this will be fun. Have you flown in the saddle much before?" Dashiel settled into the seat in front of her.

"A bit."

The saddle was longer than Kife's had been, designed to allow more than one rider. Dashiel had selected it from a range along the wall.

"Those could be a bit tighter. May I?" Dashiel reached for Kess's flight goggles.

She nodded numbly and they adjusted the buckle on one side.

"Anything else you need?" they asked.

"My legs, they aren't strong enough to grip. I need to be strapped in." And she wanted to be strapped in.

If they were taking Kess to be tossed away, she wanted to make it as hard for them as possible.

Nobody argued or made a fuss though, and Vance tossed her a harness from the range of tack. Although designed for some other purpose, Kess fastened it over her dress and found enough points of connection between the leather strips and buckles to the saddle to feel secure.

Then they were moving. Dashiel had full control of the massive creature beneath them, leading it out of the stall and toward the open flight deck at the end of the long space.

Kess turned back, eyes on the princess, trying to ascertain her motivations in allowing this. Had what she'd assumed to be flirting between Eslinde and Vance actually been some silent communication of their plan to take Kess away and kill her?

They could have arranged it after the ceremony while Ulfren talked to me. I should have refused this offer.

But then the length of the flight deck ended, and the dragon's wings clapped out on either side, and they were in the air.

Kess's stomach bottomed out as the dragon rose sharply, leaving the city behind in the blink of an eye.

She is fast!

Dashiel called over the rushing air, "All good?"

Kess ran a hand to the top of her boot, feeling the knife still there. If they thought they could get rid of her easily, they were mistaken.

Her fingers shook. "Fine."

"Ready to go full speed?"

Kess balked. "She goes *faster*?"

Dashiel's laughter mixed with the gusting wind and whoosh of the dragon's pumping wings.

Lowering themselves closer to the dragon's neck, Dashiel barked voice commands and tugged a twin set of reins.

If Kess hadn't been strapped in, she would have been left behind in the burst of speed that drove them hurtling through the sunset-tinted sky. The golden scales scintillated under the hot sun like sparks of fire with each motion of the dragon's muscles.

Below them Draekhanhelm was a dark spot on the land, between charred wastes on one side and a sparkling sea on the other. Dashiel turned the dragon, taking them out over the water, and the scent of ocean salt and a cooler breeze hit Kess.

They dove, bringing the speeding dragon down to skim the waves before swooping back up into the clouds so fast Kess felt she'd left her soul behind amongst the seafoam.

Her heart raced, in awe of the dragon's speed and in anticipation of Dashiel's upcoming attack.

Dashiel leaned sideways and called over their shoulder. "What do you think?"

Kess kept an eye on Dashiel, making sure they weren't turning all the way around to face her. "The dragon? She's incredible. But she's still ..."

"Still what?"

The trembling anxiety and sense of imminent death within Kess left her bold, so she said, "Still tamed."

There was a long silence. "What else could she be?"

Kess didn't know how to explain to a dragonlord what a dragon could be. How Dracuni had been so lively, so loyal, so kind. How even Kife's dragon, when freed, hadn't destroyed everything around it when it so easily could have. The way Dracuni's mother had flown from her home in the ocean to starve in the mountains in an ill-fated attempt to keep her eggs safe.

Creatures with their own minds, unfettered by the control of humans.

Kess replied, "Something whole. She could be something whole."

The dragon slowed, gliding in air cleared of smoke by the sea breeze.

Dashiel shifted suddenly, leaving Kess's heart shuddering and hand reaching to her boot. The rider twisted to face her, then with one hand holding the reins taut, they stood up in the saddle.

"What are you doing?" Kess snapped. The person was going to get themselves killed rather than her.

Dashiel balanced upright on the saddle and grinned. "Do you want a turn in control? Shuffle up."

"Are you serious?"

"Have you ridden before?"

"No. Not really. Not *airborne*."

"It's fine, I'll talk you through it." Dashiel stepped over her to the back of the saddle, leaving Kess no choice but to move forward or have nobody in control of their steed.

There was enough give in her harness straps for Kess to pull herself forward into the empty rider's position. Dashiel handed down the reins and dropped casually behind her as though they weren't high in the air.

And Kess was in control.

Raze it all, I'm flying a dragon.

Already overwhelmed, Kess flinched when Dashiel pressed up close behind her. But there was no following attack. They reached forward and showed her how Viska had been taught to respond to motions from the two sets of reins and how to apply pressure against the dragon's neck for additional maneuverability.

"Vance doesn't use the reins at all, but since he doesn't fly much anymore, it's good to have rein training available for others who ride her," Dashiel said.

It was nothing like trying to get Kife's dragon to follow her commands through touch alone. The reins did make it easier, but also simple in a way that had none of the joy of riding Kess dreamed of.

Once she felt more confident that they weren't about to plummet from the sky, Kess held the reins in one hand and reached for the dragon's neck, pressing her hand to the warm scales.

It only took a few minutes for Kess to pick up the basics and get a feel for how the dragon responded. The thrilling connection of action and reaction felt so much like how she rode with Griskin that it made Kess's eyes water beneath the goggles.

Only, the dragon had no choice but to respond. A servitude rather than a partnership.

Having Dashiel behind her kept Kess on edge, and she kept waiting for the tip of a blade to pierce her back or the slice of a knife that cut her attachments and left her tumbling into the ocean below.

I could strike first. I have my knife. I could slash the rider's throat and take this dragon and be free.

But to murder and steal unprovoked was dishonorable. Kess couldn't bring herself to act against the apparently cheerful young dragonlord. No. She would wait for their false show to end. And when they sprung their trap, she would be ready.

Dashiel leaned close, calling in her ear over the wind, "Come on. No way you've never flown a dragon before. You're a natural!"

"Only once. Sort of. But it's a lot like my wolf."

"Your *what*?"

"I ..." A strange rush of both shame and pride tangled

in Kess's chest. "I used to have a wolf that I rode."

"Really? Stars, that might be the coolest thing I've ever heard!"

Dashiel's enthusiasm almost cracked through Kess's worry, but her hands shook more than ever.

"There's the palace flight deck." Dashiel's chest pressed against Kess's back as they leaned to point past her. "Think you can bring Viska in to land?"

The palace below was a silhouette of angular gray blocks and spires against the rainbow hues of the setting sun.

The tremors hammering through Kess were getting worse. *When will they strike? They're running out of time. Why haven't they made their move?*

"No. You should."

She wanted them in front of her again. She was too vulnerable this way. They were going to kill her, throw her away ... any moment. Any moment now.

"Okay, switch." Dashiel pressed their hands on Kess's shoulders to help themselves up, then stepped over her in the saddle.

Kess slid back, hands gripping tight around the harness straps. The angular blocks of grand fortresses and apartments of the dragonkeep rushed up toward them.

Dashiel brought Viska into a slowing spiral, drifting round, then round, as the looming steel and ashy stone walls of the palace came up on all sides.

They came to a stop on the upper flight deck, a smaller aerial entrance reserved for royals.

Kess found herself gulping air, her heartbeat thundering in her ears louder than the wind had.

Where's the trap? It never came. It has to. What are they going to do?

She roughly pulled her goggles off, and they dropped from her rattling fingers and hit the floor with a crack. The sound echoed through the cavern-shaped space.

A few dragons were chained to one of the walls, but otherwise, they were alone.

Maybe they intended to finish her off here.

Dashiel turned to her. "You're shaking. I'm sorry, was that too much? Are you okay?"

No. They were going to kill her. Betray her. Abandon her. There was no other explanation. Panic burned through Kess and she fought with the buckles on the harness, tearing at them to get free.

"It's alright. Slow down." Dashiel frowned, reaching to help.

Kess got the last connection undone and pushed herself from the saddle. She slid sideways, skirts tangled.

Dashiel caught her arm. "Careful!"

"Let go of me!" Kess shrieked, swinging in their grasp.

She wrenched her wrist free, clinging to the dragon's side. Her fingers slipped against the dragon's scales, weak from the unstoppable tremors.

She tumbled past the dragon's front leg and landed with a thump on her back.

Dashiel leaped down beside her, staring down as she lay prone and vulnerable, easy to kill.

"Do it!" she spat.

"Do *what*? What's going on? Are you alright?"

The care in their voice blocked Kess's throat and her words came out between sobs. "Why aren't you ... why aren't you trying to kill me?"

Dashiel froze in place, face twisted in confusion. "Was I ... expected to?"

"Yes!" Kess roared, the cry reverberating around them. "It's what everybody does! I haven't been in a dragon's saddle that I haven't been thrown from."

Dashiel's eyes went round and they stepped toward her.

Kess pressed up into a sitting position but couldn't find the strength to try to escape. Tears flowed as uncontrollably fast as her body shook.

Words gasped from her as though in a need to explain, to convince the person before her that they couldn't possibly be expected to do anything *other* than kill her. "Nobody, nobody has ever been kind to me without it being a trap."

Dashiel came down slowly, tentatively, kneeling beside Kess. "It's okay. I'm not going to hurt you."

"You are! You will. Somehow. If not now, later."

"Stars," Dashiel whispered. "What has the world done to you?"

Somehow those words of compassion hurt Kess more than any hidden blade the rider could have gutted her with. And they disarmed her utterly as they wrapped arms around her, pulling her shuddering body into a tight embrace.

A choking, gasping wail broke from Kess's mouth like a death cry. She remained limp in their hold, unable to process a single thought or force her body into fight or flight.

Then she brought her arms up and clung back, crushing the rider's body into hers as though the pressure could stop the waves of tears and rattle in her bones.

But they kept coming, a release of every pain and humiliation Kess had suffered throughout her life.

Dashiel said nothing, just held her there on the floor beside the motionless talons of the golden dragon.

As finally some control returned to Kess's body, a shadow shifted near the entrance of the flight deck, and Kess lifted her head, peering over Dashiel's shoulder through tear-heavy eyes.

Down the long, dark room, a woman approached. Slowly at first, but once Kess lifted her face and met hers,

the strides became fast and determined.

The grayglim armor could have been any royal guard in the palace. But the long whip of hair swinging behind the woman and the twin blades, one in each hand, could only be Lady Hjelzahn.

Kess's whole body went cold.

It might not have been Dashiel intending to kill Kess that day, but it didn't mean she wouldn't die.

Nine

Kess pushed Dashiel away and snatched the sharpened cheese knife from her boot.

"Whoa." Dashiel held their hands up. "Sorry, I thought we were having a moment there."

"Get on the dragon, quick. Get out of here!" Kess urged, shifting forward to face Lady Hjelzahn.

"Why?"

"She's going to kill us!"

Dashiel turned to see the woman striding swiftly down the length of the flight deck.

They folded their arms and pouted. "Really? Or is this part of the whole 'everyone wants to kill me' thing?"

The grayglim was close enough now that Kess could

see a contemptuous smile twisting her lips at the sight of Kess's makeshift blade.

Kess knew she had practically zero chance of hurting the woman with it. She'd been skewered more than once by much sharper blades back in the underground and it hadn't slowed her down. But if Kess could just buy a chance for the dragonrider to escape, she'd take a shot.

There wasn't enough time for Kess to get onto the dragon as well. "Listen to me now and believe me later! Get onto the dragon!"

"Why would a grayglim be after us?" Dashiel remained still, glancing at Lady Hjelzahn again. There was enough threat in her advance that they frowned.

"She's after me and won't care that you're in her way."

The grayglim had her hands on the hilts of twin blades. Not the same ones she'd been disarmed of underground. Not nearly as finely made. But surely as deadly in her hands.

And then her advance halted and she scowled.

Kess dared a look over her shoulder, following the woman's line of sight. Two dragons flew in, landing beside Vance's golden etherflame.

Each had a grayglim rider on the front, and elaborate enclosed palanquin balanced lower down the dragon's back. One of the riders whistled loudly, and from the end of the flight deck, a half dozen servants appeared, wheeling mobile staircases over beside the dragons and lining them up to the palanquin doors.

Eslinde emerged from one, along with Vance, having managed their private moment after all, and looking only more awkward and unhappy from it. From the other came Ulfren, along with an additional two grayglim that had ridden in the enclosed seating with him.

He's serious about his protection. And probably for the best.

Kess narrowed her eyes on Lady Hjelzahn, waiting to see what she would do. The woman's expression left Kess chilled. There was something so lifeless and dark in her gaze as her face twitched, eyes darting over the appearance of the four other grayglims. She casually sheathed her swords.

As Eslinde approached, Lady Hjelzahn bowed low.

"Your Highness. A lucky chance meeting you here. We've yet to reschedule our meeting."

Eslinde blinked at the scene before her, Lady Hjelzahn addressing her in formal normality, Dashiel looking utterly confused, and Kess on the ground, face swollen and wet.

Kess tucked her hand holding the scrappy piece of sharp metal behind her back.

Eslinde stepped forward, Vance on one side.

"Kverra. Lucky indeed. I was so moved by the sad story of your missing children. How goes the search?"

Lady Hjelzahn straightened. "It continues. I hoped

connections in court might have brought me news of them."

Yensen followed not far behind the princess, wheeling Kess's chair to her.

Dashiel helped her into it, and while they were close, whispered, "Okay, that was weird. I admit it. I saw the murder in her eyes."

"Pretend you saw nothing. Take Vance and go," Kess whispered back.

Ulfren and his grayglim milled about near their dragon, and Kess wondered whether they were trying to eavesdrop. She didn't care as long as they stayed nearby. She was certain it was only the safety of their numbers that stopped Lady Hjelzahn from killing them all as she'd attempted underground.

Eslinde's voice was soft with care. "Any useful leads so far?"

"Some gossip about a group seen around old Alderkin shrines including some that match their description."

Kess inhaled sharply.

"Although there are too many contradicting stories." The woman's void-like eyes turned on Kess. "It can be hard to know what to believe when some people enjoy sharing harmful rumors. But I am undeterred by such hindrances."

Kess glared back. The grayglim could take her thinly veiled threat and stuff it into one of the holes left behind

from their last fight. If the woman wasn't prepared to reveal her murderous intent in front of everyone there, Kess wasn't prepared to be cowed by her words.

Unfortunately, it seemed as though Ulfren had decided nothing interesting was forthcoming from this meeting and was marching away, taking his three grayglim with him.

Kess inched her wheeled chair toward Eslinde.

The princess inclined her head. "Well, I'm sure you will find your children soon. As a grayglim, you must make short work of uncovering secrets."

In a low, icy voice, Lady Hjelzahn said, "I know many secrets. A kingdom's wealth of them."

Kess shivered.

Then the woman's voice softened. "But nothing is more important than getting to my children."

Kess brought her chair beside Eslinde, angled so her back was to Lady Hjelzahn. Ulfren and his guard were almost off the flight deck.

Kess looked up and whispered, "We have to go. Now."

Eslinde's eyes passed briefly over Kess, and she smiled beatifically at Lady Hjelzahn. "I'm afraid we're running late to another appointment. But if there is anything I can do, please let me know. Speak with Olva or Falden to arrange another meeting."

Dashiel moved next to their brother and grasped his

arm, tugging him toward the golden dragon. "We've got to get back home, too."

"Do we?" Vance grumbled.

"Yup." Dashiel continued to drag him away, waving with their other hand. "Hopefully we'll see each other again soon."

"I hope so too," Eslinde replied.

"And I," Lady Hjelzahn said with a low bow.

Kess turned her chair and led the way out of the flight deck as the Zarram siblings lifted off on their dragon.

Eslinde walked in long strides to keep pace and whispered, "Why the hurry? What has upset you?"

Kess glanced back. Lady Hjelzahn remained motionless in the middle of the vast space as servants bustled about to secure the newly arrived dragons and return the mobile stairs.

Kess pushed faster, to get her and Eslinde closer behind Ulfren and the protection of his grayglim, but not close enough that the forward group could hear their whispered conversation.

"Lady Hjelzahn is dangerous. She isn't trying to find her children to reunite with them. She wants them dead and has tried to kill them already."

Eslinde scoffed. "For what possible reason?"

"I don't know, but I know Aishena and Benjin are keeping away from her on purpose."

They wove their way from the flight deck through corridors of ash gray and lightning-blue lamplight.

Eslinde's brow furrowed. "What of the eldest brother, Yoskar?"

Kess eyed the grayglim over Eslinde's shoulder, knowing he would hear everything said. "There was a fight between the family when I saw them in the Alderkin undercity. Yoskar was already dead by Kverra's hand when I arrived. I didn't witness it myself, only ... the aftermath."

Although traveling as fast as she could, every time there was even a small step or threshold in their path it slowed Kess down, and soon Ulfren and his men had disappeared ahead. Kess tossed worried glances over her shoulder, expecting Lady Hjelzahn to ambush them again at any moment.

Would the strange, cold woman dare attack a first heir? She had watched both Eslinde and Ulfren with a calculating gleam in her eyes.

They reached a short flight of stairs and Eslinde gestured for Yensen to help Kess down them, her frown deepening. "I can see Lady Hjelzahn has upset you greatly, but you couldn't be mistaken? There could have been some miscommunication."

Kess's body bumped as Yensen eased her wheeled chair down each step. She didn't want to explain that her splotchy, swollen face and remnants of tears were from an entirely different upset.

"No, I don't think so." The way Lady Hjelzahn and Aishena had battled throughout that crumbled cavern in furious flashes of steel and crystal held no hesitation in their attempts to end the other's life.

"Lady Hjelzahn wanted her children dead and was willing to kill everybody else around them to do so."

"But for what reason?" Eslinde pleaded again, a hand at her chest and face distraught.

Kess's tongue went dry, words sticking in her mouth. "Unfortunately, I was too busy betraying the Hjelzahn kids and their friends for my own interests to get the full story."

Eslinde tutted. "Quite the tangled history you have, Kessara."

They came out into the courtyard Kess had begun to recognize from her few trips through the palace and then up into the statue-lined hallways leading to Eslinde's chambers.

Eslinde paused at the base of the steep flights of stairs, giving Kess a long, assessing look. 'Do you mind if Yensen carries you up? I want to be in my rooms as fast as we can. We can collect your chair later."

Kess nodded. She wanted to be able to speak with Eslinde privately, to tell her more. She'd been so focused on Kife, and what threat he could pose to Dracuni, that she hadn't considered that Lady Hjelzahn's filicidal ambitions could be an even bigger threat.

But doing anything to stop her was going to mean sharing even more information with Eslinde. Kess decided then that she was willing to take a risk on one cloistered princess over an unstoppable grayglim.

When they arrived in Eslinde's chambers, Yensen placed Kess on the lounge and Eslinde swiftly sent him out again with the order, "Go back for her chair, and send for Falden."

Yensen hesitantly crossed the threshold, leaning back toward them and giving Kess a wary glance. "Given the situation, it seems prudent I remain on guard rather than distancing—"

"Work it out," Eslinde snapped and closed the door on him. She ran her hand over the wall beside it, fingers drifting in a nervous fashion. Soft thunking sounds echoed around the chambers.

"There's something else important I have to tell you," Kess said.

"I'm sure there is." Eslinde spoke with a hard clip.

The sun outside had dipped below the horizon and the chambers were gloomy, barely enough light to see. Eslinde marched to one of the wall lights and flicked a toggle beneath it and it sparked to life with a soft *zzzt*.

Kess flinched. "The remaining Hjelzahn siblings, they

are who your daughter is traveling with."

Eslinde froze with her hand resting over the next lamp's switch. "Lyrrin? She's with Aishena and Benjin?"

"And ... some others."

Back in motion, Eslinde flicked the switch carelessly and then rubbed her thumb over her lips. "The girl, she was in grayglim training with her mother before the kids vanished from Hjelzahn keep."

"You knew them?"

"I knew *of* them. They're my great-great-something, great-niece and great-nephew, after all. Still, this is good. You said Lyrrin was well protected, and even a young grayglim is fine protection indeed."

Another soft *zzzt* as the next light illuminated.

"What's less good," Kess said, adjusting her skirts and scating from how Yensen had placed her down, "is that Lady Hjelzahn is a danger to her children and, therefore, also to Lyrrin."

"She'd go so far as to murder an eight-year-old bystander?"

"Without a doubt." Kess pulled a stray book out from underneath her and tossed it onto the low table nearby. The pitcher of water and glasses Eslinde kept there clinked, and Kess leaned across to pour herself a drink.

Eslinde meandered across the room toward the unlit lamps closer to Kess. "What about you?"

"What about me?" Kess lifted the glass to her mouth. "Is Lady Hjelzahn a threat to *you*, if you know all of this about her? If she knows you know?"

Kess paused there, glass at her lips, and thought about how the woman pretended she never intended even a harmful word once more witnesses showed up. *Whatever her game, she doesn't want to reveal herself when the odds are against her.*

"She already tried to kill me once for what I saw. Whether she's still keen to snuff me out I would have known for sure if you hadn't arrived at the flight deck when you had."

"How can you be so flippant about it?" Eslinde rounded on her, mouth agape.

"Pretty easily." Kess gulped some water, trying to cool the hot flush crawling up her neck from how she'd just moments before cried into Dashiel's arms because the burden of fear of death and betrayal from every angle had become too much. "My question is, what can you do about her?"

"Without proof? Nothing much, I'm afraid."

Kess swung around to stare over the back of the lounge at the princess. "Nothing? I'm proof. I'm telling you she's a murderer."

"And who is going to believe you, or even me, without

some form of evidence? Kverra is both an heir and a grayglim. And my brother Hjelzahn the First would not take kindly to me accusing any of his heirs, or the grayglim wife they took. He already doesn't like me."

Eslinde flicked the final lamp switch. There was a loud, crackling pop and it didn't illuminate. Kess startled at the sound, choking on her water. The remains in the glass sloshed over her fingers.

Eslinde sighed. "It's fine, they do that sometimes."

Kess's eyebrows crept up as she wiped her hand dry on her skirt.

Eslinde strode to the lounge, shaking her head. "I noticed you haven't been using the ones in the guest room. They're perfectly safe. Just ... don't touch the switches with wet fingers."

Kess continued planning to not touch the switches at all.

Eslinde reached the lounge and stopped in front of her, one hand out expectantly. "Now, speaking of safe ... I'm afraid I can't allow you to keep it."

"Keep what?"

Eslinde wiggled her fingers. "The knife, Kessara."

"If I *did* have a knife, wouldn't you be worried I'd use it on you if forced to hand it over?"

"Please," Eslinde mocked flatly.

139

She swished her skirt sideways to reveal a long slit pocket access, reached in, and withdrew a brilliantly polished length of steel. An exquisitely crafted epee with narrow swirling cross guard. With an equally liquid motion she thrust it back into its hidden scabbard.

"Right. Okay then." Kess pulled her dully pointed cheese knife from her boot and placed it in the princess's waiting hand.

Eslinde brought it close to her face to examine it, shaking her head and muttering.

"It wasn't meant for you," Kess added, mortified. "Although clearly it wouldn't have mattered if it was."

Eslinde snorted softly and tossed the makeshift weapon onto the low table amongst the stacks of books and glasses. "Us Firsts have to keep ourselves well protected. But mostly it's from each other. Why do you think Ulfren keeps three grayglim with him?"

Kess shrugged. "Desperate paranoia?"

"Accurate assessment of risk. My siblings, they've been quietly assassinating each other or scheming to remove our father from the throne for decades. As the youngest it doesn't mean much to me, although there has been a worrying increase in murdered lower generation heirs recently. And a few Firsts."

Kess remembered how Eslinde had laughed at the

concept of her father ever leaving his throne, willingly or otherwise. "You're not worried someone will succeed in removing the king?"

Eslinde straightened her skirts and lowered herself elegantly onto the lounge beside Kess. "Not at all. As much as the heirs like to plot, my father will remain safe. He protects himself by being the only person who knows where his store of silvernix is kept. If he dies, it likely all goes with him."

"And you're not worried about yourself? If Firsts are being assassinated ..."

A coy smile lifted one side of Eslinde's lips. "Have you found any way out of my chambers yet? During the times I've left you locked in? Yes, of course you've tried."

Kess grumbled begrudgingly, "No. I haven't found any way out."

"Then suffice it to say there's no way in either." Eslinde stared at the entrance door, a strange sadness in her eyes. Then she shook her head softly. "Plus, there's my ever present grayglim bodyguard. I don't trust at all that he isn't acting on my parents' orders rather than my own, but he does protect my safety. And he is *very* good."

A loud rap on the door had Eslinde on her feet again.

A familiar woman's voice announced Falden had arrived. Eslinde hurried to let him in and greeted him warmly at

the door. Olva followed, the elderly handmaiden carrying a wide tray with a dinner spread. Glistening dishes held a large rolled roast of dark meat, steaming vegetables coated in golden spices, and glass carafes of sunshine-yellow wine.

"I've brought you that information you were after, Your Highness," Falden said, his voice croaky with age.

"You have?"

"About the Heithorns?"

"Oh, yes." Eslinde beckoned him to the table by the window, away from Kess.

Falden took a seat and waited for Olva to place the tray down. Although Kess was sure it had been intended to be her and Eslinde's dinner, Falden took a glass and held it up to be filled.

Taking a sip of the pale wine, he smacked his lips. "Yes, yes. The Heithorns. A minor dragonlord family who chose to live in a walled estate far out to the west, which unfortunately was destroyed, the lord and lady amongst the dead, survived only by their son."

Kess scowled and called over from her place on the lounge. "Not only their son."

The younger handmaiden appeared as well, face red and breathing hard as she pushed the heavy wheeled chair over to Kess's side.

"Well, yes, there was a daughter too. One with ... aah

..." Falden blinked his pale eyes at Kess as she worked to move from the lounge to the wheeled chair. "A particular obsession with dragons. That was the impression those few who met her had."

"Oh, I'm sure," Kess muttered.

That was the impression. Where was this guy getting his information? Or did he simply find it too distasteful to speak the truth.

"But she's been missing and presumed dead for many years now."

Eslinde waited as her glass was filled, staring at Kess. "Quite a tragedy, by the sounds of it all."

Kess settled into the hard seat of the wheeled chair but didn't attempt to move it closer to the others.

Eslinde gave the older man a pitiful look and said, "I'm afraid I have another tragedy to turn our attention to now, though."

Falden took another sip of his wine and perked up.

Eslinde continued. "You must have heard of Lady Hjelzahn's attempts to find her missing children."

"I have, I have. Terrible matter. Has a bounty on them and all, and still no luck."

Olva worked to lay out the remaining food and serving plates, but Eslinde shooed her away. She went and joined Jillisa by the door where Yensen remained at watch.

Lowering her voice, Eslinde said, "But there's some gossip that the children might have been seen near Alderkin shrines? What do you know of that?"

Falden tugged the white strands of hair at the side of his head. "It's very worrying. Blasted criminals and cannibals of the wilds have been congregating around the old Alderkin structures for some reason. I pray for the sun's blessings those poor children aren't trapped in such a place."

"Are they so dangerous?" Eslinde glanced to Kess.

Kess rolled her eyes and shook her head.

Falden nodded vehemently. "Oh yes! Dreadful! They are pits of evil, filled with monsters worshiping cursed Alderkin magic, that are causing the shadow dragon's blight to get worse."

Eslinde's lip twitched and she drew a long sip of wine. "Surely, they are simply desperate people who've been unable to seek shelter in a dragonkeep. Perhaps they can be reasoned with, convinced to stop any dangerous activities?"

She swirled the liquid in her glass and set it back on the table. "Or if the Hjelzahn children are kept there, that they could be released? If I were to draft some messages, could they be delivered out to some of these shrine settlements?"

"You have a kind heart, Your Highness, but those animals can't be reasoned with."

Eslinde reached across the table to take Falden's hand

in hers. "There are so few I can trust these days. You've always been my favorite advisor, always ready to assist me. Couldn't we at least try?"

Falden's lips jiggled between a prideful grin and attempted humility. "I suppose communication could be attempted. I could arrange that for you."

"And keep me informed of where Lady Hjelzahn is whenever possible? So any news we might receive about her children can be passed on." Eslinde got to her feet, offering a wide armed gesture that Falden should join her.

"Of course." He hastily put his glass back down as Eslinde herded him away from the table.

"You are an absolute treasure," Eslinde said as she whisked the old man back out the door again. With a word to her handmaidens that she needed nothing else that evening, the door was closed again, followed by the echoing sounds of locking.

When the princess turned back her way, Kess clapped slowly and quietly. "Masterful."

Eslinde offered a tiny bow.

Pushing her chair around the lounge, Kess headed for the dinner spread. "You know, if those messages do reach the shrine settlements, and then get to your daughter and her friends, they're only going to think it's some kind of trap."

"Possibly. If they even realize the messages are for them.

I'm going to have to be so subtle with my language ... But I have to try." Eslinde joined Kess at the table but didn't serve herself any food. She seemed deep in thought as though already composing those coded messages in her mind.

Kess reached for the roasted meat. A long carving knife rested beside it, almost as though in mockery of Kess's previous effort to arm herself. Kess sliced a thick slab, dumped it on her plate, and stabbed the blade back into the remaining roast.

Kess picked at the juicy meat. *Griskin would love this.*

Eslinde's attention returned to her. "Now, you obviously already knew about these shrine settlements. And more. You have been open with me, but I know there is much you're holding back."

Kess munched on the meat. "I know plenty of things. You'll have to be more specific about what you want to know."

Eslinde's shoulders dropped, and the regal fire in her tone vanished. "I must play games with everyone in my life, Kessara. Please don't make me play them with you as well. You have brought a treasured truth into my life. But you are keeping a secret from me, something you're holding tightly to, something I know is important."

Kess's insouciant chewing slowed. In the lightning-hued glow of the lamps, Eslinde's face was drawn thin, sharp lines between her pale brows. A war of rebellious hope and learned hopelessness visible in her eyes.

I have to give her something. But I can't give her Dracuni.

"It's not the shrines or the people around them that is worsening the shadow dragon curse."

Eslinde waited, unmoving.

At the precipice, the words felt like treason, but Kess forced them out. "We think it's caused by the taming of dragons."

She remained still, waiting the princess's reaction, eyeing the carving blade, just in case.

"Is that all?" Eslinde seemed disappointed.

"Is that *all*?" Kess repeated in disbelief.

"It's not new information, I'm afraid." Eslinde reached for a carafe and refilled her glass, still avoiding the food. "I've known for quite some time."

Kess's words coughed out. "You ... what ... how?"

"I was initially shocked too. And I tried to spread the information, back in my rebellious phase. Back before all of that was crushed out of me." Eslinde's eyes fluttered and she took a long drink of her wine. "Nobody believed me, of course. Who would believe silly little Eslinde over the lies Yeonard Draekhan has been spreading for decades about it being an Alderkin curse?"

"The ... the Dragon King ... he knows too?" Kess could only stutter words out. How many life-threatening secrets was she now privy to? She reached for the carafe of wine and filled a glass for herself.

"I understand it must have been a big revelation for you, but as you think it through, what does it really mean? Not much. What could we do? Dragons are here and they are tamed, people aren't going to stop using them. They need them, for almost every aspect of our society." Eslinde gestured to the humming lights along the wall.

"But it's ... the tamings are causing the shadow dragon blight. We could end it, reclaim the land from the undead."

"Yet we need dragons as well for protection from those revenants. We are in a bind."

Kess took a long drink of the sweet wine, inviting the heavy effect of it flooding her veins.

What could they do? Was there no solution?

"No. It doesn't have to be this way." Kess thumped her glass down again. "There are other ways to live. Without dragons. They don't use them in the Alderkin undercity. And the settlements around the shrines. There is a magic there, but a good magic. It keeps the revenants out, and the people there are living peacefully."

Eslinde paused at that, raising her eyebrows. "Really, what life could they have without the assistance of dragons, out there?"

Kess remembered what she saw, as she'd chased her prey from shrine to shrine, of those small communities thriving within the standing stone rings. "It's a simple life, but they seem happy. And maybe people in the keeps could be too, without dragons. They could start small, untame a few—"

"Sorry, untame?" Eslinde leaned closer, eyes round.

"The dragons. They could be untamed." Kess watched the princess's stunned expression. "They can be freed, made wild and independent again. You didn't know?"

Eslinde was breathing heavily, pale eyes glimmering in the cool light. "No, Kessara. That is new information to me. And that is something I want to see for myself."

TEN

Dashiel jittered with nerves as they waited at the street level entrance of Zarram Dragonhold for Eslinde's arrival.

The racist slur that had been painted upon the wall beside the grand iron gates didn't help. It wasn't the first time, but was the biggest and boldest. Singe marks blackened the stone beneath it.

"Stars, did someone try to start a fire?"

"Good thing Zarrams don't burn so easily," Vance replied.

He'd been out waiting even earlier than Dashiel. He gave the wall a dark look. Servants hastily scrubbed to remove the crude message before the princess and her guest arrived.

That strange, wounded girl.

Dashiel hadn't been able to stop thinking about her since their flight after the investment ceremony. That had been a crazy day, and weeks later no answers had surfaced for the strange taming spike, fake silvernix, murderous grayglim, or what pain Kess's history held that had her so broken.

Dashiel could guess at some of it. Their brother hid their prosthetic leg from most people for a reason. Maybe the visit today would provide more answers, although Eslinde's communications had been vague in the extreme.

Still, Dashiel found themselves wanting to know more about Kess, wanting to help her see that not all the world was cruel.

She was a natural in the saddle, too. Imagine what she could do with some proper training.

Perhaps that was what this visit was about.

A black carriage approached down the cobbled street. Elaborate silver filigree accented the edges of the doors and windows, but it was the forest-green treedart drawing the carriage that identified it as one coming from the palace. Only the royal family had silvernix to spare on taming dragons for tasks that other livestock could perform.

"Here they come," Dashiel called to their brother.

Vance grunted at the unfinished cleaning work and moved to stand by Dashiel's side.

The carriage rolled to a stop.

Eslinde emerged first, gliding down in an elegant step. Her shoulders were back, chin lifted in a fiery countenance that had normally accompanied her when she was younger and she'd visit to talk about the most rebellious ideas.

She even smiled, very slightly. More in her eyes than her thinly pressed lips. She pointedly remained turned away from the half-scrubbed paint on the wall.

"Thank you for accepting our company today. I hope we aren't taking time from your training." She offered the siblings a shallow bow.

Dashiel returned the bow deeper. "Not at all."

They didn't elaborate as to the great pains they had gone through to skip training that day. But their mestra's great disapproval was nothing compared to missing out on seeing what had to be two of the most interesting people in the city.

Kess appeared then at the carriage door. She had the skirts of her courtly gown bundled up near her waist, revealing well-worn leather pants beneath, the kind a hunter or guard might wear. She kept the fabric out of the way as she shuffled right to the edge of the bench.

The grayglim Yensen moved about the back of the carriage, then brought the wheeled chair around beside the door.

Dashiel was about to offer assistance when Kess neatly climbed down and lowered herself into the seat. After straightening out her skirts, she rolled the chair over more smoothly and swiftly than she'd managed before.

Dashiel bowed down to her eye level. "It's good to see you again."

Kess leaned away from the words and fussed with her skirts some more, eyes averted. "You too."

Vance gestured to one of the nearby servants to direct the driver on where to park the carriage.

"Go with the carriage, Yensen. You can await our return there." Eslinde didn't look toward her grayglim as she commanded him.

"Your Highness." Yensen's eyes passed over the remaining graffiti, then Kess and the Zarrams. "I cannot allow you to wander such a facility unaccompanied."

Vance stepped forward, looming over the warden.

His voice held a low growl as he said, "I can guarantee Eslinde will be safe with us in the dragonhold."

Stepping between them, Eslinde said, "Oh, I'm sure he's far more worried that I'm the one who's going to steal a dragon and fly away and leave him to explain to my father how he lost his unruly daughter."

"Your Highness," Yensen said again, pained.

"I'm not going to run away. I'm visiting friends and

you aren't required. Unless of course your true intentions are to spy upon me?" Eslinde turned toward him then, keeping him held in her icy stare.

He swallowed visibly, jaw twitching. "I will wait with the carriage."

Eslinde turned on her heel, triumph on her lips, and led the way inside, leaving the rest of them to follow.

Kess kept up easily with the swift march but allowed Dashiel to assist when they reached steps.

"Now, I'm afraid our visit isn't strictly social," Eslinde said.

"I hadn't assumed so," Vance replied.

"Where can we speak with utmost privacy?" Eslinde said, eyes on the numerous staff and servants moving about the corridors.

"This way." Vance took the lead.

The entry level of the dragonhold was largely for administration, meetings with trade partners, and services for the humans within the hold, as opposed to those for dragons. It was all gleaming and gilt with the finest furnishings the dragonkeep capital had to offer.

The squeaking of Kess's chair echoed down the hall.

Dashiel leaned toward her. "So ... Has anybody tried to kill you lately?"

Kess flushed red. "No. Although I may feel the need for murder if you bring that up again."

"You'd murder me for my curiosity? Maybe you could look into that reaction as a place to start if you don't want everybody trying to kill you."

Kess gave them a dull glare.

Dashiel grinned in return, pressing a hand innocently to their chest. "I just want to know what the deal with that strange grayglim was."

"Oh. That's all?"

"What else?"

"The ... crying?" Kess hissed under her breath, turning even redder.

They reached a short flight of stairs, and Dashiel took the back of Kess's chair. "That? That was nothing. You should see me when I witness someone who's a better rider than I am. Tantrum central. Lock myself in my room and cry for days."

Kess scoffed.

At the bottom of the stairs, Dashiel leaned over Kess from behind. "It's lucky it's been a few weeks since our flight together. I only emerged tear-free yesterday."

Kess gave them a flat look, but there was a softening in her shoulders and eyes as they searched Dashiel's face, the smallest hint of smile. "You needn't coddle me."

"Wouldn't dream of it." Dashiel beamed.

"Yes, this will do." Eslinde inspected the room Vance

had led them to from the doorway, then entered.

Vance's office. Letters and leatherbound folios were stacked to one side of the modest desk—paperwork Vance had fallen behind on, as usual. Vance was many things, but he wasn't made for doing paperwork, despite how much Lord Zarram thrust upon him.

There were no windows, and the small room was farthest from the rest of the offices. Once an old storage room for the nearby hatchery, it had been converted when Vance's accident changed his career path.

The Zarram siblings had initial hopes that Vance would fly again, that the office space was only temporary, but their father had other ideas.

Vance struck an oil lamp alight, and Dashiel closed the door behind them.

Patting the heavy stone, Dashiel said, "The walls are thick here. It must be quite a secret you have to share, considering how keen you were to get rid of your grayglim."

Vance offered Eslinde the one chair in the room, but she shook her head and remained standing.

"Yes, well, asking one's friends to attempt to untame a dragon does feel like a thing that requires secrecy," she said.

Dashiel choked. "Sorry ... *what* do you want to do?"

"Kess can perhaps explain the process better, but she believes—"

"She has witnessed," Kess clarified.

Eslinde continued. "Kess has *witnessed* a dragon's taming being reversed. And it is something I wish to witness for myself. Which is why I've come to ask those I trust the most whether they would attempt to untame their dragon for me."

Kess gave them a description of the process, and Eslinde confirmed that she brought the required silvernix with her.

Dashiel took the sole seat in the room then, dumping down into it with a sigh.

"Taming can be reversed?" They leaned their head into their hands, laughing.

"What's so funny?" Kess asked.

"It just would have been nice to know a few weeks ago, would have saved me the trouble of faking Shiff's taming." Although, Dashiel conceded, they wouldn't have wanted to ever drive that stake in, even if they knew it could be reversed.

"Dash," Vance growled in warning, too late.

"If Eslinde trusts us with this request, I trust her to know that I never tamed my dragonling."

"I suppose that means we can't use her to test the process then," Eslinde said, eyebrows raised, but offering no other judgment. "I was hoping for something small."

"Apart from Viska, every other dragon here is allocated and owned by someone who will notice if it suddenly becomes wild again," Vance said.

Dashiel leaped out of the chair again. "Then we try with Viska! You said you regretted having to tame her. This is your chance to undo it."

"Regretting that doesn't mean untaming her now is a good idea. What would happen to her?" Vance folded his arms and directed his questions at Kess.

She shrugged.

"Would she still heed commands? Would she listen at all?"

"Hard to say."

"Would she be dangerous?"

"Likely."

"How can you be sure she'll survive the process?"

"I can't."

"What do we even do with a dragon once it's untamed?"

"The other one flew away," Kess offered.

"Flew away? No. We can't do this," Vance said. "How are we going to explain even Viska's loss from our stables? I'm sorry, I can't take that risk."

Kess lounged back in her wheeled chair, giving Eslinde a look. "Maybe you were right. We can't even convince your friends to give up a single dragon."

"You did make it sound so appealing," Eslinde chided.

"I was being honest. Thought you'd appreciate it."

"Well, luckily there is one other dragon in your hold

that won't be missed." Eslinde circled around the desk, bringing herself in front of everyone. "Mine."

Kess gave the princess a long, assessing look. "You'd give up you own dragon?"

"Of course. He's been idle for years anyway since I haven't been allowed to fly. And this is important."

Dashiel turned to their brother. "Her dragon is a good pick. Only those on the feeding and cleaning rosters might notice his absence, and you could adjust the paperwork to cover for that."

"Great, more paperwork," Vance muttered.

Eslinde moved around the table to stand directly in front of him, staring up into his face with a tilted head. "Please, Vance. For me. I have nobody else I can turn to with this request."

A growling grumble came from low in Vance's throat and his nose twitched. "Fine. For you."

Even with the agreement, Vance continued to try to find reasons not to, or to delay, but only helped them solidify their plan.

What if the dragon tried to get away? They would chain it down first.

What if the dragon was dangerous? They would do the untaming in one of the old flamesong stalls where it could be contained.

Why were they even risking it? Eslinde promised to tell them more, if it worked.

Down in the lower levels of the old building, Dashiel took Kess into Shiff's stall while Vance handled bringing Eslinde's dragon into another nearby.

"You really didn't tame her?" Kess asked, approaching the wild dragonling without any fear.

"You don't mind?" Dashiel asked.

"I ... I knew another dragonling that hadn't been tamed. She made tamed dragons seem so much less interesting." Kess held her hand out.

Still and calm? Shiff sniffed at Kess and her rolling chair warily.

"No, at ease." Dashiel patted the dragon's snout, then smiled back at Kess. "Wolves, wild dragons, legions trying to murder you ... You make my life feel so boring."

Kess shrugged. "You try living alone in the wilds for five years and I'm sure you'll also have plenty of tales to tell."

"Is *that* where you came from?" Dashiel could hardly imagine it.

They'd flown a little way out over the lands around Draekhanhelm but had never landed beyond the walls. They wanted to ask Kess so many questions, like whether she'd ever seen a rev close up, but didn't want to admit to the fierce young woman that they hadn't.

Shiff slithered to her feet, prowling forward. She scratched at the wheel of Kess's chair.

"Shiff, back." Dashiel swirled a finger at their side. "Sit."

The dragonling skittered over and sat at attention.

"You've trained her too?" Kess's eyes sparkled.

"Vance doesn't think it's going to hold as she gets older, more independent and savage. I guess we're about to have a full-grown wild dragon to test my training skills on soon."

"We're ready!" Vance called from across the hallway.

"Shiff, come." Dashiel clicked, and the dragonling followed at his heel.

They figured having the dragonling around might help communication efforts once Eslinde's dragon was untamed. Inside the next stall, Eslinde and Vance waited, looking over the medium-sized dragon before them.

Dashiel always liked Eslinde's snowshimmer. He was a blue the color of a smoke-free sky, and it had been an honor to keep a First's dragon stabled, even if it seemed a formality for a dragon that had for all intents and purposes been retired.

Vance worked on hauling a second set of chains across and locked them around the dragon's neck. "Just in case."

Eslinde patted the dragon's cheek. Dashiel didn't know why she no longer flew or whether she'd named her dragon. It was young when it had been stabled with them, eight years ago.

Kess talked them through the process again, and Vance found some pliers.

"Once the spike is out, it might take a while for the dragon to come back to itself." Kess placed herself just inside the opened doorway. "It did the other time. You'll see why."

"I certainly hope to." Eslinde moved around, lighting a few extra oil lamps to brighten the solid stone chamber.

"I just hope we aren't making a terrible mistake." Vance paused with the pliers around the end of the spike.

Dashiel elbowed him and said softly, "But you're going to do this anyway. It's for Eslinde."

Vance growled and grumbled under his breath. Then he pulled the taming stake.

It was a slow, torturous process, but the dragon didn't react. Finally, the stake slipped free, and Vance threw it and the pliers on the ground outside the stall.

Dashiel had the princess's silvernix at the ready. As they let the drop fall onto the wound, they held their breath.

What if the silvernix is fake again?

But then there was a shimmer of light, glowing between the dragon's scales.

Vance and Dashiel joined the other two at the doorway.

"So we just wait?" Dashiel asked.

Kess's eyes were on the air above the dragon's lowered head, and she nodded.

"There!" Kess said.

Eslinde gasped, and then Dashiel saw it too. Dark wisps of smoky mist, descending through the stone ceiling toward the motionless snowshimmer.

"What is that?" they asked.

But then the dragon was moving. Moving without a command or a rider. Slowly, at first. The twitch of an eyelid, the turn of a neck. Then the chains rattled as the dragon's whole body snapped to life and he roared.

Eslinde clutched her forehead and cried out, "He's screaming! Screaming in my head!"

What happens? Dragon talks!

Dashiel frowned. Could all dragons communicate normally if they weren't tamed?

Poor Shiff. What a strange, silent world where every dragon around her was mute.

They didn't know how to explain why that was.

"Can you communicate? Try to calm it," Kess ordered.

Eslinde's knees buckled, and she leaned against the doorframe. "He's so angry!"

The dragon thrashed again, tail whipping behind him. One of the chains locking him in place snapped like rock candy.

"Whoa!" Dashiel dodged a piece of flying metal. "Is the other one going to hold?"

"I'm not sure," Vance replied. "The chains are designed to stop people stealing the dragons, not to hold dragons down. There isn't usually a need."

Blue scales shimmered in the lamplight as the dragon's body convulsed, swaying and arching, eyes rolling wildly.

The second chain cracked, metal groaning as it tore free.

"Out! Get out!" Vance bellowed.

Dashiel raised their hands toward the snowshimmer. "We just have to calm her down, communicate—"

The dragon's head swung around, locked sights on Eslinde, and its mouth opened. A sparking blue glow built at the back of its throat.

Oh no.

A jagged streak of lightning shot out. Dashiel froze, the scene searing into their eyes in the harsh glare.

Vance dove, pulling the princess into a rolling tumble with him. She fell out of his arms as the beam caught up with him, and Vance howled.

"Vance!" Dashiel's feet were fixed to the ground.

"Go! Move!" Kess hissed, pushing into Dashiel from behind with her chair.

They stumbled together out of the room.

The snowshimmer snarled, eyes turning, taking in the solid walls on every side and only exit ahead.

Stop. Sit! Still and calm! Shiff rose onto her back

legs, wings outstretched like a shield in front of the humans and her chest puffing.

Dashiel grabbed for the emergency release on the wall. "Shiff! Come!"

The dragonling darted from the chamber with the snowshimmer snapping at her tail. The moment Shiff was out, Dashiel pulled the rope, and the heavy drop-gate slammed down.

Dull roars echoed through the solid steel. Then scratching and the thud, thud, thud, of the dragon trying to batter his way out.

"Vance? Are you hurt?" Eslinde crouched over Dashiel's brother, hiding him from view with a curtain of silver hair and satin gown.

The parts of Vance that were visible had a faint twist of smoke rising from them.

Dashiel rushed over. "Is he okay?"

Vance groaned. "My whole mouth tastes like copper."

"Alive then, at least." Dashiel laughed in relief and helped pull Vance to his feet.

Vance stumbled, and Eslinde caught him under the shoulder.

"Careful," she scolded. She helped him cross to a wall so he could lean there.

Vance grumbled. "I'm fine. It's just ..."

He leaned forward, pulling the hem of his pants up. The metal joint of his prosthetic leg smoldered, fused solid. "Raze it."

Eslinde jabbed him in the side with her fist. "That was reckless, moving in front of the lightning like that."

"You're welcome." Vance coughed.

Eslinde stepped in front of him then, brushing fingers over a singed piece of hair near his cheek and berating him in a long string of accusations.

Dashiel smiled softly and stepped back.

"Is he going to be okay?" Kess asked.

Dashiel squatted down beside her, taking a few deep breaths of recovery. "Oh yeah. I'd say so. He's probably loving this."

"Why would he?"

Leaning onto the armrest of Kess's chair, Dashiel whispered, "Vance has loved Eslinde for most of his life. Although he'd gnaw off his remaining leg before he'd ever admit it. Even to himself."

Kess blinked once, and for a moment, there was such a devastating clarity of pain in her eyes that Dashiel was worried she'd somehow been hurt by the dragon and was about to die in front of them. Then she blinked again and her face turned stony.

Before Dashiel could question it, Vance said, "You've

definitely done what you set out to do. That's a wild dragon in there."

The snowshimmer continued to roar, the sound reverberating through the solid door.

"Will that hold?" Eslinde asked.

"It's designed to block an exploding flamesong, so I'd say so," Dashiel answered. They stepped up to rap on the door, but considered the snowshimmer might use its lightning breath and thought better of touching the metal. "Although I'm going to have to work out a way to feed it … Maybe it will calm down, after a while."

Very angry, Shiff thought.

Eslinde stared at the door and shook her head softly. "It really worked."

"I did say it would." Kess shrugged.

"Are you ready to tell us what this is all about now?" Vance asked.

Eslinde laced her fingers together and brought them up in front of her lips, took a deep breath, and then explained.

She'd already spoken vaguely to Dashiel and Vance in their childhood about how she didn't believe the shadow dragon was caused by an Alderkin curse. But to hear the truth of it left Dashiel shaken.

But also excited. "How many? How many dragons would need to be healed to stop the shadow dragon? If

we did all of ours—"

"Dash," Vance warned. "That's not going to happen."

"Why not? If it was enough ..."

"I doubt it would be enough," Eslinde said softly. "You have a few score dragons in your hold, but there must be hundreds, thousands across Elundrae. Each one is making the shadow dragon stronger."

"So each one must weaken it. We should at least stop taming more or ..." Dashiel's words shuddered to a stop and their mouth went dry. Frowning, they jogged over into Shiff's stall.

"What is it?" Kess asked.

"You've got to see this," they called out as they removed the loose paving stone. They retrieved the bundle from the hollow beneath and returned to the others. Dashiel unwrapped the cloth, explaining about the fake silvernix from the taming ceremony.

The strange crystal taming spike no longer glowed.

Dashiel held it out to show Eslinde and Kess. "This is strange, right? Like maybe someone else is doing something to the tamings. What do these markings mean?"

Almost in unison, Kess and Eslinde replied, "They're Alderkin runes."

Kess shot Eslinde a look. "When have you seen Alderkin runes?"

Eslinde's eyes narrowed, and she took the stake from Dashiel. "In study. You know I read a lot."

Shiff came to sit at Dashiel's feet, disturbed by the echoes of the snowshimmer's attempts to free itself.

Dashiel reached a hand down, patting her neck, imagining what might have happened if they'd used that strange spike. "But why—?"

"I'll look into it," Eslinde said and dropped the spike into a hidden pocket in her gown. "Don't tell anyone else about this or about the untaming. At least for now. We're flying into dangerous skies."

The snowshimmer roared through the barrier of its cell, a long, echoing cry that eked out into a high whine.

Dashiel shivered. Eslinde's expression suggested that having a full-grown wild dragon caged in their basement was the least dangerous thing they might face soon.

ELEVEN

Yeonard Draekhan. Dragon King. Tamer of dragons. The ever youthful. The man who could no doubt have Kess killed off on a whim if the desire took him, regardless of anything Eslinde said. Somebody that Kess really didn't want to be in the same room with.

Let alone presenting evidence that directly challenged the Dragon King's source of power.

"I don't think you need me for this," Kess said, gripping the wheels of her chair to slow down.

Eslinde kept up her swift march, pushing Kess along with her. "Nonsense. You are a vital witness. I know he's turned us away already, but I'm not taking no for an answer anymore."

Grand double doors lay ahead, inlaid with golden filigree forming the design of a massive dragon's head. From the center of its forehead, swirling lines and beams shot forth like a sunrise. A palace guard stood on either side.

"His Majesty has not requested your presence," one of the guards said in a confused, boyish voice.

"You must be mistaken. Yensen? Get the door." Eslinde didn't slow her pace.

Kess worried that the princess would use her and her chair as a battering ram, but her grayglim moved faster, pushing the double doors wide for their passage before either of the guards could react.

The two men were left stuttering in their wake as the grand doors swung closed again.

Inside the private advisory chambers, all heads turned their way.

Kess straightened in her chair and tried to straighten her expression as well, which was twitching into an anxious sneer.

She recognized Eslinde's mother, Queen Vellira, a brazen beauty with a glare so icy it could have taken the spark out of dragonfire. Falden, the old advisor who had visited Eslinde, sat alongside her, plus another half dozen elders Kess didn't recognize.

Ulfren the First was there, along with another white-haired man, the same Kess had seen walking with him in

the courtyard weeks ago, hovering at his left. They leaned over the central table where a map of Elundrae was spread. Some tokens and figurines were spread around the central range of Eishowl Peaks, where the Alderkin undercity was.

On their side stood Yeonard Draekhan.

"Eslinde. Your presence is unexpected." Although speaking softly, his voice seemed to boom and echo through the coolly lit chamber.

The Dragon King's eyes were dark and piercing, with bright, glinting middles, almost as though the iris and pupils had been reversed. Kess found she couldn't look at them for long without shivers racking through her.

Eslinde seemed to have no such trouble.

"Well, we are here now regardless. Continue. I can wait my turn." Eslinde slowed her pace, pushing Kess to a respectable distance from the table and stopping there.

The princess remained standing, and her grayglim had become a shadow along the wall where other similar shadows lurked.

Craning her neck, Eslinde peered at the map. "Planning another incursion into Elgartha?"

Ulfren scowled and scooped the pieces off the side of the parchment, then roughly rolled it up. "We were done."

Eslinde raised her eyebrows and smiled politely. "I'm sure if anyone had managed to smuggle living unicorns off Elundrae, and somehow kept them alive in captivity, there would have been news of it by now."

Yeonard strode around the table to Eslinde and Kess's side. Floor-length robes of watery-silver fabric hung straight from elaborate shoulder guards of gold and gemstones, forming a high-necked collar in the center.

He clasped fingers laden with heavily ornate rings in front of him. "And what are you doing toward finding solutions for the silvernix shortage?"

So even he is worried about silvernix running out? Even with how free a supply Eslinde has had access to?

Kess wondered how much there still was in the Dragon King's hidden stores. But she knew no matter how much it was, someone like him would always want more.

He can't find out about Dracuni.

The ageless man stood in front of her. Kess frowned, turning her eyes to the polished floor, her breath quickening at the nearness of the Dragon King.

Kess hated the roiling feelings within her. She hated being someone who could be cowed.

What would Riony do, if she were here?

Probably say something inappropriate.

Kess's lips lifted, picturing the fiery giant throwing a joke at the Dragon King about his amma.

Dashiel's words echoed within her. *Vance has loved*

Eslinde for most of his life. Although he'd gnaw off his remaining leg before he'd ever admit it. Even to himself.

Kess's frown returned, pinned down painfully as though by knives.

Could Kess admit it, if there was such a thing to admit? It didn't matter anyway; there was nobody to admit anything to. She clutched the acorn at her neck.

But she also raised her head, locking eyes with the nigh-immortal ruler of their land. And it was he who turned away.

Eslinde's voice remained pleasant. "I do have news, actually, which is in a way relevant to our supplies and use of silvernix."

Kess hissed under her breath, "Now? Shouldn't we—"

"Everybody here knows the true cause of the shadow dragon already."

Ulfren scoffed again, pointing the rolled map at her like a weapon. "True cause? You've no proof. Must we listen to these delusions again?"

Yeonard Draekhan tilted his chin upward. "I had thought you'd grown beyond your tendency toward conspiracy, dear daughter."

Eslinde's fingers entwined in front of her. "Is it conspiracy that the shadow dragon curse is worsening? No. We've all seen the reports of burned revenants rising a second time.

Of revenants congregating in great numbers. My companion here has seen it with her own eyes."

"You can't take the word of some peasant from the wilds on these issues," the other silver-haired man said.

"*Peasant*?" Kess grumbled.

"Hjelzahn, I understand you must struggle with trust while there is so much happening within your family line." The sympathy in Eslinde's tone sounded almost real.

Kess eyed the man. He had looked vaguely familiar. Kess had once in her life been in the same space as the Hjelzahns, back before she'd been cast out of her noble home.

Yoska, Aishena, and Benjin were a number of generations removed from Hjelzahn the First, though. Even Kverra wasn't related to him by blood and had given her children her darker skin. Hjelzahn the First was pale like his father, silver hair in only two braids at the front and loose at the back, and a single plait in the center of his small beard.

Eslinde strode forward, leaving Kess behind as she approached the table. Reaching into her pocket, she tossed the tarnished spike that had been pulled from her snowshimmer onto the surface.

"But I can trust Kessara's word because she has brought me information that I've been able to test and confirm myself. That tamings, the cause of the shadow dragon, can be reversed."

"Reversed?" Ulfren choked on the word.

"Reversed," Eslinde confirmed. "In a similar process, with a drop of silvernix, we can take back from the shadow dragon that which is strengthening it. We could end its blight once and for all."

Kess held her breath as she waited for the reactions of those who could make or break all their lives, those who had the power to change all of Elundrae, be its salvation or downfall.

There was shocked silence at first and then quiet mutterings shared with those nearest. Falden and Eslinde's mother leaned close, whispering to each other.

"So your news of silvernix is how we can spend it twice as fast, for no reward?" Hjelzahn eyed the spike on the table like it was a venomous snake. "Why would we use a precious resource to reverse something we've already invested in?"

"Because it would liberate our lands and our people from the curse of the undead," Eslinde replied.

Yeonard Draekhan's eyes glittered. "All the abundance we've brought to Elundrae, all our trade profits from metals and glass with other lands, all our technology and innovation has come from leashing the power of dragons. You would have us throw all of that away?"

Eslinde opened her mouth, but the Dragon King

continued over her. "For what? So some peasants in the wild don't have to worry about revenants? They should be serving in the keeps anyway."

"The dragonkeeps remain safe, as always," Hjelzahn agreed.

Kess sneered. They had everything in their hands, here in their castles, kept safe by dragons, from a plague caused *by* dragons. All the while forcing those without dragons to enslave themselves to those with for protection.

"So you'll surrender the surrounding lands forever? Allow everything outside your walls to be razed to ruins?" Kess asked, her voice a low rasp.

Eslinde gave her a warning glance, then addressed the room again. "If we could simply stop taming new dragons, at least ..."

"You still bring us no proof. Some rusty old spike means nothing. The shadow dragon is a curse caused by the Alderkin and is growing worse due to the sins of the unblessed and dishonorable." Ulfren made a gesture that Kess had only seen Sunblessed Monks and Taen holy leaders make in the past. A draw of his hand from the sky to his heart.

"That's ridiculous," Eslinde said.

Ulfren smacked the rolled map down on the table, disrupting the figurines and tokens. "We should have expelled all of the Rolanians from this land when we rose

to greatness upon the backs of dragons under the mighty sun, not allowed them to serve us."

A murmuring of voices rose in the room, no doubt shocked by the concept of no longer having either Rolanians or dragons around to serve them.

The Dragon King raised both arms into the air, and all voices in the room silenced.

"There is nothing useful left to say here. This audience is done."

"Your Majesty," Eslinde pleaded.

"Enough, Eslinde. You will stop pursuing these outlandish ideas. I thought you had learned your lesson last time." Yeonard placed a hand on her shoulder. His voice was almost kind, but the edge of warning in it was cold and sharp as a sword.

Ulfren glared at the closeness between his father and sister.

The elder advisors Kess didn't know moved first, clearing out of the room in a stream of swishing robes and white hair. Ulfren and Hjelzahn followed, shoulder to shoulder and in close conversation.

Eslinde's mother remained, eyes on her daughter.

Kess caught Eslinde's eye, trying to indicate she was ready to leave as well, but Eslinde gave an almost imperceptible shake of her head, and her lips pouted.

"Is Hjelzahn here looking into his missing heirs?" She placed her own hand down over her father's, holding it in place on her shoulder.

"One of the matters he's come to address, yes." The Dragon King moved to turn and withdraw.

Eslinde held tight. "I am so moved by Kverra Hjelzahn's search for her missing children. I want to assist, personally. Would you allow me to leave the city? Take a small team and a few dragons to find those poor children?"

"Eslinde. What are you playing at?" His voice rumbled.

"I only want to help. The Hjelzahn children are my family too, as they are yours, and—"

"Stop it! You expect me to give you the rope you need to hang yourself? You'll remain in Draekhanhelm, in the palace, until you can prove you've grown beyond your wild inclinations. Today has only been proof of the opposite."

Eslinde's carefully polite expression crashed down, and she flung his hand off her.

Kess had to push fast at her wheels to keep up with the princess as she marched from the room. Behind them, Eslinde's mother had her eyes on Kess, Falden whispering in her ear.

"Yensen," the Dragon King's voice grumbled, and the grayglim that had been following turned and went to him instead.

Eslinde didn't slow, storming out through the doors.

"Your grayglim?" Kess asked.

She glanced back. Yensen stood at attention for the Dragon King, who paced before him. They spoke in a snapping to and fro in voices too low to hear.

"He's hardly mine. He is the king's man."

Are any of them on Eslinde's side?

Kess had assumed a first heir would have more power, or at least more freedom. But Eslinde couldn't leave the city, wasn't listened to, wasn't respected.

How did one pregnancy lead to all of this?

Outside the chamber, Eslinde's pace slowed, and as the doors swung closed, she halted entirely.

Her breath snorted out. "The undead blight is growing worse, and our world is dying, and all any of them can think about is their ... their ... razing trade profits!"

It had been eye-opening for Kess. She'd thought there would be objections to untaming dragons, from those who were attached to their beasts, who needed them for vital work.

She didn't expect the rulers of the land to know exactly what was at stake and see it as a way to continue profiting from making the rest of the world so unlivable that people had to shelter and serve under them.

Eslinde sighed, eyes turned up to the ceiling. "Things have to change. They have to. With Lyrrin out there ..."

Kess sought for any last scrap of hope within her. Even

in her darkest moments, she'd always found a way in the past. She just needed to know her next steps.

"So, what are we going to do about it?"

"Do?" Eslinde laughed wryly. "What can we do?"

"Everybody already seems to be blaming me for awakening your rebellious side again, so let's go all in. We could steal a dragon, fly off and find your daughter, and—"

"Even your plan relies on a tamed dragon." Eslinde shook her head. "And the vast majority of dragons are within the keeps. How can we untame enough out there to make a difference?"

Kess's mouth slammed shut. She didn't know. It seemed impossible.

They'd tried to convince the most powerful people in the land to help, Eslinde's own family, and failed.

And in the process, all they'd done was make everyone in that meeting look at Kess as though she were the source of all Eslinde's problems.

TWELVE

It was the most terrifying thing Kess had ever faced. Her skin was clammy, her throat dry and stinging from rising acid. She grasped at her thighs, wishing there were weapons strapped there beneath her gown and finding nothing.

"Oh look, there's cloud cake!" Eslinde said brightly.

The ballroom before them was like a gigantic glasshouse, with vaulting walls and ceiling made entirely of sparkling windows, arching high above. Outside, the darkness of night cloaked them, so the panes reflected the glittering party beneath like a mirror.

Kess's last experience in a building with a glass ceiling hadn't been pleasant, but it wasn't the threat of shattering glass that scared her.

It was the people. Hundreds of dragonlords milled about the space.

Hundreds of dragonlord eyes to look upon Kess and find her wanting with one glance.

"I could have waited in your chambers," Kess said.

"Why ever would you have wanted to? We've both been cooped up in there too long. This is our chance to find some allies for our cause." Eslinde plucked a crisp swirl of pastry from a passing platter.

It had been weeks since their meeting with the Dragon King, and both were becoming frustrated by a lack of progress on all fronts. No ways to untame more dragons. No news of the Hjelzahn siblings, and thus Lyrrin, coming in from the outside world. No information of the group at all, of who traveled with them, of who was still alive …

No way to get to Kife and no weapon to kill him with even if Kess could.

Kess and the princess had spent most of their time reading and sulking.

But Eslinde had decided the ball might present opportunities.

Kess glared at the extravagantly decorated space, glittering with strings of gold that hung from the glass ceiling like sunset-struck rain. Yensen and many other grayglim bodyguards stood like statues around the perimeter of the space.

"Is this for some special occasion?" she asked.

"Oh no, just a regular gathering." Eslinde wriggled her fingers in a wave as Vance and Dashiel approached.

Like the majority of the guests, they wore shades of silver and gold, the Taen fashion. Vance's suit was on the silver end, unadorned but well tailored with a high collar, and Dashiel's on the golden end of the spectrum, a jacket of free-flowing silk over a suit designed to replicate the cut of armor.

Kess fussed with the gown Eslinde had provided her. Darker than the lustrous silvers around them, it was the gray of a tumultuous sky, shimmering with an overlay of thousands of tiny gems. But it didn't matter how fine the clothing, how close she fit into the surrounding fashion.

The other guests still stared at her and her chair in a way that made Kess feel naked.

She'd never been to anything like this before. She was rarely invited even to family dinners with her parents and Kife by the end of her stay at Heithorn estate, let alone been allowed by her family to be seen by society.

"You look great," Dashiel said, offering Kess a formal bow.

Kess scowled in return.

"No, really!" Dashiel laughed. "Don't you think so, Eslinde?"

Eslinde gave her an appraising look. "I suppose she

has rather handsome features, when she isn't puckering them all together."

Kess's lips drew tighter.

"You look like you're wishing there was someone trying to kill you right now," Dashiel murmured with a sly smile.

Kess's face went hot and she hunched over in her chair. "Would you stop perceiving me already?"

Vance elbowed Dashiel out of the way and bowed low before Eslinde.

Eslinde's gown looked as though it had been spun from starlight. It clung to her narrow frame and spilled onto the ground in a glittering train. Although the gown was sleeveless, Eslinde wore dozens of silver and gold bracelets stacked up her arms that rattled together when she moved her hands. Her earrings, however, were the same ones she always wore.

Do they have some personal significance to Eslinde? A gift from someone special ... Lyrrin's father?

Kess watched Vance closely, hoping to see some tell in noticing those earrings, but his stoic expression gave nothing away.

Straightening, he said, "Our princess's beauty this evening leaves all my other senses envious of sight."

Eslinde's eyebrows went up, and she offered a slight bow in return. "How long did it take you to think up that line?"

"It came to me right then." Vance smirked.

Dashiel shook their head and whispered to Kess, "He's had that one saved for years."

A mischievous smile grew on Eslinde's lips. "I hope you'll find plenty of flattery equal to that while speaking with the attendees tonight."

"To business then?" Vance asked.

"Yes." Eslinde turned away, rising up on her toes and looking out over the sea of nobles. "Ylva should be here tonight. She's always been the kindest to me of my siblings, so I hope she'll be willing to listen. I'm going to do a round and see if I can find her. Go and mingle, all of you, and see who we can find that may support our cause."

Dashiel moved away first. "I'm going to mingle with some snacks first. See you all soon."

"Must we all go separately?" Kess asked.

"Divide and conquer," Eslinde replied.

Kess looked out over the crowd as though it were a pack of ravenous wolves. As Eslinde slipped between the bodies and vanished, Kess recognized a familiar face.

She reached out and grabbed Vance's arm, pulling him back as he moved away. "Does the Dragon King ever attend these evenings?"

"Often, although only briefly. Why? Planning to try to convince him again?"

"No, I'm hoping that the Dragon King doesn't attend, actually. Can you see that man through there?" Kess pointed to Kife, who had yet to notice her in return.

"Who is he?" Vance asked, narrowing his eyes.

"He's trouble. Could you do me a favor and keep an eye on him? Don't let him get anywhere near the king, if he does arrive."

Vance leaned over Kess, frowning. "That's not what we're supposed to be doing tonight. Eslinde—"

"It's important. I can't explain why right now, but it's very important, for Eslinde." Kess held his skeptical gaze.

Then Vance nodded and moved into the crowd, tailing Kess's brother.

Kess took a moment to calm her nerves. Already on edge, seeing Kife had shaken her up.

She wasn't lying to Vance, not exactly. If Kife got to the Dragon King and told him about Dracuni, it would affect Lyrrin, and thus Eslinde. But more than that, Kess needed time to decide what she was going to do.

Could she attempt to kill Kife tonight? She had no weapon anymore—Eslinde had been careful to check all cutlery since her first theft.

On the day of the taming ceremony, Kess had been ready and hadn't cared about the consequences of murdering someone in broad daylight.

But now, Kess couldn't imagine stabbing her brother in front of all these people. Now, when Eslinde was treating her almost like a human being, and was doing all she could to find Lyrrin, and to alter the course of the shadow dragon curse, to change the world ...

The stakes were too high.

Kess couldn't let herself be taken out of the picture for revenge. She had to wait and be smarter.

Alone now and faced with the prospect of *mingling*, Kess found her courage and rolled slowly from her place near the wall. People parted for her as she pushed her chair between them, and yet she passed unnoticed, unacknowledged, as though invisible. All eyes turned away from her as she approached.

How am I supposed to talk to anyone if they're all ignoring me?

Shame flushed her face, and she almost turned around and left.

Then a small face appeared in front of her. A boy of no more than ten years old, wearing a suit like a miniaturized grown-up, stared at Kess and her chair with wide-eyed amazement.

"You have wheels! On your chair!" he said through a smile of missing teeth.

"Yes?" Kess replied.

"That looks like fun. Can I have a turn?"

188

"I don't think—"

"Get away from her," a gravelly voice hissed.

A man snatched the boy's hand in his and dragged him backward away from Kess as though she were plague-ridden.

A plaintive cry of "Faddaaaaaa," disappeared with them.

Kess's face screwed up tight.

How had she thought she would ever be accepted by these people? That if she had her own dragon and was a dragonrider and dragonlord again, it would make people like her?

There would still have been times when she wasn't on her dragon. What then? Would she have ridden around events like this on Griskin? Kess cursed her foolishness under her breath.

She still wished for Griskin. She missed him with a deep ache in her bones. She wished to be stalking the shadows, unseen and unheard on his back.

Still, at least if the nobles were all set on ignoring her, she was unseen and unheard enough. She could listen in to the surrounding conversations, see if she could identify anyone who may be sympathetic.

It only took a few snippets of conversation to leave Kess disheartened. She wasn't sure this was the right place to be seeking allies for their cause of freeing dragons. Everyone there was living the high life at the exploitation of others.

Dragonlords spoke with Elgarthan traders, negotiating a raise in prices for upcoming metal and glass shipments due to lower production. The Elgarthans weren't interested in excuses, as though the silvernix shortages were something the dragonlords had fabricated to get more money out of them.

They settled upon a slight increase, with the dragonlords agreeing to buy enough new human slaves to replace the dragons in their factory and keep up production.

Kess eyed the Elgarthans with fascination. She hadn't seen any of the seafaring traders in person before. Their skin was pale as milk, their eyes long and sweeping, and hair a deep blue-black, puffing out in a bundle of spirals. Their robes, in vibrant reds and purples, were the sole point of color in the ballroom.

Could Lyrrin's father be Elgarthan? She had a similar complexion.

One of the traders asked the Elgarthans jokingly about rumors they smuggled unicorns to their lands. The Elgarthan promised that if they had, they'd be doing a roaring trade for them by now.

Another dragonlord joked about smuggling themselves out of Elundrae, before the shadow dragon curse became any more dire. Kess wasn't sure he was entirely joking.

She turned to move on to another conversation, when Ulfren the First blocked her path.

"Kessara Heithorn. A pleasure to meet again."

Offering the politest smile she could, Kess bent over her knees. "You honor me again with your company."

When she rose, Ulfren moved behind her and began wheeling her to the side of the room.

"Come," he said, as though she had any choice in the matter. "There are some people I'd like you to meet."

Kess attempted to slow the chair by gripping the wheels, but her palms were slick with nervous sweat. "I really need to be getting back—"

"Here we are." Ulfren brought Kess to where a few men huddled in conversation.

Each wore the sunshine-yellow robes of Sunblessed Monks and had a chain of golden beads about their neck for each year of dedication to their faith. Kess had never mixed much with the devout, those who took Taenish mythology as law in all aspects of their life.

She nodded awkwardly to them.

At least Ulfren didn't drag me off somewhere to be killed.

"This is the most interesting young lady I had mentioned, who by some accounts is said to have spent time out in the world beyond dragonkeep walls. Is that true, Kessara?"

"It's true," she murmured, wary of the fervor in Ulfren's eyes.

A man with windswept ebony hair, square jaw, and dozens of golden chains looked down upon her. "Have you seen them, then? The Alderkin ruins. Do they stir once more into cursed power as the troubling rumors suggest?"

"Umm ..." Kess wasn't sure what to say.

She'd seen the gateway crystals working again, but apart from helping Dracuni escape her during her hunt, there didn't seem to be anything cursed about them. They were keeping the revenants away.

It seemed the men didn't require her answer, though.

An older monk clutched at his beaded chains. "More signs the curse is worsening. Something must be done."

Kess sighed internally. That is what she was there for that night.

"Actually, about that—"

"You surely don't hold to my sister's sacrilegious imaginings?" Ulfren interrupted. "You appear to be a clever young woman. Don't let her delusions draw you in. The cause is clear. Sin and dishonor are rife within our land, and it must be remedied."

The monks at his side bobbed their heads vehemently.

"And it is with great pain that I tell you that Eslinde is among those sinners. The Dragon King, blinded by her manipulations, favors her. But you must see that she defies all that is honorable with her behavior, spreading blasphemy and associating with Rolanians playing at being dragonlords."

A shiver ran up Kess's spine, and she cast a look back toward the main crowd for the Zarram siblings.

She shook her head. "It's not like that with Eslinde. The king doesn't favor her."

"No other heir is given a home under his wing, ever by his side. Not even myself, next in line to the throne." Ulfren's hand fisted closed and he slammed it into the palm of the other.

"My resplendent father is the savior of our people, bringing us into the sun's glory and power we deserve. But even he is not immune to a sinner's manipulations. We cannot allow someone like Eslinde to gain power."

Murmurings of assent came from the monks around him, all watching with zealous enthusiasm.

Kess chewed her lip. "I know I'm new around here, but I really don't think that's something you have to worry about, from what I've seen."

"And what have you seen?" Ulfren leaned in.

Kess stiffened. "Not much, really."

Ulfren sighed and crouched down before her. "Kessara, please rethink your loyalty to her. The numbers of our Taenish brethren who are turning back to the blessed sun's touch is growing every day. With my full backing and funding, we will be able to flush the sinners from the dragonkeeps and hold the curse at bay."

"And will your sister be among those sinners?"

Ulfren's face twisted in righteous sorrow. He put a hand on Kess's knee, squeezing firmly. "If she must. And any assistance from you would be a great boon. If you can help us to remove Eslinde, from the king's favor, of course, you will be rewarded greatly, both by us and the blessings of the sun."

Kess placed her hands on the wheels of her chair. Even for followers of the Taen religion, these people were extreme. She could imagine the lengths to which they would go to flush the sinners from the land. She pushed, rolling herself backward out of Ulfren's grip.

When he didn't immediately reach for her again or try to follow, she pushed back again.

"I'll ... I'll think about it." Kess knew that was the truth. The messy political corner Kess was feeling forced into was almost all she could think about.

Ulfren took a step as though to follow, but a grayglim appeared at his side, whispered briefly, and Ulfren hastily followed the woman away without another glance at Kess.

Beelining for a servant with a tray of cakes, Kess parted the crowd around her. All of the royal sibling infighting and politics had given her a headache and the need for something sweet. She took a cake in each hand and didn't bother to be polite about stuffing both in her mouth at once.

"Are you okay? You seem rattled." Dashiel had appeared at her side, helping themselves to the same cake tray.

Kess swallowed. "I just had a charming conversation with Ulfren the First and his sunstruck monks."

"Aah," Dashiel said, as though they knew exactly what that entailed. "What did you do that for?"

"Didn't really have a choice." Kess brushed crumbs off her lap. "How about you? Any fruitful conversations?"

Dashiel nibbled the corner of a sugar-crusted pastry. "No. Trying to broach the subject carefully has been a nightmare. Nobody is understanding. I just want to grab them by the ears and shake them until they realize what's at stake."

"If you thought that would actually work, I'd happily join in."

Dashiel finished their dessert and sucked crumbs from their fingers. "If I could get Eslinde's dragon to cooperate, then I could prove that dragons don't need to be tamed to still be useful. That would change minds."

"He's still angry?" Kess asked.

"Furious. I mean, I feel as though I would be too, in that situation. But there have been some inroads. Shiff has been helping me to communicate with the snowshimmer, and he's clearly intelligent, even more than I'd imagined. It gives me hope that Shiff can remain untamed long term as well."

Kess smiled at the mention of the dragonling. "I hope she can, too."

Dashiel stepped closer to Kess as a white-haired woman bustled by with a grayglim beside her. "I think, if the dragon we had untamed was one I had more experience working with from birth, then I'd be able to settle it down much faster. I was thinking of untaming another—"

"Oh no, you weren't." Vance slung an arm over Dashiel's shoulders. "No more untamings. We've enough of an issue with what to do with the snowshimmer."

Kess's eyes darted around, and she spoke softly. "What happened to the man I asked you to follow?"

Vance whispered in return, "Don't worry, I still have my eyes on him. Although he seems more interested in you than anything."

Vance flicked his chin, and Kess turned around to see Kife lurking not far behind her. She exhaled roughly. How long had he been there?

The conversation in the room changed pitch, from boisterous conversation to a low murmur, spreading through the room like a wave. Another pale-haired dragonlord was ushered away speedily by a grayglim.

"What's going on?" Kess asked.

"I'll see if I can find out." Dashiel stepped away, heading toward a cluster of nobles in the center of the space.

Yensen prowled through the parting bodies, on a mission. Kess wondered if he was looking for Eslinde, when a voice at her back whispered a little too loudly.

"Ylva the First, she was found dead, dead in a private room!"

Kess wasn't the only person to have heard, as the crowd surged suddenly, barging toward the exits.

"Eslinde," Vance growled and charged off in the other direction.

Gowned and robed bodies swished by Kess in a flash of gold and gray and she tried to push her chair out of the way. She couldn't maneuver as fast as the fleeing guests, whose focus was more on continuing their gossip as they left than on the girl in the chair they were flooding around.

After a few cursed words and rough pushes, Kess made it to the side wall. The glass panel reflected her wide-eyed face, hovering over the dark glitter of her gown. And then another face was reflected above hers.

Kife.

He grasped the back of her chair and spun it toward him. "What was that talk back there about *untaming* dragons?"

"You must have misheard." Kess's hand went to her thigh, to the backs of her forearms, out of habit, reaching for knives that weren't there. She put her sharpest edge on her words instead. "Couldn't you have enjoyed the party without following your little sister around? You've only grown more pathetic since you lost me."

The crowd had all but gone, leaving only Kess and Kife in the ballroom now. He lashed out at her, grabbing her by the shoulders and wrenching her from the chair.

"I know what I heard. Is that what you did to my dragon? Is that how you made it fly away without a rider?" Kife shook her and thrust her back against the glass wall.

The pane rattled and cracked.

"It just didn't want to be around you anymore." Kess slashed a clawed hand at his face, hoping to gouge an eye or split his cheek.

But Kife was taller, his reach longer. He leaned away from her attack and brought the hands pinning her to her neck.

Kess gasped for air as he crushed her windpipe under his grip.

"No, Kess. The one nobody wants around anymore is you."

THIRTEEN

The glass at Kess's back crackled and strained as Kife pressed her into it, hands tight around her throat. Pain shot up her neck, through her skull, and her eyes watered.

She couldn't breathe or speak or spit out any of the curses her brother deserved. She wished her legs would work for once in her life just so she could kick him.

Spittle flew from the corners of Kife's lips. "I should have killed you when you found me at Skaellakeep. I should have killed you instead of leaving you in the wilds. I should have killed you when you were a baby, before you ruined the Heithorn name!"

Gritting her teeth, Kess glared back in defiance.

The edge of a blade caught the light, flashing in Kess's

eyes as it appeared by Kife's collarbones.

"Let her go." Dashiel held the end of the dagger.

They circled around, keeping the point against Kife's neck as they came around beside Kess.

Kife grunted. "Stay out of this."

Kess's vision dimmed, spotting with floating lights.

"How much clearer do you need me to be?" Dashiel pressed the dagger forward.

Kife hissed, releasing Kess and scrambling backward. His hands had been the only thing holding Kess upright, and her legs folded beneath her.

Dashiel's arm looped around her waist, pulling her back up and into their side.

Kife spat on the ground. "Rolanian scum. Don't you know who I am?"

"I really don't," Dashiel said dully.

Kife's face twisted in rage. "I'm someone you don't want to cross."

Kess swallowed, her head spinning and throat aching. She clutched Dashiel for support, leaning her head against their chest for a moment as she worked the breath into her lungs.

Her voice came out in a painful, soft crackle. "Your dagger. Let me throw it into his eye."

Dashiel glanced at her. "Your aim is that good?"

Kess put a hand out expectantly.

The moment Dashiel placed the blade into Kess's grasp, Kife turned and bolted from the ballroom.

Kess raised her arm, intending to take a shot at his fleeing back. But a wave of dizziness washed over her and the dagger dropped from her trembling fingers.

"Easy. Are you okay?" Dashiel adjusted their hold on Kess, bringing them face-to-face with one arm behind Kess's back.

They ran gentle fingers over her neck, inhaling sharply at what they saw there. Kess could feel the bruising with her every swallow and strained breath.

"I'm fine," she whispered. "You can put me down."

Dashiel's full lips moved as though preparing to refuse, then they carefully lowered Kess into her chair. As they bent over, arms still around Kess, their cheeks touched briefly, and Kess flushed with heat.

Only one other person in her life had ever held her so gently.

She gulped and her eyes watered again. *You can't go soft for every person who shows you even basic kindness, fool.*

Dashiel remained bowed over her, a soft smile emerging under their frown. "Okay, so that's two people so far that I've seen who want you dead, but I'm still not willing to think it's *everybody*. But just so I'm prepared, how many more are we talking about?"

Kess's throat throbbed with pain, so she just raised a hand and pretended to count the numbers on her fingers.

Dashiel chuckled and straightened up. "Popular, aren't you? Come on, we need to get somewhere safe. There's at least one more assassin roaming the palace tonight."

"Ylva?" Kess choked out.

"Yeah, seems as though the rumors are true." Dashiel ducked to snatch their small dagger from the ground. Sharp and well made, but barely longer than a palm of a hand.

Kess raised her eyebrows as they tucked it away again into a hidden pocket.

Dashiel moved behind her and pushed her chair, speeding them out of the ballroom. "Yeah, I know I probably shouldn't have it here. But I always carry it with me, ever since a few years back when I got jumped by a bunch of Taens who didn't like that I'd attended their party."

A few nobles milled about in the courtyard outside, but an equal number of palace guards spread through the area, moving people along and questioning others. Dashiel dodged around them, heading for the corridor that led up to Eslinde's chambers.

"Another one of the Firsts, gone," Dashiel said softly, as though they couldn't believe it.

"Another?" Kess asked.

They turned a corner and were confronted by a wall

of guards, thrice the usual number on patrol. They had to explain who they were and where they were going, but a few of the guards knew of Kess and allowed them to pass.

Dashiel muttered, "In just the last few years we've lost Leska, Tjollas, and Nevryn. Skaella a few months back. And now Ylva. And here, within the king's city, within the king's own palace! Whoever is doing this has grown bold."

Dashiel and Kess worked together to get her and her chair up the long flights of stairs to Eslinde's chambers, and as they approached, the two grayglim at the door shifted, alert.

Yensen waved the second grayglim at ease as he recognized them and rapped at the door.

The sounds of clicking locks was followed by the door swinging open. Eslinde stood there, face pale.

"I'm so sorry, Kess. I wouldn't have left you, but ..." She glared at the grayglim.

When her eyes returned to Kess, they drifted down to her neck and she gasped. "What happened? Quick, come in, come in."

Dashiel brought Kess inside, explaining the situation, as Eslinde locked the door after them.

"It was Kife," Kess added in a rasping voice.

"Your brother?" Eslinde snapped.

"Your *brother*?" Dashiel echoed, aghast.

In the large central chamber, Vance sat perched on the edge of an armchair, and two handmaidens milled about doing busywork, shuffling piles of books around and dusting, their eyes more on Vance than their tasks.

Vance stood up at their approach. "Is that who you had me following? What was that about?"

Kess winced as all eyes fell on her. She gestured at her neck. "Just wanted ... keep him away."

"And for good reason, I'd say," Dashiel said.

Eslinde stared at Kess for a long moment.

Can she tell I'm not telling the whole truth? Kess gave a pathetic cough and looked away.

Sighing, Eslinde said, "I'll do what I can to make sure he can't get close to the palace again. Although after tonight it's going to be difficult for anybody to get close to the palace for a while."

Vance cleared his throat. "Speaking of which, now that you're safe, Dashiel and I should be on our way, before we cause a scandal of some kind or another by remaining."

The handmaidens swiftly turned their backs as though there had been nothing to see.

Eslinde nodded and placed a hand on Vance's arm, murmuring a soft thank you.

Dashiel held Kess's eyes, their gaze full of questions, but they simply smiled and said, "Always so much excitement

when you're around. I'll see you next time."

Eslinde saw them both out the door, and then with a sharp order, sent the handmaidens on their way as well. They seemed happy to go now that the princess wasn't alone in her chambers with a man. There was a question of whether any silvernix was to be requested for Kess, but Kess shook her head.

Once the door was locked again, Eslinde brought her hand to her chest. A handkerchief was crumpled within it.

Eslinde had said she was closest to Ylva of any of her siblings. Given the animosity between some of the others, Kess didn't know how close that was, but redness marred the lines around Eslinde's eyes and the point of her nose.

"You ... okay?" Kess whispered awkwardly.

A gloss of tears washed over the princess's eyes, but she smiled. "As well as can be hoped. Oh, Kess, the night had been going so well. There was news! News of Lyrrin!"

Kess's breath caught in her crumpled throat.

Eslinde swept over and took a seat in the armchair across from where Kess remained in her wheeled chair. She reached for the pitcher of water on the low table and poured a glass, handing it to Kess.

"Sip it slowly. And yes, well, not Lyrrin exactly. But it could have been the Hjelzahn siblings, from what you described."

"Who ...?" Kess choked on the water.

Eslinde's eyes were full of hope and fire. "The rider said they'd heard of a group with two young women, two young children, and a dragonling, helping the people gathering around shrines, very recently. Just as you said, Kess. It must be them!"

Kess's nose wrinkled. "Two?"

Two young women. Only two.

No third.

She's gone. Riony is really gone.

All the physical and emotional pains inside Kess spiked, slicing through her. Her face pinched inward as she tried to fight tears, but they spilled out. The glass shook in her hand, spilling water on her lap.

"Kess?" Eslinde shifted closer.

Kess shook her head in reply.

"What is it?"

"Nothing."

"It's not nothing." Eslinde reached out and placed a hand on Kess's knee. "I recognize grieving, Kess. I've mourned enough to know it. I mourn my sister now, and I've mourned my daughter, thinking her dead, and I've mourned her father."

People Eslinde loved.

Is that why? Is that why it hurts so much?

Kess struggled to speak, throat aching from the clog of tears as much as the injury. "Lyrrin's father ... Not Vance?"

Eslinde leaned back. "What? No. Why would you think that?"

Kess tilted her head.

Eslinde blushed pink and stuttered, "No. Lyrrin's father is ... Don't change the subject! Tell me. Was there someone else you were expecting to hear of in that group? Who is it that you've lost?"

Nobody. I never had anybody to lose. It doesn't matter.

Every time Kess tried to open her mouth and throw out some flippant response, her lips pursed, pulled closed by sobbing pain in her chest.

Who had Riony been to her? An enemy. The thorn in her side at odds with everything Kess had wanted, and it had been too late, too late that Kess realized she'd been wanting the wrong thing.

Worse. She'd known, deep down, what she really wanted all along.

It had never been the respect of people who'd only care about her if she owned a dragon. It only ever mattered what one person thought of her. The only person who'd been kind to her. Who had come back to save her in the caves. Who even after every horrible thing Kess had done, had stood there and offered Kess one more chance.

And now she was gone.

"I ... I loved her." It was all the truth Kess could offer.

She didn't have the words to explain the violent tangle of their past, the awful power dynamics of ownership and cruelties suffered. And the loss, the loss, the loss Kess felt in every moment even when Riony was in her life because she knew she could never have Riony in a way that was real.

The weight of that truth, spilling from her lips, could crush Kess.

Eslinde shocked Kess dumb by leaning out of her armchair and wrapping her in a tight embrace.

"I'm sorry," she whispered.

And she held Kess for a long silent moment as sobs racked through Kess and her tears poured.

It was that act of kindness, something Kess would never have expected from a first heir of the land, that drew her out of the depths of her pain. Eslinde, the Zarram siblings, they did truly seem to care. Part of Kess still anticipated a blade in her back, but she fought that feeling down.

Eslinde had shown Kess kindness and respect, and Kess vowed to return the same, as much as she could without revealing Dracuni.

"Sorry too. For Ylva," she whispered.

Eslinde pulled out of the embrace and dabbed at her eyes. "Thank you. Of all the heirs we've lost, she is the

only one I will miss."

Out at Heithorn estate, Kess had been isolated from court gossip and news. She hadn't realized how many were gone.

Wiping her eyes, she looked to Eslinde with concern. "Are you in danger?"

"Not in here. Nobody can get in here. Although if anything were to happen to me ..." Eslinde sat back into her armchair and worried at the kerchief in her fingers.

"Nothing will. I'll make sure," Kess said like a vow.

Eslinde half smiled, her gaze flickering to Kess's throat as though she doubted Kess could even look after herself.

They all underestimate me. If only I had a weapon, if I had Griskin ...

Kess knew there were parts of her that would never work the same as for other people. She just needed certain things to function as well as she knew she could. The chair was something, and she was growing used to it, but it wasn't *her* things.

Eslinde rose to her feet. "Since we have confided so much to each other, there is something important that I want to share, just in case. I can't have this secret be lost with me."

She walked toward the door, beckoning Kess to follow. Kess slowly rolled after. She wasn't entirely sure she

wanted to be the keeper of yet another secret. She seemed to know more than enough that many would be willing to kill for already.

"Why tell me?"

"You brought me the truth about Lyrrin. I think it's fair that you understand more about my daughter." Eslinde came to a stop beside the door, but she didn't reach to open it. Instead, she reached for the ornately carved panel in the doorframe that she often touched as she came in and out of the room.

"See here?" Eslinde pointed to a circular section that was a smoother stone than the dark granite surrounding it.

Eslinde ran a swift fingertip over the design there, and the sound of locks clicking echoed around the room.

"Alderkin rune?" Kess asked. Is that how she's been magically sealing her chambers?

Eslinde nodded and pried her fingertips into the edges of the circular section. She pulled and out slid a long shaft of crystal, glowing softly but darkened by paint at the ends to match the surrounding stone. Within the center was a cavity where a vial of silvernix lay.

"How?" was all Kess could say.

Eslinde slid the crystal back into the wall and activated the locking rune again. "It was provided to me by an Alderkin man who wanted to be sure I remained safe."

Kess shook her head. Eslinde was only around thirty years old, and not just in appearances like some of the heirs, but in actual age. She would have only just been born when the last Alderkin were killed in the war.

The words hurt Kess's throat, but she rasped them out anyway. "You're not that old. Not possible."

Eslinde smiled sadly. "It is. Because not all of the Alderkin are gone. My father has kept some prisoners of war in a secret prison below the palace."

"Alive?" Kess gasped.

Living Alderkin, still in Elundrae? There were always rumors some had escaped to other lands at the end of the war, but to know some existed still, below where they were now, shook Kess.

Eslinde brushed her hands over the disguised crystal again, as though stroking the cheek of a lover. "And one of them was Lyrrin's father."

FOURTEEN

Kess lay awake in the daybed in Eslinde's chambers, unable to sleep from the recent revelations.

That Alderkin still existed. That Lyrrin's father was one. That Kess had loved Riony.

That she still did, but it seemed more certain than ever that Riony was gone.

Only two young women, the rumors had said. Certainly, something could have happened to Aishena or Niskina, making them the missing number of the three, but that was wishful thinking on Kess's part when she'd seen exactly what had happened to Riony.

At least Dracuni seemed to still be with the group and well.

And two children. Lyrrin was okay then, also. Riony would be happy to know that, and Kess noted that she wanted to find a way to continue honoring what Riony would have wanted.

Eslinde said there had been no replies yet to her messages, her attempts to communicate with Lyrrin.

Lyrrin ... who was half Alderkin.

Kess's brain continued to spiral when a sound beside her bed made her sleepless eyes snap open.

Eslinde stood there, finger to her lips.

"What under the sun ..." Kess hissed.

A few days had passed, and her throat still ached, but had been healing well enough that she didn't require silvernix to repair it.

"Come on, quickly." The princess ghosted toward the door. Her night dress was covered with a sweeping satin robe, and she carried an oil lamp in her hand. "No time to get dressed."

"Are we in trouble?" Kess's eyes darted as she shuffled to the edge of the bed where her chair sat.

The night outside the windows was pitch, no sign of morning light, and only a few stars sparkled through an ashy sky.

"No, we have an opportunity." Eslinde glided to the entrance and unlocked it.

Kess hurried to catch up, swinging her legs off the bed, then hoisting herself into the wheeled chair. Her nightgown was thin, and the autumn air was chilly. A robe would have been nice both for modesty and comfort, but Kess guessed her clothing was the least of her concerns.

Kess rolled to Eslinde's side as she pushed the main door open. Outside in the hallway, an unfamiliar grayglim slumped near the door.

Kess's heart pumped hard in dread until she heard a soft snore rattle from the older man's throat.

Eslinde placed a finger to her lips and spoke softly. "Yensen has to sleep sometimes. And this grayglim who took his shift tonight isn't the most reliable. I had Olva offer him a nightcap that may have had a little something extra in it."

"Why?"

"Because it's time I go somewhere I haven't been in a long while. Somewhere a grayglim would surely block me from reaching." Eslinde moved behind Kess's chair to assist her down the stairs.

"I don't think it's safe to be going anywhere without someone to protect you," Kess said.

They reached the final landing and Eslinde moved beside Kess. "I have you."

Kess snorted. "Like there's much I can do."

214

"Your preference is toward throwing knives from what I've gathered. Correct?"

Kess kept pace with Eslinde, rolling along the quiet, unlit corridor. "They've worked well for me in the past."

Eslinde stopped suddenly, thrusting an arm to stop Kess as well. Up ahead, a guard crossed the intersection, a warm globe of light traveling with them. Once they were gone, Eslinde turned to Kess, holding her gaze.

"I can trust you, can't I?"

Kess balked. "Can I trust you?"

Eslinde sighed and reached into the deep pocket of her bedrobe. She withdrew a stamped metal case and tossed it onto Kess's lap. "I just want to know one of those won't end up in me."

Kess raised her eyebrows as she clicked the book-sized case open. Inside, on plush black velvet, lay three exquisite throwing blades.

"They're beautiful," Kess's words rushed out on a breath.

"Yes, indeed. Please use them with discretion." Eslinde marched ahead again.

Kess pushed the wheels of her chair hard to catch up. As the chair rolled freely along the glossy floor, Kess hid one of the thin blades up each of her sleeves and the third down between the upholstery of her chair seat.

They took a corner into a bare, dead-end room, then

Eslinde pushed against the wall, which swung smoothly in an arc away from her.

"Where are we going?" Kess asked.

Eslinde held her oil lamp high against the darkness of the rougher stone tunnel ahead. "To visit the Alderkin."

"Oh. Good. So not only can I know the information about them which is probably enough to get me killed, but we're going to go and break into the secret dungeon where they're kept?"

Eslinde gave Kess a sly smile in return. "This is the sort of trouble I used to get myself into all the time."

"Why? Just an inner need to be rebellious?" Kess muttered.

The tunnel curved sharply, then dropped down a steep slope. Eslinde helped Kess from having her chair run away with her.

"Curiosity, at first. I was always interested to know everything there was to know in court and managed to discover that Fadda was keeping Alderkin prisoners. Those strange, savage people who had waged war with humans for decades with their terrifying magic. I had to see them for myself."

"Why?" Kess asked again.

She felt no such compulsion to see them, even now on their way to meet those prisoners. She disliked the tunnels more than the undercity caves she'd hunted Dracuni in. The ceiling was low and claustrophobic, and the air was dank and filled with a rotting smell like sewage.

"I needed to face them, to prove to myself I was stronger than them. Better than our enemies." Eslinde let out a long sigh. "Instead, as I spoke with them, all I heard was sense. Sense I didn't hear anywhere else in court. They were so humble, so wise, and the more I learned their stories, the more rebellious I became. And then I fell in love."

"With an Alderkin?" Kess had never seen one herself before.

She had no idea how human they were ... or weren't. She knew Eslinde had said Lyrrin's father was one, but she hadn't elaborated on the technicalities.

"Alleem. He was the youngest of the four, by Alderkin standards at least. Oh, Kess, he was so beautiful. Inside and out. A soul of pure radiance, he could make anything sound like poetry and had eyes that made you feel both worthy and humble in a single glance."

A wry smile formed on Kess's lips as she thought about the kinds of things that came out of Riony's mouth.

Poetry indeed. To each their own, I guess.

Eslinde pressed one hand to her stomach. "I never thought ... When I became pregnant, I tried to hide it, but the truth came out. My mother worked it out first, and then the Dragon King had his spies reveal the whole story. Allem was killed. Almost everybody who knew anything about it at all was killed."

Kess had wondered how a single pregnancy could lead to a first heir losing their freedoms, and almost their life. But it made sense now.

They rounded another corner and came to a wider section where a guard, the regular palace variety rather than a grayglim, sat slouched in a chair, chin nodding against his chest. The only thing different about his uniform was a crown-shaped badge upon his shoulder.

"Did you drug him too?" Kess murmured.

The guard jolted, snorting back awake and squinting into the light Eslinde carried.

"Your Highness? You're not allowed to be down here." He stood up and straightened his leather armor and sword belt.

Eslinde gave him one of her coy smiles. "And you're not supposed to be sleeping on the job. But perhaps we can ignore both transgressions."

Clearing his throat, the guard stepped in front of the steel grated door he'd been snoozing beside. "You'll have to forgive me. But there were rumors. That the last lot on guard down here who let you through were all executed."

A flicker of concern pulled at Eslinde's brow, then she drew herself up tall. "Then we will have to be sure that nobody finds out that I was here. And if you don't let us in, then I will make sure the wrong people *do* find out that I was here and that you allowed it."

The guard looked over his shoulders, as though checking for any other eyes on them. But it was only him, the princess, and Kess in the empty early hours of night. He swore three times under his breath, then unlocked the metal grate. "Nobody will find out, right?"

"Not a soul." Eslinde tapped him on the nose as she strode by him into the opened passage.

Kess followed Eslinde through, marveling at how adept at manipulation she was. Ulfren's warning about Eslinde manipulating the king, about her being delusional, echoed in her mind.

But she's been honest with me, hasn't she? If anything, too honest. And she was leading Kess to proof of her words that very moment. Kess checked her access to the knives in her sleeves, just in case. Knives Eslinde had gifted her. But old habits of distrust were hard to bury.

Beyond the metal gate, a short corridor came to an end in front of them, with a few doors on each side. Although the doors had barred windows, no light came from within.

"Yrik?" Eslinde called softly.

A rustle of motion came from Kess's left, bringing with it wafts of stomach-curdling stench.

A face appeared through the bars, then a husky woman's voice. "Eslinde? Is that you?"

Kess squinted through the darkness, but in the low

light the face was just a pale oval.

Eslinde rushed to the door and reached her free hand to the bars. "Priyune! I'm sorry, I'm so sorry it has been so long. Is Yrik ...?"

With Eslinde's lamp brought closer, the face became clear. High, knife-edged cheekbones swept down from eyes too large and too bright to be human. They sparkled like emeralds, matching to hair just as green, although matted and tangled around the woman's forehead and pointed ears.

The Alderkin woman's hand reached back through the barred window to hold Eslinde's, and Kess withheld a gasp. The fingers were long and came to sharp, angular points.

Just like she'd seen of Lyrrin's, when the wild girl had scratched through Kess's bracer.

A voice as low and gravelly as an avalanche came from the same cell. "I still live. Shael also."

The first Alderkin, Priyune, withdrew and a man came close to the bars. He too reached a hand to Eslinde, tipped with long blue claws and marred with a hatched mess of scars and untended wounds.

"Who has been hurting you?" Eslinde cried.

Yrik only grumbled in response, turning his face to the side and eyes low. Blue hair tangled long down his neck.

"I should have come back sooner. This is awful." Eslinde clutched his hand, squeezing hard. "When was the

last time someone cleaned down here? Are they feeding you well? Why are they torturing you?"

Yrik stared out the small hole in the door, brilliant blue eyes hooded and dull. "The slayer of unicorns has found a use for us, and he uses us as and when he sees fit."

"The Dragon King?" Kess asked. "What use would he ..."

Eslinde seemed to have worked that out already. She reached into her pocket and withdrew the fake taming spike the Zarrams had given her. She held it up to see.

"Are you making these for him?" she asked without any condemnation.

The man stepped back out of sight into the dark cell, and his voice was low. "He forces us. He brings crystals, and we must create with them what he wishes. We tried to deny him, at first, but ..."

"It's not your fault," Eslinde said.

"But it is our shame. He wanted another way to tame dragons, for when he had no sacred blood left. More dragons, each one growing the curse of the lost souls, and at our hands."

"Could the king be so short on silvernix?" Kess asked.

Eslinde scoffed. "I don't think so. He probably just wants to reserve all use of it for keeping himself immortal. And if everybody runs out of silvernix, he will have the only method in Elundrae to tame dragons. As he always

wanted. He never wanted that power shared."

Kess shook her head. "A way to tame dragons without silvernix ... we can't even wait for it to run out then, as a way to stop the shadow dragon curse, because he'll keep taming dragons anyway."

Eslinde's hand squeezed tight around the crystal spike. "He won't be able to let the silvernix run out entirely. The Alderkin crystals need to be imbued with magical charge, which they can get from being kept close to silvernix."

So that's why she kept a vial of silvernix with her locking crystal, Kess thought. She'd considered at first that it was just a convenient place to stash some extra.

Yrik's face reappeared at the bars. His features drooped as though exhausted. "Are you and your friend here plotting something, dear child?"

"Not quite. Only hoping for change, as ever. But these new crystal spikes will make things more difficult."

"We have submitted to making them because we must, to survive. But we only persist because we are the last and it seems we must strive to not vanish into the earth's embrace." The man's blue eyes glistened. "But if coming to our end gives you some chance to put a stop to the curse on the land, we can accept that."

"No, no, no." Eslinde grasped for the bars again as though she could break them apart in her hand. "Don't

say that. The land needs you. I need you. And ..."

Eslinde turned then to Kess. She moved behind her and pushed Kess's chair closer to the cell door.

"This is my friend, Kessara."

Friends? Is that what we are? Kess's lips pursed.

"Kess, Yrik is Alleem's grandfather. Yes, I know he seems young, but Alderkin age much slower than humans." Eslinde moved back to the bars, and the lamplight flickered in her glossy eyes.

She tilted her head and took a deep breath. "The reason I stopped coming, the reason my father had Alleem killed, is because I became pregnant, with Alleem's child."

Two other faces pressed in beside Yrik's then, all three vying to peer through the small window. The emerald-toned Priyune, and the third, Shael, with hair and eyes the color of an ice-melt stream, a shimmering pale aqua.

"A child?" Priyune said.

"Could it be possible?" Shael asked.

"Did it survive?" Yrik exhaled in a rush.

Eslinde clutched at the fingers that reached through the bars to touch hers. "I didn't think so. For years I thought she was gone. But Kessara brought me news that she still lives."

"A child!" Priyune said again.

"A child of Alleem's." Yrik's face dropped and he turned away from the bars.

"So young. Alone in the world," Shael cried.

"Not alone," Eslinde reassured them.

Kess gave an encouraging nod.

"Alone from her Alderkin people, separated from us. We must go to her. We must find a way!" Shael said. Then she reached a hand through the bars. "The crystal! The one you brought. Let us have it."

"It's already runed." Priyune tsked.

"Still, there may be something we can do with it, some compatible runes we can mark it with. The slayer of unicorns won't allow us charged crystals. Any crystal could help us find a way free of this prison." Shael's fingers flexed.

Eslinde held the crystal up. "I think it still has some charge. But it's not safe to leave. Not yet. We still don't know exactly where the child is."

Then she placed the crystal down into the awaiting hand. "But as soon as I know, then it will be time. And I'll do what I can to get you out."

Kess held her breath as she watched the exchange. Was the princess truly reckless enough to attempt to free these people, clearly the most valuable prisoners the king held?

It would be a good move, though. If the Alderkin were gone, they wouldn't be able to make more taming spikes for the king, and the dragonlords would run out of silvernix faster. They could cure the land of the shadow dragon curse.

Kess bit her lip. When had she ever had designs upon saving the world? *Raze it all, Eslinde is getting into my head!*

Eslinde paced, talking through a plan. "If I can find a way for all of us to leave, we could try to go to the Rebel Riders for asylum."

"Wait, the Rebel Riders?" Kess had been reading some of the chapters of those tales during her time in Eslinde's quarters. "Those are just fiction, aren't they?"

Eslinde smirked. "Not entirely. I was in the beginnings of communications with them before everything went wrong with the pregnancy. They hadn't trusted me enough at the time to offer their location, but perhaps I could attempt to reopen communications."

Kess wrinkled her nose, unable to believe it. The stories she read were outlandish fantasies. Romance like that never happened in reality.

"We could work alongside them, find and destroy silvernix stockpiles, keep the Alderkin away from the Dragon King. Stop people taming any more dragons. We could do this."

Yrik reappeared at the window beside the two other Alderkin. His sharp cheeks were streaked in tears. "You let us know when, dear child, and we will be with you."

Eslinde beamed at them all, the fire in her eyes brighter than the flickering flame of the oil lamp.

Fight the dragonlords, free the prisoners, destroy silvernix, save the world.

Kess's head and heart ached. It was too much, all too much. How had she gotten caught up in all of this?

Her goals were once so simple. Become a dragonrider. And even after that, when they'd changed, it was only to take revenge on Kife and keep Dracuni safe.

What would the princess do if she discovered Dracuni was a stockpile of silvernix in and of herself?

Would she need to be destroyed too?

Kess had gotten in too deep with Eslinde and her rebellious plans, which felt more and more like they would only ruin Kess's own.

Maybe she should consider Ulfren's offer. She had more than enough dirt on Eslinde to pass along.

Kess fidgeted with the fabric of her sleeves, feeling the knives beneath.

Could she really betray Eslinde, who had put so much trust in her? Even if it was to keep Dracuni safe, the last thing Kess could ever do for Riony?

FIFTEEN

Dashiel didn't like having to steal. As much as they justified they were only taking what belonged to their own family, it felt wrong to be sneaking around Zarram Dragonhold like a common thief.

But Dashiel needed the silvernix, and if he asked anybody for it, he'd have to explain what it was for, and it would never have been allowed. Not even by Vance.

He should understand how important this is.

Dashiel had been raised from birth to be a dragonrider. And a dragonrider's core purpose was to serve Elundrae in the fight against the shadow dragon's revenants. That was the war they fought.

But what if they could do something to end the war

once and for all?

The Zarrams still had a reasonable supply of silvernix, which they used primarily for taming dragons, or the most extreme of illness or injury only. Although even when Vance had his accident, their father erred on the side of frugality, deciding that it was too late to save the leg anyway.

Dashiel thought they should have tried regardless, but that silvernix dose was one more dragon that could be tamed within their collection, to continue growing their wealth.

And now, Dashiel decided that the one dose of silvernix he'd just stolen was what should have been spent on their brother's leg.

It wouldn't be missed. Not immediately anyway. At the next accounting day, the loss would be noticed, but Dashiel hoped by then he would be able to show everyone proof that he could retrain an untamed dragon.

Dashiel was sure they just needed to start with a dragon they'd already worked with. One they reared and trained and already had a connection with.

Moving through Zarram Dragonhold, Dashiel often received surprised looks from the staff and workers at the dragonling slinking along at their heels. As far as they all knew, Shiff was tamed now and acting under verbal commands.

But there were often mutterings about how they'd never seen a hatchling take to training so quickly. It normally took months or years to get a tamed dragonling to follow verbal orders.

"That's Dashiel for you, though. One of the best trainers I've seen," an older feed manager told their assistant as Dashiel strode by.

"I still don't like how it looks at me," the assistant whispered back, just loud enough for Dashiel to hear.

One day, Dashiel would be able to reveal to all of them that Shiff was well trained because she was able to think for herself. One day soon.

Shiff was a few months old now and getting big. Her thoughts came through clearer than ever, and there were times she challenged Dashiel's commands, making them worry they were losing control over her. But even if Shiff didn't want to follow orders every time, Dashiel could feel they'd developed a bond, a relationship beyond master and servant.

All the other dragonriders invested at the same time as Dashiel trained their dragonlings together. Dashiel had been provided special dispensation to train Shiff alone, being as they lived at the dragonhold that housed the hatchlings and had trained dragons before, and because Zarram training methods were proprietary information.

At least, that's what Dashiel told their mestra.

Dashiel led Shiff down toward the bottom levels where they had stashed a red etherflame that had recently been taken out of breeding rotation. She had looked like strong stock, but her offspring continued to be born with malformations, so she was going to be sold on to industrial use.

But while the dragon wasn't being bred and wasn't yet sold, she wasn't being paid much attention to and was Dashiel's best option to untame.

It was a rest day, and there were only core servants working. As Dashiel and Shiff went down the final flight of stairs into the disused flamesong stalls, Dashiel thought they noticed the shadow of someone behind them, but when they looked back, there was nothing.

"Vance?" Dashiel called.

No reply. Their brother was the only other person who came down there, but only when Dashiel brought him down to see Shiff. Dashiel had taken over all care of Eslinde's now untamed and increasingly furious dragon.

The snowshimmer's roar echoed through the heavy steel barrier, and Dashiel eyed the rope and pulley system keeping the door weighted closed. Only once so far had Dashiel dared lift the door even a little to throw in food. Luckily, mature dragons didn't need to eat regularly, but it couldn't be helping the dragon's rage.

Hurting. Shiff narrowed her eyes at the door. ***Wants sky.***

"Let's hope the next one is a bit more understanding," Dashiel said.

Another? Shiff's forked tongue darted out, and Dashiel could sense her eagerness.

It had been largely due to Shiff's questioning and urging that Dashiel made the decision to try to untame another dragon. They'd noticed Shiff lingering near the door holding the snowshimmer captive, and at times, Eslinde's dragon calmed at her presence.

Shiff often came away from those encounters with a strong mix of conflicting emotions. Dashiel greatly wished for the small dragon to have another of its kind that it could speak to in a positive way.

They reached the stall right at the end where the etherflame waited senselessly.

A big dragon. A fire-breather. But one Dashiel had helped raise, had always treated well.

Would she remember?

"I think it's going to work. How about you?"

Shiff flicked the end of her spike-tipped tail.

Dashiel had taken as many precautions as possible this time. The dragon was muzzled with a makeshift contraption made from harnesses and straps. The chains holding her in place were thicker than those used on

Eslinde's dragon. Ones used for locking in special guests' dragons, in a show that the Zarram stables were especially secure for their customers.

The collar was even stamped with the Zarram crest, a dragon holding a star on a shield, to make sure their customers remembered where they were. Dashiel's father always put great consideration into appearances.

The dragon's breath puffed out in a steady rhythm, smelling like the remains of a forest fire.

She really is a big one, Dashiel thought, swallowing their fear.

"This is worth trying," they said aloud and left the door open behind them in case they needed a rapid escape.

Snatching up the pliers they'd left there earlier, Dashiel approached the dragon, commanding her to lower her head.

She did so in a smooth, instant response.

It took a couple of tries to get the pliers around the end of the spike, and tugging it out was far, far harder than Vance had made it seem. It seemed suctioned in, and Dashiel was panting and sweating from strain by the time it even budged.

And then it slipped free in a swift, slurping motion.

With fumbling fingers, Dashiel dropped the spike and pliers on the floor and hurried to apply the silvernix to the open wound.

As the magic spread its light through the dragon's body, sparkling below its scales, Dashiel imagined the dragon's brain knitting itself back together, repairing itself in a way it had never been able to before because of the steel stake within it.

And as before, the spiraling ribbons of dark shadow drifted down through the ceiling and into the dragon. And the dragon awoke.

"Easy, easy," Dashiel said in a soft voice.

The etherflame's eyes snapped wide open and neck pulled up. Chains snapped taut. Eyes went wider again. Her mouth strained against the muzzle. One leather strap tore.

Angry also, Shiff thought, body lowered as she skulked away from the bigger dragon.

"Yeah, yeah, I noticed, thanks."

The etherflame bucked against the chains clamped around her neck, and in a swift and easy stretch, the chains broke.

Far easier than the stockyard chains they'd put on Eslinde's dragon. The etherflame wasn't that much bigger or stronger, but the chains had snapped like a dry twig.

A piece landed near Dashiel's foot, and they could see that although the chains were thicker than the others, they were made of cheap, friable metal.

All just a show for the customers, hey, Pabba? That was like so much of how their father had gone about making

their fortune. They should have known.

The dragon reared back, eyes whirling in their sockets, taking in the corners of the dark, enclosed space.

Scared. Scared.

The voice in Dashiel's head wasn't Shiff's. It came from the etherflame, more a surge of childish emotions than words or language, the way Dashiel had felt the connection when Shiff had been newly hatched.

Sparks flickered from her nostrils.

"It's okay. You're safe," Dashiel urged, unsure how much the dragon could understand.

Safe. Safe, still, and calm, Shiff added.

Dashiel lifted both hands in a calming gesture and kept their eyes on the dragon's.

A few huge breaths pumped the dragon's chest like bellows, and then she turned wild eyes to Dashiel. And her breathing slowed.

She remembers you.

"Really?" Dashiel's voice cracked, too high-pitched. "In a good way or ...?"

Red scales across the dragon's shoulders shivered and twitched, but her eyes stayed on Dashiel, lids lowering.

The hot glow around the dragon's muzzled snout dimmed.

Dashiel let out their own long exhalation. "That's it. You're good. You're going to be okay."

A flash of metal passed by Dashiel's eye, followed by a harsh, scraping thunk.

Dashiel frowned, unable to understand what they were seeing. The handle of a dagger, sticking out from between the etherflame's chest scales.

"What in the stars?" Dashiel spun around, searching for the source. A shadow fled up the corridor behind them.

Muted by the muzzle, but no less filled with fury, the dragon roared.

Dashiel didn't have time to turn back around.

Free of her chains, the dragon lunged forward. Dashiel raced her, trying to get outside of the door before she did. She stampeded through, knocking Dashiel out of the way with her flank.

Dashiel tumbled, crashing into the doorframe, barely missed by stomping, taloned claws. The etherflame galloped out of the stall, smashing an oil lamp on her way.

Flames flickered from the spilled oil and Shiff hissed at it, dodging back into the now empty stall for shelter.

Scrambling back to their feet, Dashiel didn't worry about the small patch of fire. The floor and walls were stone and there was little else to burn.

They were far, far more worried about the panicking, untamed etherflame charging up the wide stairwell into the rest of the dragonhold.

"No, no, no. Come back!" Dashiel raced after it.

The dragon moved faster, tail disappearing in an elegant swish around the corner ahead.

Stars, what do I do?

Even if Dashiel caught up to the dragon, could they calm it down again? It had been going well, hadn't it?

Who threw that dagger?

A scream came from up ahead and Dashiel sped into the chamber beyond, where a couple of servants had their backs pressed to a wall as the dragon bore down on them.

The muzzle suppressed the fiery breath, but more straps strained and snapped, sending the workers fleeing in terror. The creature's bloodred scales gleamed ominously, neck straining against the heavy collar around it, broken chains dangling and clattering like off-tune windchimes.

She forged on, her colossal form hammering down storage barrels and shelves in her path as she continued upward, as though sensing her path to freedom.

She's heading to the flight deck.

"Close that door!" Dashiel yelled through the chaos.

The workers beside the wide double doors froze, gaping at the dragon, uncomprehending.

Dragons didn't just *move* on their own.

The etherflame plowed forward. The passages within the dragonhold were designed for the passage of large beasts, but in the dragon's wild rush, she smashed her sweeping tail against the doorframe, shattering the hinges and crumbling stone.

A woman was knocked aside, a trickle of blood on her forehead. Panic spread among the servants, their shouts blending with the dragon's roars.

With each step, Dashiel's heart raced. They felt the pulse of the dragon's emotions, a chaotic blend of fear, anger, and an innate longing for the open sky.

The flight deck opened out before them.

"Stop! Please!" Dashiel cried, breathless.

"What in the stars is going on?" Vance appeared, running beside Dashiel in a lopsided stride.

Dashiel gave their brother a pained look.

"You didn't!" Vance growled.

They both ran harder.

On the precipice of the open flight deck, the behemoth of flaming red spread her wings wide. The muzzle couldn't stifle the determination burning in her eyes.

Dashiel slowed their pace, holding their hands out, pleading. "Don't go. Please. You can be safe here."

Dashiel could feel the lie on their tongue. Now that the dragon had been revealed, could she be safe anywhere?

A wave of emotion returned, roiling and shifting but mostly **hurt, hurt, hurt.**

Like the crack of a whip, leather bands snapped around the straining jaw. The torn scraps fell free and the dragon opened her mouth in a deafening roar that echoed back through the flight deck.

With a powerful beat of her wings, the dragon swept off the flight deck ledge. Uneven at first, as though still finding her ability to move her body freely, but strong and determined.

The creature soared into the sky above the capital city.

Vance ran a hand down over his face and growled, "We are utterly screwed."

SIXTEEN

Dashiel stared at the retreating etherflame for a few heart pounding moments.

"I can fix this. If I can recapture her ... or bring her down outside of the city or ..." Dashiel wasn't exactly sure how to fix this.

Had any rider battled with a full-grown wild dragon since the early days when humans hunted wild dragons instead of breeding them? Dashiel's chest contracted trying to imagine what they were about to face.

But still they turned and ran back toward the stalls.

"I'm taking Viska," Dashiel called back.

"You razing aren't," Vance replied, hobbling after. The run up through the dragonhold would have been hard on his missing leg.

Dashiel reached Viska's stall. The golden dragon wasn't saddled or harnessed. There was no time to do either. Dashiel climbed up her shoulder and settled into the bare scales at the nape of her neck, above the powerful muscles of its wings.

They had ridden bareback before, but never on a ride like this.

Vance blocked the exit to the stall, standing firm with arms crossed.

"Let me do this. Pabba can punish me all he wants for this mess." Dashiel gestured to the broken stalls and shocked servants. "But if I can do something to stop the etherflame before anyone else realizes what's going on, I have to try."

"Not without me you aren't." Vance stepped forward.

Dashiel adjusted their seating. They'd flown Viska plenty of times, but nobody knew her like Vance.

Still, they hesitated. "This isn't on you."

Vance blew out a low whistle, and Viska dropped, lying flat against the ground. Moving around beside the dragon's shoulder, Vance reached a hand to Dashiel.

"Fine." Dashiel reached back, helping their brother up onto the dragon's back.

Vance settled in front, and the moment he leaned over

the dragon's neck, pressing hands against her scales, the dragon burst into motion.

Powerful legs scrambled beneath them as the dragon launched out of the stall, scaring the nearby servants again with the rush.

Down beside the stall entrance, Shiff trotted closer, looking around, confused, having finally caught up.

Going?

Many eyes in the area turned to the dragonling, roaming apparently on her own, then to Vance and Dashiel's hurried launch.

Dashiel cursed. "Get back to your room, now!"

Fly?

"No!"

They were almost to the edge of the flight deck, but the hurt from Shiff still came through as the dragonling turned and left.

Dashiel kept their eyes turned behind them at the wreck of the stalls and flight deck area, as Vance kept his forward, preparing the dragon to fly.

As Shiff exited the space, Lord Zarram entered, cheeks flushed red and chest heaving.

"What under the blessed sun is happening in here?" he roared. "What happened? Where are you going?"

Dashiel turned away, teeth gritted, and Viska took flight.

Air slapped Dashiel in the face as Vance pushed the golden dragon fast right off the deck. They hadn't even taken long enough to grab goggles.

Searching the sky with squinting eyes, Dashiel saw a blur of red.

"Above and to the right."

Vance turned Viska, soaring toward the heavy clouds.

The red dragon hovered still in the sky on massive wings, looking over the city. As dragons of the plains, etherflames had the widest wingspan of all breeds, built for hovering above the herds of the grasslands, picking their prey.

Dashiel whispered a quiet prayer that the red wasn't picking something from the city below as her target.

As they got closer, the dragon's emotions encroached into Dashiel's, a high level of bewilderment and panic. Freed jaw hanging open and eyes wide, her head swiveled, seeking escape in the open sky.

"Why isn't she leaving?" Dashiel yelled in Vance's ear.

But then they saw it too, so ever-present that they hadn't at first noticed.

A sky full of dragons. There were always at least a few, gliding over the dragonkeep. Dragonriders on patrol, or slower steeds transporting civilians and cargo. It was an everyday sight to Dashiel.

But to a wild plains dragon, it must seem like threats

all around.

Viska was almost upon the red, and Dashiel's heart raced, unsure whether it was their own panic or the dragons.

"Slow down!" they yelled at their brother. "Don't approach so fast."

But the red etherflame noticed Viska then, shooting toward her, and brought her wings snapping back into her sides. She swooped in a swift dive away from them.

Vance sent Viska into the chase.

Both etherflames, the gold was faster than the red, through her mixed breeding, and Vance brought Viska down like a dart toward the fleeing dragon's back.

Viska's talons touched against the red's spine, and she snarled, spinning into a roll, belly up. As her head turned a full circle beneath the Zarram siblings, she loosed a long gust of fire.

The flames spiraled, scorching the air around them. Vance swore and turned Viska so sharply that her wings cracked like thunder.

Banking hard, Vance slipped from his seat, prosthetic leg kicking out as he tried to regain grip. Dashiel kept their thighs tight around Viska's spine scales and grabbed Vance by the back of the shirt, pulling him back into position.

They circled out and back around toward the dragon again, closing in fast.

But the massive burst of fire above the city had drawn attention. Four riders brought their dragons speeding their way.

The red etherflame beat her wings hard, aiming toward the dragonkeep walls and freedom beyond, but one of the city guard riders came back toward her, head-on. Blasting another short puff of flame, the red changed course, dipping lower, penned in.

"Try to direct her out of the city!" Dashiel yelled.

"It might be too late for that." Vance growled back.

Two more riders came in from the left.

Another moved in close enough to Dashiel and Vance to call down to them, "Has that thing got no rider?"

"Just let her go out—"

"Keep back, we'll handle it," the female rider waved her hand above her head in a series of signing motions, and two nearby riders saluted back.

The red put on a new burst of speed, aiming out toward the sea. The city guard riders barreled in toward her on their smaller, faster steeds, flanking her on both sides and forcing her to turn around again.

She swiveled her head, snapping at the air around the pursuing dragons. A rider on the shimmerdart to the left sent a shot of ball lightning blazing back toward her. The red dove under, dropping lower to the city again.

Dashiel kept their hands on their brother's back, keeping

him steady as they pushed faster. Vance maneuvered Viska down into the small gap between the shimmerdart and the red escapee, then turned toward the dragonrider, forcing them to back off with the bulk of Viska's golden body.

But as they dropped back, the rider on the red's other side pushed their attack, bringing their snowflame down onto the red's wing, clawing at the leathery membrane.

The red etherflame keened as her wing tore, and she tumbled in the air. Turning and turning, she spiraled faster and faster toward the rooftops. Wings continued trying to flap but were tangled around her body in the twisting fall.

Scared. Hurt. Scared.

The terrified scream the red cried chilled Dashiel's spine and made their fingers clamp tight around Vance's shoulders.

Fire burst out around the dragon as she flamed and flamed again, desperately trying to burn her attackers, until the red etherflame looked like one giant fireball, plummeting toward the earth.

The riders pulled back, regrouping high in the sky.

Vance dove hard, one last time. Dashiel held their breath. If they could get to the red in time, catch her in Viska's claws, slow her descent ...

The red hit a tall, spired building in a crashing explosion of stone and glass and fire.

She smashed straight through, catching everything

flammable in her wake, then demolished a smaller warehouse with the slide of her huge body. She came to rest in a wide square, surrounded by fire and debris.

Screams echoed from the streets and buildings below. Vance shot Viska's wings out, catching the air and bringing their speeding descent jarring to a stop to avoid hitting the rooftops themselves.

Dashiel stared at the scene below, speechless with horror.

"We should get out of here." Vance leaned to turn Viska around.

Dashiel could sense the fallen dragon's pain and fear surging through their veins and couldn't leave the creature, not like that, not alone to her fate.

Reaching both arms around their brother's waist, Dashiel pressed the commands for landing and yelled them aloud for good measure.

"What are you doing?" Vance pushed back, trying to recover control, but Viska was already level with the rooftops and a second later skidded to a stop on the cobblestones of the square.

The red lay twisted and broken and panting before them. Dashiel leaped down from Viska's back.

A group had gathered, pulling bodies from the destruction of the burning warehouse. Dashiel could feel the rising heat on their back, and the flames glistened over the scuffed and torn scales of the red etherflame.

Screams and shouts surrounded them, and Dashiel moved fearlessly toward the downed dragon.

Tears streamed down their face as the red's chest lifted sharply and compressed, lifted again, then all the smoky air inside her wheezed out in a long, final breath.

"I'm sorry. I'm so sorry." Dashiel put a hand against her snout, still hot from the remnants of dragonfire. "This was all my fault."

Dashiel's face twisted, fierce with frustration and anger.

But it wasn't only their fault. It wasn't their actions that had led to this moment, not entirely.

Pushing past the dragon's slumped neck, Dashiel stepped over strewn bricks and smoldering timber to the dragon's chest. She lay belly up, exposing the wide underbelly scales and the dagger stuck between them.

Vance stumbled up beside them as Dashiel grabbed the handle and yanked it out.

"What is that? Did you do that?"

"Would I have done that?" Dashiel glared back.

"Then who?"

Dashiel opened their fist, staring at the knife in their hand. A finely crafted blade, larger than those designed for throwing, but serving the purpose well enough. On the pommel, a solid letter *H* was stamped, surrounded by a ring of thorns.

Heithorn?

Smoke gusted around them from the roaring ware-house fire.

"Sabotage?" Vance growled.

Dashiel clutched the dagger tight again, bringing it flat against their chest, lips twisting with fury.

It might have worked. Without the sting of this blade, keeping the untamed dragon calm and safe might have worked.

But now Dashiel would never know. And a dragon, and any number of people Dashiel couldn't bring themselves to turn and see, were dead.

Through the surrounding smoke, large shapes rushed in around them. City guards on small treedarts. They barked orders to the remaining citizens gawking at the downed dragon and some split off to manage the fires and shattered buildings.

"You should go," Dashiel said heavily.

"*We* should go," Vance snapped back.

Dashiel's eyes lingered over the heavy collar on the dragon's neck, stamped with the Zarram crest. "Someone needs to stay and claim responsibility. I'll do what I can to keep our family from feeling the consequences of all this."

Vance rested a hand on Dashiel's shoulder. "Not with-out me."

A squad of six guards approached cautiously, eyes on the

siblings and the stationary bulk of Viska behind them. Too late for any escape that didn't add more guilt to the scene.

If Dashiel had thought that their standing as acclaimed riders and dragonlord nobles within Draekhanhelm was going to shield them from punishment, that hope was quashed by the glee on the lead guard's face as they took in their dark, tanned skin and Rolanian features.

"Zarrams?" the pink-skinned Taen man asked, a twang in their tone mocking of a strong Rolanian accent.

"Yes," Dashiel said, straightening up and staring up at the guard in his saddle.

Looking over the body of the red etherflame, the branded collar at its neck, and then up into the sky to make clear they'd seen everything that happened, the guard's grin widened. "Wild dragons? Is that what you keep in your unblessed dragonhold?"

Dashiel firmed their jaw and remained silent.

The head guard pointed to the riders at his side, and they climbed off their steeds.

"I don't know what tricks and cheats you Rolanians have been up to in your hold. But it's all come crashing down now."

The two guards on foot approached, manacles in hand. There was nowhere to run, surrounded by treedarts and fire on every side.

Dashiel sought their brother's eyes. He returned a look, solid and determined, and nodded once. Zarrams didn't run. Zarrams didn't burn. Zarrams would face their fate with honor.

Dashiel still shivered, scared for Shiff, all alone, and Eslinde's dragon, and Eslinde herself if the truth of untaming came out, as the heavy steel was clamped about their wrists.

SEVENTEEN

Kess was drenched in sweat by the time she, Eslinde, and the princess's grayglim reached the audience chambers. She'd worked hard to keep up with the racing pace Eslinde set, charging down through the palace from the moment the news arrived that the Zarram siblings had been brought in shackled with chains.

A guard at the ornate doors opened his mouth at their approach.

"Don't you say a word," Eslinde commanded without slowing. She swung the double doors wide and marched in.

An angry hum of voices filled the chamber. Everyone was on their feet, hands flailing with emphatic gestures. Only the grayglim wardens guarding with their backs to the walls remained still.

Lord Zarram was there, red-faced and towering. "What trouble have you brought down on us? It's only by the graces the Dragon King has bestowed upon us that you aren't in a noose already."

Dashiel and Vance stood shoulder to shoulder in front of their father, hands clasped and locked in heavy iron before them. Dashiel's golden hair was dulled with ash and their face hanging, drawn long and pale. Vance held his chin high.

Neither responded.

"I don't know what ... How did you ...? Where ...?" Lord Zarram sputtered.

Across the room, Ulfren the First and Hjelzahn the First stood with a flock of Sunblessed monks like a spill of yolk, bright in the coolly lit room.

They listened, muttering horrified exclamations and prayers as a guard gave them a report. A number of the elder advisors in darker robes listened in from the fringes.

Eslinde stepped between the Zarram siblings and their father. "Perhaps I could have a moment with them. It seems something terrible has happened, and I would be honored to offer what aid I can to the Zarram household."

"Your Highness," Lord Zarram bowed deeply. "I am most honored and can assure—"

"A moment with them *privately*." Eslinde smiled pleasantly.

Frowning, Lord Zarram backed away. "Of course."

He wandered over as though to join the group headed by Ulfren, but from the looks he received in return, he pivoted and moved around to fidget with the corner of the table in the center of the space.

Kess moved in close beside Eslinde, forming a tight group with Vance and Dashiel.

Ulfren glared at their huddle from across the room, especially at Eslinde.

Eslinde wiped a finger across Dashiel's cheek, smearing a smudge of ash.

She spoke softly, "A wild dragon from your dragonhold attacked the city—that's all I have heard. Was it mine? Did she escape?"

Vance grunted. "No."

Kess eyebrows went up. "You untamed another one?"

"I did. Alone. Everything that happened is my fault." Dashiel's hands squeezed and released over and over in front of them. "Everything except ... It was *working*. The dragon was calm, was listening. And then ..."

"They were sabotaged," Vance growled.

"How? Who would?" Eslinde gasped.

Dashiel's eyes met Kess's for the first time since they came in. "There was a dagger, thrown at the dragon while it was confused and vulnerable. A dagger with an *H* surrounded in thorns."

"Heithorn." Kess crossed her arms, grasping at the wrists where two of the knives the princess had gifted her were hidden, as though doubting herself whether it could have been her.

She hadn't been there. The knives she had now had no crest. Yet it was so like the betrayals and cruelties she'd committed in the past that the doubt came easily. But she knew who it had to be.

Kess snorted out the words. "Kife. My brother."

Dashiel nodded, eyes still locked on Kess's. There was no judgment in their expression, only regret. It stabbed Kess deeper than if she'd betrayed Dashiel herself. She didn't need to throw the blade herself. Her mere presence in their lives brought tragedy.

"Why? What is that man's problem?" Eslinde snapped, nostrils flaring.

Kess flinched away. The princess knew she was still withholding secrets from her, but there was still one she refused to tell. "He's angry at me, and he's determined to do anything to take his revenge on me and anyone around me. Dashiel saved me from him after the ball."

"You think he wanted to get back at me?"

"No doubt. I also think he overheard us discussing

untaming dragons."

Vance's shoulders lifted and rolled, and his face worked through a few dark expressions before he said, "And then he saw proof and took a chance at making a mess of everything."

"But he's your brother?" Dashiel shook their head.

Kess looked at the two Zarram siblings standing shoulder to shoulder, and her nose stung.

What would it feel like to have a brother who treated me with that kind of love and support? She couldn't answer, only turned her head down and rolled her chair back just a fraction, out of the tight group.

"Remind me to tell you how Kessara and I met, and then you won't be confused any longer at the state of the Heithorn siblings' relationship. But for now, do you have the dagger? Perhaps we can use it to our advantage," Eslinde said.

Dashiel lifted their empty hands upward. "It was taken off us. I don't know where it is."

"What other proof do they have? Explain to me everything and—"

"Enough colluding!" Ulfren pushed in between Eslinde and Vance, sweeping his arms to break up their group.

The back of his hand knocked Eslinde's chin, and Vance stomped a step forward.

Head still tilted back, earrings swinging, Eslinde gave him a warning look and he stilled.

She said, "I'm only comforting our family friends over what must surely be a misunderstanding."

Ulfren's long face turned to her, his dark eyes fierce. "Don't treat me as a fool. You last were in this room asking for us all to untame our dragons, and now what has been set upon the people of this keep? A savage, untamed beast. Is this the blasphemous world you hope for?"

"She didn't have anything to do with this," Dashiel said.

Kess wasn't so sure of that. Eslinde was the one who shared with them the possibility of untaming, and it was Kess that knowledge first came from.

Ulfren's voice dropped, deep and dangerous. "No. I know where the blame lies and where punishment must be served."

Hjelzahn stepped up behind him, nodding fervently. Around the other side, one of the elder advisors shuffled in, voice warbling in distress. "Let's not accuse so freely. There are still so many unclear details as to who was behind this and how it transpired."

Dashiel stepped into the middle of the building crowd. "It wasn't her, it was m—"

Vance elbowed them and spoke over the top, saying not much of anything, a grumbling philosophizing about the nature of dragons and guilt.

Ulfren's voice rose again, and Lord Zarram returned, defending the honor of Zarram Dragonhold more so than his offspring. And soon everyone was speaking all at once as voices grew louder and louder.

Kess's chair rolled backward. Slowly at first, and she clutched the wheels, worried somehow that it was rolling away on the perfectly flat floor. But the chair continued, backing up, then turning. A grayglim had taken control of it and was swiftly wheeling Kess toward a side door.

"*Excuse me!*" Kess exclaimed.

The grayglim said nothing.

Turning as fully as she could in her chair, she looked back toward the others, all so deep in argument that they hadn't noticed Kess being slipped away from beneath them.

Should I raise my voice? She wasn't sure they'd even hear her, and surely she was making a fuss over nothing. The grayglim wasn't Lady Hjelzahn and Kess was fairly certain she was the only one who wanted her dead.

As they reached the side door, another grayglim opened it and Kess was pushed through.

"Where are you taking—?"

Before her, Dragon King Yeonard Draekhan turned from the floor-to-ceiling window to greet her with a steely expression. The small room was bereft of furniture, the

glossy stone floor and walls decorated only by glowing lamps and silver and red pennants of shimmering silk.

Eslinde's mother stood motionless in a shadowy corner, dress draped about her like an elegant statue.

Kess swallowed a dry mouth, and the grayglim closed the door behind them.

The Dragon King took a single step closer, placing himself in the center of the room. "Do you know, Kessara Heithorn, how many people died today in my keep?"

Dropping her eyes down and bowing as best as she could from her chair, Kess said, "I do not, Your Majesty. But any number is too many."

He hummed. "True indeed. It is fortunate that it was a rest day, so few were in the warehouse that was destroyed. The reports make it clear what happened. All that is left to decide is who will take the blame."

A shiver ran up Kess's back, and she kept her eyes low. "Have you made that decision?"

And why did he bring me to him as though I could help make it?

The king moved closer, pacing languidly before Kess so her vision was filled with the sweep of his silver embroidered robes swishing back and forth, reflected in the tiles beneath.

"Perhaps it needn't be my decision to make. The Zarrams' trouble, alas, affects my daughter, which in turn affects me."

Kess couldn't fathom the entirety of the political fallout from what had occurred. But even what she could imagine seemed dire.

She tried to keep her tone even, logical, not pleading in panic. "Then blame nobody. Make it go away. Say it was a wild dragon only and an unfortunate accident that it was brought down over the city."

"But the people are angry. And they need a target for their fury." The Dragon King's voice echoed in the small space. "Look at me, child."

Kess turned her eyes up, breathless. "Your Majesty."

The Dragon King's dour face was framed between the ornate, twisting metal collar of his robes and the sharp pointed crown upon his head.

Kess felt a little relief that there was no anger in his expression. If anything, he seemed bored and annoyed that this issue had been brought to him at all.

He sighed. "Eslinde had been doing so well recently, before all of this."

Had she? Kess bit the thought from escaping her mouth.

The Eslinde Kess had first met was a living ghost, wasted away and wan inside and out.

It had been months since then, and Eslinde was only just regaining color and softness to her body, although the fire inside her returned much faster. But clearly that fire was all her father cared about and wanted extinguished again.

His strange, darkly bright eyes settled on Kess. "She had been doing well, before *your* arrival."

She held the Dragon King's gaze. "You believe it's my arrival that has affected her so?"

"You and the information you brought with you. Spurring Eslinde into illicit activities."

Kess's lips drew tight.

"Yes, I know about it all." His sparkling eyes narrowed, glinting like stars.

A terrible, cold sense of courage rushed through Kess. The kind of vibrating, anxious daring she used to feel in the wilds when facing death. She folded her arms, clutching at the hard metal beneath her wrists.

The Dragon King turned away from her then, striding to the window.

"My daughter is beloved." He cast a glance across to Eslinde's mother, still motionless in a shadowy corner. "The Zarrams are valuable partners. And you ..."

Kess could hear all the possible endings to that sentence in her mind. She was nothing. She wasn't important. She was a shame and embarrassment to even have around.

She was expendable.

Through the massive expanse of crystal-clear glass, the sky was a tumultuous swirl of dark clouds, curdling over the

roofline of the city. Smoke rose from a district to the east.

Kess released her grip on her forearms and the knives hidden there. There was no point in fighting.

Her life was already over.

"You," Yeonard Draekhan said thoughtfully and turned back to her. "You could admit that you were the one who freed the wild dragon to frame the Zarrams. Given your unique history, it will be understandable that you craved revenge on the dragonlords and riders who refused to let you fly with them. We even have a Heithorn dagger covered in dragon blood for proof."

Kess lifted her chin. "Is this what you've decided?"

"Oh no. This is your decision, Kessara Heithorn. You can confess, and I can make everything better for the Zarrams and Eslinde. Or choose not to, and the punishment for the crimes committed can be spread far and wide."

The sweat dampening Kess's gown from their rush to the meeting had cooled now, and Kess shivered.

Her attempt to keep her voice stable failed. "And what would happen to me?"

"You will go away to prison. I have a number of places to put people where they will never be seen again. For that you should be grateful, that you won't face the direct wrath of the populous. I may not be able to be so generous in swaying the outcomes for the others."

The Dragon King raised a hand then in a swift wave, and Kess was moving again. The grayglim had her chair under his control and rolled her back out into the audience chambers.

The king clearly felt no need to await an answer from Kess.

Did he not really care? Or did he already know the outcome?

The arguments within the room continued on. Her presence, or lack of it, went unnoticed.

The grayglim released her and Kess pushed herself slowly back to Eslinde's side, weighing the decision within her.

Kess had always wanted a dragon. To be a dragonrider. But that had always been the means to an end. To have the power to do good in the world. To gain respect and friendship and love.

Did she have any of that from Dashiel, Vance, or Eslinde? Maybe. Sometimes it felt as though she did. The flickering connections of friendship, the considered actions of respect ... Love? No. Not love.

But they definitely had that for each other, and if Kess didn't do something, they were all going to be ruined. They seemed as close to good people as Kess hoped to find. They were important—to Kess, to each other, and the world.

And me ... I'm not.

She didn't matter. Even Griskin had given up on her.

And the person she most wanted to matter to was dead and gone.

The Dragon King strode into the room then, silencing the raised voices.

Folding his hands together, he showed far more concern than he had moments before in the privacy of the side chamber. "We've all heard what must be heard on this matter. Now, we must hear directly from the source of this trouble and decide upon the consequences."

Ulfren practically frothed at the mouth with glee.

To one side of Kess, Eslinde's eyes darted, calculating and troubled. She gave Kess a nervous smile.

To the other, Dashiel had a fierce and sickened expression on their raised face, and Vance hissed commanding whispers in their ear.

Dashiel shook their head once and opened their mouth.

Kess yelled into the room, "It was me. The plot to release a dragon upon the city was mine."

EIGHTEEN

Kess sold her guilt as best she could. Offering up the tale of revenge and feigning delight at the destruction it wrought, as though her plot had played out exactly as she wished, and she simply couldn't contain herself any longer from letting everyone know from where that wrath had come.

Eslinde, Dashiel, and Vance, of course knew she was lying, and of all the expressions of surprise in the room, theirs were the most shocked.

"What are you doing?" Eslinde spat from the corner of her mouth.

Dashiel tried to raise their voice over Kess a couple of times, but Vance kept them quiet.

Kess lifted her chin high and bared her teeth.

"I would have had every one of you burn in dragonfire if I could have, but because these cowards"—Kess glared at the Zarrams and Eslinde—"wouldn't be drawn into my plans, I was only able to free a single beast. But even still, I wanted you to know it was me who burned your city."

Kess found it remarkably easy to fill her words with spite. She put into them all the hurt and torment she'd ever suffered, and from the horrified stares of the elder advisors, she'd hit her mark.

Ulfren, however, gave Kess a withering glare. "This is ridiculous. How could she have done any of this?"

The Dragon King gestured to one of his grayglim, who brought forth the Heithorn dagger, holding it up on display.

"This was found with the downed dragon, and we have the girl's full confession as to how and why and that despite her evil influence she was unable to gain any collaborators." The Dragon King offered Kess an almost imperceptible bow of the head. "That seems to me all we need to know."

Lord Zarram pressed a hand against his chest. "And my children? Zarram Dragonhold?"

"Both free to leave. If there were damages to your property, we can discuss reparations at a later date."

With one wave of the Dragon King's hand, two grayglims approached and released Dashiel and Vance from their shackles.

"This isn't right," Dashiel murmured, dark brows low

over pleading eyes as they looked at Kess.

Seeing them freed, a lightness came over Kess, and she breathed easier.

She offered a wry smile and whispered back, "It might be the rightest thing I've ever done. Let me do this."

"Kess." Her name sounded like heartbreak on Dashiel's lips.

Bowing repeatedly, Lord Zarram wished every blessing and honor upon the king, then forced Vance and Dashiel swiftly from the room.

Kess stared at the door they left through, a spike of emotion twisting her face. The thought that she may never see them again hurt, but she stilled herself, transforming the lines of her grief into a dull glare.

Eslinde looked pained enough for both of them. "And what of Kessara? What is her fate for ... for what she's done?"

Playing along now too, are we? Kess wasn't surprised. She was the perfect scapegoat.

"Into custody and transported to permanent imprisonment tomorrow. Someone like her cannot be allowed to return into society." Yeonard Draekhan looked over the elder advisors and Sunblessed Monks as though seeking their say on the matter, although Kess knew it was already decided.

There were quiet mutterings of approval from them all.

Except Ulfren. "There are still—"

"The matter is concluded," the Dragon King boomed.

He turned to leave, but Eslinde fluttered in a rush to his side.

She spoke brokenly, as though finding her thoughts as the words tumbled from her mouth. "Allow me ... Tonight, let me be responsible for Kessara's custody tonight. Her final night of freedom."

Yeonard Draekhan turned, frowning softly. His voice was warning, but gentle. "Eslinde ..."

She reached out and clasped his hand. Whispering, but still loud enough for all to hear, she said, "I know she's done a terrible thing and I ... want to be sure she receives what she deserves, personally."

Pulling his hand free, the Dragon King sighed. "She's your responsibility for the night. See that you remain responsible."

Eslinde nodded, steel in her eyes, then rushed back to Kess. The Dragon King turned the other way, heading to the side chamber.

Ulfren snarled, chest heaving with seething breaths. "Your Majesty?"

The king didn't slow, and the door closed behind him, blocked by a grayglim.

Turning to Hjelzahn instead, Ulfren hissed, "I won't stand for this blatant favoritism."

"Move, quickly," Eslinde whispered to Kess, then walked fast for the exit.

Kess followed, Yensen at her back.

"This can't be allowed! I know the truth!" Ulfren yelled at their backs.

They were two corridors away, where no one else was around, when Eslinde dropped back to walk beside Kess instead of leading.

Her narrow white eyebrows pulled together. "Oh, Kess. Why?"

Plenty of reasons came to Kess, of how she wanted to help, of how she was the one link in their chain that wouldn't be missed, but only one reason needed to be communicated, and urgently.

"The king, he knew, *everything*, and—"

"Lady Eslinde!" Falden rushed toward them from the corridor ahead. "I was looking for you. I have news!"

"Falden?" Eslinde slowed her pace, openly surprised for a moment. "Is this about the Zarrams?"

The advisor hadn't been at the meeting with the others, but he bustled toward them with red-faced urgency. "Zarrams? What about them? Did something happen?"

Kess coughed out a laugh.

Eslinde resumed her march toward her chambers, gesturing for Falden to follow. "Never mind. Tell me what your news is."

"As you know there have been plenty of rumors circulating

about the Hjelzahn children. After a great deal of trouble, I managed to track down an eyewitness from an attack on a smelting factory. I wasn't sure it was relevant at first; however, this guard has quite the eye for faces." Falden patted about his body, then extracted a few sheets of parchment from a pocket.

"I believe we've been having trouble tracking the children because they've been dyeing their hair and disguising themselves. I can't understand why. Almost like they don't want to be found! But look at these faces. Surely it is them."

Falden thrust two of the sheets out, and Eslinde took them. She held them up so both she and Kess could see.

The guard had a good eye indeed. The sketches of black charcoal and white chalk captured Aishena and Benjin's faces perfectly. But unlike the steely-toned hair they'd had in the undercity, their locks were now dark.

Eslinde continued walking as she glanced back at Kess for confirmation.

Kess nodded.

The parchment trembled in Eslinde's hands as she asked, "And who else was with them? I want all the details. Perhaps they are being coerced."

Falden shuffled the other loose sheets, trotting at Eslinde's side. "Ah, there was a mixed-race young woman and a big redheaded Rolanian, an odd-looking dragon, and another small girl."

Eslinde snatched the final sheet from his hands, staring intently.

But Kess's eyes had glazed as though streaked with grease. She choked out the words, "When? When was this?"

Falden replied, "I spoke with the guard just now and came directly."

"No. The attack on the factory. When?" Kess rasped.

"The attack? It's not recent, I'm afraid."

Kess's heart turned sluggish, refusing to beat properly. "*When?*"

Falden counted upon fingers. "Summer's end, a bit more than three months ago."

Kess went rigid, her chair stuttering to a standstill.

"Although not current, the information that the Hjelzahns are disguising themselves is very useful. Thank you," Eslinde said.

Eslinde and Falden strode ahead, continuing the conversation, until Yensen cleared his throat from behind.

"Kessara?" Eslinde returned to her and crouched in front of the chair. "What is it?"

Kess's whole body struggled in a war between laughing and crying, relief and pain.

Three months. *After* she'd been locked away in Kife's cellar. After she'd met the princess. After Kife stabbed Riony in the back. *After.*

"She's alive?" Kess couldn't believe the words on her own lips.

Eslinde's information from the contact at the ball had been more recent, telling of only two women. Kess couldn't know what that meant. But Riony hadn't died from Kife's blade, and that awoke in Kess a startlingly painful hope.

When Kess gave no further explanation, Eslinde frowned and stood back up.

"I'm afraid my friend has had quite a day." She reached for the remaining drawings. "May I keep these?"

Falden released his grip reluctantly.

They had reached the base of the stairs, and Eslinde gestured for Yensen to help Kess up them.

Eslinde took a few steps herself before turning to Falden. "Thank you for this information. Hopefully we can use it to bring those poor children home. You haven't shared it with anyone else?"

"I came straight to you with it."

She offered him a respectful bow. "I would appreciate it most sincerely if it stays between you and me. Now, please excuse us, we are retiring early."

"Your Highness." Falden bowed in return.

They had reached Eslinde's chambers by the time Kess could breathe again.

Eslinde closed the door on Yensen but didn't lock it.

She strode in, eyes still on the parchments, on the hooded face of a young girl looking back from the sheet on top.

Then her gaze fluttered to Kess, all too knowing.

"You have the look about you of someone who has discovered a person they grieved has come back to life." She smiled softly. "It's familiar."

Kess couldn't reply. She didn't know what to say. Of everything that had happened that day, a scrap of information which mightn't mean anything shouldn't be what affected her the most. She was now a criminal to the crown and tomorrow would be locked away forever.

Eslinde kept the portrait of Lyrrin and tossed the remaining sheets onto the low table in front of Kess.

And there was Riony, looking back at her. The guard had made her look fierce but still captured the ever-present smirk at the corner of her lips. For her portrait alone, they'd added color. Vibrant red for her flaming hair.

And Kess found herself explaining everything.

How she knew Riony from her past, when she was only Pony to her, but had become so much more. Of how she'd hunted them, but still Riony came back for her, gave her another chance, and another, when she deserved none of them. And of how she'd believed her dead by Kife's hand.

She explained everything except for Dracuni.

Shaking her head, Kess moved closer to the table, eyes

locked on the portraits. "But I still don't know that she's alive now. What you heard at the ball ... there were only two young women with the group then."

Eslinde sat down on the lounge opposite and gave Kess a look so intense it engulfed her like a wave. "That could mean anything. You've told me before how you feel about her. What's most important now is deciding what you will do with your feelings. If she is alive, what would you do?"

Kess confronted those emotions within her, trying to name them and draw out answers. The fear of seeing Riony again and facing up to her crimes and betrayals. The way her heart had cracked open and changed forever when she saw Riony crying under the waterfall. The guilt for every pain she'd caused. The ache, ache, ache of impossible love.

Anything. I'd do anything to make amends for everything I have done.

Kess shook her head. "There's nothing I can do. Not anymore."

Eslinde brought Lyrrin's portrait up to her chest as though embracing it.

"I never ... because of my views and ideas, I never had close confidants before. Other than Alleem and the Alderkin. You and Vance and Dashiel, I want you to know what it has meant to me, having people around me who believe as I do and feel how I feel about the world. And now I fear I'll lose everyone. Again."

"You won't lose Dashiel and Vance," Kess said.

"I don't want to lose anyone." Eslinde stood up and marched toward the entrance door.

Stopping beside a cabinet, she rummaged in a drawer and pulled a dark metal key. She dangled it from the ring with one finger.

"I need to leave for a while. There are plans to make with this new information. Yensen will be with me, and ... I will manage my sadness if you aren't here when I return."

"I can't leave," Kess said.

"You might not find it so impossible as usual. I know you are capable. I know you've survived worse."

"It would mess everything up. I'd be hunted."

Eslinde smiled. "Sounds like that would be a change, for you."

Kess coughed something between a laugh and a sob.

"Best be fast about it, then you'd have until morning before anyone starts looking for you." Eslinde opened the door, then glanced back at Kess with eyes sparkling with tears and said, "You've gotten me closer to reuniting with what I've lost than I ever dreamed possible."

Then she closed the door behind her.

The sound of the key sliding into the lock and turning was so different to the usual chorus of clicking and thunking

of magical closures.

The princess had left Kess with only a normal lock as the barrier between her and freedom.

She could leave. She could escape.

Kess turned her chair and rolled into what she'd come to think of as her room.

The wheels squeaked softly on the polished marble, and Kess brought herself beside the window.

Although one of Eslinde's piles of books obscured some of the view, the capital dragonkeep spread out into the distance before her, shrouded in bruised clouds and pattering rain.

Often when Kess gazed out that window, she would see the shadow dragon, futilely descending upon the keep where there was no dead for it to raise, and she would feel the cursed creature's mourning presence.

It wasn't there that evening, but the torment inside Kess felt the same.

Although it had left her shaken, the hope that Riony may still be alive meant nothing. Because tomorrow Kess was going away forever.

Because she would do anything for Riony. And Eslinde and Dashiel and Vance and this was what she could do for them all. She could save them by giving herself up. She would be saving Lyrrin's mother, and if that was one thing she could do for Riony, that would have to be enough.

Kife hadn't killed Riony. He'd stabbed her, yes, and Kess still wished a death of a thousand flaming humiliations upon him for that alone, but if that's what someone who stuck a blade in Riony deserved, Kess deserved it ten times over.

And if Riony was still alive, she'd still be able to protect Dracuni. So Kess wasn't required there either.

Kess settled into her chair and listened to the thunder breaking across the lightning-streaked sky and prepared to wait for morning.

Through the low grumbles of the storm, another sound turned Kess toward the main chamber. A soft sound again reverberated from the entrance door.

Was Eslinde back already?

The sounds at the door weren't the same as before. A harsh scratching and clinking of metal.

Kess had decided she wasn't going anywhere, but somebody was trying to break *in*.

Nineteen

The door to Eslinde's chambers swung open and two pale-haired men stepped inside.

Kess's breath hitched, and she pulled herself in behind the stacks of books, folding at the waist to lower herself enough to be hidden.

"I told you they wouldn't be here yet. It must take them a terribly long time bringing the chairbound girl up the stairs." Ulfren the First swept into the chambers he expected to be empty. "The route we came up will give us plenty of time to do what we must."

Kess felt for the knives hidden in her sleeves, considering for a moment dispelling his gross underestimations of her. How much more trouble could she be in, after all?

Although assassinating two first heirs may lead to a swift execution rather than a life in prison. Assuming she could trust that was where she was going. Maybe the place the Dragon King hid prisoners who held no value for him was in a pyre.

Does it matter either way? If I'm gone, I'm gone, and I'll be gone soon enough. What hope am I lingering on?

Hjelzahn followed his brother in, more cautiously, casting his gaze about the space. As he stepped to the door of her room, Kess ducked lower, away from the gap she was watching back through.

"If anyone was here there'd be a guard on the door," Ulfren said.

"There may be servants," Hjelzahn responded.

"They would have greeted us. Stop worrying and let's be quick about this. I loathe being without my grayglim for this long."

Hjelzahn's footsteps echoed as he walked away, and Kess looked through the opening between stacked books again.

"Then you should have brought them." Hjelzahn picked up a book from the low table in the sitting area, scowled at the cover, and tossed it back again.

Probably one of the Rebel Rider collections Kess had been reading.

Kess returned the man's scowl from her hiding place.

The stories weren't *that* bad. The romance was intolerably unrealistic, but she liked the part when the characters raced dragons through a narrow chasm.

Ulfren scoffed. "We can't have any witnesses for this. Not even grayglim can be trusted, not by anyone who isn't the king. They all belong to him, in the end."

Well, you're going to have one witness for whatever you're plotting. Kess pushed her chair a fraction forward for a better view.

"Then let's hurry, as you say." Hjelzahn reached into a pocket on his embroidered robes and removed a thin vial the length of a finger.

Kess's mind turned to silvernix, but the substance within the glass didn't shimmer. It was a clear, ghostly green as Hjelzahn held it up into the light.

Hjelzahn uncorked the vial and held it out toward Ulfren. "She won't smell or taste it until it's too late."

Poison. That could be solved easily enough. Kess just had to remain hidden until they were gone, and then she could warn the princess before any damage was done.

Ulfren took the vial, giving it a tentative sniff for confirmation. "Good. There'll be no mess on our hands and the death will be blamed on the Heir Killer."

"A shame whoever has been ending heirs hasn't gotten to her already. Would have saved us the trouble." Hjelzahn stepped close to Ulfren's side. "No new leads on their identity?"

"None, unfortunately. As you say, an alliance with them could be fruitful indeed." Pushing aside a couple of books, Ulfren collected the water pitcher from the middle of the table and unstoppered it. With steady fingers, he tilted the vial over the opening.

Hjelzahn said, "Just a few drops will do."

Both Kess and Eslinde drank from that water while reading, the way they spent most of their days and nights confined in those chambers. If she hadn't been there, bent down in the shadows when Eslinde was expecting her to escape, both of them would have been dead by morning.

If she'd made her escape alone, Eslinde would have been dead without her.

"Check for any other pitchers. I want this ended tonight," Ulfren said.

The two first heirs stepped farther into the chambers, beyond what Kess could see from her hiding spot.

"What is Eslinde doing with all these books?" Hjelzahn muttered.

"No doubt reading them," Ulfren replied. "She must have something to occupy herself with when not plotting violent conspiracy with those Rolanian sinners."

"And how the king still favors her!" Hjelzahn said, and there was the slamming sound of book against book. "Eight

years now of this special treatment, keeping her here with him in the capital. He's clearly grooming her for rulership."

Kess shook her head. If only they knew the truth, would they think more or less of their sister? Find her death more or less necessary?

It wasn't worth the gamble. Better to stay hidden and wait till they were gone in order to fix their assassination attempt.

Ulfren's voice was a low grumble from the far end of the chambers. "It was outrageous even when the king began constructing a keep in her name. At least he abandoned that."

Hjelzahn gave a grunt of agreement. "She was born after the first heir cut off and shouldn't be considered a legitimate heir in any regard."

"But to see our father putting her needs first, protecting her from her obvious crimes ... He must have more planned for her."

"We can't allow her to take the throne from you." Hjelzahn sounded livid.

"No, we cannot. For our land and our honor, we cannot. And it will be seen to this night." There was the clink of glass, then Ulfren said, "Here's another. I'll check this bedroom. You check that side room."

Kess sucked in a breath and pulled her head out of view as Hjelzahn appeared in the doorway. She was thankful her

wariness of the lightning-powered lamps had meant she'd left them off when she came into the room and hoped the shadows would cloak her.

But there was a pitcher of water in that room with her, on the side table nearby, and if Hjelzahn approached it, Kess's hiding place would be revealed.

She reached behind her to where her third knife had been tucked down into the upholstered gap between seat and backrest of her chair. If Hjelzahn saw her, she could down him easily enough ... Then what? Ulfren too, or attempt to escape?

Kess pursed her lips. She'd work it out as she went, but she was ready to do whatever she had to, to keep Eslinde alive, for Lyrrin, for Riony.

Hjelzahn's footsteps plodded into the room. He must have seen the pitcher, or Kess herself, as he picked up his pace.

Then Ulfren's voice came through from the main chamber. "Who's there?"

The footsteps turned, squeaking on the tiles, and went back the other way.

Kess blew a soft sigh, then lifted her head again to see who had entered. Worry shook her that it might be Eslinde and that this was about to get bloody.

But instead, a grayglim walked alone into the space. Their shadowy armor reflected the cool light of the few lit lamps.

"Kverra?" Hjelzahn said, greeting her with all the warmth of a distant family member.

Kess's body went rigid, and her breath seemed caged in her lungs. Not Eslinde, but perhaps even greater potential for things getting bloody. Kess glanced over the thin barrier of books sheltering her and pulled the skirts of her dress closer to her from where they spilled on the floor beyond her cover.

"What are you doing here?" Ulfren asked.

The grayglim didn't reply. Turning to take in the space, Lady Hjelzahn's dark eyes held a chill that made Kess shake all over. The woman's daughter had inherited those same almost black irises, but they somehow seemed warm and bright in her face. On Lady Hjelzahn, there was nothing but abyss and void behind them.

In a tone so casual even Kess found it hard to believe he was busy poisoning their sister a moment ago, Hjelzahn said, "I had been hoping to speak with you, actually. But you've been rather difficult to pin down for a meeting."

Huffing, Ulfren approached as well, brushing a braid of white hair from his shoulder. "Perhaps you can arrange that now, elsewhere?"

Yes. Leave, leave, Kess urged silently.

Nodding slightly, Lady Hjelzahn said flatly, "I have been hoping to meet, too. I've just been waiting for the right time."

Drawing close, Hjelzahn held out an arm to direct the grayglim toward the door. "And how is now for you?"

"Are we alone?" Lady Hjelzahn asked, unmoving.

Hjelzahn raised his eyebrows. "We are ..."

"Then this moment is perfect."

There was one drawn-out heartbeat of a moment when Kess wanted to feel relief as the two first heirs moved toward the door. But only dread filled her, whispering the truth Kess hadn't seen.

The reason Aishena and Benjin hid from their mother. The reason Yoskar died.

It was only as Lady Hjelzahn drew her twin blades in a flash like liquid metal that Kess wondered, and then knew.

Heir Killer.

The man from whom Kverra had received her last name when she married his great-great-grandson died so swiftly it was likely he never even saw it coming.

Hjelzahn the First fell back, head tilting up and falling faster than his body, severed at the neck in a spray of streaming red.

Ulfren had enough time to sputter curses and confusion and to draw a sword that had been hidden beneath his robes before Lady Hjelzahn launched herself upon him.

There was no contest. Ulfren swung wildly, connecting at times with the blur of Kverra's precise blades, but more

often those blades cut through his defenses, slicing into arms, thighs, cheeks, soaking his silver robes with dark blood.

"What are you doing? Why? Why?" Ulfren gasped between painful groans.

Kess pushed her chair into motion, then thought better of it. She couldn't help save the man, even if it was a good idea. She remembered how the strange, icy grayglim woman had plucked blades from her unbleeding body as though they were less than thorns.

With a final slash, Kverra had Ulfren down on his back. She strode languidly over him, straddling across his prone form as she stared down.

She disarmed him with a flick of her boot. "Because every one of you must die."

Both her blades swung down in mirrored unison, and a sound like tearing cloth was followed by a bloody gurgle of final breath.

Kess's body seemed to sympathize, feeling cold as death all over. *Every one of who? The heirs?*

She stilled her breathing, trying to remain as silent as possible, hoping the Heir Killer would leave now that her murderous work was done.

But the woman did not. With swift and sure motions, Lady Hjelzahn hauled the bodies from the room, one after the other, dragging them into the bathroom. She returned

with towels and soaked up the blood until the living area appeared, at least on first glance, as though it hadn't been touched by murder.

And then like smoke becoming one with shadow, Lady Hjelzahn slipped into a gap between a bookshelf and a curtain and disappeared.

Kess bit off the curses building in her mouth,

She's laying a trap. She's lying in wait for Eslinde. Three first heirs in one night. Wouldn't the Heir Killer be proud.

Kess gritted her teeth. Not three. She wouldn't let the Heir Killer take Eslinde's life any more than she'd allow Ulfren to have taken it.

But she couldn't simply wait Lady Hjelzahn out. Eslinde would come back at some point, come right in and close the door to Yensen as she always did, and Kverra would have one of those blades in her.

Even if Kess came out as quick as she could and yelled a warning, it would be three of them against the Heir Killer, and Kess wasn't entirely certain the woman could be killed.

She had to warn Eslinde before she returned. The only question was how.

Glancing around the room, it was clear Kess couldn't make it back into the main chamber and out the front door. She'd be spotted immediately.

Especially in this chair.

Kess tucked her third knife away into her sleeve with the other. She didn't often feel useless. She'd always preferred to claw and spit and fight through anything in her way. But that had been so much easier when Griskin was with her. She had certain limitations, and without her wolf, speed was one of them.

Bent forward as she was, Kess slumped, putting her face in her hands.

What would Riony think if she were alive and found out Kess had let Lyrrin's mother die?

Riony never gave up. When faced with a dragon or cave spiders or a mass of revenants the size of a house, Riony had never given up.

What would Riony do now? Kess pondered, hoping for inspiration. She smiled wryly.

Probably throw herself from a great height …

Kess's eyes turned to the window beside her, unlocked for the first time, and took in the great distance down to the courtyard below.

She was going to have to jump.

TWENTY

With painstaking slowness, Kess crept her chair closer and closer to the window. Even slightly too fast and it would squeak on the polished floors. Her heart thundered in her ears as loud as the storm outside.

She hated every second. She was too slow. She pictured over and over in her mind Eslinde returning and being slaughtered before she'd even reached the window. How long was Eslinde planning to stay away? Long enough for Kess to escape, however long she assumed that to be.

Kess reached the end of her book tower shelter. Anxious energy urged her faster. Turning her chair to go around the side table which held the pitcher of water, the wheels loosed a long, low whine against the stone beneath.

Holding her breath, Kess swung around to check through the door behind her.

And Lady Hjelzahn, marching out from her own hiding place, locked eyes with her.

"Raze it." Kess pushed the wheels faster, but Kverra was already at the door.

Shifting her center of balance, Kess spun her chair around to face the woman and grasped at the glass pitcher. She eyed the unlit lamps.

No wet hands? Let's see what this does.

Kess flung the glass vessel across the room, aiming for the toggle switch closest to the door. The pitcher shattered against the wall around it.

An arc of blue light shot out from the dripping toggle.

Kverra dodged back, as crackling spread through the room, running within the walls and exploding out from the lamps. Their glass shades shattered, and blue sparks streamed from them like horizontal waterfalls.

Kess had to rush back as the lamp nearest to her exploded, and she came up against the glass with the back of her chair as the blue embers caught fire to the books they landed on.

Pulling the handle to the balcony door, it clicked easily, unlocked for the first time.

Kess rolled out backward, eyes on the burning, sparking

room, and Kverra, striding toward her through the flames and smoke.

As the back of her chair hit the balustrade, Kess glanced behind and down.

That's a long drop. It was farther than she'd thought seeing it from inside.

Whispering under her breath, Kess said, "If I am worthy to ride a dragon, then I am unafraid to fall."

With gritted teeth and shaking arms, Kess pulled herself out of her chair to sit atop the balustrade.

Riony would jump.

And she had. When she'd jumped from the rising cage over the burning slaver camp, the drop had been farther. But Kess had been there, and without even knowing why she'd done it, she'd had Griskin stretch out the canvas of a tent to catch the foolish redhead's fall.

Kess smirked wryly at how much she had lied to herself all that time. She'd always known why, deep down. Why she kept going back, why she held her throws or missed her shots, why she kept doing what she could to keep Riony alive and in her life.

She could no longer deny it any more than she could deny the fall that awaited her.

And there was nobody waiting below on the hard stone of the paved courtyard to catch Kess.

A spike of panic froze her in place.

Then Lady Hjelzahn reached the balcony door and Kess leaned back and let herself topple from her ledge into the open air.

Air rushed around Kess, dragging at the skirts of her dress that fluttered around her. She turned and tumbled, and then the fall ended with the harsh crack of bone.

A wheezing scream burst from Kess. She breathed roughly through clenched teeth, her head swimming with agony. She tried to identify the pain, catalog it: in her chest, her wrist, her leg—the most. But also *everywhere*.

Kess cried out again as she pushed herself from her crumpled tangle onto her back and stared up at the thundering clouds above, triumphant.

Because pain meant she was alive.

Rain spotted all around her, growing heavier, and from the balcony far above, Lady Hjelzahn glared down.

Kess returned a toothy, bloody grin.

"Go on," she growled. "Follow me if you dare."

The Heir Killer turned and disappeared from sight.

"Coward."

But no doubt a coward that would be rapidly heading her way down a safer route.

Kess groaned as she brought herself up to a sitting position. She felt around her sore wrist with the other

hand, where bruising was rapidly darkening. Sprained, but intact. Her ribs were tender to the touch, but she could breathe without any telltale spray of blood.

Her leg, she could tell it was broken at a glance.

But beyond the pain, she could move as well as usual.

Icy rain pelted over Kess, soaking quickly through her clothes. She'd been wearing her leather pants beneath her dresses every day as the weather had grown cooler, and she was glad for it as she pulled one of her blades and cut the tangled skirts of her dress off. She'd move much faster without dragging all that weight behind her.

She just hoped it would be fast enough.

Kess pushed hard, getting herself across the paving of the courtyard and in through the nearest entrance. It was a relief to be out of the storm, and Kess felt hot and cold all at once from exertion and feverish aches and frigid rain.

She left a trail of water in her wake as she slipped up the corridor, trying to get her bearings. The courtyard she'd thrown herself into wasn't the same they often passed through going to and from Eslinde's quarters, but it too led into the labyrinth of corridors marked by grand statues of heroes standing vigil in niches along each side.

At the next intersection, the sound of marching feet pulled Kess back. She flattened herself low to the ground, lying against the wall below the shadow of a tapestry as a troop of guards marched by.

Their eyes didn't turn from their path as they crossed hers.

When the corridor was empty again, Kess turned to look left and right to choose her path but couldn't recognize either as a better option. She leaned against the wall for a moment to catch her breath and her leg throbbed, pain robbing the air from her just as quickly as she caught it.

Trying to imagine the layout of the palace and where she was within it, Kess headed left. She had learned well how to navigate the burned wilds of the world, how to get her directions from the sky and landmarks and find her way.

But the corridors of the palace left her feeling lost in a maze. Every space was made of the same dark polished stone and gold accented carvings.

Around one more corner, Kess recognized the grizzled face and braided beard of the statue before her. One more intersection along and she'd be in the corridor Eslinde usually took to her chambers.

A guard stood watch up ahead.

Getting as close behind the man as she dared, Kess pulled a metal button from the collar of her dress and flung it down the opposite hallway.

The guard turned but didn't leave his post to investigate. Taking the next button down, Kess tried again, and this time the man meandered down to check on the noise.

Kess bit back a whimper as she pushed to cross the intersection as fast as she could. Her sprained wrist crumpled under her, and she screwed her face up against the pain and pressed on.

She'd just reached the shadows of the next hall along when the guard's footsteps returned behind her.

She glanced back to check, but the guard didn't look her way. She'd dried enough now that she wasn't leaving a telltale trail behind her.

Sweating and shaking, Kess made it around the final corner.

"Eslinde had better come back this way," Kess whispered to herself as she climbed up into the niche behind a statue of a glorious woman warrior with a thick mane of white marble hair.

Kess pulled her legs in tight to her body. She winced and tears prickled the corners of her eyes as she drew the broken one in. She felt faint and overwrought all at once.

Her hiding place wasn't perfect. If anyone paused to look at the statue she hid behind, she'd be obvious. But without knowing where the princess went, it was the best place she could hope to wait for her. She only hoped she hadn't missed Eslinde already.

Kess spent the next short passage of time doing her best to rest while not succumbing to unconsciousness, as a woozy agony built within her.

Then the mumble of low voices and footsteps approached.

Kess remained still and hidden, not daring to peek her head out to look. It was only when the people were directly in line with the niche that Kess could identify them.

"Eslinde! Here!" Kess hissed.

The princess, flanked by her grayglim, handmaidens Olva and Jillisa, and advisor Falden, stopped abruptly.

Falden blanched and pointed a crooked finger. "Fugitive!"

Clearly, he had been caught up on the events of the day.

Eslinde moved in front of him. "Kess? What under the sun?"

Kess hated how Eslinde looked disappointed in her, as though Kess hiding there was the result of her escape attempt gone wrong.

"Just listen," Kess snapped. "Lady Hjelzahn is the Heir Killer. She came to your room and has killed Ulfren and Hjelzahn the First."

Gasps rose from Falden and the handmaidens. Yensen took a step closer to the princess and placed a hand on his weapon.

"What? Why were they there?" Eslinde's expression remained shrewd.

Kess shook her head in response. She moved to the edge of the niche. Once in the light, Eslinde also gasped as she looked over Kess.

"You're hurt! Did she do this to you?"

Kess longed for the healing touch of silvernix, but they didn't have time to send for it from whatever stores Eslinde had access to. The hairs on Kess's neck bristled, imagining the murderous grayglim launching upon them at any second.

"I'm fine, I'll manage. But Lady Hjelzahn saw me escape. She knows I'm a witness. She was waiting to kill you too, but now she's probably more interested in getting me. Even more than before."

Eslinde's lips drew in and she nodded once. "Then we can't keep you here."

Falden sputtered, "How can we know any of this is true? The girl may be lying to escape the consequences of her actions."

"Will you go and check?" Eslinde asked her grayglim.

"I will not leave your side at this time, Your Highness." Yensen remained planted where he was, eyes flickering to the ends of the corridor on constant guard for approaching movement.

"Of course, it wouldn't be that easy." Eslinde tsked, then sighed. She stepped away from her grayglim, standing beside Kess, her back to the statue looming over her.

She didn't look to her grayglim, but rather her handmaidens and advisor as she said, "I am sure Kessara is speaking the truth. She's not nearly as good a liar as she thinks she is. Which means

296

it's time to leave. For all of us."

"Your Highness?" the older handmaiden folded her hands together and drew up straight.

"Ulfren and Hjelzahn the First have both been killed. In my chambers. With only someone already convicted of terrible crimes as a witness. This is all going to come down on our heads." Eslinde gestured to Kess and herself.

Kess shook her head. "It doesn't need to. I only escaped to warn you. If I'm already taking the blame, perhaps I could—"

"No, Kessara. It's time. We're leaving. And I hope there are some loyal to me here that will assist us and remain by my side." Eslinde looked to Falden.

The elderly man took a step back and blinked glossy eyes. "Our king has made it clear you're to remain here under his eye, Your Highness."

Eslinde turned to her handmaidens.

The younger bowed silently, then stepped away.

Olva lifted her chin. "Her Majesty, your mother, will hear about this!"

Eslinde straightened up, but Kess could see the hurt in the crinkled tension around her eyes. "I'd feared one of you had been disloyal all along, but it seems it was all of you."

Reaching into the slit pocket of her gown, Eslinde drew her fine epee. "Well, Kessara, I had been hoping we'd have

some assistance in escaping my grayglim, but it seems it's just you and me."

Kess tilted her head and drew in a long breath, steeling herself against her pain and the fight to come.

At least this grayglim seemed entirely human, but two versus one still weren't odds Kess would favor.

She drew a throwing knife into each hand as the grayglim drew his sword.

TWENTY-ONE

The rumble of thunder echoed ominously through the corridor and Yensen's approach was like a gathering storm, his gaze piercing and his movements calculated, sending a shiver down Kess's spine.

She adjusted her grip on the throwing knife in her uninjured hand. She didn't really want to kill the man. Perhaps she could pin him in his joints the way she did with revs, slow him enough to get away. Or perhaps there was still more that could be said to persuade him from the fight. Kess opened her mouth.

Before any words could be exchanged, Yensen halted, his steely gaze on Eslinde.

"Why would you assume we'd need to fight, Your

Highness?" His voice was low, filled with a restrained intensity.

Eslinde's brow furrowed, her gaze flickering between Yensen and Kess. "I ... I thought ..."

Her words trailed off as Yensen's attention rounded abruptly onto the others in the corridor.

Falden's hands shot up in front of him, guarding from the sword now pointed his way. "What are you doing? What about the king's orders?"

Yensen circled around them, opening a side door as he kept his sword pointed at the trio. After a quick glance inside, he waved the sword threateningly at the advisor and handmaidens.

"In," he commanded.

Kess raised her eyebrows at Eslinde as Yensen herded the three of them into what appeared to be a small office. Eslinde shrugged in return.

Once Falden, Olva, and Jillisa were inside, the grayglim closed the door on them, then pulled a short strip of metal from a pouch at his belt and jammed it into the lock.

Outraged cries came from within, and thumps rattled the door, but it remained sealed.

"You ... aren't against me?" Eslinde's voice was barely above a whisper, and she kept her sword before her.

Yensen's gaze softened, a rare glimpse of vulnerability crossing his features before they hardened once more.

"My duty is to remain by your side and keep you safe, Your Highness," he declared, his voice unwavering. "And I will fulfill that duty for as long as it takes."

"Oh." Eslinde only seemed more confused, a blush of color over her cheeks.

"Sooo ..." Kess slipped her knives back into her sleeves. "Are you going to help us get out of here or not?"

A small smile lifted on the grayglim's lips. Sheathing his sword, he approached Kess, awaited her approval, and lifted her into his arms.

"Where to, Your Highness?" he asked Eslinde with a bowed head. "Carriages?"

The princess kept her sword drawn, her fingers white around the grip, a war of emotions on her face.

"Follow me," she said and swept back down the corridor at a swift pace.

After a few turns, Kess knew where Eslinde was leading them.

This is going to test Yensen's loyalty once and for all.

Kess wasn't sure she liked that she would be at the grayglim's mercy when that time came.

Cradled in his arms, Kess winced as the journey jostled her broken leg. Twice they needed to backtrack or hide while guards marched by, and once Eslinde stopped, heading into a side room where she rustled around for a moment, then emerged with a pile of dark fabric draped over one arm.

When they reached the small, bare room and Eslinde opened the secret door to the dungeons, Yensen stopped.

Kess could feel his tension in his hold on her.

"We should be leaving," he said, low and warning.

"I'm not leaving without them," Eslinde challenged in return.

The grayglim looked like he had more he wanted to say, but he only nodded and followed as Eslinde pressed on, down into the rough tunnel.

He's really going to help?

From where she was pressed against the man's chest, Kess looked up at his square jaw, twitching in the corners. She wondered at that level of loyalty. To follow someone into any danger, to do anything they asked, to give themselves completely to that person and their cause.

Clearly, Eslinde still had her doubts, which left Kess on edge as well. But after a lifetime of betrayals and abandonment, Kess *liked* the idea of that kind of loyalty, of giving oneself. She wanted it to be real.

Riony's voice filled her mind.

I know it might be a stupid dream, but maybe we can start making it real. We could start with the two of us.

And then all of Kess filled with the kind of *wanting* that she hadn't known in a long time, back when she would have

burned the whole world down to have a dragon for herself.

Her eyes stung with the intensity of it, wetting at the corners in a way that had nothing to do with the physical pain she felt.

The steep tunnel was dark since they didn't have a lamp with them, but up ahead light glowed brightly.

In the guard station where they had encountered a single, sleepy sentinel on their last visit, now there stood a dozen, heavily armored and alert.

At Eslinde's approach, they shifted to form a barrier between them and the cells behind. Each wore the badge on their shoulder marked with a pointed crown.

"Turn away, Your Highness," a grizzled older woman said with a voice like grinding rocks.

All manners and manipulation were gone from Eslinde as she lifted her sword and replied, "Turn away yourself. I'm going to get what I came for, one way or another."

Yensen grunted softly, glancing side to side as though seeking somewhere to put Kess down.

Whispering up at him, Kess said, "I can maybe take three. How about you?"

"More. Not enough," he grumbled back. Then slightly louder to Eslinde, "There are too many."

"Yes," replied the lead guard. "Even with your grayglim, you aren't getting through. We won't have any part in your

treason. We won't be punished for your actions again. The king knows all about your visits and has made it clear you're never to go in there again."

Eslinde relaxed her stance and sheathed her sword. "That's fine then. Because I'm not planning on going in. They are coming out."

The guard rolled her head back in a scoffing laugh.

And Eslinde yelled, "Yrik! It's time!"

A muffled voice replied, "We are ready. Stand back."

Eslinde smiled and stepped away.

"What are you planning?" The lead guard's eyes widened, and she barked to the man beside her, "Get in there and see what they're doing!"

The man fumbled his keys, rushing toward the steel gate behind him that led to the hallway of cells. He swung it open with a clang, and then the air erupted into a deafening explosion.

Air blasted out, filling the space with dust, and then sucked backward again, howling through the tunnel.

Kess's unbraided hair whipped around her face, and the wind pulled against her so strongly she felt she might be ripped from the grayglim's grip.

The solid door to the Alderkin's cell cracked off its hinges, crumpling up into itself and vanishing into the deep hole of darkness that had materialized there.

Guards scattered, knocked off their feet and clawing at the ground to keep from being pulled in themselves. An unlucky few lost their grip and went hurtling into that dark, whirling space, their screams cut short as they vanished.

A deep, primal fear filled Kess, and she clung tightly to the grayglim.

The Alderkin created this terrifying magic from a single, small crystal? Kess had heard stories of the brutal war between the Alderkin with their magic and the might of riders with their dragons. But now those stories seemed so much more vivid and horrifying.

The wind eased, and Yensen moved fast, placing Kess beside a wall, then moving through the messy crowd, knocking down any guard still on their feet.

Eslinde held tight to the opened gate, white hair flying around her face and a grim smile baring her teeth. "Quickly now!"

The dark magic ended as suddenly as it began, and the three Alderkin emerged from their broken cell. They looked worse off than beggars in ragged and soiled rags, their bright hair darkened with filth and bones showing prominently through tight skin.

But they moved with purpose and strength, running over the downed guards, only a few of which still had enough sense to try to reach grasping hands at their ankles.

Eslinde stomped those hands aside, then followed the Alderkin out of the room.

Yensen quickly picked up Kess again and gave her an assessing look when she moaned at the pain shooting through her.

"I'm fine, hurry!" she snapped.

He did, chasing Eslinde and the Alderkin back up the steep tunnel.

When they emerged back into the palace, Eslinde was handing each of the Alderkin one of the dark cloaks she had taken from a room earlier.

"It was the best we could do with the crystal you gave us. It was already runed with magic to heal and stop a hole from closing," Yrik said as he pulled the hood up over his bright blue hair and long ears.

"We added runes to make a bigger, more explosive hole. We haven't done something like that before. It's lucky it worked," Priyune added.

"I'd say it worked well enough," Kess said, still rattled by the effect.

"Indeed," Eslinde said, throwing the final cloak around her own shoulders. "Now we just have to get us all out of this palace and out of this keep."

Eslinde moved to the doorway, but a shout and clamor of heavy boots sent her hiding within again.

"Could they have heard what happened below?" Kess asked, angling to see who approached from her position in Yensen's arms.

A troop of guards rushed by the doorway, jogging two abreast, grim-faced and set on the path in front of them.

At the very back of the troop, a young man whispered to the guard at his side, "First Ylva, now two more?"

"Prepare for a rough few days. They're going to take this out on all of us," their friend replied.

Kess sucked in a breath. Once the guards were gone, she shared a look with Eslinde.

"How long until the whole palace is locked down?" Kess asked.

"Not long enough for us to make it to a flight deck." Eslinde took another glance out the doorway, then turned back to the others. "If they have found Ulfren and Hjelzahn dead, they'll secure those escape routes first. Let's try for a carriage. Then make our way to the Zarrams' and fly from there."

Eslinde moved to step out into the corridor, when another figure pressed in toward her, thrusting bare hands against Eslinde's shoulders.

"Mami?" Eslinde gasped.

"You undeserving troublemaker! Of course you're here! I knew it!" The queen screamed at the pitch of a whisper.

She scurried farther into the room, pressing Eslinde back with each step. No grayglim or guards followed the woman in, and she looked harried and enraged, a flowing robe thrown on over a crumpled nightgown.

"After everything I've done for you, to keep you out of trouble, and here you are again seeking it out." She pointed violently toward Kess and then to the three Alderkin.

"I'm doing what has to be done," Eslinde said, although her voice held none of its usual strength.

The queen laughed bitterly. "You've been a fool your whole life! What lies have these animals told you to turn you to their side?"

The next thrust against Eslinde didn't push her back, her stance and jaw set firm. "Don't speak to me of lies, Mother."

"Grayglim!" the queen shrieked. "Put *that* down and get these prisoners back in their cells, then maybe we can clean all this up before anyone else knows anything happened."

Kess opened her mouth to throw an insult back at the woman, but Yensen spoke over her.

"I'm not beholden to your orders, Your Majesty." He offered a mocking bow of his head, then turned to Eslinde. "Would you like me to do something about her?"

"No," Eslinde said. "She's my mother."

The princess's arm came up fast like a striking snake and her fist cracked against the queen's nose.

The woman fell flat on her back, blood streaming from her nostrils. She wailed pitifully, but Eslinde was already moving, stepping over her body and leading the way for the rest of them.

"Nice hit," Kess said.

Eslinde shook out her thin fingers. "Well, I am the troublemaker, after all."

They raced down one corridor and the next, Kess biting her lips closed against the pain the frantic pace cost her. Then they paused, backs pressed flat against a wall as more troops of soldiers ran by, a flurry of sun-yellow robes gathered within them, wailing and growling words of fury.

News of the first heirs' deaths was spreading fast, and people were taking it as well as Kess had thought they would. The fallout would be no doubt as murderous as the inciting act itself.

"Almost there," Eslinde called back as they turned another corner, went out through a diamond-cut glass door, and rushed across an open garden.

Rain smacked against them, and their feet splashed through building puddles. One of the Alderkin stumbled, blue hair spilling from under the hood. The two women by Yrik's side lifted him back up, breathing heavily.

They weren't in condition to be running so far. Even Kess, not having to run at all herself, felt on the verge of

passing out as the shattered long bone in her shin twisted and jabbed into her muscles at each of the grayglim's steps.

Then they reached the carriage house, and inside, it was clear of guards. Clear of anybody, except for one figure, moving toward them.

Lady Hjelzahn.

TWENTY-TWO

Within the cavernous flight deck of Zarram Dragonhold, an oppressive silence hung heavy, broken by the patter of building rain and thunder from outside. A few servants moved around, glowering and wary as they worked to clear up the wreckage from the dragon's escape.

Dashiel paced, feeling a churning, hot sickness through their stomach. At least none of the dragonhold workers had been hurt, but there had been people down in the city who were injured and killed because Dashiel had chosen to untame a dragon and hadn't been able to keep it under control.

But the person they were most worried about at that moment was the young woman with the dark, lightning-streaked hair and even stormier eyes.

"We shouldn't have let Kess do that," they said.

Vance moved about Viska's stall, circling his golden dragon and checking for injuries. "It was her choice, and we're lucky for it."

The dragon had come away from the aerial chase with a few burns. More for Dashiel to feel guilt over.

Thankfully, Viska had been returned to Vance's ownership, and the Zarram family returned home together on the dragon. Lord Zarram had taken control of the flight and hadn't said a word to his children the whole way, simmering and stern. The moment they'd arrived, he'd stalked off, calling servants to his side and barking orders.

"But why? Why did she do it? This had nothing to do with her." Dashiel tugged at their blond curls.

Vance rubbed at a mark of soot on Viska's leg, then straightened up again. "Maybe she felt responsible, given her brother's sabotage."

Dashiel kicked at a splintered piece of wood left over from the dragon's escape. "If anything, that was my fault for making an enemy of him when I stopped him from strangling Kess."

"Sounds to me more like his fault for being an irredeemable asshole. But regardless, the reason why isn't important. We must honor her choice by making the best of what she gave us."

There had to be more reason to it than that. Politics

and machinations Dashiel could guess at but not confirm. All they knew was that it didn't feel *right*.

"She gave us her *life*, Vance. She will never see freedom again. We can't just let that happen."

Vance folded his arms and growled. "We can and we will. What else are we to do? I'm not going to allow you to give your life instead, nor would you let me."

"No, but—"

"Should it be Eslinde, then? Who else could take the fall for all the damage that was done?"

"Why not the Heithorn brother? We should find him and make him answer for what he's done, make him take the blame." Dashiel turned a full circle, staring into the dark shadows between flickering oil lamps that lined the stone walls, suspicious that the man could still be lurking somewhere nearby.

"Dash, look at it logically. We barely know the girl—"

"And yet look what she has done for us, to save me from my mistake. Raze logic!"

"And yet," Vance echoed, "she is one person. If we are blamed for what happened, we risk losing all of this! The Zarram name would be ruined, and any chance of any other Rolanian becoming a dragonlord would become even worse. You know how they already hate us."

Dashiel knew well. As they had returned to their

dragonhold from the palace, a swarm of protesters had been building in the streets around the Zarram property. Even with the blame officially on someone else, there would be repercussions from this, because it had been a Zarram dragon; it had been Dashiel and Vance who were first seen at the site of the devastation. And because the Taenish nobles and dragonlords hated them simply for who they were.

Vance's face softened. "Kess's sacrifice wasn't just for us, but for our father, all our family, for those we employ, for Eslinde, for Viska and Shiff. She will save us all."

Dashiel dropped down onto their haunches and put their face in their hands. "I feel like I'm going to be sick. I hate this. I hate all of it."

"Then perhaps you shouldn't have done what you've done!" Lord Zarram boomed, as loud as the thunder echoing in from the open end of the flight deck.

Dashiel shot back up to their feet.

Their father stalked forward, red-faced, eyes gleaming. He waved his arms and the few servants who had been milling about fled the area.

Lord Zarram came to a stop in front of Dashiel. His gaze flickered disapprovingly to Vance for a moment before returning his full wrath on Dashiel.

His lips curled as he said, "How did you do it? The red

etherflame? How did it become wild?"

Vance gave Dashiel a warning look.

"It just ... did?" Dashiel shrugged.

"Don't test me!" Lord Zarram held up a piece of metal. "I've just been to the old flamesong stalls."

"You've been down there?" A shiver of fear rattled Dashiel's words.

Lord Zarram threw the metal at Dashiel's feet. The taming spike that had been pulled from the red dragon.

Dashiel tried to formulate an excuse. What could they say? That maybe the spike had fallen out on its own? But before they could speak, their father held up another smaller piece of metal.

"I have. And look what I found." Lord Zarram threw the shiny disc at Dashiel's chest.

Dashiel caught it and held it in the flat of their hand. They swallowed hard.

The fake spike cap that had been hammered onto Shiff's forehead.

He knows. Dashiel looked at Vance in panic, and their brother stepped closer by their side.

Lord Zarram turned then, pacing before his children. "I went there straightaway because I had a terrible notion. I wanted to believe it was all a plot by that broken girl, but no. No. Don't think I hadn't noticed your sneaking around. But I never thought ..."

Dashiel said, "Please, I can explain—"

Lord Zarram cut them off with a fiery scowl. "My own blood has betrayed me! Lying and keeping secrets. Refusing to tame their dragon as ordered! I should never have let you keep your dragonling separate from the others. I thought that would be all I found in the old stalls but instead I find two wild dragons kept within my dragonhold!"

"You didn't open the other stall, did you?" Dashiel gulped.

"And let loose a second dangerous beast upon the city? Of course not." Lord Zarram stopped pacing and pointed a finger at Dashiel. "What have you got locked up in there? Is it Eslinde's dragon?"

"It is, but Eslinde—" Dashiel tried to answer, their words lost beneath their father's tirade.

"I'd noticed the snowshimmer missing, but I thought you'd moved her for training or exercise. What a fool I've been. I cannot even trust my own offspring."

Lord Zarram rounded on Vance then. "You've been part of this too, haven't you?"

Vance didn't cower, only lifted his chin. "If you take a moment to listen, perhaps you will understand, for once, our reasons, rather than expecting your will to be followed without reason. Not everything in this world is profit and prestige. But you forgot all your values long ago."

Lord Zarram sputtered, "You dare?"

"Anything he did, he did to support me and try to keep things safe," Dashiel said, stepping between the two.

Throwing his hands up, Lord Zarram turned his back on them. "I can't trust either of you, not anymore. Not to help me run this place. To think I had hoped to hand over control ... What am I going to do now? I have so much more work to do to manage this disaster."

Dashiel knew Vance had never really wanted to take over the dragonhold from their father, but after his accident, it was Vance's only option. Dashiel couldn't bear to see their brother lose that too.

"I'm sorry for what happened. But please don't let everything be ruined from this one mistake. It was me, alone, who untamed the red etherflame. And it wasn't violent, not until it was attacked."

"Like Eslinde's dragon, roaring and howling and scratching at the door, isn't violent?" Lord Zarram scoffed. "I'm going to have to dispose of it now, and how do I then explain to Eslinde the First that her dragon had to be killed?"

"You don't have to do that. It's not hurting anyone. I will look after it, please, Pabba," Dashiel said, reaching a hand for their father.

Lord Zarram pulled away. "You can't be trusted to deal with anything! You couldn't even do what had to be done in taming your own dragonling!"

Dashiel squeezed the fake spike cap in their fist. "You didn't do anything to Shiff, did you?"

"Not yet. Not yet. But that is my next stop. I'm going to get a spike and silvernix and tame that blasted beast myself, once and for all!" Lord Zarram lifted a hand and signaled back toward one of the entrances of the cavernous space. A group of guards emerged.

"You can't, please. Shiff isn't dangerous. She's clever and listens to me."

"For now, maybe. But when she's as big as the etherflame that rampaged through the city today? What then? How will you keep her controlled? That red dragon killed people today, Dashiel!"

The guards brought chains with them, and for a moment Dashiel wondered if the chains were for them. But instead, they approached Viska.

Vance stood firm, blocking the guards' way, but with another order from Lord Zarram, they stepped around him and began chaining the golden dragon.

Dashiel's breath came out in angry snorts, the guilt burned away by fury. "Of course, the red etherflame was angry! It had gone its whole life enslaved with a spike in its brain! Can't you see the cruelty of that? No, of course you can't. You can only see the profit it brings you."

"Wealth it brings our whole family. You're so spoiled you can't even see the privilege all my hard work has given you. Why do you think that girl took the blame for your mistakes? Because the king himself asked her to, for us, because of the respect he has for me."

Dashiel's mouth squeezed closed. Was that why? Was Kess pressured into it by the king himself?

Vance grumbled, "If the Dragon King was protecting anything, it was his own interests."

He stepped away from the guards shackling his dragon and spoke in a rough whisper. "He knows who untamed the dragon, and he also knows why. He knows that it's the taming of dragons that is causing the curse of the shadow dragon and that the curse could be removed by freeing them."

Lord Zarram took a step back, staring at his son as though he'd gone insane. "What is this nonsense? The curse is the fault of the Alderkin. Everybody knows that."

Vance laughed without any humor. "It's a lie. It's all lies, and Yeonard Draekhan has known for years. Eslinde herself told us so."

A flicker of uncertainty crossed Lord Zarram's eyes.

Dashiel seized upon it, pleading. "Consider if for even a moment that it is true, Pabba. What would you do? If freeing our dragons could stop even some of the curse, wouldn't it be the right thing to do so?"

Lord Zarram's face went even redder, head shaking as he looked from Vance to Dashiel. "It's not something we could do. We've too much invested in this. You expect me to throw it all away? We'd have nothing. We'd be beggars and slaves like every other Rolanian in the keep."

Dashiel's voice rose. "Maybe we wouldn't need to be locked away in a dragonkeep if we could end the undead curse! If we could set an example, show other dragonlords ..."

"You're fools, both of you. If we lose our dragons, then we are weak, and weakness has no place in this world. If you cannot understand that, then you are no kin of mine."

The final locks clicked onto Viska, and one of the guards came over and handed the key to Lord Zarram. He put it away in a pocket. All uncertainty had left his face now, and he narrowed eyes upon Dashiel and Vance.

"You will have no access to your dragons until I decide so. No access to silvernix. You will not leave this dragonhold. You will not speak your treasonous lies to anyone. And Shiff will be tamed. Tonight."

With a flick of his chin, the guards formed up around Lord Zarram and they all turned and marched away.

Dashiel lunged to follow after their father, but Vance grabbed their arm, pulling them back.

"I can't let him hurt Shiff. Please!" Dashiel clutched

Vance's arm in return, needing the support.

"We won't," Vance said in a whisper. "But there's no point arguing with him. It wasn't enough to save my leg; it won't be enough to save your dragon."

"I have to do something." Dashiel glared at the space their father had left in the room.

"And we will. He'll need to go and get silvernix. We can get to Shiff first." Vance squeezed his grip around Dashiel's arm and nodded.

Dashiel gave him a wavery smile. "Thank you. For everything. Although I know at least some of your choices have been made to please Eslinde rather than myself."

Vance grunted. "Don't push it or you're on your own."

Huffing a laugh, Dashiel nodded in return, and the two of them made a dash for the stairs.

The windows they passed by were lashed by rain. Outside, the storm had worsened. The wind howled like a vengeful spirit, driving the rain sideways with its force. Lightning rent the sky asunder with jagged streaks of white-hot fire.

On the streets below, the angry crowd had only grown larger, despite the drenching torrent. Flaming torches and lanterns sputtered against the deluge and shouts rang out in competition with the lightning.

One point of light caught Dashiel's attention. A runner,

coming down the hill street from the palace. They reached the crowd and were engulfed within it, and a riotous roar was unleashed at whatever news the runner had brought.

Torches and weapons were lifted into the air, and for a moment Dashiel wondered if they had brought news of Kess's supposed guilt, that they were appeased and would now leave to their dry homes.

But instead, they seemed only more enraged, raising their weapons against the gates of the dragonhold.

"What's going on down there?" Dashiel muttered.

"I don't know. As long as it stays out there, though, we're okay," Vance replied.

They hustled fast down the rest of the steps, and as they moved through the ground floor to the next descent, a panicked servant was hurrying in the other direction, muttering under his breath.

Vance put out an arm, stopping the round, older man.

"What is it? Do you have some news?" he asked.

The man bobbed his pale face. "From the palace! A tragedy has struck. Two heirs have been found dead, slain by the fugitive who unleashed the wild dragon."

"Two heirs? Which ones?" Vance growled.

"Ulfren! Ulfren the First. The other, I don't know. First heirs, though. Both of them. That's what people are saying."

Vance released the man, who bowed, then ran on to

share his gossip.

Dashiel's blood turned cold. Was that the same news the runner had brought the mob outside?

Two heirs dead.

Vance's chest heaved and his forehead twisted as he said, "Eslinde."

Dashiel's own chest constricted. "Kess."

TWENTY-THREE

There was no surprise in Lady Hjelzahn's expression at seeing the group that had arrived before her.

She must have known we were coming, tracked us here.

Kess looked around the carriage house. One carriage stood by the gate, already prepared with a treedart dragon ready to pull, but no sign of who it was prepared for. Not a single servant, driver, or guard to be seen. Had Lady Hjelzahn sent everyone away—or worse—to avoid any witnesses for what was about to happen?

With eyes as cold and dark as a lonely midnight, Lady Hjelzahn stared at Kess and Yensen holding her. Resting her hands on the hilts of her twin swords, the grayglim woman addressed Eslinde.

"Your Highness. Move away from Kessara Heithorn. She is a dangerous fugitive."

Eslinde reached a hand down into her pocket where she kept her sword concealed beneath her gown. "And as agreed with the king, she is under my custody tonight. She is well under my grayglim's control, and I don't require any other assistance."

Lady Hjelzahn seemed taken aback by that. Did she even know about the untamed dragon and judgment placed upon Kess for it? Perhaps she didn't and had simply taken the opportunity to remove two heirs when she'd seen them without any guards.

The unnatural woman shook her head. "She has murdered two first heirs."

Kess raised her eyebrows. "You're going to pin that on me? I'm just the perfect scapegoat for everyone today."

"No, I don't believe Kessara did that," Eslinde said forcefully. And then her voice softened and grew cunning. "But for my safety, being a first heir myself, let us pass so we can leave to a more secure location. We do not want to face the true killer tonight."

Eyes narrowed, Lady Hjelzahn looked over the group—the princess, the grayglim carrying Kess, and the three hooded figures—as though weighing the danger of each of them.

She took a step closer, blocking their path to the carriage. "I'm to assume then that you all know who the true killer is?"

"They don't know anything," Kess blurted. "You only want me."

Lady Hjelzahn wasn't even looking at her. She gave Yensen an assessing glance and then turned a gaze of utter, disgusted hatred toward Eslinde.

With a threateningly lazy shrug, Kverra Hjelzahn said, "It may be a challenge, but you aren't the only one I want."

One more step and Lady Hjelzahn was almost in striking range.

"Eslinde?" Yensen asked softly.

He changed his hold on Kess, and she feared he was about to hand her over to Lady Hjelzahn.

"Do what you must," Eslinde gasped back, as the ring of twin swords being drawn echoed through the carriage house.

Then Kess was airborne, thrown out of Yensen's grasp. Her mouth went wide in a gasp and she braced to hit the ground, but instead collided with another warm chest, and arms wrapped her, catching her fall.

Kess's broken leg swung and hit hard against the new body, and she cried out, eyes blurring and dimming from the surge of pain. Through her blindness came the sounds of clashing steel, a flurry of blades singing and scraping against each other and clattering against dragon scale armor.

Blinking her eyes clear, Kess saw she was held by Eslinde herself, who circled around the battling grayglims toward the carriage.

Yensen held his ground against Kverra, driving her back to clear the path. She didn't seem concerned at all, relentlessly striking back with already bloodied blades.

Was that from Ulfren and Hjelzahn the First? It seemed too fresh for that. Yensen wasn't bleeding yet either, at least not for how much blood covered the swords.

"You're in pain," Eslinde whispered down to Kess, eyes staying on the battle.

"That's what happens when you jump from a balcony to get away from a murderous grayglim."

"Kess!" Eslinde gasped.

"Just worry about continuing to get away from Lady Hjelzahn."

"Yensen has her. He'll bring the killer down."

Kess could only hope so. The battle between Aishena and her mother hadn't been as fair. Aishena had some grayglim training but was far too young to have completed it nor be as experienced as Lady Hjelzahn. Perhaps a full-fledged grayglim would have a chance.

Yensen was getting some hits in already. But Kess could see they weren't slowing the strange woman down.

"We need to get to the carriage," Kess urged.

"Go, quick!" Eslinde hissed to the Alderkin, who made a dash toward the awaiting coach.

One split off to open the gate. A flash of bright-green hair identified Priyune.

Thunder cracked from the sky above at the same time as Yensen's sword met the gray scale mail on Kverra's chest. He sent her stumbling back, cutting into the vulnerable joints of her armor as she went.

"I told you he was good," Eslinde said, cheeks flushed.

Kess's lips pursed. "It's not going to be enough."

As Yensen slashed again, slicing a line into the leather connection of the armor on Kverra's elbow, it seemed to dawn on the grayglim what Kess had already seen. Lady Hjelzahn wasn't bleeding.

Her sword shot out toward his frowning face, and he turned away from it at the last moment. A thin line of scarlet bloomed on his cheek, and Kverra's advantage became all too clear.

Teeth bared, Yensen doubled his efforts, moving faster and striking harder than before.

He was expending all his energy on one brutal assault, and when his sword struck into a gap between Lady Hjelzahn's chest armor near her waist, his bared teeth turned into a victorious grin.

The grin faltered when his sword came away clean.

"What under the sun ...?"

A boot hit his chest, sending him floundering backward.

And Lady Hjelzahn turned her fury toward Kess and Eslinde.

Kess clutched her throwing knife, but her eyesight was still swimming as the woman raced toward them, long braid of hair swinging like a whip behind her. Neither of Eslinde's hands were free to draw her weapon either, although Kess doubted she'd be a more capable swordsperson than a grayglim.

Lady Hjelzahn brought both her swords into the air and twisted her body into a spin, bringing the blades toward the pair of women with a momentum that could slice clear through both of them.

Then a dark swish of fabric blocked Kess's view of her imminent death, and a woman cried out. A twang of snapping metal was followed by the clatter of a broken length of blade against the ground.

In a reprieve of stillness, the figure turned slowly around to Eslinde and Kess. Priyune, the green-haired Alderkin woman, stared over them, her large emerald eyes unfocused.

One of her clawed hands was raised, clasping Lady Hjelzahn's sword by the broken blade. But the jagged end of that blade was lodged in her shoulder.

She stumbled onto her hands and knees in a puddle

of rain and blood-soaked fabric.

"No!' Eslinde screamed, and her grasp on Kess loosened, but she didn't drop her.

"Watch out!" Kess cried, as Lady Hjelzahn's remaining sword slashed their way.

It pulled back at the last moment as Yensen threw himself upon the woman, grappling her from behind.

"Go! Get out of here!" Yensen yelled.

Yrik and Shael rushed to Priyune's side, lifting her and carrying her into the carriage.

Eslinde hovered, and Kess understood her unwillingness to leave. Their chances of escape, of surviving whatever their next location would be, were so much lower without a grayglim with them.

Yensen wrestled the unyielding woman, holding her from behind as she struggled to get her arms free, both of them facing back toward Kess and Eslinde.

Kess squinted, focusing her wavering sight and then lifted her throwing knife.

Hold her still, just for a moment, she willed silently.

Kess sent her dagger flying, and it struck true, deep into Lady Hjelzahn's eye.

"Oh my," Eslinde gasped.

The murderous grayglim stilled, going limp in Yensen's grasp. He held her for a moment longer, as though wary

of ruses, then angled around to see the cause.

Then he let the woman go and hurried to Eslinde's side, limping slightly.

But still as she was, Lady Hjelzahn didn't fall. She remained there, swaying on her feet.

And then she slowly lifted her head to glare at Kess through her now lonesome eye.

"*Oh my*," Eslinde said again.

"That's not going to stop her," Kess snapped. "It's time to go!"

"Get in." Yensen took Kess from Eslinde.

Eslinde climbed hurriedly into the carriage, and Yensen none-too-gently dropped Kess inside as well, before slamming the door.

The sounds of him climbing into the driver's seat came through the dark timber and metal of the carriage walls, and then they lurched into motion.

The interior was dark, lit only by the frequent bursts of lightning that brightened the world outside the windows. The three Alderkin sat along one bench, Yrik and Shael seeing to Priyune's bloody wound.

Eslinde sat along the other bench, and Kess lay on the floor between them.

The pain from her leg had her feeling shivery and feverish, so she remained there for a moment, lying on her back and catching her breath.

Eslinde turned to look out the back window for a long moment, and Kess worried that Lady Hjelzahn was there, chasing them down on foot. But the princess turned back with a relieved sigh.

"How is Priyune?" she asked, her fingers fidgeting with one of her earrings.

Yrik muttered in his deep, gravelly voice, "She will survive this. The bleeding has stopped."

The hood had fallen back from Priyune's head, her green hair vibrant in the flashes of lightning. She leaned back, her eyes closed, but a smile spread on her lips. "I feel no pain, for we are free."

Eslinde's smile in return was thin and flat. "We're not quite free yet. Not until we're on a dragon and out of this keep. And even then, with the deaths of two heirs and running off with father's prisoners and scapegoat ... well. We'll see."

Kess pressed a palm to her forehead, wanting to laugh and cry. "Have we just become the most wanted fugitives in Elundrae? Because I thought I was going to hold that honor on my own."

Eslinde leaned over her, looking down at Kess from her seat.

She tutted. "Only if you had fled when you had the chance. Why were you still in my chambers when Ulfren and Hjelzahn were killed there? You had time to leave. And on that, why under the sun were my brothers there?"

"They'd come in to poison you."

"Poison?" Eslinde pressed a hand to her chest, sitting back in her seat again. "And here I had been feeling sad for their loss! Poison? Why?"

"They thought you were going to be named the Dragon King's successor. Because of all the special treatment you get." Kess lifted herself up onto her elbows, slowly shifting into a sitting position while checking on the parts of her that ached.

Eslinde stared at Kess for a long moment before bursting into laughter. "Special treatment?"

Kess chuckled too, a laughter of relief taking over as she tried to get her words out, explaining their plot, how Kess had heard it all. "I really hope nobody investigating the crime scene decides to have a glass of water."

Eslinde wiped her eyes, her face a mix of mirth and anguish. She reached a hand for Kess to help pull her up onto the seat beside her.

"Lady Hjelzahn ... *What* was that woman?" Eslinde shivered, rubbing her bare arms against the cold of the stormy, late autumn night. "She didn't bleed, didn't die. How?"

"I wish I knew. It's a trick I'd like to pull sometimes." Kess stared at the window, almost opaque with the amount of rain pelting against it.

Yrik turned their way, face shadowed by the hood still covering his head. "The woman has been touched by the shadow curse. Infected and yet still alive. I've seen it once before, during the war. A fallen human, not quite alive, but not quite dead when the shadow dragon cried its dark magic. The man went mad, still in part themselves, but driven by the shadow dragon's command."

Kess could only shake her head, believing and yet not wanting to. "So that's how you get a fully trained, unstoppable grayglim who seeks the death of all Dragon King heirs."

"And those who know her goal," Eslinde added. "You told me she wanted to kill you, but the unstoppable part would have been nice to know."

The carriage rumbled, careening around a corner so fast it skidded, water splashing up around the windows.

Kess said, "I would have mentioned it before, but the last time I saw the woman get stabbed was in a dark cave in a mess of fighting, and I wasn't sure of what I witnessed. I'm pretty sure now."

Eslinde stared flatly at her. "She had a knife through her eye, Kessara, and she didn't fall. Yes, I'd say it's pretty sure there is something strange about her."

Kess edged one of her remaining two knives out from her sleeve and rubbed a thumb over it in appreciation. "I was a bit worried I'd lost my touch."

"I'm not sure if I'm glad or not that I gave you those knives, Kessara," she said. "You're rather terrifyingly good with them."

"I'm not giving them back," Kess said, sliding the knife away again.

The carriage hit a bump, and Kess's leg knocked against the bench seat hard enough that she whimpered.

Eslinde gave her a firm look. "What is it? We have time now, so stop deflecting."

"It's just broken, I can—"

"*Broken*? Kess!" Eslinde moved closer. "We can—"

The carriage shuddered to a halt so fast that Kess and Eslinde almost slid right off their bench seat.

There was still no visibility out the window, the rain even harder than before. A moment later the door was flung open, and Yensen stood there, soaked to the bone, water streaming down his face.

"The way is flooded, Your Highness. If we're going farther, we're going on foot," he said.

The princess nodded, checking with the Alderkin who nodded their readiness in return.

"Take Kess," Eslinde ordered. "How far are we?"

"A couple of streets. We can take the narrower alleys," Yensen replied, lifting Kess into his arms and pulling her out of the carriage.

Brown water churned around his legs, almost knee-high. Eslinde lifted her gown, bundling the skirts in one arm as she climbed down into the rushing water.

While they were waiting for the Alderkin to emerge, another group of people splashed past, oil lamps flickering through the rain and weapons in their other hands.

"More unrest, even on a night like this?" Eslinde tsked.

She took the lead, wading as fast as possible through the water. The next street wasn't as flooded, and the group broke into a run. Up ahead, there was the group that had passed them before, oil lamps burning like red eyes in the dark.

They're going the same way. Kess's face pinched with worry.

Around one more corner, the familiar walls of the massive Zarram Dragonhold came into view. And at the base of those walls, hundreds of people swarmed, breaking anything that could be broken and pounding at the gates. There were no Rolanians that Kess could identify through the rain and darkness, but the large group of bright-yellow robed Sunblessed Monks were easy to spot.

Eslinde slowed. "I'm not sure we're going to be able to use the front door. Those people don't look happy."

The smaller group moving just ahead of them turned back then. Holding their oil lamps high, they muttered between themselves.

Although the Alderkin were disguised, Kess felt a cold chill at the realization of how recognizable she and Eslinde were. Far too recognizable.

If news had gotten out of the palace about Ulfren and Hjelzahn's deaths, of who was with them when they died …

"That's her! The Heir Killer!" a man in yellow robes yelled.

Safe to say they know.

A score of men broke off from the larger group. With one look at Kess, they charged toward her, weapons held high.

TWENTY-FOUR

Eslinde took a step forward, in front of where Yensen held Kess and cried out toward the approaching rioters. "It wasn't her. You're mistaken."

Whether they didn't know who she was, too muddy and bedraggled to be seen as a princess, or they knew but didn't care, the mob didn't slow their aggressive advance.

"I don't think these tamebrains are going to listen," Kess said.

She wanted to laugh at them calling her the Heir Killer. She'd unwittingly stolen Lady Hjelzahn's infamy. But there was nothing funny about the murderous rage directed her way because of it.

The mob was halfway down the street toward them,

sloshing through a deep stream of flooding water.

Eslinde retreated to Yensen and Kess's side. "Ulfren and his unblessed extremists! He'd had them all riled up already, and getting himself killed has gone and pushed them all right over the edge."

Kess blinked water from her eyes. "That, and a wild dragon destroying a city block, all of which I'm apparently guilty of."

Eslinde pointed to the larger mob, still hammering at the front gate. "Seems they're plenty angry at the Zarrams as well, regardless of your attempt to take the blame."

Yensen said, "We need to go. Find some other way out of Draekhanhelm."

Face grim, Eslinde shook her head. "We can get in the back of Zarram Dragonhold, through the livestock pens. This way."

She still had her skirts bundled in one arm and the tall leather boots beneath were dark from muddy water. She led them back along the street they had come, then turned and took them up a steep alleyway between the dragonhold walls and a neighboring estate.

Rain pattered down all around them, mixing with the cries of the rioters at their back, chasing them down. The wind gusting through the street sounded like the low howl of a wolf and Kess's heart ached.

Yensen kept a tight grip around Kess, pressing on with stern determination, but she could feel a limp in his gait, smell the sour tang of blood from his wounds. Yrik and Shael followed close behind Eslinde, supporting the third, injured Alderkin between them.

With half of their group already bleeding and broken, Kess didn't like their chances.

As they reached the peak of the hill, the stone walls gave way to a tall fence of solid iron bars. A gate of ornate wrought iron featuring the Zarram crest at the top already hung open.

Eslinde pushed it closed behind them, the metal whining and clanking.

"The lock's broken," she called through the rain.

"Here." Shael pointed to a heavy cart, loaded with sacks of animal feed.

She and Yrik rolled it across to block the gate, and then with a strong swipe of a clawed hand, Shael knocked the pin from the axel and the wheel slipped off, the loaded cart tipping to the side.

"Watch out!" Eslinde grabbed Shael, pulling her away from the gate.

A few of the rioters had reached them, arms stretching through the bars for the hooded Alderkin woman. She slipped just out of their fingers.

The mob yelled and pushed at the gate, but the barricade of broken cart and grain bags held firm. A couple began attempting to scale the barrier. One man threw a flaming torch at Kess through the fence. It landed in a puddle at Yensen's feet, fizzing and sputtering.

"Keep moving. Go!" he commanded.

Eslinde took the lead again, down through the path between the livestock pens.

The pungent scent of wet earth mingled with the sharp tang of animal musk. Bovin brayed, disturbed by the storm, churning the mud and muck beneath their hooves. It overflowed from the pens onto the path, squelching as the group ran down toward the dragonhold building.

The clamor and cries of fighting came back toward them.

Four men wearing rich leather armor, with strips of bright-yellow cloth tied around their upper arms, had a fifth man, a Rolanian wearing a guard uniform, pinned against the wall beside the dragonhold entrance. They each took turns beating the guard.

"Stop them," Eslinde gasped.

Kess's fingers twitched for her knives, but before she could draw them, Yensen handed her into Eslinde's waiting arms.

With a fluid grace, he darted forward, his sword gleaming in the faint light as he closed in on the rioters.

Only at the last moment did they notice his approach.

They turned from the guard they'd been using as a punching bag, letting him drop to the ground behind them.

The first rioter lunged forward with a bright short sword. With a deft flick of his wrist, Yensen parried the blow and delivered a swift strike to the man's jaw. The rioter crumpled to the muddy earth.

Without missing a beat, Yensen spun to strike the next man, knocking the hilt of his sword against the assailant's temple, sending him stumbling backward into the third. They collapsed together into a heap, and Yensen followed through, skewering his blade through both their torsos in a single motion.

The final man, faced with the fury and prowess of a grayglim warden, made the smartest choice of the lot of them and ran. He vaulted over a pen fence and disappeared amongst the bovin.

Kess had to admit, Yensen was good at what he did.

Eslinde took slow, heavy steps as she carried Kess closer. "Is the guard—?"

"Dead." Yensen shook his head.

"Inside then, quick!" Eslinde didn't hand Kess back and marched determinedly through the open entrance of the dragonhold. Once they were all through, Yensen closed and barred the solid gate behind them.

Inside the vestibule, the world quieted. The relief from

not being directly under the relentless hammering of rain and thunder left Kess feeling deaf and numb. Her torn dress and leather pants were soaked through from the icy rain, and she shivered in a way she couldn't stop.

Only a small circular grate in the ceiling allowed a thin stream of lightning-highlighted rain in. They all stood around the edges of the chamber, avoiding the running water, but unable to progress farther in. A second solid steel door blocked their way.

"How do we get that open?" Kess asked.

"Over here," Eslinde headed to a large crank jutting from the stone wall.

An empty chair sat beside it, with a tipped over flagon leaking a still steaming drink onto the paved floor.

Yensen turned the crank, and the heavy gate raised slowly into the ceiling above, screeching all the way.

Once it was up high enough for them to pass under, the Alderkin stepped through to the other side, looking about warily.

"Let me carry Kessara again," Yensen said, and let go of the handle.

The steel door came slamming down at an alarming speed. Yrik cried out, jumping out of the way only just in time.

Like the ringing of a gong, the sound of the fallen gate echoed through the small space.

Eslinde startled, shaking Kess and sending a jolt of pain up through her broken leg.

She gritted her teeth and groaned.

"Sorry," Eslinde said, then placed Kess gently down onto the chair, as though worried she'd hurt her again.

Then she yelled toward the closed gate. "Is everyone unhurt?"

Muffled murmurings from the three Alderkin on the other side came back through.

Sighing, Eslinde turned to Yensen. "What happened?"

"I don't know," Yensen replied.

He turned the crank again, and the gate rose as it had before. He let it up only a small gap this time before releasing the handle, and it slammed closed again.

"It only stays open with someone on the crank. Is that a security mechanism?" Kess asked, thinking of the dead guard outside and the empty seat she had taken.

Eslinde turned from the door to the crank, squinting at both. Her silver hair had fallen loose from the bun and was plastered to her head and cheeks with water. "I don't think so. It wasn't this way before. It must be broken. Is there a way to open it from the other side?"

Yrik's voice came through the steel door. "There's a crank, but it does nothing."

A cold, still calmness settled inside Kess beneath her

shivering skin.

She asked Yensen, "Do you think you can get through after letting it go?"

"Not even I'm that fast," he replied.

Kess nodded as she looked at the distance, expecting the answer. The crank was all the way across the room, and the steel gate came slamming down as fast as a guillotine. Even if she had Griskin, she didn't think she'd make it through without being crushed.

"Someone has to stay behind," Kess said. "Someone needs to keep the gate open for everyone else."

Eslinde's face turned ashy. Her voice wavered and she said softly, "Yensen?"

"No," both Yensen and Kess replied together.

"No," Kess said again. "You'll need him."

After seeing the grayglim in action, Kess knew he was the group's best defense against any other threats they might face.

"Then I'll stay behind," Eslinde said, lifting her chin. "Whatever punishment will come will be lesser for me, as a First. I will stay and see it through."

Kess laughed wryly at the princess's foolish bravery. "No, you won't. For starters, good luck getting your grayglim behind the plan. And secondly, you're the princess, someone who people might listen to, to start fixing this blighted world.

We can't risk losing you. Also, you're Lyrrin's mother, and saving you is at least a small part of the debt I owe."

Eslinde tilted her head, eyes watering. "Then ..."

Kess leaned away from her, pressing into the back of the chair and shrugging as nonchalantly as she could. "I'm staying. Obviously. You need Yensen, and the Alderkin all have to be freed as well. I'm the only one here who doesn't matter. It was clear when I took the blame for the Zarram siblings, and it's clear now."

"No." There was no command in Eslinde's voice, only a pained plea.

"It's our best option, Your Highness," Yensen said softly.

He gave Kess a single nod of appreciation and began urging Eslinde toward the closed gate.

"No!" Eslinde said more forcefully. She pushed past the grayglim and knelt on the ground before where Kess sat. "Kessara, you do matter. Please believe that. You've mattered to me. So much."

A loud thump came from the exterior door, startling them both. The shouts of the angry mob followed.

They've made it through.

Kess turned back to the princess. "I can matter by saving you. Now get out of here!"

Eslinde's face scrunched up, pushing a tear from her glossy eyes. She reached for one of her earrings, tugging it free. Holding it out, she placed the skin-warmed silver into Kess's palm.

"For your leg, or anything else you need it for. To help you survive. Please survive, Kess."

Yensen returned to Eslinde, grabbing her by the arm and lifting her back to her feet, getting her moving.

Kess looked at the earring in her hand. The long, spiraling design ended in a small cap that unscrewed. A tiny vial. Kess didn't have to open it to know what it contained.

Eslinde has been keeping an emergency supply of silvernix on her this whole time.

Tucking the precious treasure away in a pocket, Kess leaned across and grasped the handle for the gate. She began turning, putting her whole body into cranking the gate open from her seated position.

"I'll see you again soon," Eslinde called back as they stepped through the opened gate, joining the Alderkin on the other side.

Her voice was scratchy, the strain of impossible hope pulling it so taut the sound brought tears to Kess's eyes.

"Sure. See you soon." Kess smiled, and let the handle go, slamming the solid gate closed between them.

Kess took a moment to inhale a long, deep breath to settle herself for the end.

The mob outside had grown louder and larger, hammering at the barred exterior gate.

And Kess was alone, with two knives and one vial of silvernix.

She considered using it then. Her whole body was ragged with pain and without a sustained effort of willpower, the tug of unconsciousness was an ever-present threat.

But whether or not she had a broken leg would mean nothing when the angry rioters got through that door. Maybe it would mean she could down three of them rather than two before she died herself, but Kess never doubted the end result.

She'd always expected, or even hoped, she would die gloriously in combat upon the back of her dragon.

I suppose this is as honorable of a death as I deserve.

But still, she found that she really didn't want to go. She didn't feel ready.

She would never know whether Riony was still alive. She wouldn't know whether Eslinde would find her way to Lyrrin. Whether Riony would be grateful for Kess's part in that. Whether that would be enough for Riony to ever think of Kess as anything other than a source of cruelty in her life.

The cacophony of voices outside rose louder. The tone changed, from righteous anger to incensed outrage. The clamor of weapon against weapon followed.

Kess stilled, listening closer.

Are they fighting amongst themselves? Or fighting someone else.

As the voices dwindled—downed or fled, Kess didn't know—it was clear the mob was up against an opponent that could easily dispatch a whole crowd.

Even Kess's slim hopes of survival dropped away.

An opponent like an unstoppable grayglim, determined to destroy her targets.

The sounds of fighting outside ceased, and Kess slipped off the chair, pressing back along the wall into the darkest corner of the room, praying for the sun's blessing that whoever had cleared away the rioters outside would leave again.

Then the exterior gate shuddered and clanged with the force of a heavy blow.

And then another. And another.

The hinges of the gate rattled and bent as the gate was pounded with the force of a battering ram. With each earthquaking strike, Kess drew and held a breath, expecting it to be her last.

Her fingers traced her collarbone, looping around the string of leather there and drawing out the acorn pendant. She clutched it tight in her fist.

And the door groaned, hinges snapping as it was beaten free. The slab of metal slammed down flat at Kess's feet, and she turned to face her death.

TWENTY-FIVE

"You don't think Eslinde was one of the two heirs that was found ..." Vance's eyes were dark under low eyebrows, and his shoulders rose and fell with strained breaths.

Dashiel shook their head, even though they couldn't be sure. Two first heirs dead and the blame on Kess. They didn't believe that part but knew it would be easy for others to believe, especially after the guilt Kess had already claimed that day.

Whoever had died and how, it was going to mean trouble.

No wonder the people outside are riled up.

Ulfren wasn't just one of the first heirs, he was first in line for the throne. Nobody really expected the Dragon King to pass it along anytime soon, but Ulfren's murder would cause chaos.

If all that blame was going to land on Kess, what would happen to her? Would she even make it to a prison?

Lightning flashed in through a window. The storm raged, rain sheeting the sky.

Vance looked back up the way they'd come from the flight deck. "If we could get to the palace ..."

Dashiel's eyebrows rose. "The palace will be locked down. Going to charge your way through the grayglims and castle guards to see if Eslinde is okay?"

Vance grunted. "Maybe."

Dashiel placed a hand on their brother's shoulder, turning him around again. "We don't even have a way to get there. Not with the mob outside. Not without stealing a dragon. And I think we're already in enough trouble."

Vance's shoulders slumped. "Look at you, being the voice of reason for once."

"I know. Wild, right? Listen, I'm worried about Kess and Eslinde too. But right now, I'm thinking about the other trouble we're about to get into. I need to stop my dragon being tamed."

"Right. Yes." Vance got moving again, hurrying down the long corridor.

"But that also leaves us with the question of what we do after we save Shiff." Dashiel caught up to their brother, stomach churning as they watched the stern angles of his face. "I think maybe you shouldn't have any part of this. Pabba is angry now. I don't know if he's going to forgive the person who directly defies him again."

Vance's uneven pace slowed and then resumed again. "I've found, in recent years, I'm less interested in that man's favor or forgiveness."

Along the corridor, portraits of the Zarram family hung. Their father, regal and imposing, in every one. A few showed their sisters—married away in trade deals— and their mother, who had died during Dashiel's birth, refused silvernix even in the late stage lest her baby be born physically different.

The wealth the Zarrams had accumulated over the years hadn't kept their family either happy or whole, but Dashiel didn't know any life besides this and hated thinking he was dragging his brother away from the protection of their wealth too.

"If you help me, he might cut you out of the business entirely. You'd be losing all of this."

"Oh no, Dash. Don't make me choose between paperwork or my sibling." Vance smirked. "Besides, isn't our end goal to free all the dragons? I'd be losing it all anyway. And it would be worth it."

A world without the shadow dragon. Could it really be

possible? Dashiel hoped it was and that it would be worth it. But they had already seen the consequences of taking steps down that path and how many people would stand against them.

Dashiel released a long breath and clutched at their stomach. "Did I mention how much I hate all of this?"

"I can't imagine it's going to get much better anytime soon."

They reached the old stairwell down into the underground flamesong stalls. Rivulets of water trickled down them, coming in from leaks in the old building.

Vance gave Dashiel a wry, assessing glance. "Besides, if I don't go with you, what will you do?"

"Might be time to put that run-away-and-live-in-the-wilds plan into action after all? Shiff is older now. Bigger. It could work."

Vance huffed. "You haven't really thought about it, have you?"

"No. Kind of. I did wonder whether I could let Pabba go through with it. Let him tame Shiff, let things settle down, and then find a chance to reverse it later on. But what trauma would that leave Shiff with? What if she became angry and volatile like the other dragons we untamed and I lost her forever? I don't think it's worth it."

"Even if you lose everything else?" Vance leaned forward

and rubbed his amputated leg before heading down the steps. The older, more functional section of the keep didn't have glass on all the windows, and the chill of the storm blew in. Torches guttered and flickered in niches along the wall.

"Says the person ready to be a one-man army against the palace to check in on his 'old friend.'" Dashiel smirked. "I only know I have to get Shiff somewhere safe, then deal with the consequences later."

At the bottom of the stairs, Dashiel paused for a moment and let all the thoughts and worries and fears inside them settle beneath the truth that had been picking at the edges of their mind. Vance stopped too, waiting.

Dashiel lifted their hands, looking at the palms, then clenching them into fists.

"I don't think I can stay here any longer, anyway. Pretending everything is fine, knowing what we now know. How can we continue on with our lives, continue letting our father and the other dragonlords destroy the world one dragon at a time?"

Vance's jaw worked. "No, I don't think I can either. I'm with you."

They held each other's stare for a moment, then without another word moved on together again. They passed by the stall that held Eslinde's dragon, first in the row.

Dashiel wondered if they should free it too, but it was

too risky. Dashiel ached at the thought of the lives that had been lost in the city that day, no matter where the blame lay. They couldn't set another angry dragon loose.

And the snowshimmer seemed angrier than ever. She roared and scratched against the solid door in a wild rage. Disturbed by the storm or something else, Dashiel wasn't sure.

Until they felt Shiff's fear as well.

Captured! Need help!

Breaking into a run, Dashiel reached Shiff's stall. The door was open, and a guard stood in the threshold.

Behind him, the small dragon lay on the ground, a chain clasped about her neck and a muzzle strapped around her snout.

"I'm here, Shiff," Dashiel gasped out the words.

"You can't go in." The guard squared up in the doorway. He had a face like a lump of sandstone and arms limbs like gnarled logs.

Shiff got to her feet, moving forward, but was brought up short by the chain.

Captor has chained me. Chains tight! Anger edged in on the fear now that Dashiel was with her again.

"I'm sorry," Dashiel said to her, then turned on the guard. "Let her go. She's too small to cause trouble, and the chains are hurting her."

The guard pulled himself up straighter, rolling his

shoulders in a way that made him seem to double in size. "I'm under orders from your father. Nobody touches the dragon until he returns to tame it."

Putting on their most threatening tone, Dashiel said, "Move out of my way."

The guard sniffed lazily and drew a wide short sword.

Dashiel reached for their belt. From the point of untaming the red etherflame, through its escape, to returning home, they hadn't had a chance to arm themselves with a sword.

All they had was the small push dagger they normally kept on them. Hardly longer than the palm of a hand, it was useful for scaring off bullies. Not so much in a sword fight. They drew it anyway.

"I guess we're doing this." Vance grunted and lifted both fists up in front of his chest.

Death to the captor. Shiff's chains rattled as she bucked to join the fight.

"Easy" Dashiel said, both to her and the guard. "You aren't going to skewer Lord Zarram's heirs, are you?"

The guard took a step backward, herded by the approaching siblings. "Just stay back and you won't have to find out."

"It's two against one."

"But I'm the only one with a weapon. A real one, anyway." The guard gave the sword a casual swirl, lip twitching. But still, he stepped back again, unsure.

"We don't need weapons." Dashiel took a long, bold step forward into the guard's space.

The guard startled, backing up again.

Shiff growled through the muzzle.

"Because we have a dragon," Dashiel said.

Shiff pounced. The guard, now within reach of the chain, went down face-first into a puddle as the small dragon collided with his back. He cried out, screaming as her talons dug in.

"Don't kill him," Dashiel told her, as a spike of emotion disconcertingly like bloodlust and vengeance swept over them.

Why? The pale blue and purple dragon stilled, but their thoughts were a violent challenge.

"He's only following orders. And you'll just make people think those orders were justified if he dies." As much as Dashiel sympathized with the desire to extract revenge.

Vance knelt on one knee beside the guard and pinned him down.

Pain to the captor, then.

Shiff tensed her claws one more time before very begrudgingly removing them from the man's flesh and stepping away with the rattle of chains.

The guard groaned as Dashiel patted him down until they found a key in his pocket.

"Come here." They beckoned to Shiff, and the dragon moved closer, still growling and sulky.

Dashiel pulled the muzzle off, cutting the straps with the dagger, and then unlocked the padlock holding the collared chain around the dragon's neck.

Shiff shook herself from snout to barbed tail.

Freedom! the young dragon seemed to bellow in Dashiel's mind.

"We're not quite free yet. Come on." Dashiel reached a hand for Vance, helping him back up.

The guard cursed and groaned but didn't get up as the three moved away at a jog.

They were out of the old section and moving into the main building when another group of five people ran their way down the corridor.

Dashiel still held their dagger in hand, and their fingers clenched around it.

"Vance! Dashiel!" a woman's voice, high and regal, called out.

"Eslinde?" Vance picked up his pace, running with a swaying gait. "What are you doing here? What happened at the palace?"

They met at the intersection of the hallway and stairs. Eslinde reached both hands for Vance as he drew close, and he grasped them in his.

"Too much to tell right now. We need to get out of the city. Most especially the three people I have with me here. Can you help us? Can you give us a dragon?"

"And you? Are you leaving too?" Vance asked.

Eslinde tilted her head. "Yes. I can't go back. This is my chance to be free."

Dashiel caught up. They took in how wet and muddy the princess and her grayglim were. The three people with them were tall and draped in dark, hooded cloaks that obscured most of their features. Bright eyes sparkled out from the shadows.

They seemed wary of Shiff at first, and when the young dragon moved naturally, coming to sniff at the hems of their robes, they muttered between themselves.

Dashiel looked behind them, down the corridor, hoping for one more addition to the group.

"Where's Kess?" they asked.

Eslinde's face scrunched, then drew out long. "We had to go in through the back gate. The guard there had been killed by the mob, and Kess ... she stayed to hold the gate for us."

"She's down there? Now?"

Eslinde nodded. "We went through only moments ago. But ..."

"Then we need to go and get her," Dashiel said.

"We couldn't get the gate open from the other side."

Dashiel wiped the sweat from their forehead and prepared to run again. "There's a trick to it, but it can be done. We'll go and get her, and then we'll all get out of here together."

A loud crash punctuated their final word, and a roaring cheer of screams came from the direction of the main entrance. A percussion of stomping feet and smashing objects followed.

"They're inside," Eslinde gasped.

Flickers of torch flame and long shadows emerged at the end of the hallway Eslinde had just come down. The way that also led to the broken vestibule gate.

"There are too many of them. We won't be able to get through," Vance said in a growl.

"Then how do we get to Kess?" Dashiel asked, but they already knew the answer.

"We have to get to the flight deck. We have to get out of here. I'm sorry." Vance grasped Dashiel's shoulder, turning them toward the stairs on the other side.

The first rioter stepped into sight at the end of the corridor, yelling a hunting cry at the sight of their prey. A clamor of footsteps followed.

Vance reached for Eslinde, but the grayglim stepped between them, helping her race up the stairs. Vance grunted and jogged after. Dashiel hesitated another moment, as the rioters charged down the corridor and Eslinde's three companions went up the stairs.

Burn and claw? Shiff asked almost gleefully as she watched the approaching mob.

"No. Run. Quick." The words dropped mournfully from Dashiel's lips. They turned and bolted up the stairs toward the flight deck with the dragon at their heels.

As the group spilled out of the stairwell and into the cavernous space, the booming voice of Lord Zarram competed with the storm drumming through from outside.

He stood in the center of the space, all remaining guards of Zarram Dragonhold around him. He barked orders, splitting them off into groups that went running one way and another to deal with the invasion.

"What is this?" he roared as the siblings and followers ran in.

"Princess Eslinde came to us for safety and needs a way out. We need Viska. Give us the key to my dragon." Vance stopped before the man, holding his hand out.

Lord Zarram stepped back. "You cannot trick me into treason. I know the Dragon King has a rule about how and when the princess is allowed to fly."

"Can't you hear what's going on? The rioters are in the dragonhold. We have to leave." Dashiel held their father's gaze, pleading. "Come with us. It's not safe here."

Lord Zarram scoffed, chest shaking into a laugh. "Not safe? Our guards will have it all under control soon enough. I won't leave everything I've ever worked for because a few idiots kicked our door in."

Vance raised his voice. "Haven't you seen how many there are? They will overwhelm our guards in no time. You've only sent those men to their deaths."

"If there are so many, then the Dragon King will send assistance. He will assure our protection."

"I doubt it," Eslinde said. "If he were going to, he would have already. You raise fine dragons, my lord, but there are plenty of other dragon breeders he will happily turn his favor to."

Lord Zarram's cheeks turned red and his head shook violently. He backed away from their group, glaring at the dragonling skulking at Dashiel's heels. "I will not leave. And I will give you no key. Help will come!"

"Pabba," Dashiel called out.

With a narrow-eyed glare at the Rolanian word, Lord Zarram turned and stepped into a side room, and the loud click of the door locking behind him echoed out.

"Raze it," Vance growled. "I don't think he chained the other dragons, but I really didn't want to leave without mine."

"Show me the chains," one of the robed figures spoke. A woman, with a deep, musical voice.

"Over here," Vance said, frowning but leading the way.

At Viska's stall, the golden dragon waited in vegetative stillness. The robed figure stepped up to the dragon without hesitation and grasped the chain. The hand that reached out of the robe was tinged a pale, icy blue, and the fingertips ended in dagger-sharp points.

Dashiel shared a wary glance with their brother, but no explanations were offered.

The woman reached those sharp fingertips between the links of the chain, squeezed, and pulled. There was a screech of tearing steel as the chain link cut and snapped against the woman's strange hands.

And Viska was freed.

"No time to saddle her. Will you manage?" Vance asked.

"I'll be fine. I'm not sure about my friends," Eslinde replied.

"Not once in our long lives have we ridden one of these great beasts," a deep, gravelly voice replied.

Dashiel turned on the spot, checking the other stalls. "The orange etherdart there is saddled for multiple travelers. I can take them and Shiff on it. You take Eslinde and her grayglim."

With nods of agreement, the group split off, mounting the dragons.

Vance pushed Viska out of her stall first, golden scales flashing. Dashiel took a longer moment, helping the three strangers onto the dragon's back and getting Shiff into a secure position.

Own wings should fly, Shiff thought petulantly.

"You're not quite there yet. We need to be fast and travel far," Dashiel said, then commanded the orange etherdart out of the stall.

The rain hit hard as they swept into the air from the end of the flight deck.

Viska circled above, only a little over the dragonhold rooftop parade grounds. Dashiel brought the etherflame in front of Viska and yelled over the rain, "I'm going to check the back gate!"

Vance signaled back an affirmative, and Dashiel curved their flight path down and around the building. Rain poured over the walls and out of dragon skull-shaped spouts like waterfalls. Bovin in the livestock pens bleated and moaned.

Dashiel couldn't get too low, but they could still see enough.

Exactly what they didn't want to see. The exterior gate had been broken through.

A few bodies lay outside it. Perhaps Kess had fought back. Or maybe the guard there had. Dashiel wasn't sure. But there had been rioters there, and they had gotten in to where Kess had been trapped, alone.

Dashiel's fingers felt numb and their heart cold as they brought the orange dragon back up beside Viska.

Eslinde covered her face in her hands as Dashiel reported back with a silent shake of his head.

"Dragons, rising from the palace," the grayglim yelled.

Vance caught Dashiel's eye and signaled for them to follow.

Dashiel nodded back, grateful that the soaking rain hid the tears running down their cheeks.

Viska took off at speed, a golden streak through the glistening rain, and Dashiel followed, flying away from their home and all they'd ever known.

TWENTY-SIX

Lightning flashed through the open, destroyed doorway. Purple radiance filled the vestibule, and Kess squinted into it, seeing the monstrous figure there, holding a glowing blade.

"*PONY*?" The word squealed from Kess's mouth.

Shaking rain from her red hair, Riony stepped into the shelter of the room, stomping over the fallen door.

"Sparks. I thought I'd regret this, but I didn't realize I'd regret it quite so quickly."

Kess clasped a hand over her own mouth at the slipup, the name Riony hated. She'd promised never to use it again, swore it to what she thought was a ghost. Now, she wondered if somehow her mind had broken again, seeing the woman impossibly standing before her.

"I'm sorry. I'm ... what ... how ... *HOW*?"

"We came to find you, you dumb gremlin." Riony hoisted her huge Alderkin sword and rested it on her shoulder.

It clinked against the shoulder guard. She wore an almost complete suit of mismatched plate armor, glistening from the raindrops dripping off it. Only her upper arms were bare.

"We?" Kess's other hand remained clamped around the acorn at her neck, and her body trembled.

From behind Riony, Griskin padded forward out of the stormy night.

He sniffed at Kess, whined, and then shook the water from his coat. It rainbowed in the glow of Riony's sword, and then the wolf jumped in one swift leap to Kess's side.

"Gris?" Kess's voice was strained and high, unbelieving as her wolf licked at her cheek.

She wrapped her arms up around his neck, the fur wet but warm. A choked, laughing sob escaped her throat and her fingers shook.

Turning back to Riony, Kess gaped. "Am I dreaming?"

"Ew, gross. Don't make this more awkward than it is by suggesting that you dream about me." Riony wiped the water dripping off her chin with the back of a hand. "I know I must be looking unrealistically hot right now, but I am real, and so is the wet pup. You can't dream a smell like that."

Kess's face scrunched up in painful relief and confusion. She pressed her forehead to Griskin's and held him in a grip that denied any prospect of ever letting go again.

He lowered himself down onto the muddy floor beside her and panted joyfully. He still had her saddle and bags strapped on, and she checked the buckles, making sure they weren't rubbing against him badly. The soft touch of the leather and earthy scent of the wolf's fur felt like home.

All Kess's pains were forgotten, and her head was light and woozy from a rush of emotions.

"You ... came to save me?"

Riony lifted her sword again and gestured at Kess with it. "Who says this is a rescue mission? Maybe I followed your hairy mutt to find you for revenge. You left me hanging after I was all emotionally vulnerable, and it hurt my feelings."

Kess stared at the ridiculous woman and her heart ached. "That's what you'd seek vengeance for? Not for being stabbed in the back?"

Riony shrugged. "What's a knife in the back between traitorous acquaintances?"

Words burst from Kess in a pleading rush, and she leaned forward, drawn toward Riony with the intensity of them. "It wasn't me. Please, I need you to know it wasn't

me who did that to you. It was Kife."

"Yeah. I kind of figured." Riony's eyes flickered down to the acorn at Kess's neck, and she frowned. "If it was you, you wouldn't have missed my heart."

The words reverberated in the space as though taking up all the air, and for a moment, Kess couldn't breathe. Tears and wonder and confusion warred through her, and she could almost smell the morass mercy again, scared she'd never left her nightmare-filled cell and everything, everything had all been a dream.

And if it was, she'd welcome it for this moment. To have Riony back.

Then Riony continued yammering, big mouth filling the void in a way that also held the yearning ache of home and felt so real.

"Of course, I had a dagger in my back so what could I know? I was never really sure what happened: why I got shanked, where you went, why you weren't appearing around every dark corner to steal Dracuni. Unsolvable mysteries everywhere."

Riony kicked at the fallen door, scowling at the rain blowing in onto her back. She moved farther into the space, not really looking at Kess as she spoke. Turned to the side, a dark pattern was visible on one of her biceps.

A tattoo?

"But then the wolf showed up. Alone. Clearly trying to get me to follow and help. That's when I put the pieces together. Realized the only other person who'd have fun playing backstabbing games who was there that day, and I figured Kife had taken you away and ..." In the soft purple glow, Riony's cheeks darkened. "I didn't like the idea of that."

She cleared her throat. "Plus, when a wolf comes to you for help, you don't turn it down."

"So ... you did come to save me?" Kess confirmed, uncertain.

Riony winced and rubbed her temple. "Do we have to say it out loud?"

She hates me. She clearly still hates me, but she came to save me anyway. Kess stared up at Riony over Griskin's shaggy fur. She stood with her sword resting effortlessly in one hand, armor gleaming, every inch the hero Kess had always dreamed of becoming herself.

The one thing Kess wanted. Like she'd never wanted anything else.

She bowed her head and spoke with a sincerity she hoped wouldn't be misunderstood.

"I'm sorry. For everything. I may not have wielded that dagger, but I brought Kife into the hunt. It was still my fault that he hurt you, and I thought you were dead, and

...” Kess's throat closed up.

And even if Kess thought Riony was alive, she never thought anyone would come to help her. She'd been sure that even Griskin had abandoned her.

But it seemed as though he hadn't. He'd gone to find help. He'd gone to the person who had saved him from the net in the slavers' camp. Who had reunited Kess and Griskin in the caves.

The one person who always tried to help Kess, even when Kess never deserved it.

“Clever boy,” Kess whispered into his fur.

He whined and licked her chin some more.

“Listen.” Riony's shoulders lifted and fell, jangly and awkward, her eyes averted. “You helped save Dracuni, and you saved my life. I owed you. And you never did reply to my offer, so it still stands. One last chance.”

Kess leaned back against the wall and scrubbed her face with her hands, an almost hysterical laugh burbling from her lips.

“One last chance? After all I have done to you ... every cruelty and betrayal ... you return and walk into the burning ruins of my heart as though you could not catch on fire.”

“I mean, you don't have to be so dramatic about it.”

Kess did laugh then. “You ... you followed a wolf across Elundrae ...”

Riony groaned. "I didn't think it would be such a big deal. Would have been much faster and easier if the pup could have pointed out which gateway to travel through, but nooooo. Sparking *weeks* of walking."

"On foot?" Kess gaped. "And broke down a door ...?"

Riony lifted a hand palm upward, as though confused why Kess was questioning it. "Pup wanted insies."

Kess's face tensed, caught between laughter and tears. Riony appearing there felt like *everything* to Kess, but she could see, for Riony, it was just another day. It was simply what Riony did. She saved people, any people, without once questioning the pain or hardship it cost her.

Stupid, beautiful fool.

"And like I said, you don't say no to a wolf." Riony turned, squinting through the rain at the few bodies scattered through the livestock area, groaning in the mud. "Plus, like, *everybody* is out there smashing stuff tonight. What under the stars is going on in this dragonkeep?"

Kess couldn't work out where to start so she simply said, "Trouble."

"Fantastic. I'll fit right in. Aish says if trouble was a currency, I'd be the richest person in the land."

There was a fondness in Riony's voice as she spoke of the Hjelzahn girl and Kess refused to let the way that made her feel show on her face.

Then, suddenly worried, she asked, "The others, Lyrrin, Dracuni, are they okay? They aren't in the city, are they?"

"They're fine and far away. I know I'm not the smartest, but you're the dumbass if you thought I'd bring them on this mission with me."

Kess released a relieved breath.

Riony continued. "I was still fifty-fifty that this was all some elaborate trap you'd set to lure me to my painful death. And then Aish, Lyrrin, and Dracuni all declared my death upon return as well if I let you hurt me again. So I'd be dead four times over. A record, even for me."

"But still, you came," Kess said. She shook her head, laughing mirthlessly. "You always were a glutton for punishment. You don't still think it's a trap?"

"After seeing that dull look of acceptance in your eye after I knocked down the door, I'm pretty sure you really did think you were about to die. Also why were you holding my pendant like that, and how the sparks do you have it?"

Mortified, Kess clutched the acorn again as though hiding it in her hand could make it disappear. Her first impulse was to lie, to say it was nothing, meant nothing, wasn't Riony's at all.

But she owed Riony more. "I found it. It ... brought me comfort. I want to keep it."

Riony raised an eyebrow and muttered, "We'll see about that."

Shouting in the distance drew a line of tension down Riony's neck. "But how about we get out of here first? Get on your wolf. I've cleared the way out through here. For now."

Kess shifted into a more upright position and retested the current pain levels of putting her broken body into motion. Still witheringly high. She inhaled deeply and prepared to lift herself onto Griskin's back.

"No, we're not going that way," she said. "We've got to get through this door here. Or at least, you do."

"Umm, why?" Riony stepped closer, eyeing the solid steel door.

While her gaze was turned away, Kess took the opportunity to hoist herself up. She gasped a silent scream as her bruised rib cage twisted and as she pulled her broken leg over the top of the saddle, then folded over and sobbed without a sound into Griskin's fur.

"Kess?" Riony's voice came softly from beside her.

Lifting back up again, Kess schooled her face. "The door ... It only stays open when someone holds the crank. That's why I'm here. I stayed to let some important people through. People you need to catch up to."

Up the path that was now more a muddy stream than paving, torches flickered through the rain near the livestock yard entrance. More rioters moving around.

"I'll keep the gate open for you. Go and find them. You'll know them when you see them."

It hadn't been long since Eslinde and the others went through. Riony should be able to find them.

"And you?" Riony glanced at the growing crowd up the hill, frowning.

"Don't worry about me. I have Griskin. I'll work it out." She could run now, with her wolf. Hopefully fast enough to evade an entire city who thought she was the Heir Killer.

Riony gestured up and down toward Kess's body. "Sorry. I thought I had found Kessara Heithorn. Who are you?"

Kess held Riony's gaze. "Somebody who has learned from her mistakes but will still do anything I have to do for what I want. And I want you … to get through this gate."

"Don't go getting all self-sacrificing so quick. I'm good with doors. Let me have a look."

Riony checked the handle, giving it a few pumping turns, then letting it go. The heavy gate boomed down. Humming, Riony assessed the solid steel structure.

Dropping her sword, she took two leaping steps toward the gate and kicked up to grab the high mantle. Hanging by one hand, she wedged herself into the corner between door and wall and angled her head to stare into the gap above.

A solid backplate, stamped with an embossed design of fire-breathing dragons, covered the triangle of Riony's back where the knife had so easily pierced before.

Kess stared, part of her still unbelieving. "When Kife stabbed you ... How did you survive?"

Riony turned back and gave Kess a dumfounded look. "I literally have an entire dragon friend made of silvernix."

"But you fell. You fell and didn't move, and they said you weren't breathing."

"Yeah." Riony chuckled as though remembering an old joke as she reached her arm into the gap where the gate slid into the ceiling above. "The dagger missed my heart, but it hit something vital inside. Blocked me up real good. But once Aish pulled it out, the silvernix did its job."

There was a grinding sound, then a click, then Riony dropped back to the floor. "Try that."

Kess turned the handle, lifting the gate knee-high, then letting go. It slammed closed again.

Riony swore, then pouted back Kess's way. "You really thought I was dead?"

Kess could only nod and try not to cry.

"Exactly what form of celebration did you choose for the moment? Cake?"

"I mourned you, you intolerable oaf!" Kess snapped.

"You always have such sweet and kind words for me."

Riony stooped to reclaim her sword. "As much as I'm loving this moment more than the last time I loved your amma, it's time for us to move, one way or another."

Riony pointed her blade out through the broken door. Lightning flashed, and dozens and dozens of torchlights glowed through the storm, moving closer.

A horde of rioters trudged down the slick ground through the livestock pens toward them.

TWENTY-SEVEN

"I don't think we're getting back out that way. Not both of us, anyway. I'll open the gate for you," Kess said, getting her hands onto the cold steel of the crank wheel again.

Riony gave her a shrewd look, then nodded. "Okay."

Something small inside Kess crumbled at Riony's willingness to leave her. She'd wanted more time. But Riony had done what she'd come there for, reuniting Kess with Griskin, and Kess had to do the right thing for Riony in return.

Kess's strained wrist ached as she turned the handle as fast as she could, racing against those marching their way.

"Stop it there," Riony called back when the door had

lifted to just under her chest height.

She slid in underneath it, pressing her back to the doorframe and one shoulder against the base of the door.

"Okay, release it, just a little."

Kess kept her knuckles tight around the handle. "What? No! It'll crush you."

"That's why I said *a little*, tamebrain. I'll see if I can hold it before giving it a chance to turn me into jam. Just do me a favor and do as I say for once in your life."

Kess bit her lip and let the wheel reverse freely half a turn, keeping her hands close in case she had to catch it.

The heavy gate came down on Riony's shoulder and she braced, knees bending and legs shaking. A huff of air exhaled from her. Steel groaned. The crank stopped spinning on its own.

"I've got it. No problem." Riony wheezed. "Let it go and come through."

Kess grabbed the handle fully again, taking the strain off Riony. "What? No! Just get out of here. Or ... or at least use your sword to keep the door up."

"And risk shattering my baby? I'd rather invite all our new friends there to take turns rearranging my face." Riony flicked her head toward the rioters almost upon them.

The men and women at the front of the crowd had spotted them now, turning from where they'd been smashing through gates and freeing livestock.

"We don't have time. Do it!" Riony snapped.

Kess let the wheel turn freely, her hands loosely around it as it spun in case she needed to halt the door's fall.

But it only moved a fraction, then stilled. Riony let out a groaning roar. The armor on her back screeched as she slid down the doorframe, then held again. Her sword lay on the other side of the gate and she pushed both hands up against the heavy metal, arms shuddering from the strain.

"Would you stop gawking and *get through the door already*?" Riony howled.

Nodding, Kess pressed Griskin into action, and they flew on swift paws, ducking under the low doorway.

The moment the wolf's tail was clear, Riony grunted and released the weight, diving clear in a clattering roll.

The gate slammed down like a landslide. Riony lay panting at Griskin's feet.

Kess stared down at her. "You didn't have to do that."

"Oh, really? Sparks, well, let's get this door open again and I'll just pop you back on the other side where you were." Riony remained on her back for a moment and screwed her eyes up as she cricked her neck and stretched her arms.

Closer now, the tattoo on Riony's sweat-sheened bicep was clear. Four rings. Two blades. One candle. Kess didn't know what it meant. She shook her gaze free from it and swallowed.

"I mean … thank you." Kess leaned over in her saddle and extended a hand.

Riony gave her a look like she'd just been offered a sack of squirming eels. "What was I going to do? Come all this way, then say, 'Oh well, have fun dying to flames and pitchforks'?"

Angry screams and the pounding of fists and feet came through the steel. The rioters had reached the chamber.

Riony didn't take Kess's hand. She rolled over, reclaimed her glowing sword, and rose to her feet. "Let's get moving. That charming gathering is going to work that door out in no time and have plenty of people to keep it open."

On cue, the door lifted, and great cheer went up from the crowd on the other side. Then it slammed down again to the sounds of boos and jeers.

Kess cast her eyes about the space. It wasn't the wilds she was used to tracking in, but it wasn't hard to spot the wet and muddy trail left by Eslinde and the others.

"This way."

She took off, keeping Griskin at a pace that Riony could keep up with. The wolf didn't whine or resist traveling down the enclosed corridor. He still panted happily, tongue lolling as he ran.

Kess rubbed his ears. Her chest filled with air in a way it hadn't for a long time. She was whole again.

"What's wrong with your leg?" Riony asked, almost casually, in a huffing breath from Kess's side.

When did she notice?

"It's broken," Kess said, and when Riony gave her an expectant glance, she continued with, "It's a long story."

"I bet. Are you good? Not going to pass out? You're looking peaky."

"I'm fine. I'll manage." Kess pressed a hand to Eslinde's silvernix in her pocket.

If they had a chance to stop soon, or when they caught up to the others, she could use it and relieve all the aches and agony shooting through her. But not yet. Not until they'd seen their way clear of the danger. It wouldn't do to heal herself only to be stabbed again before they got out.

And the rumblings of the mob still chased after them.

The trail of muddy footsteps was enough to get Griskin going, but once he had the scent, Kess didn't need to watch the path or keep her eyes forward, trusting him to take them where they needed to go.

Instead, she found she couldn't keep her eyes off Riony.

How had Kess ever believed that washed-out hallucination she'd shared a cell with was real? Her morass mercy visions were a pale substitute for the vital vibrance of the real thing.

Wild red hair hung wet over her face and was twisted at the back into that same single short braid she'd always worn. Her lips turned up in a smirk as though running from a revolting horde was a good time. The purple glow of her sword lit her eyes.

Riony. There and real and alive.

If Kess was going to pass out, it was from how her heart hammered in her chest every time her eyes turned Riony's way.

More shouts and the crash of breaking furniture came from all around in halls and rooms they passed as they sped through a more modern portion of Zarram Dragonhold.

The rioters must have gotten in through the front as well.

Through the shouting, a familiar voice broke through.

"What I know will smooth everything over. It's worth enough that everyone will be back on your side."

Kess brought Griskin to a stop.

The path that Eslinde took split off, going up the stairs, but Kife's voice came from ahead.

"Is that who I think it is?" Riony said, bringing her sword up, her knuckles tightening around the hilt.

Kess eyed their two paths. "I don't think he's told anyone else about Dracuni yet, but—"

"But maybe I want to see how he feels about getting a blade in the back, regardless? I feel like it would be a good way to keep him quiet."

"For once we agree." Kess turned Griskin, taking him

at speed along the corridor.

Portraits lay knocked from the walls, frames cracked, and canvases slashed.

"Just give me one dragon. I'll take what I know to the Dragon King and then send help," Kife said.

Kess scoffed. *Sure he will.*

"I don't know what it is you think you know, boy, but Yeonard Draekhan will send aid regardless. It must be on the way already," the booming voice of Lord Zarram followed.

The hall the two men stood in was narrow, lit by one lamp still attached to the wall and another fallen and cracked on the ground, flame sputtering over a pool of spilled oil, encroaching onto a woven rug.

The glow of Riony's weapon flooded over the scene, overwhelming the small flames. Lord Zarram and Kife turned to see who approached. The light flickered over the gold trim on Lord Zarram's elegant storm-gray jacket.

Kife reached for the sword hanging from his hip below his blue-and-red dragonrider armor.

He glared from Kess to Griskin to Riony and back to Kess. "What are you doing here?"

Riony answered first. "I'd say I came all this way to kick your ass, but that'd be a lie. It's just a nice little side bonus."

Kess lifted her chin, catching Lord Zarram's eye. "Did you know this is the man who set off the etherflame who attacked the city? He sabotaged your family."

Frowning deeply, Lord Zarram's eyes moved more intentionally over Kife, assessing his face, the sword and daggers on his belt, and the crest stamped into their pommels.

He moved away from the dragonrider. "I can't trust any of you."

"You haven't even met me," Riony cried after him as he scuttled off in the other direction.

She turned to Kess. "Do I look untrustworthy to you?"

"You look like someone who should be dead," Kife spat.

"Did I ask you?"

Fuming, Kife drew his sword. The metal sang. "You've been begging me to put you in a pyre since you first plagued Heithorn estate. This time I'll make sure you stay dead."

Riony grinned. "To the death it is, then. I was going to offer you a battle of wits, but you're clearly unarmed."

Leveling his sword her way, Kife growled, "How I look forward to silencing that mouth of yours forever. Again."

The confidence in his tone concerned Kess. Faced with both of them, she thought he might run. But the corridor was too narrow for them to take him on at the same time.

Kess readjusted her seating, grimacing as her broken leg bumped Griskin's flank.

She nodded to Riony. "I'll let you rough him up first if I can finish him off."

Riony's eyebrows went up and she cooed, "That might be the nicest thing you've ever said to me."

The slice of Kife's sword ended the conversation. Riony brought hers up to counter just in time. The clash of metal meeting crystal burst around them.

She swiped his blade to the right, taking the chance to jab him in the ribs with her left fist.

"Careful," Kess hissed, barely a whisper.

Riony left herself open with that punch, and Kife's sword slid down the length of the crystal blade as he pulled back and thrust into the gap. The lightning-fast lunge seemed clear to hit, and Kess held her breath.

But Riony readjusted just as fast, parrying with the long unicorn horn-shaped pommel of her Alderkin weapon.

Kess watched as the parry, thrust, parry of the fight picked up, and her smile grew. Had Riony actually learned how to use a sword?

Catching Kife's latest lunge in her cross guard, Riony also caught Kife's face with her fist, splitting the skin under his eye.

The knock back put Kife against the wall. He bumped into a hall table, and the vase on it fell and smashed.

Kife spat blood. "Don't look so cocky, slave. I survived a one-on-one with you before. I'm sure I'll win this time."

Riony twirled her massive sword once and moved into

an elegant fighting stance. "That was before I had sword training from Elundrae's hottest grayglim."

Kess's smile faded a little.

Beneath her hands, Griskin's skin twitched. It had been so long without feeling those sensations beneath her fingertips that Kess almost missed it, almost forgot what it meant.

Griskin sensing something, far earlier than Kess could.

Griskin sensing trouble.

Kess strained to hear, and faintly over the clash of the swordfight, there it was.

Footsteps, and a lot of them, coming their way.

She pulled one of the fine, sharp knives Eslinde had gifted her from her sleeve. "Enough, Riony. We need to finish this."

"Just ... one ... more ..." Riony punched Kife three times in the stomach as she held him pinned to the wall.

There was a cracking sound with the fourth. "That was for bleeding Dracuni."

Griskin growled. The footsteps were clear now. Flames flickered from the end of the hall.

They were going to get cut off from Eslinde and the others if they didn't leave now.

Kife slumped in Riony's grip, and she had a wild, feral sneer on her face. She pulled him back up to her level and got the edge of her sword against his neck.

"And this is for stabbing me in the back and framing your sister for it."

"Enough!" Kess couldn't get a clear angle on Kife with Riony in the way, and she wasn't throwing a blade anywhere near her direction. Never again.

Riony spun around, angry at first, but then her expression cleared. Then she looked over Kess's shoulder.

"Oh sparks. Go, do it!"

Riony dropped Kife and broke into a run back the way they'd come.

Kife fell slumped and groaning against the wall. Kess's eyes narrowed, and she breathed to steady her shot.

But then Griskin was moving beneath her.

"Wait!" she growled.

He grumbled a growl back, turning them both around and bounding down the corridor after Riony.

Oh no. The rioters were far closer than Kess had thought. Middling noblemen wearing strips of yellow cloth around their arms were led by Sunblessed Monks, chanting in the name of Ulfren, their lost leader.

The stairs Eslinde and the others had taken were in the middle of the corridor, and both groups raced headlong at each other from each end.

Kess judged the distance. She knew how fast Griskin was, relishing in the speed as they broke ahead of Riony.

They could make it there first.

Riony's heavy steps thumped, falling behind. Her breathing, already labored from the swordfight, came thick and fast.

We can make it. But she can't.

Kess cursed. Pushing her hands into Griskin's fur and twisting her torso, she skidded him to a halt, pivoting him around.

"Back the other way, quick!"

"We can ... Nope, we can't!" Riony yelled, turning herself as well.

The mob passed the stairs, blocking their access to it entirely and continuing to charge.

Kife had just gotten himself halfway to sitting upright when they barreled back his way. He curled up in a fetal position. Griskin growled as he leaped over the top, and Riony hit him with a glancing kick on her way.

Hopefully the mob will finish him off. Not nearly as satisfying, but still a job done.

Kess and Riony were herded forward, keeping just out of reach of the rioters. They hit some steps, slick with water flooding in, and hurried down. Kess recognized where they were now. She recognized the older, rough-hewn stonework and musty scent.

They were heading into a dead end.

TWENTY-EIGHT

Griskin's paws splashed down the muddy steps toward the old flamesong stalls. The rough descent jarred Kess's broken leg and she gritted her teeth. Water pooled and flowed down the stairs, trickling in from holes in the old stone walls.

Kess whipped her head around, checking if there was a chance for them to still turn back before being cut off down there, but the first few rioters were already there, blocking the way.

"Raze it," Kess hissed. "We might end up having to fight our way out of here. There's no other way through."

Riony hit the bottom of the stairs first, frowning as she took in the short hallway and the end in sight. There were eight dragon stalls down there in total, some with doors open, but one important one still had its door closed.

Eslinde's dragon raged from within.

Riony turned again to face up the stairwell. "Sorry I spent too long punching your brother. But also not sorry."

Kess swung Griskin around to meet their fate.

The very act of the two young women—one with a very large, glowing sword, and one with a wolf—turning around to face the rioters, made their pursuers hesitate at the top of the stairs.

"I'm sorry," Kess replied. "That you had to come here and get caught up in this. And for before that."

Riony brought her sword up, pointing it threateningly at the growing mob. "You're going to have to be more specific."

"For everything." Kess turned and held Riony's gaze. "Everything."

Riony frowned as though she couldn't comprehend at all what Kess was saying.

"Heir Killer!" a haughty woman cried down the steps.

Riony raised her eyebrows. She pointed to herself, then Kess, mouthing, "Me or ...?"

The first few brave souls charged down the steps toward them, the others hanging back.

"Hey." Riony turned to Kess and winked. "Check this out."

Riony brought one hand off the hilt of her sword and traced it over a carving on the crystal blade.

The cool purple glow flared, bursting brighter in hues of vivid magenta. Pink-and-red-tinted flames rushed up the blade, crackling and swirling.

"Lyrrin worked out an upgrade for me."

The few rioters rushing down the steps halted in their tracks. One slipped, skidding a couple of steps down through the water, then hastily clambering back up again. There were additional gasps and rumbles of muttering from the mob, and although edging closer, they remained wary of the burning blade.

The heat from the weapon radiated out, warming Kess's cheeks that felt too cold from a rush of dizzying pain.

"You couldn't have done that before?" she asked.

Riony whispered back, "This is kind of designed for revs. I don't actually want to burn real living people, and I didn't know you were leading us into a dead end!"

"Add it onto my debt. Think you can scare these idiots off?"

Riony shrugged, then took a couple of steps up the stairs, swinging the flaming sword in front of her. The rioters at the front of the crowd cringed backward, but there were too many people behind them who couldn't directly see the blazing carnage coming their way for the path to clear.

"For Ulfren!" a man bellowed in a deep voice, and a flash of silver flew through the air.

Riony shielded herself behind the thick width of her blade, and there was a soft clink as the dagger glanced off, followed by a wet thunk and string of increasingly more obscene curse words.

A dagger had wedged itself into Riony's inner elbow.

Her flaming sword lowered as she kept ahold of it with her injured side and reached for the hilt with the other hand.

"Don't pull it out!" Kess snapped.

Riony grimaced. "You think I want to leave it like that as a souvenir?"

"That's going to bleed, and a lot, the moment there's nothing wedged in there."

Even with the blade stuck into the flesh, blood swelled around the wound with every small motion, running thick over Riony's sienna skin.

Riony pouted at the jutting hilt but retracted her hand without touching it.

"I will make them bleed in return." Kess rifled through Griskin's bags, sighing when she found a supply of bone daggers. Five, without a more thorough search she doubted she'd be allowed time for.

Riony got her sword back into her good hand and stepped clear of Kess's aim. "Aw, are you jealous somebody else got a knife in me?"

Kess sent the knives flying, one after another, a hailstorm of pointed bone. One, two, three, four, five rioters fell, screaming and clutching their wounds.

It wasn't enough to dissuade the others to give up though.

Having drawn Riony's blood, the crowd at the top of the stairs surged and grew bolder.

Kess's own stomach surged seeing the red staining Riony's skin. The blood dripped down onto the sodden ground.

Kess narrowed her eyes at the rioters and the stairs, all soaked from the storm.

"Listen. I have a plan to get out of here. But it's risky. Reckless even."

"I love it. Let's do it."

"I haven't even told you what it is!"

Riony shrugged. "As long as it gets us out of here, I'm open to anything."

The front line of the mob pressed forward again. Kess nodded and eyed the surroundings, calculating whether they had any chance at all. She considered the thickness of the rope and pulley and weight attached. The one small dry patch of shelter.

Their chances were low.

"Get up into that niche." Kess pointed to the carved-out section of wall where a torch flickered.

"Okay?" Riony deactivated the magic on her sword that made it flame, returning it to its cool purple glow, then lightly jumped up into the narrow space.

She hung out over the edge while she pulled the torch from its sconce and threw it away so she could fit in without burning herself.

Kess prepared Griskin to follow. "And make room for us."

Riony's forehead wrinkled, but she pressed herself as far into the gap as she could.

Griskin leaped, back paws scrambling against the wall beneath the niche as he tried to fit onto the too-small ledge before he found his balance. The three of them pressed together on the small shelf, barely covered by the wall on each side. Riony had to duck to avoid her head hitting the arched top.

The mob approached, still cautious, but without the flaming sword blocking them they edged closer.

Kess drew one of the fine blades Eslinde had gifted her. She lined up her shot.

Riony's voice was close to Kess's ear. "I sure hope that's some kind of secret magical weapon that fells a hundred foes with one blow, but you know you're not even pointing the right direction, yeah?"

The knife flew through the air, nicking the rope beside

the closed gate, but not severing it.

Kess only grunted.

Riony's eyes followed where the knife went and then in a slow voice asked, "Kess, what's behind that door?"

Drawing her final remaining weapon, Kess exhaled slowly. She had to cut the rope with this shot. But the rope was thick, and the angle from where they sheltered in the niche was bad.

Still, she threw. The rope split, frayed. But held strong.

"No!" Kess grunted. "I'm out of knives."

She searched hastily through another of the saddlebags but nothing came up. The mob was growing bolder and was almost on them.

"Umm. We have one more." Riony held out her arm, the dagger stuck in it on display.

Kess's heart clenched. She didn't want to see Riony hurt. But she had silvernix. As long as they could get somewhere safe and Riony didn't bleed too fast, it might be okay.

She nodded once, lips thin.

Riony yanked out the blade. A spray of arterial scarlet followed, and Riony folded her arm, pressing the wound closed. Still, blood flowed far too fast.

Riony groaned, "Make it count."

Kess took the warm blade from her. Her heart hammered. "The angle isn't good. I need to be farther out."

She tried to lean out from her saddle, but almost slipped off Griskin's back entirely, and then he almost slipped off the shelf of the niche.

Riony grasped Kess's free arm with hers, each clasping the other's wrist. Riony whimpered as she used her wounded arm to hold the empty torch sconce to steady them both, and Kess winced as Riony squeezed her sprained wrist.

But it steadied Kess, and she leaned out at an almost horizontal angle.

That was it. A clear line of sight. She stared from the blood on the blade to the frayed rope and ignored her pain and the angry mob at her back and threw.

The blade slipped through the last strands of the rope. The counterweight fell, the gate rose up, and the bright, furious eyes of Eslinde's snowshimmer glittered from the dark space within.

"Pull me back in!" Kess gasped.

Riony did, and they pressed against each other, chest to chest in the small space, eyes wide and drawing fast breaths as an earthshaking roar filled the stairwell.

Blue-white lightning streaked through the air.

The dragon's attack lanced out, hitting a burly man at the front of the assault. The crackling energy dropped him and then leaped across the wet ground, arcing to the people beside him. It shimmered over their soaked clothing, their bodies tensing, jerking, then falling as well.

The effect rippled out and up the stairs and scores of twitching rioters fell to the ground.

Riony's words breathed over Kess's ear. "Sparks. That's what you were planning? You weren't playing around."

There was a mad scramble of remaining bodies and their screams almost overwhelmed the dragon's next booming roar.

"That was the first half of the plan. The second half is praying we don't get eaten."

Griskin whined. Kess reached back and tucked his tail into the niche to make sure as much of them as possible was hidden in the crammed space.

Eslinde's dragon emerged from its cell. Cautious at first, head swinging side to side, eyes taking in everything. It sniffed the air, then broke into a run. Its claws scraped and stomped over the paved floor, building speed as it reached the stairs.

When its head was level with the niche hiding space, the dragon loosed another bolt of lightning. Kess flinched back, pressing her cheek to Riony's shoulder.

More screams followed. A cacophony of footsteps and crashes reverberated down as people scattered, and the dragon gave chase. Its barbed tail flicked by, glancing over Kess's leg like the brush of wind, and then it was gone.

Kess leaned back as far from Riony as she could, a hot

flush over her cheeks. "Come on. Let's try to get out of here before our luck runs out."

Riony flicked the acorn at Kess's neck and said, "I'm feeling lucky."

She pushed past and jumped down first. Her sword glowed in one hand and she kept her bleeding arm folded and close to her chest.

Kess urged Griskin to follow. Once out of the niche, they moved into a sprint up the stairs.

The acrid, fatty smell of smoking bodies made Kess screw up her nose. Most of them still groaned and twitched, stunned but alive. Only the burly man who led the charge and got hit directly seemed far too charred to have survived.

Griskin understood their path, and Kess turned back to check on Riony. Despite keeping her arm folded, blood streamed from her elbow and her face was turning ashy.

"Not much farther!" Kess called.

Hopefully they'd find Eslinde on the flight deck, and her grayglim could protect them while they saw to Riony's wound. Kess checked her pocket again, the silvernix still there. She blinked pain-bleary eyes.

Riony stumbled over the top step onto the flight deck, and Kess and Griskin bounded ahead.

There were a handful of rioters who had made it there, piling up anything flammable they could find onto a

growing bonfire. Kess launched Griskin at them, scattering them with a growl.

Then she passed an empty stall and her heart sank. Viska was gone. Eslinde and the others were already gone.

"We're too late." She snorted a breath.

Riony leaned against the entrance of a stall, her chest heaving and eyelids drooping. "Sorry. Kind of felt like the faster I ran, the more blood squirted out of me."

The blood covered Riony's armor in a crimson flush and dripped from her clothes. Her gaze was unfocused.

Kess chewed her lip and looked around her for options, feeling pain blurred and heavy with disappointment and worry. All she could think was she had to get Riony to safety.

"It's okay. We're still getting out of here. We'll take a dragon," Kess said.

Riony ambled closer in an uneven stumble. She pointed with her sword. "Snowflame? They're fast, right?"

It was a pretty beast with ice-blue scales and gold-tipped wings and horns.

Kess raised her eyebrows. "Yes. They are. I'm surprised you know that. I thought you didn't care about dragons."

"I just remembered it was the one kind of dragon you didn't want to own, and I've got to get my digs in somewhere."

Kess huffed a laugh but turned Griskin toward the snowflame. It was already saddled with a small single saddle. The snowshimmer/etherflame hybrid was medium-sized but should carry them all. As long as Kess could command it.

Moving closer, Griskin whimpered.

Kess rubbed his ears. "Don't worry, boy. No claws for you anymore."

She maneuvered Griskin toward the back of the stall and had him run up the dragon's lowered tail and to its shoulders. Griskin's claws skidded on the scales, but he managed to balance there. Kess lowered him down onto his belly across the saddle.

"Get on behind him," Kess called down to Riony as she slipped off Griskin and onto the dragon's neck in front of the saddle.

She groaned as she slid her legs down and she leaned forward to catch her breath.

The brightening of the purple glow announced Riony had joined her. "Are you okay there?"

Kess nodded. She looked around from their perch and for a moment, there was peace. All the screaming was at least muted and distant, for now.

She reached into her pocket and blinked heavy eyelids. "Let's get you fixed up before we move. The princess gave me silvernix."

Riony shuffled in her seat behind Griskin and the saddle, her head wobbling. "I think maybe I have lost a lot of blood because I thought you just said a princess gave you silvernix."

Kess held it up, fingers fumbling as she worked to unscrew the earring vial.

"Hold on a second." Riony leaned out of Kess's reach. "If anyone is using it, it's you. You look like you're about to pass out, and I don't want that to happen while we're airborne. I have no idea how to fly a dragon."

"And you look like you're going to bleed out, and I need you to hold Griskin in place. I'm not losing either of you again."

"I'm fine," Riony protested, and then she slumped forward, armor clattering. Her chest flopped over Griskin's back and head bumped into Kess. Then she shot back upright again.

"I'm *fine*," she repeated more firmly.

"Fine," Kess sneered back. "Just hold on to Griskin for me as best you can."

She held up her own hand and made a show of tipping the silvernix toward it.

Riony smirked and nodded a lolling head. She reached one arm over Griskin's shoulder.

Kess let the drop of silvernix fall into her own palm.

And then lashing out, she grasped Riony's outstretched hand in hers.

Riony jerked back, but Kess held tight, and the opalescent fluid pressed between them.

Light sparkled out between where their hands met, and then with a flush of moonlight glow, the illumination washed outward, engulfing them both entirely.

Kess cried out as the magic churned and worked on the broken and cracked bones beneath her flesh. Riony's jaw tightened, and her eyes remained locked on Kess's face, but she didn't make a sound.

It was a gamble, trusting there was enough silvernix in the dose to heal them both.

But as the light cleared, Kess sighed in relief at the absence of pain. Riony shook out her injured arm, still slick with blood, but no longer flowing freely.

Shaking her head, Riony pulled her hand free from Kess's.

"You're such a sneaky pain in the ass, Kessara."

"You're welcome, *Riony*."

Kess only got a glimpse at the reddened, dumbstruck look on the woman's face as she turned around. A thrum of nervous delight filled Kess at the thought of surprising Riony again. She could imagine the expectations Riony had for her, and she planned on shattering them all.

All the relentless determination she'd put into getting a dragon of her own, all the grit and single-mindedness she'd put into hunting Dracuni, were all turned now toward a new goal.

Repaying an impossible debt.

Kess's heart beat firm and steady as she leaned forward and pressed her hands onto the dragon's neck.

The snowflame reacted instantly, standing up and moving forward in a slow stroll. Out of the narrow stall, Kess leaned and adjusted, testing the motions.

"You've got this, right?" Riony asked nervously.

Kess grinned to herself and pushed the dragon into a run.

It galloped up the cavernous space toward the open flight deck. Screams and gurgling cries followed them, closer now.

They were at the edge when Kess glanced back.

Dashiel and Vance's father, Lord Zarram, ran up the length of the room, panting and stumbling. A horde of rioters followed at his heels.

Kess swore, trying to adjust, but the dragon's talons were already over the drop and into open air.

The change in Kess's motions left the dragon confused, and for a moment they dropped.

"Kess?" Riony yelled in an increasingly higher pitch.

Kess refocused. The dragon's wings snapped out, pumping at the air around them. They lifted, shooting forward into the darkening night.

Kess turned the dragon, taking it back to pass in front of the flight deck exit. She could no longer see Lord Zarram. Only a messy swarm of raging rioters.

Too late to go back.

The storm had eased. An odd flash of lightning brightened the blanket of clouds above them, but the rain had stopped, and Kess brought the snowflame high above the city, hovering there for a moment as she caught her breath.

From the back exit of the dragonhold, Eslinde's dragon burst into the sky with a roar and soared out toward the ocean.

And beneath them, Zarram Dragonhold burned.

TWENTY-NINE

Kess circled once, twice, her breath held as she tried to decide their heading, tried to spot any sign of where Eslinde had gone. The dark sky and city below were clear and sparkling, washed clean from the storm. Only a couple of other dragons flew since the rain had stopped. But they mostly moved around near the palace, on guard after the trouble of the day.

"What are we looking for?" Riony asked.

"A golden dragon, five-to-seven passengers." Kess hadn't seen Vance or Dashiel anywhere in the chaos of the dragon-hold. She hoped they'd gotten clear. With Viska gone, she assumed at least one of them did. She hoped they both did.

Riony sheathed her sword over her shoulder and pulled a

palm-sized crystal from a belt pouch. Invoking the Alderkin magic, the milky crystal turned glass-clear, and Riony held it up to her eye.

"There." Riony pointed southwest.

Kess narrowed her eyes at the gloomy horizon. Far in the distance, under a burst of storm-light, golden scales glittered—Viska, and another dragon, speeding away.

Kess's heart raced in turn. She adjusted her position on the dragon's neck and pushed it into pursuit.

She took it gently at first, getting a feel for the control and speed. Dashiel had taught her so much on their flight together, but this was a different dragon. And their seating was precarious.

Kess was wedged in between the dragon's neck and saddle. She wasn't tied on at all, and even the slow turn left her worried she was going to slip right off. Griskin's fur was warm at her back, and she could feel the tension in his soft whines. Behind them, Riony was off the saddle as well, hanging on to the straps with one hand and Griskin with the other.

Once Kess had the dragon pointed in the right heading, she pushed it faster.

"All good back there?" she called over her shoulder.

"Yeah." Riony's voice was muted by the rushing wind and a thickness of some emotion. "Sparks. I think I might

get why you were obsessed with this."

Kess's chest rose and fell with a soul-filling breath, and she pushed the dragon faster again.

If Viska was going full speed, she doubted they'd catch up. But the others didn't seem to be moving too fast, whether due to the second dragon's abilities or the passengers. The sleek and smaller snowflame gained on them.

Out past the dragonkeep walls, the sky cleared. A bright moon shone down between clouds onto the plains below, turning them patchwork with light and dark.

A gust of wind buffeted them from the side, and Kess slipped from her seat. But a hand grasped the damp clothing at her back and held her in place.

As they came up behind the two dragons, the moment they were spotted was clear. Viska maneuvered abruptly, twisting away from their flight path and circling out and around, coming up behind the snowflame so fast that if Kess had been an enemy, she suspected they'd have been burned from the sky before she could blink.

She was proud she could keep a dragon in the air and on target at all. Could she ever dare to dream again of becoming a dragonrider with that sort of prowess, after all her misplaced ambitions?

Whether the rider recognized the Zarram dragon, or Kess herself, their fiery end didn't eventuate. Instead, Viska

came up alongside them, flanking wingtip to wingtip.

The second, orange dragon slowed and leveled out with them on the other side.

They were close enough that faces became clear in the moonlight. Kess waved, filled with relief.

On Viska, Vance, Eslinde, and the grayglim signaled back with varying levels of enthusiasm. On the second dragon rode Dashiel and the three Alderkin. They'd made it. All of them.

"These are your friends?" Riony called into Kess's ear.

"Yeah. They are." The words warmed Kess as she said them.

People who had been kind to Kess, who offered her respect and friendship, even when she had no wealth or dragons or anything to her name. People she was proud to call friends.

Kess had only ever studied dragonrider technique in books, and it had been years ago. She did her best to make the correct hand motions to indicate the others should follow them. Vance and Dashiel each replied with a sideways pump of a fisted hand, affirmative, and Kess began bringing her dragon out of the sky.

Blessed sun, I hope I can land this thing.

"If we're heading down, I want to be near a shrine," Riony yelled. "Kind of still want an escape plan. No offense."

"Okay, let me find one." Kess slowed the dragon, gliding

over the dark ground below, getting her bearings. From the mapping and tracking she'd done with Kife, she was fairly sure there was a shrine just over the low hills ahead.

"Really? No argument?" Riony asked.

"Really."

They came closer, and within a valley of twisted trees, a ring of standing stones glowed in a shaft of moonlight. There was no settlement around it, and the shrine building within the center was almost entirely collapsed, exposing the crystal ring standing within the crumbled walls.

"Is that one any good?" Kess asked.

"Yeah, it's activated," Riony confirmed.

It wasn't one that had been working before when Kess chased them across the land, and it was a fair way on foot from where most of those ones had been. Riony and the others had been busy.

"Time to see whether I can land."

"Sorry, WHAT?"

Kess already had the dragon at a slow glide. In theory, she just had to slow it down more, angle it right, and get it in the correct landing position. All things Dashiel hadn't covered on their flight together.

There was a clearing around the shrine, and Kess aimed for it. Despite pulling the dragon back slower, and slower again, the ground came up fast toward them.

The hand at her back appeared again, clenching into what fabric there was left of Kess's dress.

Leather wings clapped as they filled with air. The sound punched into Kess's eardrums, then they hit the ground. The dragon skidded, falling forward onto its chest, and Kess bounced from her seat, hanging beside the dragon's shoulder by Riony's hand.

They came to a stop with a final bump. Cloth ripped, and Kess slipped down and landed on her back.

Staring up at the sky and the two other dragons elegantly coming in to land, Kess laughed.

Griskin let out a ruff and jumped down beside her, licking her cheeks. She wrapped her arms around his neck and let relief fill her to every tingling extremity.

Riony climbed down from the snowflame, groaning as she got her feet on the ground. "Sorry, I didn't mean to drop you. Although if I knew you'd find it that funny, maybe I would have done it on purpose."

Kess wiped her face, still chuckling. "I'm just happy to be alive. That we're all alive."

Riony eyed the descending dragons. "And who are these special people we risked our lives to catch up to?"

Kess's laughter faded, overtaken by nerves. She hadn't wanted to tell Riony before who they were following. Whether she'd said Lyrrin's mother or a first heir or escaping

Alderkin, it was all too complicated to have dealt with in the moment.

But that moment was upon her now.

"You'll see." She climbed up into Griskin's saddle and waited.

As Viska and the orange dragon landed in a soft rush of air around them, Riony's face twitched, and she moved to put her back to the gateway crystal. Reaching to her belt, Riony swiped her finger over a stone in a netted bag there. It illuminated the clearing in a bright glow of cyan light.

Dashiel was the first off their dragon. They ran for Kess, then hesitated at the looming wolf beneath her.

"He's safe," Kess said.

Dashiel raised their eyebrows, but still moved closer and wrapped her in a hug. "I thought we'd lost you. I'm so sorry we left, and you ... you took the blame for me, and ... Raze it, Kess."

They squeezed her harder.

Kess raised timid arms to hold them in return. "I'm sorry, Dashiel. Your father ..."

She explained in a rushed whisper what they'd seen as they left. "The mob, they were there for me, because they thought I was the Heir Killer. If it weren't for me ..."

Dashiel shook their head. Their voice was thick. "No. That's not the only reason. Those people had been waiting for any excuse to destroy us."

"I'm still sorry."

Pulling away, Dashiel's eyes were red, and they gave Kess a small nod before turning toward their brother. The siblings moved to the side together, speaking low and holding each other. Shiff was also there with them, Kess was happy to see, and the young dragon curled at Dashiel's feet.

Eslinde approached Kess next as though she were going to rush in for an embrace as well, but then her eyes locked on Riony.

And Riony's in turn were stuck to Eslinde.

Eslinde's eyes flickered briefly to Kess and over Griskin. "How? What happened?"

Kess patted her wolf, but her eyes were also on Riony. "They came to find me."

Eslinde nodded, her head tilted and expression softening.

"It's her," Riony said, as though to herself. She'd gone pale again like she'd been when losing blood.

"You recognize me?" Eslinde ran her hands nervously over her damp dress, the silver fabric darkened with mud. Her moonlight hair hung loose, wispy as it dried.

Riony rubbed the back of her head, a soft color over her cheeks. "The person I stole a baby from? Yeah, you kind of made a lasting impression."

Eslinde's back straightened. Yensen stood on guard

beside her shoulder, and the three Alderkin were behind him, shadowed by cloaks and ominous. Vance and Dashiel simply exchanged matching nonplussed looks.

Riony took a step back and held both hands out in a calming gesture. "Also, really sorry about that, by the way. I can explain ..."

"No need. I understand. I know what happened. Although I hope to hear it in your words one day, too. But now, please tell me, is Lyrrin safe?"

Riony shot Kess a look as the girl's name emerged from Eslinde's lips.

"How much did you tell them?" Riony snapped in a whisper.

Kess gave her head the smallest shake. "Only what she deserved to know, about her daughter."

Riony flinched but nodded.

Eslinde moved closer, her voice strained. "Tell me, please, is she safe?"

Giving the woman a long assessing look, Riony sighed. "She was, as of a few days ago when I last checked in."

"Checked in?" Kess asked.

"It's not like I was going to abandon them all for the entire time I was chasing a wolf across Elundrae. We have a system. The others let a trusted friend know where they are, in code, whenever they moved locations. So anytime

me and Griskin were near a shrine, I could go back and find them. Make sure everything was okay."

Eslinde pressed her hands to her chest. "And where is Lyrrin now? Can we go to her?"

"Whoa. Hold on. Beyond being the woman who gave birth to Lyrrin, I don't even know you, let alone trust you." Riony made a point of looking over the seven figures standing across from her in the clearing.

Frustration flashed over Eslinde, but she pulled her lips in and said, "Introductions, then."

Kess couldn't understand exactly how the two women before her felt. A mother who had missed the first eight years of her daughter's life, faced with the person who had been there for all those moments. And the person who raised the child as family, faced with the person who could claim a bond of blood.

But she knew emotions would be high.

She moved Griskin in between them and spoke in a slow, careful tone. "Riony, this is Eslinde. Eslinde the First."

"Oh." Riony grasped both sides of her head with her hands. "Oh shit."

She took another step back as though ready to activate the magical gateway and flee.

Eslinde mirrored Riony's earlier gesture, palms forward. "Please. I only want to meet my daughter and have no intention of harming you or any of the people who kept her safe."

"What about Lyrrin?" Riony stilled, and her expression grew dark. "How do I know you aren't planning on getting rid of her, to finish what your mother started when she ordered the baby, me, and my amma murdered."

"I wouldn't. Please tell her I wouldn't." Eslinde turned to Kess, expression pained and pleading.

Kess shrugged. "If you think she trusts me any better, you're out of luck."

"Yeah, I'm afraid you're going to need something more than the word of this traitorous goblin."

Eslinde glanced behind her, then gave Riony a long, hard look. Her silver eyes glittered in the cyan light.

"You can trust I mean my daughter no harm because I know exactly who she is. And why she was born different." She beckoned to the three cloaked figures.

They stepped forward and, at her urging, drew back their hoods.

Riony let out a rush of air. "That's … something alright."

Her eyes roamed over their bright-blue and green hair, vibrant eyes, and long clawed hands. Especially the hands.

The Alderkin each stared at her in return, at the glowing stone on her belt, and the hilt of the crystal sword showing over her shoulder, faces equally questioning.

"These are Alderkin," Eslinde said softly. "As was Lyrrin's father."

Her eyelashes fluttered as she glanced with flickering brevity across to the Zarram siblings. Vance frowned, but there was a softness of compassion in his eyes.

"Alderkin," Riony breathed the word. "Sparks. It makes sense, but also ... how?"

"That's a far longer story, for later." Eslinde drew up straight. "Now, I have trusted you with the biggest secret in all of Elundrae."

"Yeah. Biggest. Sure." Riony choked.

"And also my own greatest secret. I have extended that trust to you, midwife daughter. And all I ask in return is to see my child who I believed dead, whom I mourned and missed every day."

Riony dragged her attention away from the Alderkin.

She swallowed visibly as she frowned at Eslinde. "Okay. Maybe I could take you, you alone, to go and meet her. No grayglims or dragonriders."

Her eyes narrowed on Yensen, Vance, and Dashiel as she spat the terms.

Vance moved up beside Eslinde, but Yensen spoke first. "Eslinde isn't going anywhere with you alone."

The princess tsked, but Vance gave her a quelling look.

"I am free of the palace and my parents but still you

restrict me? I only want to meet my daughter! Why must you all make this difficult?"

Riony shrugged. "Sorry, princess. Let's tally up how many times we've each been literally stabbed in the back and maybe it will explain the trust issues. But ..."

Eslinde's shoulders slumped, her mouth opened as she waited on Riony to finish her thought.

Riony's shoulders lowered as well. "But this isn't really my decision to make. It should be Lyrrin's."

The two women stared at each other in silence for a long moment as owlettes hooted from the surrounding trees.

"I'll go and tell her you're here. Then the rest is up to her." Riony turned away.

Eslinde cried, "How long? How long will you be?"

"Shouldn't be long at all." Riony bent down to the base of the geode ring, then rose back up as the symbols all around the edge lit up.

Gasps came from the Alderkin, and they muttered between themselves. Kess only caught a few fragments.

"How does she know ...?"

"Shouldn't be possible ..."

Kess's eyes remained on Riony as she stepped toward the glowing magic.

There were so many more symbols illuminated now than Kess had last seen. Almost all of them.

Riony tapped the one Kess recognized as the settlement near the glass factory.

Without saying anything else, Riony stepped through, and the gateway closed behind her, taking the light and all the air in the world with her.

Kess's chest ached. She wanted to have gone with Riony, stayed by her side, never left her side again. But if Riony had wanted that too, she'd have invited her.

If she didn't intend on returning, would she have said goodbye?

Without the cyan glow of light, the night was so much darker. Kess shivered and leaned into Griskin. Somewhere in his packs there would be a spare shirt she could replace the remains of her gown with, but for now, Kess only wanted the warmth of Griskin's fur.

"I missed you so much," she whispered.

He groaned a low whine in reply.

Eslinde appeared at their side, ghostly in the moonlight. She approached confidently, but when Griskin sniffed at her, she stopped and took a step back.

Looking to the geode, she asked, "Can we trust her? Will she do as she says?"

With all the revelations just dumped upon Riony, she may decide it was safer to take her adoptive sister and flee Elundrae entirely. Especially with Dracuni in the mix.

Kess wasn't sure what she'd do if the gateway didn't open and bring Riony back to her.

But even the one time Riony had tricked her and left her for dead, hanging from a cliff over a monstrous mass of revs, she'd returned.

"I trust her. I don't know if she'll come back. But I hope so."

A soft smile played out over Eslinde's lips. "I can see why you like her."

Kess scowled in return. "It isn't some childish crush. I owe her my life. I owe her repayment for years of blood and torture and cruelty. I owe her a debt so large I could spend my lifetime giving my body, heart, and soul to make amends and not come close to being what she deserves."

Eslinde's eyes glittered. "But it is clear you're ready to try."

Looking at the unlit gateway geode, Kess prayed to the blessed sun that Riony would give her that chance.

Eslinde moved closer, reached for Kess's hand, and squeezed it in hers. "Thank you, Kessara, for getting me this close, so close, to fulfilling dreams I'd thought long dead."

With a final, melancholy smile, the princess left and joined the Zarram siblings. No doubt they'd have questions for her. The Alderkin kept to themselves in a small huddle, gathering crystal shards from the broken shrine and strappy weeds, and seemed to be using both in some kind of ritual on the injured Priyune.

And Kess settled in on Griskin, facing the gateway, and waited.

After a while, Eslinde paced, then fumed, arguing with Yensen and blaming him for losing her only chance at meeting Lyrrin as he worked on a small fire to keep them warm.

Kess remained apart from the others. Her fingers shook and grew cold. Griskin's fur had dried and was warm beneath her, and although the few twisted trees around the standing stones were naked of leaves for winter's approach, it wasn't the chilled air that affected Kess.

It was the worry that Riony wouldn't come back, but also, if she did, what was going to happen next between them. What Kess had planned.

But Kess had waited for what she wanted before.

It was hard to tell how much time passed. The moon and stars hadn't moved much overhead but it seemed like an eternity.

Then the gateway shimmered into life, and Kess sprang upright in her saddle.

Cyan light rippled over the magical surface, and Riony stepped through, brightening the area.

And from behind her, hiding near her hip, a smaller body followed.

"Lyrrin?" Eslinde ran forward, stopping a respectful distance away. She covered her mouth with both hands.

"That's her," Riony said softly, a hand on Lyrrin's shoulder. "That's your amma."

The girl stepped out from Riony's shadow, lifting her face. She had her own glowing stone and a range of other crystals along her belt. Her hood was off, showing a strip of blue along the roots of her hair, and no gloves over her hands.

The Alderkin approached then too, Yrik falling to his knees and Priyune and Shael crying and smiling into each other's shoulders. Lyrrin's eyes went round as the full moon when she saw them.

And then the gateway rippled again.

Yensen tensed as more bodies followed.

Aishena stepped through, her face grim and her hands on the crystal daggers sheathed at her belt. Her hair was roughly cropped at the chin and darkened with dye. Then Niskina, almost as heavily armored as Riony, her expression firm but eyes bright with emotion. And Benjin, holding a glowing staff and standing a foot taller since the last time Kess had seen him.

But larger again was the final shape pushing through the magical space. Dracuni's head emerged, high off the ground and large like a horse's. Her singular golden horn had grown long and sharp like a blade, and as the rest of

her body followed between the sharp ring of crystal, she had to push and shimmy to squeeze through.

"You didn't say they had a dragon," Yensen hissed to Kess.

"I didn't think they'd bring her," Kess shot over to Riony with a concerned look.

Riony flinched and shrugged. "Everybody wanted to come. And does it look like I can stop her doing what she wants to do now?"

From farther to the side, Dashiel murmured, "She's not tamed?"

"No, but she'll stay friendly as long as you and your dragons stay friendly," Riony replied.

The Alderkin watched the unidragon as well, with an intensity to their bright eyes that made Kess worry.

Dracuni snorted, an almost embarrassed look in her lilac eyes as her back hips got stuck, then she finally popped the rest of the way through the crystal ring.

Then her attention shot straight to Shiff and the other dragons. The larger three, all tamed, made no response. But Shiff perked up immediately.

Riony tilted her head. "Looks like you've got a little untamed one too."

Dashiel crouched down and stroked the forehead of the pale-blue and muted-purple dragonling. "She wants to meet your dragon, closer up. Is that okay?"

"You can hear her?" Riony grinned and jabbed a finger in the air toward Dashiel. "Oh, we are having a chat later."

Dracuni was clearly communicating with Riony as well, and she nodded the go-ahead for the two young dragons to meet.

Shiff was half Dracuni's size, but far bolder. They edged closer, and Riony's jaw was tight with tension, until each young dragon trilled happily.

Eslinde stood still and patient across the clearing, her eyes never having left her daughter.

Riony sighed, then with a gently push to Lyrrin's shoulder's, she whispered, "Go on."

As Lyrrin took a couple of hesitant steps forward, the princess knelt to the ground, her muddy-hemmed gown pooling around her. She outstretched her hands, then took no further action, waiting for Lyrrin.

The girl moved slowly but finally lifted her own hands and placed them in her mother's. The long blue nails were quickly engulfed in the woman's embracing fingers and Eslinde beamed, tears trickling down her cheeks.

Mother and daughter spoke to each other in low, cautious voices, and a smile grew on Lyrrin's face as well.

Riony watched, chest rising and falling in heavy breaths. Then she turned away with an expression of a multitude of emotions. One that sought comfort. And she turned straight to Aishena.

The two of them clasped hands together, tight between their chests, and Riony leaned in, pressing her forehead to Aishena's. They whispered softly to each other, and there, on the Hjelzahn girl's forearm, Kess saw a tattoo. Four rings. Two swords. One candle.

Matching to Riony's.

Oh. Kess's heart shuddered weirdly.

As long as she's happy. All that matters is that she's happy.

Kess waited for the tender moment to pass and then moved so she could speak to Riony without Eslinde or the others hearing.

"I didn't tell them anything about Dracuni. She could have remained away, remained secret."

"Dracuni isn't so easy to keep hidden these days," Riony murmured back. "Generally, nobody has had any reason to think she's anything other than a dragon. We just try to be careful and hope we can trust people."

The unidragon was bigger than a horse now. Around the size stories told that unicorns once were. But there was still a playful frolic in her step as she engaged with Shiff.

Dashiel and Vance seemed fascinated by her, and Kess could see them speculating about her breed already. Dashiel's eyes were bright with an enthusiastic smile.

"These are good people. I think you can trust them," Kess said.

"And what about you? Can I trust you?" There was an edge to Riony's voice, something akin to exhaustion and vulnerability and worry all at once that left the words clipped.

Kess held her gaze and then turned in her saddle, lowering herself down to the ground.

"What are you doing?" Riony balked. "Is this some weird revenge plan to stab me in the toes?"

Kess's body shivered with nerves. She couldn't quite kneel. Not neatly, not formally. So she prostrated herself on the ground, bowing low at the feet of the woman who was once her slave.

"Riony ..." Kess hesitated. No longer an Uf'Heithorn, she didn't know how best to address her. But the effect of even using that name rather than the old, hurtful pet name was enough.

She swallowed a dry throat and went on. "By all my honor, I pledge my life to you and your cause. For whatever good it can provide you. However you wish to expend it. My life, my hands, my blades are under your command. It is the least you are owed."

Kess tried to imbue her voice with every fiber of sincerity she had. "I don't ask any forgiveness. I only ask that you let me serve you."

Her words came out broken and scratchy. "I am yours."

Kess remained there, forehead to the dirt, waiting. No reply came.

Turning her face upward, Kess felt a small amount of satisfaction that for the first time in her life, Kess had rendered Riony speechless.

EPILOGUE

The world blurred back into focus in a whirl of pain and nausea. Kife wrestled weakly against the hands that grasped his arms.

They continued to drag him forward.

Kife groaned and slumped. Only a thin slit of vision was present between swollen eyelids and hot liquid tickled as it ran down his temple.

"Where ... where are you taking ..." Kife's tongue was thick and tasted tangy and metallic. He'd lost a tooth somewhere along the way.

The mob had beaten Kife to the last breath of his life, but he'd held tight to that breath. Now he feared he'd been rounded up with the criminals to be punished again.

This is Kess's fault. How many times must the wretch ruin my life? I'll kill her. I'll kill her and her Pony and everybody who'd ever raised a hand against me.

Polished floor skidded by under Kife's limp feet as he was dragged along. And then they stopped.

"Advisor Falden and two handmaidens have been found in a chancellor's office, all dead in the same manner as Ulfren and Hjelzahn," a man's voice spoke in a low, confidential voice from nearby.

"More dead? Under my own roof!" A deeper voice boomed in a way that seemed to rattle Kife's aching ribs.

"Why can none of you tell me where my daughter has gone? Or find who killed two more of my sons?"

Only a murmuring of apologies and excuses followed.

Then, "Who is this you've brought me?"

Kife was pulled forward a few more steps.

"We found him in Zarram Dragonhold. He has Heithorn crests on his weapons."

"Heithorn? Are you part of this plot, along with Kessara?"

The blurred form of a silver robe stopped in front of Kife.

Kife lifted his pounding head.

The draping fabric led up to a wide chest covered in golden scale plate armor. Silver hair spilled down in long braids around a familiar face, one Kife knew from the profile stamped on every coin in Elundrae.

His split lips bled and cracked ribs ached as he grinned wide, laughing silently.

"Your Majesty, my Dragon King. I have been waiting so long to speak with you."

To Be Continued
in
Secret of the Dragon Born

GLOSSARY

Including pronunciation guide

CHARACTERS

Riony Eyfarr (Ree-OH-nee AY-far) – Rolanian, Daughter of Eylin and Farrad, born when servants to the Gyrstein Dragonlords, then sold on as a family to the Heithorn Dragonlords, and since living as fugitive slaves. Trained as a midwife and herbalist. Sword enthusiast.

Lyrrin Eyfarr (Li-rin AY-far) – Daughter of "The Guest", an unknown dragonlord woman, and an unknown father. Taen and Elgarthan? Has some unusual features. Likes animals and magic.

Kessara Heithorn (Kess-AH-ra High-thorn) – From the once wealthy Heithorn dragonlords with strong dragon riding traditions, estranged. Taen. Rides a wolf.

Kife Heithorn (K-eye-f High-thorn) – Elder brother to Kessara, dragonrider. Taen.

Dracuni (Drak-YOU-nee) – Unique hybrid between unicorn and dragon, created from the use of silvernix on a broken dragon egg, and something more?

Griskin (Griss-kin) – Large gray wolf, male, for some reason abides Kess's company.

Aishena Hjelzahn (AYSH-ena Hyel-zarn) – Delver, Middle sibling of three (remaining), fifth generation heir, grayglim in training. Taen.

Benjin Hjelzahn (BEN-jin Hyel-zarn) – Youngest sibling of three (remaining), fifth generation heir. Taen.

Kverra Hjelzahn (Kv-errar Hyel-zarn) – Grayglin warden and wife to Vori Hjelzan, fourth generation heir to the Dragon King. Taen.

Yeonard Draekhan (Yeh-nard DRAKE-arn) – Dragonking, ruler of Elundrae. Taen. First to tame a dragon.

Eslinde Draekhan (Ez-Lind-eh DRAKE-arn) – Last of the dragon-king's first generation heirs.

Alderkin (ALL-der-kin) – a secretive and powerful race of elven humanoids. Masters of rune crystal magic. Extinct.

Alderkin Depths – Massive underground cities once inhabited by the Alderkin. There are five known Alderkin Depths across Elundrae.

Alderkin Runes – Magical symbols carved into crystal items, which, when somehow charged, allow for a range of magical functions. The runes must be traced in the right sequence and direction of strokes in order to be activated and deactivated.

Alderkin War – A twenty-year war between the Alderkin and the Dragon King's forces, ending thirty years prior to the events in these books. Prompted by the human's slaughter of unicorns, and the Alderkin's attempts to protect them.

Athame (Ah-Thahm-Ay) – A dagger of varying size, made from crystal, and powered by various Alderkin runes for utility or combat.

Breachers – Undercity dwellers who brave the aboveground world to scavenge resources, highly dangerous but sometimes

required.

Delvers – Undercity dwellers who brave the dangers of the Alderkin depths to salvage useful artifacts to be sold in the undercity. A risky but lucrative profession.

Dragon Glass – Glass manufactured with the use of dragon's fire to melt the base ingredients.

Dragon guards/riders – Those trained to ride dragons, generally for combat purposes. Either born to or hired by Dragonlord families who own the dragons.

Dragonhold – A building with multiple facilities for dragon keeping and raising, including hatchery, stables, and training areas.

Dragonkeeps – Walled in cities protected by dragons. The Dragon King has built and gifted a dragonkeep to each of his first generation heirs.

Dragonlords – Those who have the riches and resources to own their own dragons. Not necessarily royalty.

Elgarthans – A sea-faring race, pale skinned, they will visit and trade with Dragonkeeps for the riches of steel and glass provided through dragon labor, but rarely remain in Elundrae due to the dangers.

Elundrae (Ell-Un-Dray) – The continent in which the story takes place. Nearest neighboring country being Elgartha, across the seas to the East.

Rebel Riders – Title of a popular serial fiction, published and distributed in chapters.

Revenant/Rev/Shadow Revenant – Any undead creature raised by the Shadow Dragon's curse. Generally defeated by fire or dismemberment.

Rolanians – Once ruling large cities throughout Elundrae, most Rolanian settlements were destroyed as the Shadow Dragon curse spread through the land. As very few Rolanians became dragonlords, they had to buy into protection from those who had dragons, often at the cost of their own freedom. Generally presenting with a warm array of darker skin tones, and hair ranging from blonde, through reds and browns.

Shadow Dragon – a cursed and mysterious creature of smoke and sadness that brings the undead blight to the land of Elundrae. Wherever the Shadow Dragon touches

ground, the dead rise.

Silvernix – Unicorn blood. Miraculous healing qualities, a single drop can cure a body from near death. Can only be stored in dragon glass, otherwise loses potency within minutes. Opalescent liquid.

Taens – Generally dark-haired and light-to-mid-brown skin-tones, Taens were once a warrior like clan of horse-riders, taking residence through the north-west of Elundrae. When the Dragonking rose to power, Taens became favored and more likely to become dragonlords, and soon became the dominant race across the land.

Taming – The ceremony in which all dragons are subjected to in order to be domesticated, similar to a lobotomy. Performed not long after birth on dragons bred in captivity. Utilizes silvernix in the process.

Undercity – A human settlement, established in the large upper cavern of the Central Alderkin Depths, as a refuge from the dangers of the aboveground world.

Unicorns – Ethereal, horned horse-like creatures. Driven to extinction in the race for the riches of their blood.

Herbs

Carrowmy – culinary.

Corpsefoot – used for contraception, dangerous in high doses.

Genjermint – sleeping tea.

Hennen – for hair dye.

Morass Mercy – powerful sedative with bad side effects.

Plumeberry – tart, seedy berries, poison detox.

Shillgrue – to condition leather.

Tinctoria – for hair dye.

Weftweed – a sticky (both in appearance and sap production) antiseptic.

Dragons
Natural subspecies

Etherflame – Plains dragons. Golds and reds, large size. Fire breathing for clearing grasslands/cooking herds, and big wings for hovering. Blood itself is flammable and is aerosolized in breath weapon. Most common dragonrider mount.

Seasong – Sea dragons. Silvers, greens, blacks, largest size, big lungs creates big surge of air/sound to stun schools of fish, and bigger mouth for feeding. There are tales they once

sang, but never have in captivity or once tamed. Mostly used for interbreeding and beasts of burden.

Snowshimmer – Mountain dragons. Whites-blues, medium-sized, fast build for snatching up rare prey. Big talons, lightning breath attack, rare and solitary. Used in industry for power and interbreeding.

Treedart – Forest dragons. Yellows, browns, purples, camouflaged scales. Smallest type, with concentrated fire bolts for individual prey. Considered pretty basic by breeders and dragonlords, mostly used for interbreeding. Main/only dragon still in the wild because of size.

Dragons

Interbred selective breeding species

Etherdart – Etherflame/Treedart cross. Medium size, tough but slow, big fireballs. A basic combat dragon.

FlameSongs – Etherflame/Seasong cross. Largest size, high-capacity fire-breathers, used mostly for industrial uses, not used as mounts because they can spontaneously explode.

Seashimmer – Seasong/Snowshimmer cross. Large size, cold, icy breath used in ice making and food storage industry.

Shimmerdart – Snowshimmer/Treedart cross. Small size, with small ball lightning darts, dangerous for single targets but not great against mass undead, bred for speed as scouts/communications/assassinations.

Snowflame – Snowshimmer/Etherflame cross. Medium-large size, white "liquid" fire, fast, considered a great dragonrider mount, but short lifespan as breath weapon deteriorates their health fast.

Treedart/seasong – don't interbreed successfully.

Bantam Ferrets – Mouse sized ferrets.

Bovin – A large (twice human height) buffalo or yak style creature, docile, used to be in large herds that supported wild dragons. Moved into farming for captive dragons.

Carrion Birds – Massive scavengers with a cry like a wolf's howl.

Cave Otters – A large sized otter with specially adapted claws that allow them to climb sheer walls easily, pale colors to match limestone surroundings.

Cave Spiders – Head-sized spiders, nonvenomous.

Dreer – Deer with Armadillo like scales, that grow as large as giraffes. Also popular prey for wild dragon populations in the past.

Glowflies – firefly-like bugs, finger sized, live in large swarms and light up when disturbed.

Mouse Deer – Cat sized deer with fangs.

Olm – Just like real olm, but larger than human size and carnivorous.

Owlettes – Cave dwelling owls that feed on small rodents and insects within the caves, the size of a small hand.

Rope Worms – Just a worm, but much larger. Delicious when fried.

ALDERKIN RUNES

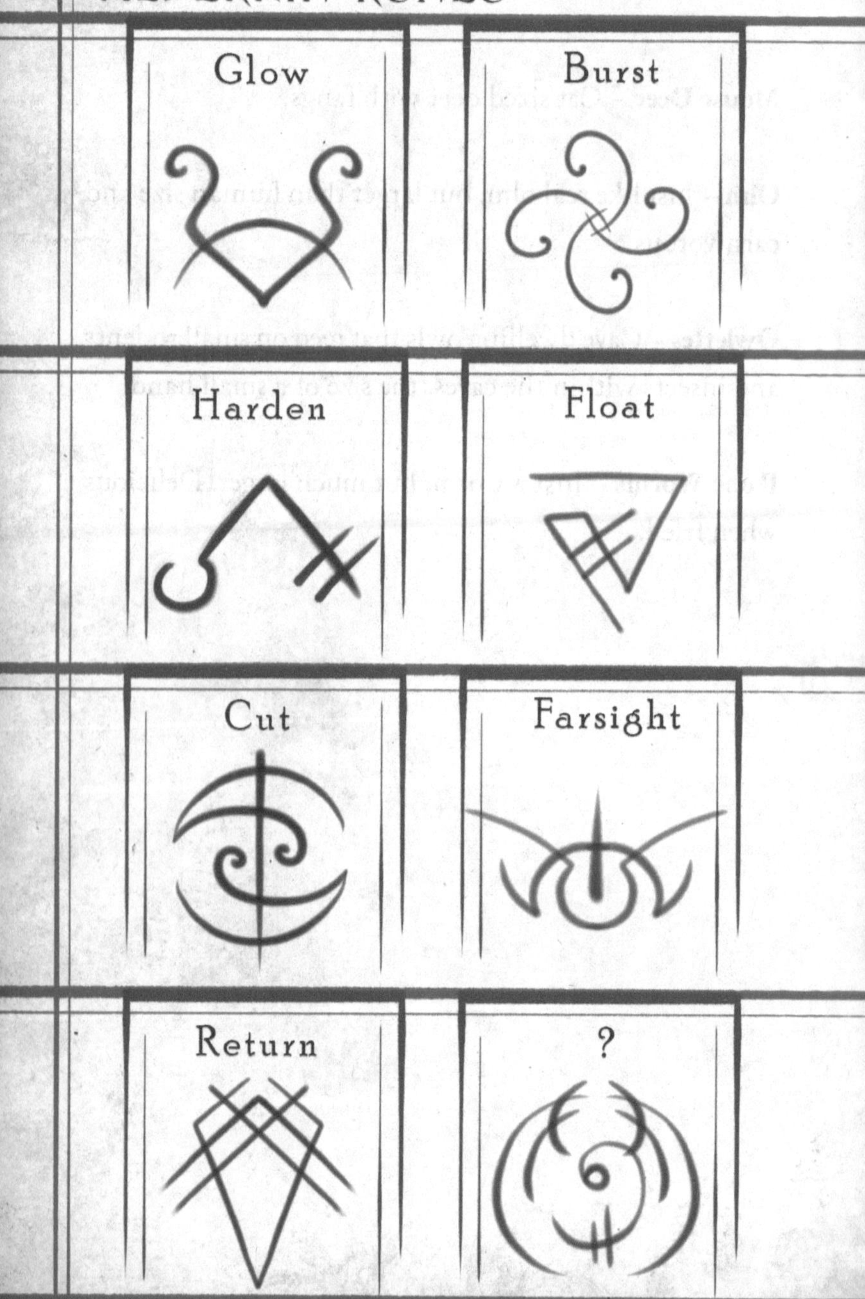

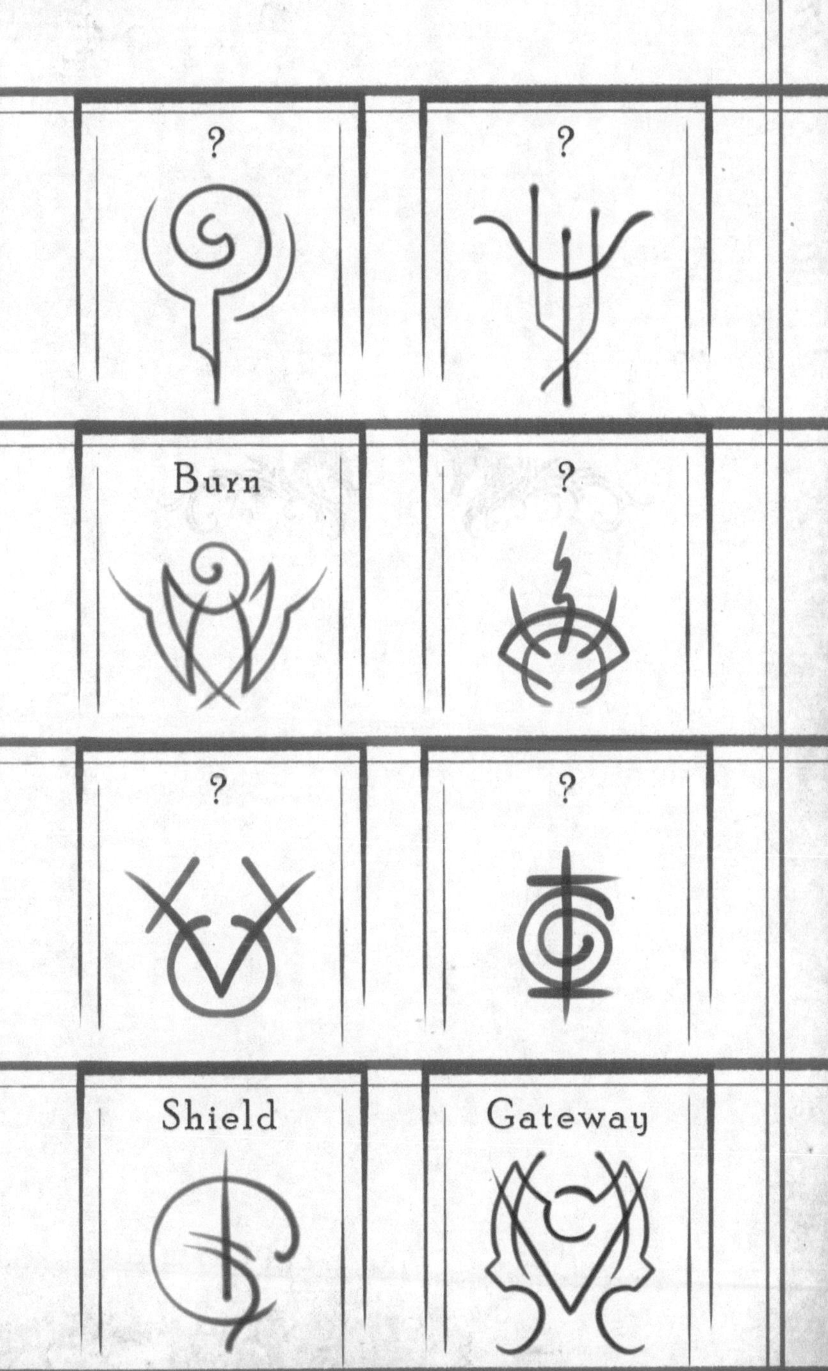
?
?
Burn
?
?
?
Shield
Gateway

Tree Dart
Sea Song
Snow Shimmer
Ether Flame

About the Author

Professional daydreamer, Selina A. Fenech writes "adorably dark" Epic and Urban Fantasy for teens and adults. Filled with sweet and quirky characters, laugh out loud moments, and perilous adventures, her magical worlds are perfect for readers who love daring twists and happily ever afters.

A cancer survivor determined to live life to the fullest, she is an escape room enthusiast, avid gardener, foodie and self-proclaimed geek, residing in Australia.

In addition to literature, Selina applies her unique take on the dichotomy of light and dark as a professional fantasy artist working under the name Selina Fenech and has published many illustrated books, oracle decks, and colouring books.

Find Out More About Selina

OFFICIAL WEBSITE: www.selinafenech.com

Memory's Wake Trilogy

A modern girl lost in and hunted in a fairy tale world.
An illustrated young adult portal fantasy with
Arthurian and Victorian themes.

Empath Chronicles

Teenagers with superpowers fueled by emotions ... what
could go wrong? A young adult superhero romance.

More Books by Selina A Fenech

Beshadowed

You have been lied to. Werewolves, vampires, ghosts …
they aren't what you think. What is really lurking in the
dark? A spooky urban fantasy.

Heartsblood

Her blood is irresistible, but is it worth the cost? A
vampire romance for adults.